# The Bright Lights

## *Also by Frank Swinnerton*

Frank Swinnerton

# The

# Bright

# Lights

Doubleday & Company, Inc.

Garden City, New York

1968

# Contents

# The Curtain-raiser

I

I<small>T</small> was a stormy day on the south-east coast of England. The
month was February; the year 1900. In Wilmerton, a small
town on this coast, unless by chance some member of the family
was in the Army, nobody without access to newspapers would
have supposed that Britain was at war thousands of miles away
in South Africa. Khaki was not to be seen; no recruiting posters
nor flags nor patriotic symbols were shown upon walls or in the
windows of marine villas. The place was very much as it had
been for nearly a hundred years.

This immunity arose from the fact that the Boers had neither
navy nor allies. Dwellers around the English coasts feared no
attack by water, and of course no attack from the air. They were
concerned only with their own age-old battle with the elements,
against which they fastened their shutters. They sat in drawing-
room or kitchen or bar-parlour, talking slowly, the women
sewing or knitting, the men smoking pipes or drinking ale from
tankards, the small boys and girls chanting lessons in the local
school, and the infants huddled into multiple garments to protect
them from draughts.

'Rough today,' said the men; and 'listen to that wind!' said
the women. 'A-a-a-ah!' crooned or bellowed the babies. Their
progenitors had uttered the like sounds ever since Napoleon had
been packed off to St Helena to meditate upon his wrongs.

Out at sea, passing ships were often hidden by tremendous
surges of grey water. Waves reaching the shore of breezy

Wilmerton scattered high-flying spray and shingle over the deserted coast road; and not one resident, nor even a dog, from the town risked his life there. At this season a resort which had still to become fashionable lacked visitors to pretend, while shivering, that they enjoyed the bluster. Drenched and wind-swept houses, together with a couple of unambitious stucco-surfaced hotels on the sea front, appeared as lifeless as the streets of Pompeii, and in their present sodden state were as wretched as rocks half-submerged in a tormented sea.

Inland, beside a churchyard wall of ancient stone, a little girl was running on tiptoe, crouched to escape notice; while the thin cry of another, younger, child, who was invisible, struggled vainly against the afternoon's turbulence.

'Con-nee! Con-nee!' was the burden of this cry; and the little girl, ejaculating 'Bother', bent lower as she ran, until her chin almost touched her knees. This was the very pursuit she had schemed to avoid. Pen, like the artful monkey she was, must have been watching, and just caught what eyes less sharp would have imagined to be the shadow of a wind-blown bush in the Rectory garden. Pen really was *awful*!

No picture of British soldiers fighting, dying, and suffering the horrors of dysentery interfered with the excitement of evasion. The names of Kruger, Botha, Rhodes, Buller, Ladysmith, and Mafeking, if they had been glimpsed in the headlines of her father's quickly-hidden *Times*, would have been meaningless to the runner. Nor had she any knowledge of her father's views on the War and its origins. They were never mentioned at meal-times. Her parents, for reasons entirely domestic, were deter-mined to keep all familiarity with the idea of carnage from children too young, they believed, to accept such horror.

If there had been any significant reference to events overseas, the little girl was sharp enough to have grasped and remembered every detail; but being ignorant of most other things and people she was absorbed in her own affairs. She, Constance Rotherham, was all-important. What she did, planned, and thought was paramount. Nobody had the right to stand in her way. Let them beware of trying! She would cr-r-r-rush them!

Neither Constance nor the British people as a whole could foresee at this hour that within her lifetime the Rectory at Wilmerton, place of her birth, which she regarded alternately as haven or prison, would be demolished by enemy bombs.

At last a tall yew hedge, growing just within the last yards of her protective churchyard wall, provided a complete screen from what she knew must be Pen's observation point, a small mound near the Rectory's back door. She was able to stand upright. In standing, however, she exposed herself to the roaring wind which swept directly from the sea. It stifled her breath, flicked her hat into the air, and made her overcoat heavy as a blanket against her body. Imprecations ceased. She swooped upon the hat before it could escape, turned her back to the storm until breath became normal, and when she once more faced it held the hat with both hands. This thrill was just what, in escaping Pen, she had hoped to receive.

The little girl was not quite twelve years old. Her coat was of grey tweed, and the rescued hat was of grey felt. Curly golden hair was gathered at the nape of her neck in a bow of navy ribbon—sole relic, for this was a Saturday, and as a day girl she was released from bondage, of her school uniform. Her eyes were unusually wide apart under distinctive eyebrows much darker than her hair; and the eyes themselves were of a curious blue which in some lights became almost impenetrable black. She had a straight, broad nose and full lips; and when, as now, the lips were parted in animation, it could be seen that her teeth were large and white. She was not yet beautiful; her most obvious characteristic was determination.

At this moment she was very determined indeed. Nothing would force her to go back to the Rectory for at least an hour. Nobody there, except Pen, would guess that she was out. Her aim was to defy the storm, and to exult in her defiance.

Pen, she knew, hated wind and the unruly breakers. They

made her hysterical. She always screamed, clutched at the nearest hand or sleeve, and wanted to run away, to safety. She would have wanted to do that this afternoon.

'Oh, Connie, do let's go home! Connie, do come! I'm frightened!'

Silly little coward! Baby! Pest! Thank goodness she wasn't here!

On the whole Constance disliked Pen. She did so particularly this afternoon, because that frightful hullabaloo might have roused the Rectory, brought Father from his study, and Mother from her bed. She would have had to pretend to be sorry. There wouldn't be a row; because there never were rows. What happened was that Mother would look ill and worried; while Pen watched with a little smile upon her lips, quite silent, but with something like contempt in her eyes. The one thing in Pen's favour was that she wasn't a sneak. She never went grizzling to anybody, and when Constance made her excuses she didn't interrupt, saying 'Oh, Mummy, that's not true. She's telling lies!' No; having failed in her screaming chase, she always went quietly back to the nursery and played with her dolls.

She treated the wretched things as if they were really her children; made them cough, gave them medicine and cups of tea, asked if they felt better, or were comfortable, and wrapped them in bits of stuff which she said were blankets. The dolls were great invalids. When they were all snuffling and wailing it was like being in a hospital.

Constance had never cared for dolls. She was never going to have any children. Babies smelt of milk, and dribbled. They were disgusting. Pen, being seven years old, was now past that sort of thing; but at first she had been awful. To have her dumped on your lap, to look after while Mother was busy doing something else, was torture. That was what had first made Constance dislike her.

If Pen wasn't playing with her dolls, she was making believe to read one of her books. She had been read to so often by Mother and Father that she couldn't, even now, read very well by herself; but she remembered what she had heard, and said the words to herself as she looked at the pages. She had a very good memory. They both had good memories, not for sums and history, but for poems, and sometimes for quite long paragraphs in ordinary writing. Constance was always being made to recite at school. She liked this. The other girls didn't mind, either, because while she was reciting they could write notes to each other.

Without warning, the storm became violent. A whirlwind rose, lashing the waves to madness, and sweeping over the breakers with such fury that it caught her as if she had been a piece of paper, and flung her against the wall surrounding a public garden. She did not fall; but her hand was scratched by the rough bricks, and for a moment, being taken off her guard, she was terrified. Only when the gust fell, and she knew she was not to be carried high over the roof-tops, did she recover enough to laugh in bravado.

'Lovely! Splendid!' she cried; trembling, but vaunting her courage. It was wonderful, with this buttress of wall, to look out over the sea at great clouds of spray like cascades of pearls against the lowering sky. A roaring of storm and the rattle of innumerable pebbles filled her ears. She hadn't really been a bit afraid, she told herself. Salt was upon her lips; her cheeks tingled; she bared her teeth in defiance.

'"Blow till thou burst thy wind!"' she declaimed, pretending to be the boatswain in *The Tempest*. '"What cares these roarers for the name of King?"' Carried away by enthusiasm, she added less-noble words from a lately-read book: '"Overboard you go, miserable snivelling cur!"' A pirate had said that. Pirates were grand cruel creatures. They cared for nobody. Thinking of them, she felt a cutlass by her side, and about her waist a belt full of pistols. The sensation was magnificent.

Nevertheless, she kept her back against the wall, fearing that she might be blown off her feet and perhaps carried by the back-wash of a huge wave out to sea. She did not want to be drowned. That would spoil everything. She wanted to be a great actress, playing glorious parts that made people stand up in the theatre, shouting and clapping. When they did that she would bow gravely, again and again, first this way and then that, until they were beside themselves with admiration.

Love, also. They would all be in love with her, offering marvellous suppers, parties, champagne, ices, exquisite flowers, chocolates, peaches, rides in hansom cabs, and, of course, their hearts. She would be an ice-cold beauty, smiling at their passion.

'"Bah! You're heartless! I shall shoot myself!"'

'"Must you, really? Please don't do it in my boudoir, Edward. It makes such a mess. I abhor messes!"'

In the midst of this passionate scene the wind again swooped upon her. She was going. She was being sucked from the wall. There was nothing to hold on to. Nobody would see her or hear her. She would be drowned. Screaming, she threw herself face downwards, lying spread-eagled on the pebble-strewn pavement until this latest gust had passed. In the lull, much shaken, she crawled upon all-fours until she reached the end of the wall and was safe under its lee.

She never forgot that moment of terror and confusion, which made her heart beat fast and loud, like a roll of drums. The after-excitement was thrilling. Having escaped, she believed, the most dreadful death, she was alive and excited as she had been after a toboggan race, almost longing for it all to happen again. It had been absolutely marvellous: She began to laugh.

And then she caught sight of her wet and muddy coat, and a great gash in the right stocking, where blood was already dripping from her knee. She was in a disgusting state. It wouldn't be possible to hide such damage. She must quickly invent a story to account for it.

There would have to be two stories; one for Mother, the other for Pen, who would probably be watching from the nursery window, or standing at the top of the stairs. But Mother was lying down, and would see nothing. If she crept in by the church-yard and the back door, and tiptoed past Father's study, she might escape. Her coat might be less muddy than she feared; the knee could be bathed; the stocking could be darned without anybody knowing.

Pen would know. Pen was like the Recording Angel. Limping homeward beside the churchyard wall, with the wind behind her, Constance worried about Pen. At one moment she decided to brush her aside with imperious words, at another to tell her, rather boastfully, what had really happened. She would say, as was true, how *terrifically* she had enjoyed the experience, how she had seen the splendid waves rearing like mountains and swooping over the promenade, and how she hadn't been at all afraid.

To a voice within, which said: 'You were frightened out of your life,' she boldly answered: 'No, I wasn't. You don't know anything about it. And I'll do it again tomorrow. You jolly well see!' When the voice continued: 'Pen won't believe a word of it, you know,' Constance grew angry, shrugged, and pretended not to hear. But she knew the voice was right. Her quick walk dropped to a thoughtful dawdle. The wind grew cold. The afternoon's darkness became twilight.

## 2

At one point in later life Constance claimed to have been born in 1890. As a year that was nice and round; and as, in stress of emotion, she wanted to escape a charge of abnormality, it . scotched any suggestion that her character had been affected by shocking mischances in the lives of her parents. When the emergency passed, she was delighted to revert to the truth. It held more public credit.

She had really been born in the spring of 1888, when, as she amusedly discovered, Bernard Shaw was music critic to a new halfpenny London evening newspaper called *The Star*, and A. B. Walkley, afterwards a pontiff on *The Times*, wrote theatrical notices for the same paper. Meeting both men in her first hour of London triumph, she anticipated a later infatuation with what was called 'simultaneity', and likened herself to Beatrice, in *Much Ado about Nothing*, who said that at her birth a star danced.

'In my case,' she laughingly exclaimed to Mr Walkley, 'it was three stars. Two up on Beatrice!'

She thus pretended to be part of a brilliant constellation. And yet it might so easily have been otherwise. She might not have been born at all, or, if born, delivered in a state of sickliness or deformity. Terrible things had happened successively to her parents in the Winter of 1887. There were three of them.

First, a midnight fire destroyed their home and all John Rotherham's manuscripts. This dreadful accident was followed by the second; Mr Rotherham's almost fatal descent, in a moment of inspiration, from the top of a thirty-foot embankment to the railway line below. The third, of a different variety, will appear later.

Mr Rotherham had just, he was convinced (for this was a time of ferment in clerical doctrine, and he was a man of speculative intelligence), discovered the meaning of the Universe. Crying, like some modern Archimedes, the one word 'Eureka!' he leapt ecstatically in the air, arms raised, eyes fixed upon the glorious heavens. He then stumbled, overbalanced, clutched frantically at grass tufts in the appalling sandy slope, and slithered head first downhill until he landed with great force upon the rails. There he lay unconscious for perhaps a quarter of an hour, at the end of which time, just as the evening express was due, he was luckily seen and rescued by two of his parishioners.

The men thought immediately that he had been struck by an earlier train, and assumed him to be dead. Some muttered words from the corpse, however, startled them; and as the express thundered by he was dragged to safety and carried on a stretcher to the local hospital. By the time this haven was reached he had become speechless.

A more self-important cleric would have ascribed his rescue to miracle. John Rotherham was too humble in spirit to do any such thing. Indeed, he knew little about it. Long illness followed, in the course of which he entirely forgot what his discovery had been. Incoherent efforts at annunciation were thought to be symptoms of delirium, and sedatives completed total forgetfulness of all that had preceded his tumble.

When told afterwards of delirious ejaculations, he looked blank, almost ashamed. 'Strange,' he murmured. 'Strange of me to insist so stubbornly that I *knew*. It was rude to accuse others of wilful disbelief. I can offer no explanation. They were the ramblings of a sick man.' He tried, naturally, to recapture the assurance, in vain. For him, as for Bully Bottom, a wonderful experience had become incommunicable.

'"I have had a dream, past the wit of man to say what dream it was ... Methought I was—there is no man can tell what. Methought I was,—and methought I had, —but man is but a patched fool, if he will offer to say what methought I had. The eye of man hath not heard, the ear of man hath not seen, man's hand is not able to taste, his tongue to conceive, nor his heart to report, what my dream was."'

The third blow, and to Mrs Rotherham morally the worst of all, was the arrest, conviction, and imprisonment of her only brother, Terence, for large-scale fraud. While for her husband this was no more than a summons to further stoical endurance, it was almost fatal to a prospective mother. Mrs Rotherham had already suffered from fright and horror. Now she was appalled by an event which, at first greeted with incredulous indignation as a monstrous libel, became almost unbearably shaming. The climax of distress was reached when she visited Terence in prison and found her passionate disbelief met by a cheerfully nonchalant admission of guilt.

'Don't cry, my dear Lucy,' said he, laughingly. 'I was unlucky enough to be found out. Something went wrong. But I had a magnificent time while it lasted.'

Was this bravado? Did Terence not realise that what he had done was immoral? Was he impenitent for having robbed those who trusted him, and for bringing disgrace to them all? It seemed not. As she turned away, weeping, he gave her a kiss and one of his old rallying slaps on the bottom. He even hummed, not an appropriate dirge, but a popular comic song of the day.

The Rotherhams, sunk in gloom, had then to decide, while the energetic Constance, not yet born, kicked lustily in augmentation of her mother's pain, whether to leave at once the small Northamptonshire town where they and their affairs were known to all. Mr Rotherham, a stoic, would have endured it; his wife, agonised in mind and body, begged that they should go. They went.

Less than a month before Constance was born, therefore, they were imperfectly settled in the bleak south-eastern coastal townlet of Wilmerton. Here, in what they hoped would be a haven from disaster, Mrs Rotherham paid in temporary paralysis for all the agitations she had endured. For several weeks she could not move her arms and legs; and although supported by a robust constitution she knew little of the days preceding Constance's birth. When well enough to see her daughter, she learned that the child was already baptised.

'A beautiful baby,' declared the nurse. 'As bright a little Christian as I ever saw!'

Constance, at the age of seventeen, had this observation repeated to her for the first time. She laughed heartily, as she did whenever she thought of it. She then found that her sex had brought thankfulness to the mother because, if she had been a boy, she was to be named after her wicked uncle. Being a girl, she escaped the fate; and was plain 'Constance Rotherham'.

'Thank you, dear God!' whispered Lucy. 'Thank you for not sending me a son. Little Constance will not be branded for life. Even the stigma attaching to John's name will pass when she marries. This dreadful shame will be erased.'

The scandal was already forgotten. Gay Terence Wilberforce,

whose life had been delightfully adventurous and enjoyable, was dead, having developed pneumonia in prison. He disappeared with no more than brief mention in the Press; and nobody in Wilmerton associated him with the Rotherhams. Only his sister Lucy cherished the picture of him as a dazzling, uncontrollable boy, defiant of authority and reckless of consequences.

This part of memory held secret admiration. The rest appalled Lucy to the end of her life. Whatever she read of poor people defrauded she saw a thousand haggard ghosts; whenever she was defied by her elder daughter she dwelt in terror upon Terence's comparable unruliness and feared that it was born again in this beloved child. Could there be truth in the scientific notion that certain diseases, certain characteristics, were transmitted through the mother to some or all of her children? Could she, unwittingly and unwillingly, have bred in Constance the taint revealed in her brother's unrepentant villainy?

When strongly roused, this fear produced in Mrs Rotherham a total obscuration of sight by what seemed to be a curtain of blood. Her sanity was not affected; the red blindness signified only the onset of profound agitation; but its sequel was a *migraine* so intense as to be almost insupportable. The attack, lasting for a week or more, was accompanied by an irrational conviction of responsibility for her daughter's naughtiness.

Constance, therefore, was never punished. She grew up thinking herself a model child.

3

One of the supposed advantages of Wilmerton was its healthy climate, which led to the establishment there at the turn of the century of several boarding-schools for girls. These were not, at first, the famous places they have since become; and their proprietors were glad to accept day scholars as well as boarders. The boarders, in turn, living in a world of pleasantly divided social classes to which the modern disease of anxious self-importance was unknown, felt no snobbish disdain of those who arrived every morning with satchels over their shoulders. Indeed, the daily arrivals were sometimes envied for their freedom, and welcomed for the edible gifts they brought to hungry exiles from home.

Constance and Penelope, seen off by their mother after early breakfast with a fond kiss apiece, waved as they reached the rectory gate, and walked sedately through roads leading further inland. Mrs Rotherham, watching from the porch, felt proud of both. They held themselves really well, she thought; and although Constance refused to hold Penelope's hand the fact that they were dressed alike in the dark blue school uniform was deeply reassuring. They looked all that a good clergyman's daughters should do.

A good clergyman's daughters; not the nieces of an un-repentant criminal. True, the ways of Constance were sometimes alarming. But Lucy Rotherham had faith. Dear John's influence must in the end prevail. Constance would grow out of every difficult characteristic. She was fundamentally good, funda-mentally sweet.

As for Penelope, who had been born in 1893, when peace had settled at last upon the household, she was the offspring of marvelling spiritual relief. The attribute which her parents noticed and cherished in her was that of simplicity. They thought her docile. Small, very dark, light-footed, and more obviously sensitive than Constance, she bore no resemblance at all to her uncle. Terence had been fair, slightly florid, and, in the heyday of his fortunes, substantially built. Pen was none of these things. She was truthful, scrupulous over pocket money, and ex-quisitely unselfish.

She adored her sister. It was beautiful, thought Mrs Rotherham, to see them together, the one, whatever her occasionally dis-gusted grimaces, really protective, the other happier in Constance's company than at any other time. It was also extraordinarily pleasant to hear neighbours say: 'What a delightful pair they make! Such understanding! Such charming affectionateness! You really are a very lucky woman, Mrs Rotherham, to have two such daughters. I wish *my* children . . .'

The school the girls attended was called Pickering's, because its founder, Robert Pickering, was a rich free-thinking printer in Birmingham who wanted to improve female education and at the same time to create a job for his only sister. He was justified in both aims. Miss Pickering, as astute as her brother, and highly gifted in the choice of subordinates, made a success of the school. She was learned; she was able; a woman with no domestic inclinations, who had been born to rule.

Husbands would not have satisfied her; she could neither submit nor cajole. On the other hand she had a considerable understanding of those much younger than herself. Each one of them represented a human entity, to be developed, encouraged, and given a strong sense of duty. Accordingly Miss Pickering taught her older pupils so wisely that the school had a higher percentage of loyal members than any other on that stretch of the English coastline.

Younger girls were naturally dealt with by mistresses junior to Miss Pickering herself; but Miss Pickering knew almost everything about them. She seemed to be omnipresent. This displeased Constance Rotherham, who, never a grateful person, regarded Miss Pickering as an intrusive rival. Constance had quickly adopted the school habit of referring to their headmistress as 'Picky', and she invented disrespectful nicknames for the other mistresses. When her reports showed a lack of enthusiasm she was not abashed; she merely attributed such faultfinding to jealousy.

'She's really a frightful old woman,' said she to her troubled mother of Miss Rowland, whose comments were a little tart. 'Well, I mean she must be thirty, at least. She's never pleased with anybody. We all hate her.'

Since Miss Rowland knew many things which she omitted from reports, this perhaps explained why Constance was never a prefect at Pickering's.

The truth was that her interest in the curriculum was fitful. Boldness made her popular, especially with younger girls. She had strength and grace, flashes of considerable intelligence, and in general good manners; but she exasperated nearly all the mistresses, who recognised at sight an unbiddable child. Miss Batchelor, who taught elocution, could detect 'real talent'; Miss Prince, who taught English, brought herself to say 'Constance has taste; but must work harder at grammar and spelling': otherwise praise was grudging. Miss Rowland was particularly severe on what she thought an obstinate refusal to apply a superficial mind to problems of arithmetic and algebra. She said bluntly: 'Constance makes no attempt to understand what is uncongenial to her.'

In private discussion with Miss Pickering, Miss Rowland was equally emphatic.

'The only way I can get the wretched child to attend,' said she, 'is by giving every problem a personal application. If she can think of it as something affecting *herself*, she's bright enough; but the abstract's a closed book. She won't open it.'

Miss Pickering, with a smile, murmured kind words to Miss Rowland. She liked the girl's parents, considered Miss Rowland capable but unimaginative, and had known many egotists. Not all of them had a bent for mathematics.

Penelope was a new pupil, in what was called the Junior School. She was smaller than other girls of seven, and was jostled by those who were born thrusters. As yet, having been so short a time at school, she had no bosom friend; but she was already marked down for invitation to parties by little girls whose mothers insisted that all guests should be 'nice', which meant that they would romp in a seemly manner. Pen was quite obviously seemly.

She was approved, without enthusiasm, by the mistresses,

who, with one exception, thought her a well-behaved nonentity. The exception was Miss Gosling, who tried hard to make Miss Pickering's little girls understand the arts, as well as the delights of dancing. It was Miss Gosling's first job after leaving Madame Boncour's Academy for Ballet; and her ambition was high. She wished to be a second Madame Boncourt.

Alas, she felt herself to be, at the age of nineteen, a person doomed for life. Not only had she been lamed by an accident which destroyed all hope of success as ballerina, but she had been unchivalrously jilted by a young man of temperament. She was in great need, therefore, of somebody to love. Penelope Rotherham was the one child at Pickering's who could be envisaged as a substitute for herself, or as the child she might have borne to the faithless lover. The other girls were clodhoppers, fit for nothing but country-dances.

Watchful elder mistresses had already exchanged cryptic remarks upon Miss Gosling. They said: 'Picky will have to warn Beryl about that kid.' To this, Miss Rowland, the eldest of them all, added: 'I've already spoken to Miss Pickering.' And Miss Pickering, unknown to the others, had already spoken to Miss Gosling. No unpleasant words were used; Miss Gosling, although she flushed under the warning, had been able to say, truthfully, that her enthusiasm for the little dancer had been rigorously concealed; and for the present all was quiet.

Fortunately, Penelope herself was too modest to penetrate and exploit (as Constance would have done) the young mistress's aesthetic joy in her. She was no more elated by her dancing prowess than by more painstaking efforts to learn her other lessons. She was satisfied to adore Constance, and to point her toes with the anxious attention of a beginner.

As the end of term approached, it was usual for the girls at Pickering's, as elsewhere, to be drilled into giving an entertainment for their mothers and fathers. This was a miscellaneous affair, composed of pianoforte or violin solos, the singing of madrigals, the dancing of a gavotte in old-fashioned costume, the recitation of short poems, and a speech by Miss Pickering at the end of which either the head boarder or the smallest of all the small girls, curtseying, presented her with a bouquet.

The whole school enjoyed this occasion, which involved dressing up, rehearsing, and an escape from desks. Some of the older girls pretended to think it a bore; but for the younger ones it was a first experiment in the showing-off which was so firmly suppressed in general. Discussions as momentous as Cabinet Meetings took place between members of the staff who had to decide not only as to rival artistic skills but on the imponderables of character. The last were judged by Miss Pickering herself.

She was a tall, deep-breasted woman, almost black-haired, with rich grey eyes under black brows; and when she looked round at the assembled faces, it was clear that she understood the pupils, their parents, and every mistress in the school. She knew that Miss Rowland, impatiently strict, suffered from ambition, that Miss Batchelor was over-eager, Miss Prince lacking in fundamental sagacity, Miss Gosling too easily discouraged, short-sighted Miss Thomas, who had rabbit's teeth, in danger of neuroticism, Miss Trent a good solid system of instruction like a temperature chart, the rest pilgrims upon the endless way of self-sacrifice to an ideal.

None of these perceptions was betrayed. As a consequence all, including the opposites, Miss Rowland and Miss Gosling, felt complete trust in their leader. They spoke, with assurance, cautious tentativeness, or, in Miss Gosling's case, breathless timidity, the truth about what was in their minds. Miss Pickering, surveying them, felt as a gardener does when, leaning for a moment upon his spade, he sees robins or blackbirds at his feet, confident of the treasure he has revealed to their bright eyes. She smiled.

'What I should really like to do,' said Miss Prince, feeling bold, 'is to end the programme with a play—a morality, or a pastoral—we've never done that before; and I think it would inspire the girls.'

'Inspire their jealousies,' objected Miss Thomas. 'Fill them with silly vanity.'

'Nonsense!' cried Miss Batchelor. 'There's plenty of emulation in class.' She had embraced Miss Prince's notion at once; and was ready to fight for it.

Miss Prince frowned slightly, not welcoming this particular ally. However, she looked for decision to Miss Pickering. Miss Pickering, addressing the shy Miss Gosling, said:

'What do you think, Beryl?'

Miss Gosling, who had not expected her opinion to be asked, caught her breath. A flush rose to her cheeks.

'I just wonder if they have the necessary talent,' she stammered.

'You can leave that to me,' said Miss Prince. 'Most girls learn to act in their cradles.'

'Not act; dissimulate,' snapped Miss Thomas. 'You're thinking of Constance Rotherham. She must have done that. You should see her—hear her—pretending she knows a little Latin, when she can't construe one single sentence. It's quite a performance.'

'Yes, grammar's not her strong point,' agreed Miss Prince. 'That's rather peculiar, as her father's supposed to be a scholar.'

'Well, his head's in the clouds. He's incapable of teaching her anything, unless it's tripping over a mat. In any case, she won't be taught.'

'You don't need grammar—or even brains—to spout lines. She does that remarkably. But as a matter of fact I hadn't thought of her.'

This was a lie, detected only by Miss Batchelor and Miss Pickering. A demure glance passed between them. Miss Thomas spluttered.

'I warn you that you'd be playing with fire,' she said, 'if you gave parents any reason to think our idea of education was a theatrical performance.'

She herself disliked all plays, all recreations. She was interested only in examination results. Because of this, she had favourites;

and because of it she thought nobody should tolerate the sight of girls making fools of themselves. Parents, who paid good money to have their daughters' minds trained, wanted to see those daughters collect prizes; and the girls saw in prizes tangible rewards for effort. She had good prize earners in mind—Mabel Sadman, Emily Raikes, Sarah Cohen . . . Rowland might say they were dull; but they were workers; and a school's reputation rested on its workers. Not on conceited little apes like Constance Rotherham! Why talk about the child at all?

'If it was a pastoral,' said Miss Gosling, feeling tremendously bold, 'they'd have to be very graceful. And they're not. The only thing they can dance is the polka.'

'Still, we've always had—before you came, Beryl—a minuet or a gavotte,' objected Miss Rowland. 'They could manage that, couldn't they?'

'The trouble is,' grumbled Miss Thomas, 'that Sally Prince wants to show off Constance Rotherham; and Beryl dreams of little Penelope doing the fandango.'

'Do you know what a fandango's like, Agnes?' laughed Miss Rowland.

'No, I don't,' snapped Miss Thomas. 'Except that it's foreign capering of some sort.'

'Agnes would like to re-introduce the back-board,' said Miss Prince.

'Better the back-board than the back-cloth! You'd put all sorts of notions into the head of Constance Rotherham. She's already an affected little devil!'

'Sh, sh, sh!' Miss Rowland, enjoying this passage, pretended to reprove the combatants.

Miss Pickering, having followed every speech with interest, thought irrelevancies had continued for long enough.

'Don't let's slang the girls,' she begged. 'They're individuals like ourselves. And don't let us summarily dismiss the idea of a performance. I always feel morality plays are de-humanised and dull. And, for pastorals, you need not only graceful movement, as Beryl says, but extraordinarily good speaking of verse. Sometimes lovely singing. I should like us to do, let's say, a Purcell; but somehow I can't . . . I wonder if we could try some scenes from *A Midsummer Night's Dream?* Not the lovers; but the yokels and the fairies. Genevieve Scholes would make a charming Titania.'

'I'd love to clap an ass's head on Cynthia Fleet,' muttered Miss Rowland. 'She's got one there already; but you only know that when you try to drive something into it.'

'What a fiendish idea!' Miss Batchelor immediately developed fanciful notions of other suitable decorations for offending pupils. 'I suppose it would be too obvious to make a tableau of little asses. Everybody would laugh, of course; but the mothers . . .'

'Cynthia would roar splendidly,' said Miss Prince. 'Like a foghorn.'

Miss Thomas snorted.

'A cracked foghorn. Her parents would think her voice had broken. A terrifying change of sex! It does sometimes happen, I believe.'

'If we did the fairy scenes,' Miss Gosling was in a reverie, 'I should love to see Penelope as Robin Goodfellow.'

Miss Thomas raised her eyes, her eyebrows, and her arms in mute protest.

4

This discussion had far-reaching effects upon the girls at Pickering's, and especially upon the two who had been most heatedly mentioned. By Miss Pickering's suggestion, the school included extracts from *A Midsummer Night's Dream* in its breaking-up entertainment; and the part of Titania was played by Genevieve Scholes, who looked exquisite and was fallen in love with by every male in the audience, one of whom married her three years afterwards, almost straight from the classroom.

By Miss Rowland's cynical wish Cynthia Fleet wore the ass's head of Bottom, and ever afterwards bellowed like a drill-sergeant, which she became (to her parents' relief) in the W.A.A.C. during the War of 1914–18.

Because Miss Prince so wished it, Constance Rotherham played Oberon with such magnificent swagger that she could have been principal boy in any pantomime if she had not set her heart upon such heroines as, successively, Beatrice, Portia, Lady Macbeth, and others less famous. And as a result of Miss Gosling's reverie little Penelope Rotherham abandoned her wish to become a nurse.

As if to disconcert the grumbling Miss Thomas, every child in the school rallied to the supreme game of make-believe. All were absorbed in their parts; all helped each other; all laughed uproariously at the comic situations, and heard the magic words with half-comprehension. The clowns, kept in order by Miss Prince, forgot to show off and be silly; Genevieve was so lovely in her fairy costume that the small girl fairies ceased to hate her as a tyrant at games; and Bottom, in her ass's head, which appeared only at the final rehearsal after its thrilling red mouth had been finished in the sewing class, looked so frightening that the awkwardness of her acting, which prevented a stampede, proved quite fortunate.

Miss Prince, gathering the cast together behind the scenes, read a lecture.

'Don't giggle, girls. Remember your words. Remember that each one of you is not herself but a clown or a fairy in a play. You, Peaseblossom, must only come forward when it's your turn. You mustn't push the others. Titania, do remember to vary your tones as I've taught you to do. It's all a lovely piece of nonsense; and that's what you've got to make it seem.'

Miss Gosling made no speech. She was too deeply affected to think of anything to say. But she had shown the fairies how to flit on tiptoe, and although at first they had made her weep by hopping like the giant robins of pantomime they gradually learned to imitate her light steps. By the exercise of great self-control she had been as firm with Robin Goodfellow as with the others; and Miss Prince had coached Robin so well in her speeches that both teachers were content.

'In fact,' Miss Prince murmured to Miss Gosling, 'I'm half inclined to think you were right all along, Beryl. I didn't at first, you know.'

'I just pray,' was all that Miss Gosling could answer.

The excitement was great, both in front of and behind the curtain. Mothers in their new clothes, fathers cramped by the seats and hoping they were not going to be made to appear foolish, rustled and whispered as they waited. All the mistresses helped with the dressing and grease-paint. Miss Thomas, after much scowling and muttering, began to share the fever, and having already, before the platform was converted into a stage, enjoyed her own triumph in summoning the prize-winners, checked instinctive hostility to the rouged cheeks and shining eyes of her pupils.

At last the performance began. Miss Prince, as stage manager, stood in the wings; Miss Gosling, keyed to the agony common to artists, whispered under her breath all the words as they were spoken, and watched with the dreads of a mother each movement of the fairies. As the audience laughed, her eyes filled with tears. And when, at the end, Robin Goodfellow, without slip of the tongue, uttered the actors' final plea—

> ' "If we shadows have offended
>    Think but this (and all is mended),
>    That you have but slumbered here,
>    While these visions did appear . . .
>
>    So, good night unto you all
>    Give me your hands, if we be friends,
>    And Robin shall restore amends—" '

as if they came from the heart of a gay and mischievous fairy, the tears brimmed over and ran down the teacher's cheeks. This was what she had prayed for; a triumph for her darling.

It was a triumph for everybody. The girls, elated, crowded the platform-stage, bowing in unison as they had been taught to do; and the proud audience, who had seen their own children transfigured, clapped with all their might. Miss Prince was drawn by her cast to the centre of a very pretty picture, and was cheered; Miss Gosling hid lest she, too, should be called, and was in fact called, to the satisfaction of the fairies. She would have resisted entreaty if Miss Rowland had not given her a great push, exclaiming: 'Go on, Beryl! Don't be a goose!'

When all was over, and, still radiant in their make-up, fairies and clowns were allowed to dart through the crush to their parents, the atmosphere represented joy for all save two persons. The first was Miss Thomas, that equivalent of the Wicked Fairy, to whom the applause was a repellent din. The second was Constance.

Knowing that she had done well, assuming that she had done better than anybody else, and confident of loving praise from her mother, whom she had seen, with Father, in seats towards the middle of the fourth row, she now saw both parents surrounded by other people. Pressing towards them, she found her way barred by two strangers who stood in the aisle.

They had their backs to her, and both were large and majestic, the man wearing a finely-trimmed black beard, and the woman having a voice almost as deep as the man's.

'Quite remarkable,' drawled he. 'I was hardly bored at all.'

'I wasn't for a moment,' retorted she. 'I was transported.'

'On fairy wings?'

'Fairy indeed. I thought the Titania beautiful, the Oberon both handsome and sonorous—obviously well-drilled. But as for little Puck, I was enthralled. She was the best Puck I've ever seen. Exquisite!'

'Certainly charming,' agreed the man.

'Exquisite,' insisted his friend. 'Delicious movements. A voice to break your heart. A born actress. In fact I'll make a prophecy about her. It's that she'll be in the West End within twenty years.'

'Twenty,' repeated the man, as if exactly noting the period.

'I'm serious.'

'You're always serious, my dear,' came the indulgent reply. 'And sometimes right. So I'll make a note of that prophecy—which I endorse without qualm—in my tablets.'

He produced a pocket diary, in which he scribbled something while the woman looked at his moving pencil.

Constance, seeing the next row nearly empty, pushed past them and into it. Somebody detached would have recognised the man's seriousness as badinage of a too-sanguine woman. Constance was not detached. To her, in this hour of great excitement, when all she wanted to hear was admiration of her own performance, the prophecy had the effect of a Doom. They had dismissed her as sonorous and well-drilled. It was Pen whom they . . .

Pen? This about Pen? What could it mean? Pen wasn't an actress at all. She'd never wanted to be one. She mustn't be one. She was going to be a nurse . . .

Her own triumph was destroyed. In its place, for the first time, came the dread sickness of melancholy.

# From Wilmerton to Wilmerton

# The First Disillusion

I

I T was a Summer day, two years later. The boarders at Pickering's were away on holiday, some in France, some in Scotland, some in their own beautiful or less beautiful homes in various parts of England. Wilmerton itself was half dead, at least for a girl of fourteen-and-a-half, whose only friends were her schoolmates.

Constance was very lonely. As the Rector's daughter she was shunned by crudely shy fishermen's children; and those of her own class were either little things who gabbled and giggled foolishly with Pen or young ladies of eighteen or nineteen who made it clear that they wanted nothing to do with somebody four or five years younger than themselves.

Constance resented this disdain. She felt herself to be quite as grown-up as her elders; cleverer, better-looking, and better-mannered. Yet they had the fun, often in magical London, to which the Rotherhams went but seldom; and they spoke tantalisingly to each other in low voices, with silly titters of conceit, about fascinating creatures whom they called 'fellows', inept conversations with whom they retailed at length—'He said,' 'I said'. Much laughter. Many arch glances. And then, nothing to say to Constance. Idiots!

She hated them most fiercely of all because they had what she needed most, fun and young men friends with whom they danced or played tennis and croquet. Young men, boys, or 'fellows'. She now thought of boys all day long, dreamed of them at night, imagined wonderful scenes in which they were completely baffled by herself, the 'serpent of old Nile', who laughed at their bafflement and airily kept them guessing. Unfortunately she had nobody to baffle. If the most desirable boy in the whole world, dark, flashing-eyed, and attractive, had appeared on the promenade when she took her solitary walks, she could not let him so much as speak, lest a local woman, seeing her in agreeable company, began a cascade of gossip.

'I see Rector's daughter 'sarfernoon with a BOY!' 'Did you really? Oh, dear! She's beginning early, ain't she! What is she; twelve, thirteen? My word, a Boooy! Rector's daughter! 'Stead o' setting a good example! I reckon her mother ought to know about that . . .'

Disgusting creatures.

If Mother were told about any such thing, there would be no row, such as the girls at school complained of regarding their own parents. Father, being so tall, like a lamp-post, would squint down through his spectacles, push them up on to his forehead so as to examine her directly with bloodshot faded blue eyes, make that funny sound in his throat which reminded her of a big dog's 'wuff', and—say nothing. He would then sigh heavily, and return to his study.

He never said anything, except in the pulpit, where he was as dry and cloying as an arrowroot biscuit. Pained inspection was as far as he ever went in comment upon her perversities. Constance was sure that he disapproved of her and bemoaned his fate at having such a child; but as he always preached the virtue of charity she supposed he then summoned charity to his aid.

'Isn't there something in the Bible about thorns in the flesh?' she asked herself. 'Or is it in the pot? I'm his thorn.'

When Father had vanished, Mother, looking as if she were going to be ill again, would give mild, earnest warnings against boldness and any relaxation of high principle. The warnings would be accompanied by sad shakes of the head and mysterious references to mishaps and misfortunes which Constance did not understand.

She herself, trained not to protest, would hold her tongue, as she always did under rebuke. And the precious imagined friendship with a boy would end. He would loiter near the Rectory for ten minutes, hoping to see her, while she, hidden, watched from an upper window. Then he would go away. If she saw him again she would have to pretend that they had never passed delicious minutes together.

'Wait until you're older, darling,' Mother would say, very seriously. 'Then you'll understand why you must be so careful, even with the nicest boy. Not all boys are as good and noble as Papa. Above all, I trust you never to do anything clandestine.'

'Wait until I'm older,' muttered Constance, in quite a different tone, when she was by herself. 'Then I'll show them!'

All the same, the word 'clandestine' had a delightful sound. It made her picture herself as a girl born to be rebelliously wicked.

One day her longings were half-answered. A Mrs Smith, a regular churchgoer, given to good works and kindness to all God's creatures except flies, ants, and silverfish, came to tea at the Rectory. She often did this, with a great air of respectful affection for Mrs Rotherham and awe of the Rector; but Constance doubted these protestations. They were too often accompanied by furtive glances of suspicion at Constance herself.

Mrs Smith always wore black. Her long face looked like that of a stupid horse, and her strained voice of piety was hateful to one whose ear was already alert to the music of words. She spoke of 'Gard-ah . . . our soools . . . carnduct . . . woorship . . . the laave we ought to *bear* one another, although I'm *afraid* too many don't feel that laave . . .' Alone in her room, Constance briefly, and in disgust, repeated the phrases and imitated Mrs Smith's gestures.

As always, her entry to the drawing-room was reluctant. She heard from outside Mrs Smith's voice pitched in lingering monotone, and the sight of Mrs Smith's uncomfortable forward-stretching pose filled her with constraint.

'Sickening old girl!' thought Constance. And then she caught sight of a second visitor, who took her breath away. This visitor was young. Moreover, she wore a delicious frilly full-length and tight-waisted white dress in the latest possible fashion, and an equally delicious chiffon-decorated hat as large as a perambulator wheel. She was the smartest young lady Constance had ever seen. She was entrancing.

'Ah!' moaned Mrs Smith. 'Here is dear Constance! How are you, darling? You always look so sweet. So healthy. And now I have a treat for you. This is my niece, my dear sister's child. You've heard me speak of my sister. Saach a loss to me. I mourn her in my soul!'

The lovely girl was like a thrilling splash of moonlight in the old brown room, where ancient mahogany and a heavy chandelier of aged brass put weights upon the spirits of the young.

'How splendid!' silently exclaimed Constance, like the captain of a privateer sighting a white-sailed treasure ship on the horizon. 'A prize! A prize!'

In the same instant she was just quick enough to notice that the visitor, without moving her head, showed interest in Mrs Rotherham's daughter by the merest flicker of very long eyelashes. The flicker, revealing acute judgment, gave place to a charming smile as they were named to each other; and although the smile remained the charm diminished when Blanche supposed Constance's attention to have been withdrawn. The effect was thrilling.

'I must practise that,' thought Constance.

Hitherto, in assuming expressions before the mirror, she had concentrated upon the more positive, such as anger, fear, or grief. Raised eyebrows, lofted and melancholy eyes, downturned corners to the lips, and such horrible grimaces that sometimes they forced her to stop through laughter, had been her chief concerns. Because Miss Prince believed in training her girls to declaim Shakespearean parts, Constance had ardently defied the elements, pleaded for her client Antonio before the Court of Venice, or lamented service to her King rather than her God. Such rôles, magnificent in their periods, involved no delicate *nuances* of facial expression.

Out of class she had taken the available models, still within a limited range. Mrs Smith was one of them. Oddities in local speech, or the mannerisms, such as they were, of the mistresses at Pickering's, had amused fellow-pupils rushing from the class-rooms. When alone in bed, she had invented strange ribald sharpnesses from Miss Rowland or Miss Thomas, or hypo-critically pious drawlings from Mrs Smith; but had never seen her face while so engaged. If she had dared to do so, she could have given ludicrous impersonations of her mother and father, making the one perpetually lachrymose and the other absent-minded to the point of woolliness and self contradiction in the pulpit. But these were commonplaces of vocal mimicry. Now, for the first time in her life, she beheld an artist.

She saw at once what could be compassed subtly with and behind eyelashes, and the fitful visitations of charm; how bore-dom could be hinted or hidden by a turn of the head or the lift and depression of mobile lips; how alertness could be simulated while attention had really passed to a shadow on the wall or the swaying of a lace curtain in the afternoon breeze. Everything was immediate, conscious, and secret. It was wonderful.

Constance remembered Blanche's *finesse* all her life. It became the foundation of her art. In one of her most highly praised character studies she reproduced it, drawing, of course, on later understanding, so exactly that she gave life to a dramatist's puppet and made the dramatist's fortune.

Sitting at a distance from the others, and only half observed by the elders, at least, she concentrated all her attention upon the new and fascinating visitor. Her first belief was: 'She's French!' Not because Blanche resembled Mademoiselle, at school, for she had no moustache and seemed to have no diffi-culty with the English words 'with' or 'how', but because none of the girls there, and none of the women of Wilmerton, had such curious buoyancy, such *chic*. But was she French? Mrs

Smith called her 'my niece'; and she was as pale as her aunt. Her face was milk-white, and she had Mrs Smith's heavy dark eyebrows and thin lips. Indeed, there was an extraordinary resemblance between them.

Unlike her aunt, however, Blanche was not angular. Her bones were invisible. She moved hardly at all, yet she contrived to give an impression of vivacity, which Mrs Smith never did. Her cheeks were round; her jaws a little square; her teeth small and pearl-like. She was also built more compactly than her aunt; and whereas Mrs Smith was gauntly shapeless from breast to hips, as if her flesh had eroded, Blanche had extraordinarily agreeable curves. She was perfect!

Her voice was low, and its pitch gratified the ear. Mrs Smith's, which was never raised, had an undercurrent of harshness. Where Mrs Smith unctuously drawled, Blanche, speaking no more quickly, gave her words colour. This, too, was something to be copied. It made what was said much more interesting. Used as Constance was to the level tones of Wilmerton, and the shrieking loudness of the girls at Pickering's, she found this discovery exquisite. If only she could have such a paragon for a friend!

2

Listening avidly, Constance discovered that the visitor was at school in France, was on the verge of seventeen, was thought to be very clever, had arrived two days earlier, and was staying with Mrs Smith until the time came to visit some grand friends in Somerset. When this last fact was mentioned, Blanche again glanced swiftly sideways.

That was a very curious glance indeed. Constance felt that only herself could understand its meaning. She saw at once—

not only from the glance but from something which might have been either a slight compression of the lips or an additional curve in the cheeks—that Blanche was anticipating no amusement from her stay in Wilmerton, though much from her visit to the grand friends; that Blanche was saying to her, but to nobody else in the room, that she found Mrs Smith a complete bore; and that she was already, after two days, impatient to bring her stay to an end.

Constance wanted to respond: 'I know exactly what you mean about Mrs Smith; I shouldn't want to stay with her even for a day!' She glanced in turn, with what she hoped was a perceptible flicker of the eyelashes, at her mother. The signalled meaning was: 'You see my position? I'm also rather bored, although mother's a dear. But what can I do?'

She realised how cleverly, while seeming to attend only to her hostess, Blanche had all the time been taking stock of her hostess's daughter. She could not imagine how it had been done; but she read with ease the faint smile which again changed the contour of those softly-rounded cheeks. The smile was something Constance would have given all her elocution prizes to command. In retrospect, long afterwards, she likened it to that of La Gioconda; but today, supposing it to be Blanche's private achievement, she felt enthusiasm comparable to that felt by ardent amateurs for the placid cunning of the original.

Her joy in the belief that she alone saw and comprehended the smile was ecstatic. She was sure her mother, whose delicate pallor was almost transparent by contrast with the milk-white of Blanche's cheeks, and whose mild brown eyes held no art, could not have seen what she saw.

The Rectory was ancient; one of the oldest houses in Wilmerton. It was outwardly Georgian; but much of the building belonged to pre-Georgian days, so that besides being cold and draughty it was full of old stairways, recesses, and almost cupboard-like rooms at extraordinary angles. The floors creaked, corners jutted awkwardly, the upstairs ceilings were low. But it was picturesque. Its eccentricities excited would-be archaeologists, who goggled in awe at supposed priest-holes and smugglers' and highwaymen's hide-outs.

'Marvellous! Marvellous!' they exclaimed. 'How lucky you are to live in a place like this! It's real history. In its way as evocative as Pompeii or Herculaneum!'

'I do weesh,' said Mrs Smith, in a pause, 'dear Mrs Rotherham, that Blanche might be allowed to see your woonderful house . . .'

'Oh, yes!' Blanche herself, turning with significantly vivacious shoulders, supported her aunt's prayer. Indeed, Constance could not check a sudden belief that there had been a silent appeal from niece to aunt for remembrance of a promise. Hints! Mrs Smith was always hinting. Hints ran like mice through her conversation. Mother and Father never hinted. That was one of the nice things about them.

Had Blanche peeped through those lashes at her aunt? It was impossible to tell. Both the Smiths—but obviously Blanche's name couldn't be 'Smith'; it must be something very noble indeed, like Mowbray or Cecil—had the air of keeping their real minds hidden. It was a resemblance between them, like the eyebrows. In Mrs Smith's case the reserve was almost sinister. There was an unpleasant contradiction between her beseeching tongue and fixed grimace of benevolence and her cold, grey, examining eyes.

There was something else, too. Constance clearly remembered an incident of two years earlier. She had been sent with a message from her mother to the little cobbled house in a back street where Mrs Smith lived. Receiving no answer to her rap, she had ventured to raise the latch and step within, at the same time calling to announce her presence. The door opposite, which led to a back room, was half open, and she caught a glimpse of what lay beyond.

Her glance was quite innocent; the Rectory was so immediately at the service of any visitor that she had intended no intrusion; but the glimpse she had was of dirt, a bare floor, a broken chair, and a wall from which ragged strips of paper hung. Disconcerted, she called again, and would have withdrawn if at that moment Mrs Smith had not come in behind her, from the street, hurried across the open door, slammed it, and turned with a look of fury.

'You've no business to come into anybody's house like that!' cried Mrs Smith. 'It's most impertinent!'

'I'm very sorry. I thought you hadn't heard. I did call you . . .'

Anger remained in the eyes; the smile was imposed as before. Mrs Smith heard the message, gave a reply full of gratitude to Mrs Rotherham, and, apparently thinking to erase memory of her savage rebuke, rummaged to find some sweets for her visitor.

The sweets were refused. Constance said goodbye. Memory, so far from being erased, was confirmed. She had never told anybody of the scene or the glimpse; but she had never forgotten it.

She jumped up.

'Whenever you like to come,' she said.

'At once!' Blanche rose with a swirl of skirts. She moved very rapidly indeed, so that Constance could hardly dart in time to open the door for her.

How wonderful that they were going to be alone together! The house became a treasure to be revealed, from its crooked stairs to its wide hearths and cavernous chimneys. And Blanche, eager for the strange, would listen attentively to everything that was said, and exclaim and ask questions, and examine beauties more closely with that lovely grace of hers. Time would pass; they would still be engaged when Blanche was called to go home; and perhaps . . . perhaps Blanche would suggest coming again, again and again, from affection for her new friend . . .

While Constance was breathlessly imagining the scenes that would follow, she heard Blanche exclaim close to her ear, in a whisper.

'Thank heaven! I thought we should never get away! Aunt's such a tortoise!'

While yet astounded by the frank words, Constance caught a faint odour of scent. How lovely! Scent was not used at the Rectory. Father wouldn't have liked it. How Parisian a charm it gave! Something more to remember! And the words spoken were an echo of the impatience in her own heart. Old people— so slow; young people—so ready to see and speak quickly! She gratefully acknowledged the communication with a smile. Blanche would understand that. Blanche understood everything. Blanche was a shaft of light into one's confusions.

Nothing could be said, of course, about her feelings.

'That's Father's study,' she explained, pointing to the door of a room behind the one they had just left. 'We don't go in there while he's at work; but it's just an ordinary room, with French windows opening on to the terrace. Rather dark, like most of the house. It's crammed with books.'

'He must be very clever,' sighed Blanche, as if in envy. 'Very learned. Is he famous? Oh, how I should love to be famous!'

'I'm sure you will be. We never think of Father as clever. We think of him as Father. I don't think he's at all famous. He's kind, you know; but . . . well, rather far away. He just comes in to meals; and goes back to his study. It's where he sees parishioners.'

Blanche's attention had strayed. She pointed to a little flight of stairs leading directly to the first floor.

'Aren't they quaint!' she exclaimed. 'Do they lead anywhere?' As if she did not hear Constance explain that the stairs led to her parents' bedroom, she cried: 'Oh, it's so romantic! So unexpected and inspiring!'

Constance, passing to another staircase, felt a momentary constraint.

'I suppose it is,' she agreed. 'Sometimes I wish it wasn't so old. On windy nights . . .'

'It creaks! Oh, yes, how well I understand. But if you compare it with Aunt Sarah's dull little house. Tiny. Cramped. Dismal beyond description!'

Constance hurried to the narrowest staircase of all, which wound so curiously that it was like the ascent to a belfry.

'Mind your head!' she warned. 'And your dress against the walls!'

They clambered up the uneven steps, and at last reached a small landing, from which two doors opened; and Constance led the way into a room with a ceiling which sloped almost to the floor. In the one straight wall was a window giving an almost complete view of the long garden. Two or three gnarled apple trees could be seen growing above very long grass, while in the grass hundreds of dandelions reared their golden heads.

Constance was proud of the little room. It was her own. Here were her own white bed, bookshelves, and dressing-table, her white-framed reproductions of pictures by Landseer and Millais, and the patchwork rug which she had made in the previous Winter. Until her fourteenth birthday she had shared a front room with Pen; but Pen no longer dreamed of monsters, and Constance had been liberated.

'This is mine,' she said modestly, hoping for praise.

'All of it?' Blanche glanced hastily round the room, pouted at the Landseer, and added: 'Are you artistic? I am, very. I'm going to be a painter.'

'That will be lovely.' Constance could not bring herself to say that she hoped to become a great actress.

'By the way, how old are you?'

'Nearly fifteen.' Constance, disconcerted by a tone in which she imagined condescension, added several months to the real tally, standing as it were on tiptoe to touch a star.

'Only that? I hoped you were older.'

'I think I'm old for my age.'

The lashes flickered.

'I expect you do.' The words were careless; they wounded. 'You have a sister, haven't you?'

'Oh, Pen's only a kid. Not ten yet.'

'What a long interval! I wonder why? Didn't they have any more? Is she clever?'

'Yes,' cried Constance, loyally. 'Very clever. But not a companion. She used to be an awful nuisance.'

'What, clutching? It's a bore when people clutch! I've had a lot of that.'

Constance realised from the fastidious distaste implied that if she seemed to clutch ever so little she would lose this exquisite butterfly. With a great effort, she said:

'Pen's better now. She's got friends of her own age.'

'Haven't you?'

'At school; but most of the girls there are boarders. They come from all parts of England. There's nobody I like in Wilmerton.'

'No boys? Young men?'

Blanche's expression changed. She looked directly into Constance's eyes, reading there—what? The longing for boys? The longing for friendship with one whom she must not bore by clutching?

'How can I?' asked Constance. 'There aren't any in Wilmerton.'

'Not at this season?'

Constance shivered.

'I don't know,' she said.

Blanche's face expressed nothing but enigmatic indifference. Her eyes became exactly like Mrs Smith's, or those of a cat looking into the sun. She said abruptly:

'Let's go down again, and see the garden?'

'It's nothing really, you know.'

·'Never mind; I want to see it.'

'You don't want to look at any more of the house?'

'Not now.'

Blanche had turned quickly to the low doorway. She began impetuously to descend the stairs.

'Mind!' cried Constance.

It was too late. The beautiful hat had been knocked sideways; and in catching at it Blanche caught her elbow against the door-post. Her face was distorted. Her pretty teeth revealed not a smile but anger.

'Oh, damn!' she exclaimed. 'You ought to have told me!'

Constance followed her visitor down the winding stairs. She was painfully disconcerted.

## 3

The distress increased when Mrs Smith and Blanche were gone. Neither had looked back as Constance, waiting, stood by the gate, ready to wave. With their heads together, as if they were whispering unkind comments on the visit, they hurried away. She crept indoors again, with a terrible sense of failure.

Mrs Rotherham added to misery by asking innocently if Mrs Smith's pretty niece had enjoyed her exploration of the Rectory.

'I expect it was a treat to her,' she remarked, looking fondly at Constance.

'Oh, no.' Constance transferred Blanche's indifference to her own tone. 'She's seen much more interesting places.'

'Mrs Smith said she'd been wild to come here,' murmured Mrs Rotherham.

'She didn't show any wildness.'

'I expect that was just good manners. She's been very strictly brought up. In a convent. But she's not a Catholic, Mrs Smith says.'

Exasperated, Constance made no reply. Only after a silence did it become possible for her to add:

'She knocked her elbow.'

'Oh, poor child!' Mrs Rotherham, still apparently unaware of her daughter's stifled despair, exclaimed in true regret. 'I'm so sorry. I wondered why she was so quiet at the last. Was she badly hurt?'

'I don't know. She's not the sort of person to say.'

'She's like you, then.'

'She's not a bit like me.'

'Not in other respects. I know. But I had hoped you and she would be friends. You did like her, didn't you?'

'Yes, I liked her.' Constance's tone was sulky; she was almost in tears. 'She wasn't interested in me. I'm too young.'

'Connie!' Mrs Rotherham was horrified. 'But you're not silly. Far from it.'

'She might think so. I think she did think so.'

'Then she's not as nice as she seemed. But of course girls of her age do sometimes exaggerate their own maturity.'

'It wasn't that at all. Nothing of the kind.'

Unable to utter another word, Constance turned away in anguish.

A few minutes later she went mournfully to her bedroom, where further distress met her. Within twenty minutes the room had changed. It was no longer an exquisite sanctuary; but merely an expanded cupboard. The pictures—especially the beloved Landseer—had been revealed as proof of childish taste. The white paint was insipid. The books, by Louisa Alcott, Fenimore Cooper, Clark Russell, Stanley Weyman, with *Jane Eyre* and a few odd volumes of Shakespeare, were infantile. Blanche had seen them as nursery tales. Worse still, she had shown scorn of a girl who could not produce a troupe of boy friends.

With trembling lips, Constance protested against that contempt.

'I can't help it. I can't *make* boys come to a wretched place like Wilmerton. It's too dull. She ought to know that. She simply doesn't want to know *me*!'

Depression grew black. Always subject to collapses of high spirits, Constance now did what she rarely did; she wept. The tears were hot upon her cheeks.

## 4

Twenty-four hours passed. Forty-eight hours passed. At the end of the second day rain began to fall, and a biting wind from the east chilled every corner of the Rectory. It became clear that Blanche did not intend to return.

A desperate thought occurred to Constance that her mother might be persuaded to send her with some message to Mrs Smith. She dismissed it. Mother, already suspecting the wondrous Blanche of unkindness, would shake her head. Besides, Blanche hated those who clutched. Besides, again, with rain blackening the grey walls, and running furiously in the gutter, it was no weather for calls. Another snub from Mrs Smith would be intolerable. Nothing but misery would result.

Weary and spiritless, she sought her usual distraction, and shutting her bedroom door began to study and memorise a long part. This time she chose that of Portia, the charming lady of many suitors, whose address so cleverly outwitted Shylock and saved the life of gloomy Antonio. How wonderful to be like Portia!

> "'Come, Nerissa. Sirrah, go before.
> Whiles we shut the gate upon one wooer, another
> knocks at the door.'"

From Pen's bedroom, next to her own, came shrill laughter. She ignored it. The laughter rose again, high-pitched and merry. There must be two of that child's friends there, playing in carefree sport. Probably, because strange wailings also arose, they were amusing themselves with dolls, brushing their hair and smacking them for being naughty. Silly kids! And yet, happy. Pen always seemed to be happy. She was very superficial . . .

> "'Ay, but I fear you speak upon the rack,
> Where men enforced do speak anything.'"

'That's "enfor-ced". But the rack: what a diabolical torture. She and Bassanio were only pretending. She knew he would guess right. What if he hadn't? She'd have cheated. I should. I should like to talk about that with Blanche. Grown-up talk. How I wish I could impress her!'

The pages of her book flicked over. A later speech, made by Jessica about Portia, caught her eye:

> ' "The poor rude world
> Hath not her fellow." '

Blanche! Blanche! Deep sighs followed this impulsive comparison. Portia faded from her thoughts. When laughter came again from the little girls in the next room, she shivered. Her heart seemed to fill her whole breast.

Almost exactly upon the seventieth counted hour, when wind and rain had travelled west and the sky was blue, the Rectory door bell was sharply pulled. Since Pen, in the drawing-room, was nearest, it was she who scampered to answer the caller, while Constance, drudging out of doors with the tangle of weeds, heard nothing.

Her name was called. 'Con-nee! Con-nee!' She was reminded of days when Pen, beseeching companionship, cried wildly after a crouching fugitive. But Pen's voice this afternoon held no wail. She was excited, almost joyful.

Constance flung down her gloves. The weeds were abandoned. With sudden hope she hurried towards the house, where light-footed Pen was pirouetting as she had done in the part of Robin Goodfellow. Pen ran towards her.

'Oo, hurry, Connie!' Pen was breathless. 'She's here. She wants you to go out with her!'

'She'? There could be only one 'she'! 'Just because I'm all hot!' thought Constance, ashamed of what she supposed must be her scarlet cheeks. She passed her sister without remark, and ran into the drawing-room.

Yes, it was Blanche; Blanche in a pale blue flounced dress and another large hat which shaded her immaculate face. She was attending in her most grown-up manner to what Mrs Rotherham said; but her quick smile towards Constance was extraordinarily sweet. Every charm of the first visit was reproduced. She looked deliciously cool and self-possessed, like one who had never in her life pulled a weed or, for that matter, knocked an elbow.

'Hullo, Connie!'

'Run up and change your dress, dear.' It was Mrs Rotherham who gently spoke, while Pen gazed at the visitor as if intoxicated by the sight of so much beauty. 'Blanche wants you to go for a walk with her, and to tea afterwards with Mrs Smith. Be quick!'

Constance, not knowing that her flushed cheeks gave her remarkable brilliance, returned Blanche's faint smile with one of startled rapture. She darted from the room, scrambling up the narrow stairs, washing her face and hands at high speed, and in spite of unsteady fingers slipping into her best dress and brushing the ample golden hair. She was in a dream; but in her dream she did not fail to reflect that the dress would make her look much more grown up than she was. Her last act before running downstairs again was to seek assurance from the small mirror upon her dressing-table.

'Hm. Red. I hope Blanche won't be ashamed of me.'

Her jubilation gave a glow to face and manner. The wonderful thing had happened. Blanche had proved her sweetness. Mother would be pleased. Everything was splendid. It would continue to be splendid, as long as Pen didn't spoil the afternoon by wanting to come with them. 'Con-nee! Con-nee!' That would be awful!

5

It was all right. Pen had made no attempt to change her dress. She still sat on the floor, listening to Blanche's soft voice as one who hears the nightingale; and although, at Constance's coming, she scrambled to her feet, she obviously had no thought of intrusion. On the contrary, she withdrew like a shadow into the background, quietly observant, a thin, dark little girl, rather odd, but certainly pretty.

What happened next? What did Blanche think of this new dress? It was of plain blue cotton, with a narrow white hem at the neck and wrists. They had all—Constance, Mother, and Pen—helped to make it; and it had never been worn before. Blanche must have examined the dress in one instant of lightning observation, without, of course, betraying the fact.

'Yes,' she was saying politely to Mrs Rotherham. 'Auntie's cottage is really charming. It's so compact. I tell her it's a castle in miniature. She likes that.'

An enigmatic smile played upon her lips as she quoted herself; and Constance, marvelling at the praise, wondered whether it was sincere. Mrs Rotherham seemed to have no doubt at all. She responded to Constance's expectant look of inquiry with a little nod of approval, and returned at once to Blanche.

'I'm glad the cold wind has dropped,' she said, in her gentle way. 'Constance will be able to show you the most interesting walks. We're particularly fond of one to the Downs.'

'Which aren't real Downs,' explained Constance, fearing Blanche's ridicule of the rough hillocks stretching inland for a mile. 'That's only what we call them.'

'They'll be real enough to me.' Blanche smiled at Mrs Rotherham. 'England's a lovely uneven country. I feel April must be in the air and soil all the year round.'

'We sometimes think Wilmerton's prevailing month is February,' said Mrs Rotherham. 'However, it's notoriously healthy.'

'So my aunt says.'

'Are you fond of climbing?' asked Constance.

'I don't climb for choice—except to the stars. But I love walking. Next to riding.'

'Ah, you ride?' Mrs Rotherham showed innocent marvel.

'In the Bois, I expect!' suggested Constance.

'Not at all. The Bois is for fashionable people.'

'Aren't you fashionable?'

There was an arch flutter from Blanche.

'You must be very brave,' said Mrs Rotherham. 'Though I love their beauty, I've always been nervous of horses.'

'That's because they put their ears back at you, and show their horrid gums.' Pen took her hearers by surprise, as she had meant to do. Constance quelled her at once.

'It's really Mother's tender-heartedness,' she explained. 'She can't bear the thought of bits and bridles.'

'Oh, you have to dominate the brutes.' Blanche's little white teeth were set, as though she actually rode a difficult steed. 'Otherwise they play tricks.'

'Aren't their mouths awfully tender?' asked Pen. 'Like Mummy's heart?'

'That's why one's able to control them,' said Blanche.

They were out of the house and in the beautiful sunshine, walking side by side with no great difference in height but, Constance felt, extraordinary differences—all to her own dis-advantage—in carriage and thought. She had noticed Blanche's dainty shoes, which were now hidden by the long skirt, and had contrasted them with the boots she visibly wore. Now she became aware of the difference in the way they walked. Blanche's steps were unseen, and therefore fairy-like, so that she seemed to progress without effort. Blanche's shoulders, too, moved easily; while her own, from constraint, were rigid. Blanche's hat was superlatively lovely, very large and shady; her own, less large, and revealing her forehead, gave no shade or secrecy to the eyes.

She could not deceive herself into the belief that she looked like a young lady.

Knowledge of these contrasts made her tongue-tied. She longed to say something witty, or startling, as Pen had done about horses, silly though Pen had been. Alas, no words suggested themselves. Blanche, on the contrary, looked about her with composure, and spoke with ease.

'Your mother didn't like what I said about horses,' she remarked. 'Nor did your little sister.'

'They didn't understand. They've never ridden.'

'Have you?'

That was disconcerting.

'No, I haven't. I never escape from Wilmerton, remember.'

'Where there are no horses, it seems, but only wind and rain.'

'Those are what we generally have.'

'What, all the year round? We're lucky, then, today. I felt I couldn't stand my aunt's hutch for another hour.' (Constance thought "A palace in miniature"? Was that the only reason she came for me?' She dismissed the thought as Blanche continued:) 'I told your mother it was delightful, because I didn't want her to hint to my aunt . . .'

'Oh, Mother never hints . . .'

'No; but my aunt might ask . . . She's fond of asking questions. Well, so am I, for that matter. It's one way of finding things out. Not the only way, of course.'

'No, not the only way,' agreed Constance, intoxicated by this sense of intimacy with her idol. 'Can I ask *you* a question?'

'Certainly.' Blanche showed interest by a shrewd glance.

'Do you go much to the theatre?'

'All the time. I love it. Another world. Do you go a lot?'

'Not as often as I should like,' acknowledged Constance. 'There's only one theatre in Wilmerton. We get touring companies. Some of them are quite good. Mr Hurd has been here several times, in Shakespeare.'

'Oh, Shakespeare.' Blanche's tone was disparaging. 'We have to read his plays. Pretty boring.'

Constance, after that, could not say 'I love them.' She ventured: 'We did *A Midsummer Night's Dream* at Pickering's. Not all of it, of course.'

'Let's go along the promenade, shall we?' suggested Blanche, with an implied yawn. 'I'd rather watch the people.'

'Oh, you like watching people?' Constance caught a flicker of those expressive lashes, which showed amusement at her *naïveté*; and being abashed, hastened to add: 'I like watching the sea, especially when it's rough. I feel I'm defying it.'

'I shouldn't think there's much defiance at the Rectory. It's so calm.'

'You mean, dull?' asked Constance, anxiously.

'I didn't *say* "dull",' replied Blanche, demurely.

The sun shone. The sea glittered. The waves, with little fringelets of lace, played upon the shore as if they could never rise boisterously to storm.

'This is what I call "calm",' observed Blanche, with an air of patience which was belied by the quick movement of her eyes in other directions. She was closely observing the people on the promenade, who, owing to the hot sunshine, were more numerous and much smarter than usual. They were strolling along under parasols, or—if they were young men—leaning upon the shabby balustrade and quizzing the passers-by. One or two common girls looked at the young men invitingly; an immodesty which made Constance feel quite hot.

She herself was shrinking with shyness at the knowledge that she and Blanche would have to endure the quizzing; but Blanche showed no hesitation.

'Let's walk along there,' she invited, which meant, for Constance, 'past those staring fellows.'

Eyes down, Constance did her best to keep in step. She saw the cruelly-watchful young men, who wore high linen collars and the straw hats known as 'boaters'; and the envious young women in waisted frocks with spreading skirts coming well below their ankles, some with sun-veils, and nearly all with hats as big as bicycle-wheels. Blanche's hat was much the prettiest. So was her exquisite pale blue dress, which was as closely waisted and as full below the hips as all the others, and evidently in the latest fashion. How wonderful she was!

Of course the lovely dress must be Parisian. It attracted all eyes to the wearer; and Constance felt proud, amid her own self-consciousness, to be the friend of one so irresistible. She peeped to see whether Blanche was at all embarrassed by the attention she provoked, only to be baffled by her companion's air of composure.

'If I wore a dress like hers,' thought Constance, 'I should know everybody was ogling me. And everybody would know I knew it.' Aloud, for the sake of continuing the conversation, she asked in a low voice: 'Is your elbow better?'

'What?' Blanche's tone was quite sharp, as if the question had been irrelevant. 'Oh, yes; it was nothing. I've forgotten it.'

Had she also forgotten her anger, and the fact that she had sworn?

'I was so sorry. I tried to warn you—just too late.'

There was no reply. Blanche, preoccupied, was looking ahead, to a point where the short promenade began to lose width and become a track irregularly paved with flat stones which soon gave way to tufted sand.

'Would you like to turn back?' asked Constance. 'There are no more people; and if we go on I'm afraid your shoes will be spoiled.'

She might as well have left the words unspoken; for they were ignored.

While Constance, perplexed by the incomprehensible, tried to account for this new vagary, Blanche spoke again—with decision.

'We'll go on,' she said. 'It looks attractive.'

They stepped from the last flagstone into the uncertain path. It meandered here and there, like something made by the steps of a drunken man, away from the sea, among hillocks where rocks showed their grey heads. The sun disappeared behind cloud, and a sharp breeze arose, making the afternoon so chill that Constance shivered. Wouldn't Blanche now want to turn back, even if that involved fresh encounter with those alarming stares?

It seemed not. Constance, looking up at the darkened sky, was reminded of a day when she and her mother had been caught by a storm at this very spot. She also remembered something else with which the dunes were associated. It was little Miss Gosling's dog, Beastie, who was often brought along here by his mistress.

'I wish we had a dog with us,' she exclaimed. 'One of the mistresses at school has one. She brings him this way in the mornings. Of course I mean during term. She's away now. I think she lives in Wales.'

'Dogs are dirty, disobedient things,' declared Blanche. 'Very rough.'

'Oh, Beastie's not rough. He's a dear little Scottie. He just runs about, looking for rabbits; but he never finds any.'

'And gets muddy paws.' Blanche, who loved horses, evidently took no interest in uncontrollable dogs. She was frowning.

Constance held her tongue. She had been unlucky enough to displease. Therefore she tried desperately to think of some other subject, to bring back that fascinating smile. Shakespeare, stormy seas, and now dogs had all failed. Her heart grew heavy.

It was at this moment that she noticed how remarkably Blanche's step had quickened. Yes, the smile had returned! It was sweeter than ever, full of animation; and it proved that they were true friends, at ease, and in harmony. She was exquisitely happy.

But Blanche seemed to be looking towards a spot where two heads showed for an instant above higher ground. The heads disappeared at once, hidden by ground still higher; but they presently reappeared. Two boys, or young men, coming from the opposite direction, were suddenly visible. What a nuisance! They would meet in the path, and the boys would have to step aside to let them pass. She glanced at Blanche with a little grimace of resignation which she thought would seem quite grown-up.

To her astonishment, Blanche had become visibly coquettish. Her head was lifted; her flounced skirt swayed from the dancing impetuosity of her steps; she was a changed creature. Did she then know these boys? It seemed not; for she took no notice of them as they approached, but turned vivaciously towards Constance, saying:

'What was that you told me about your schoolmistress?'

'Oh, that she had a little Scottie.' But Constance was not deceived. She knew that Blanche had been really impatient in speaking of dogs; and therefore that the inquiry was an improvisation, to suggest that she and Constance were engrossed in conversation. Blanche must know the boys; she was waiting for the appropriate moment to recognise them.

Doubt passed altogether when the taller, and elder, of the boys threw up his hand, at the same time shouting something unintelligible. His mouth, which was large, spread in a broad grin.

Constance could see that he was about twenty years of age, slightly built, very dark-skinned, with teeth showing whitely between lips that were almost brown, and black eyebrows which met above the top of his nose. If he had been less handsome, these eyebrows would have given him a sinister appearance; but there was great charm in his gaiety. Obviously he must be French; for his assured manner was as different as possible from the stiffness Constance had noted in English boys when they met girls on the promenade.

The young man's companion was different. He was not more than sixteen, with wavy light brown hair and fresh colour; and he was as shy as the elder boy was confident. He did not take part in the greeting; but stood a couple of yards away, looking at neither Blanche nor herself. He was very clean, as if newly scrubbed, and his clothes were scrupulously neat.

'This is something we don't tell my aunt,' murmured Blanche into Constance's ear. Aloud, with apparent surprise, she exclaimed: 'Good heavens! What brings you to this stony region? Are you walking from Land's End to John o' Groats?'

The dark youth continued to smile.

'I have always known England to be a land of romance,' he said. 'Of happy accidents!'

As he pronounced this last word, it seemed to Constance that he and Blanche exchanged a glance of understanding, on his part mocking, on hers warning and quickly veiled. Accident? Or pre-arranged? The injunction to herself not to mention it to Mrs Smith suggested something thrillingly clandestine. She instinctively drew away, supposing that they were to pass; but was checked by Blanche's next speech. It was:

'Where do you go from here?'

'We are strolling,' answered the stranger, with the same arch-ness as before. 'My friend lives two–three miles from here. We have all the time in the world.' He looked directly into Blanche's face, so boldly, so impudently, that Constance drew a quick, nervous breath. Surely Blanche would come away at once? But no.

'This is my friend Constance,' she said, with a glance equally impudent. 'Constance, this is François. As you can tell, he is from France—for better or worse.'

'I'm enchanted.' François bowed ceremoniously.

'Good afternoon,' returned Constance. She was abrupt; and her discomfort was increased by suspicion that he and Blanche shared immediate ridicule of an English girl's gawkiness. They seemed to know each other well. She remembered: 'This is something we don't tell my aunt.' But supposing they were seen by a gossip from the town? Mrs Smith—Mother—conceal-ment—betrayal; the disturbing thought darkened delight.

'And this, if you will allow me to present him, is Tom. Tom; it is a good name; a good English name, I think. You know? Tom Brown, Tom Sawyer, Tom Moore, Tom Thumb . . . You'll say they're not all English. There has been no King Tom.

But who knows? A King Tom would be very popular. Like
this Tom . . .'

Constance found the flood of words and allusions confusing.
When she could bring herself to turn to the boy Tom she saw
that he also was confused. He was not handsome. He had very
heavy eyelids, and she thought he grinned sheepishly. The grin
passed, however; he frowned as if he found the party not to his
taste, but could not summon words of protest.

'Yes,' continued François, 'Tom. I commend him to you.
Always the firm upper lip; the refusal to admit defeat; the strong
silence . . . But why do I tell you these things? It is enough to
say that he is English.'

Tom was not amused. Only Blanche considered the rallying
delightful; and having laughed she shook her head faintly to
François, warning him to stop. Silence fell upon them all.

Suddenly Blanche made a decision.

'Let us walk,' she said, falling into step beside François, and
quite obviously leading the way along a path already determined,
among the hillocks and away from the sea and people. It was
fringed with scrub and furze which developed into occasional
masses of woodland. Tom and Constance were expected to
follow.

Constance, averting her face from Tom, obeyed this assumption; Tom did not. He hesitated. When at last he joined her he
looked sulky, and remained quite two feet away, as if fearing
contamination. She did not know what to do or say.

Because this was the first time she had ever been alone with a
strange boy, her heart was beating fast. Here indeed was the
clandestine adventure against which Mother had warned her;
but it was different from all secret imaginings of such a thing.
It was also marred by suspicion that Blanche and François were
conspirators. Tom's distant behaviour suggested that he was as
uncomfortable as herself, perhaps from the same reason.

Blanche and François, chatting with animation, walked very
fast, seeming bent on out-distancing superfluous companions.

'Blanche! Blanche!' No notice! She was like Pen, in former days! What was to be done? Either Tom or she must speak. He seemed unable to do so; she could think of nothing to say. He might be a nice boy; but one could not be at ease with someone who scowled.

'Do you know François well?' she asked, in desperation.

'Yes.'

That was all. She tried again.

'He's French, isn't he?'

'Yes.'

'Blanche has just come to stay with her aunt. This is only the second time I've seen her. She's lovely, isn't she?'

No answer. At last Tom said, in a tone of reproof:

'Your bootlace is undone.'

'Is it? Oh, excuse me.' Convicted of being a sloven, she knelt and re-tied the lace, while Tom, having taken a few steps, stood uncertainly looking out to sea. So they were both shy; and his expression showed that he did not like her. Probably he thought that she ought not to wear such heavy boots. Or did he think her in the habit of trailing their laces? It was terribly embarrassing.

The delay had been particularly unfortunate, because by the time she stood upright again Blanche and François were not to be seen. They had run away, with cruel indifference. Only rough grass, bushes and clumps of stunted trees lay ahead.

What was Tom thinking as they stopped, scanning the distance? He was so speechless, so much like a boy who had been tricked into association with a distasteful girl, that Constance was at a loss. Her impulse was to say: 'I'm sorry if you don't want to be with me. It's not my fault, you know'; but he would not believe her, and the words would not come. She continued to take step after step; but her heart was heavy. Should she say: 'This is just as bad for me as it is for you'? Should she suggest turning back?

All at once Tom resolved the situation.

'I must go now,' he said, abruptly. 'Goodbye.'

And with this he turned at right angles across the land, leaving her alone, astounded, humiliated, with burning cheeks and tear-filled eyes.

## 6

She stood in consternation for several minutes. What was to be done? Should she go after the others alone? No! She would never force her company on those who did not wish for it. And yet Blanche, who had supposed—sweet girl as she was—that Tom would stay with her, would be shocked to know of his desertion.

This wasn't Blanche's fault at all. Nothing was Blanche's fault. That mischievous François had hurried her away; no doubt laughing in triumph at having shed two children. When she discovered what had happened, Blanche would be furious. If Tom had not forgotten his manners, they could have gone, laughing, in pursuit; and when at last the truants had been overtaken all would have been happiness. She and Blanche would have come home in high spirits at the adventure.

Meanwhile she couldn't stay here. Some horrible man, noticing her, might try to scrape acquaintance. Somebody from the town would recognise her and make up a story. 'I see that girl, Rector's daughter . . .' 'Ooh! What was she a-doin there, then? I lay she was up to mischief, naughty girl, tryin' to get picked up . . .' Disgusting!

Shaken by a sob, she began miserably to drag heavy feet back towards the promenade, turning again and again to look for the fugitives. They were not to be seen. Only a small, moving object, far away to the right, might be Tom, trotting home, away from somebody he disliked.

Oh! Oh! The lovely afternoon was spoiled!

Slipping into back streets, to escape the staring crowds, she made a long détour to avoid Mrs Smith's horrid little cottage and the observation of Mrs Smith's spying eyes; and at last crept through the Rectory garden to the kitchen door, opening it noiselessly. If Mother was lying down, and Father was in his study, she might escape observation and reach her room unseen.

Hardly breathing, therefore, she moved along the passage with her ears strained to catch any sound. In her progress she had to pass within a short distance of the drawing-room door, which was ajar; and so she became aware of a voice, of voices, within the room. Curiosity led her to stop, listen, and at length go nearer, in order to see the speakers. One of the voices was like Blanche's, and hope sprang to her heart. Could Blanche, having missed her, be here? That would be wonderful!

On reaching the open door she saw something that filled her with amazement, anger, almost horror. There was only one small figure in the room, arrayed in flowing skirts and an absurd hat made from tissue paper spread and crumpled to represent headgear of the latest fashion. Pen! But what was she doing?

She was languidly strolling about the room with an air of extraordinary affectation, stopping to pirouette, sitting down with exaggerated grace, and cocking her head in a way to suggest a mixture of pride, simpering insincerity, and vulpine cunning. It was a fantastic performance. Moreover the voice Pen used was not her own. It was full of strange cadences, in which the accent of a fine lady alternated with saccharine deference to what, apparently, had been said by some other person, invisible and inaudible.

The tones did not always reach the point of articulate speech. They were just such murmurs as a parrot reproduces. But as Constance, with gathering indignation, recognised a parody of movements and speeches made in this very room no more than an hour ago, she heard Pen say, with ruthless mimicry:

'Yaice, mai aunt's ha-oose is laike a witch's castle, where she eats little gairls for breakfast. Ai laike eating little gairls, too; but ai prefer raiding. Ai make horses obey me. Ai pull the bits

against their tender ma-oothes—so. It's a laavely sensation. Ai
do it with aiverybody. *Otherwise they plaay tricks!*'

The speech was followed by a swift fluttering of the eyelashes; and it was this fluttering, so grotesque, so diabolically
observed and burlesqued, that drove Constance frantic. She
rushed into the room, tore the paper hat from her sister's head,
and smacked the elfin little face.

'You wretched child!' she shouted, blubbering. 'Wretched!
Wretched! It's not a bit like!'

Pen did not cry. A mischievous smile remained upon her face.
Worse still, she uttered no sound, and gave no sign of emotion.
Only the slapped cheek shone red below eyes glowing with
satisfaction at having given a perfect example of the mimic's art,
and received the tribute of anger from one who thus testified to
its perfection.

Fiend! Fiend! Deeply agitated, Constance felt the torments of
shame and despair. She ran, crying noisily, from the room.

Flinging herself in agony upon the bed in her little room, she
fought to stifle hysterical sobs by burying her face in the pillow.
Her muffled ejaculations were sometimes those of anger, sometimes those of wild wretchedness. She hated Pen for having
listened with pretended admiration to Blanche, while at the
same time mocking her speech and with frightful malice watching
every gesture. She hated Tom for his boorishness, which had
unbearably wounded her pride. She hated François for tempting
Blanche into treachery. But chiefly she despised herself for a
triple defeat. Pen would never forget that slap and all it betrayed.

Deceitful little devil! Pen was artful to the core! Her performance had been as clever as it was shocking. Those people at
school had called her a genius. This proved them to have been
right.

'She's got genius. I haven't!'

The humiliation was overwhelming. It was confused by
sudden jealousy. Horrible little beast! There was something vile
about her. Always pretending to be so good; clinging like a burr

for as long as she needed protection; but now—independent—
a danger to peace, hope, ambition.

'Perhaps she mimics me like that? Makes those other little
beasts laugh like hyenas!'

Even Blanche had been soiled, especially by the charges of
cruelty to horses and resemblance to that hypocritical creature,
Mrs Smith.

'It's not true!' screamed Constance, wildly, beating the pillow.
'I don't and I won't believe it!'

Beneath the cry an inner voice, heard many times before and
throughout life, whispered doubt. Pen's mimicry could not be
dismissed. She heard it anew, with all its insinuations. The
whisper became clamour. Blanche's behaviour was revealed in a
new light. Blanche, having made a convenience of her, had left
her open to Tom's affront, and given Pen the opportunity for a
disgusting show. Blanche, therefore, was involved in all three
humiliations. Ghastly, ghastly humiliations!

'Never again!' thought Constance. 'I won't be made a fool of!
I shall never again trust anybody, as long as I live.'

SCENE TWO

# Discovery of a Mother

I

ONE afternoon, shortly before her seventeenth birthday,
Constance, who was declaiming silently in her little bedroom, was roused by clamour from below. It was caused by
Mrs Muffin, the fat old woman who came to the Rectory to scrub
and polish; and Mrs Muffin was screaming as she battered at the
study door.

'Sir! Sir! Come at once! The mistress is dead!'

Constance flung her play-book aside and jumped the short
flight of stairs at a bound. She was in time to see her father,
drowsy with sleep, make a haggard appearance in his dressing-
gown, blinking uncomprehendingly and muttering words that
Mrs Muffin could not understand. They were: 'What is this dis-
graceful noise? I don't understand you. I'm too old.' At sight of
Constance he showed relief. 'What is the woman saying, Connie?
She shouts so, I can't . . .'

'Mother. Ill.' Constance darted away from him, and into the
drawing-room.

There, all was darkened by thunder-clouds out of doors and
the weight and size of the old mahogany furniture within. Her
mother, collapsed beside an armchair, looked like a hastily
thrown brown dress; and she was filled with terror. Then love
for this brave and much-enduring woman (which she had not
known before that she felt) swept every other feeling aside. She
was at once by Mrs Rotherham's side, kneeling, and tenderly
embracing a body which was rigid with pain.

'Mother; can you hear me? Let me help you!'

'I'm so sorry, darling,' came a faint voice. 'So sorry to be a trouble to you.' Overcome by the effort to speak, and seized with violent nausea, Mrs Rotherham would have sunk to the floor but for Constance's embrace. For an instance their heads were together as they had been in Constance's babyhood.

'Oh, dear; oh dear.' It was the Rector who added a second groan. Some other words, perhaps a prayer or an apostrophe to his wife, seemed to follow; but, still in his ungirdled dressing-gown, he was obviously incapable of lending assistance. 'Oh, dear, dear. What did you say, Connie?'

'Doctor, Father. At once! Don't forget to put on your coat.'

To her satisfaction, he understood, turned at once, and tip-toed from the room.

'Why,' exclaimed Mrs Muffin, as they raised and supported the almost lifeless body, 'there's nothing of her! Oh, poor lamb, she's passed away!'

'She hasn't!' shouted Constance. 'Be quiet! Help me to get her to the couch. Then we can loosen her clothes. That's what she needs.'

Mrs Muffin was quelled. She marvelled at Constance's presence of mind; and Constance, knowing that she did so, was strengthened. Within three minutes, while they still struggled with their task, they heard the Rector close the front door and saw his shadow flit across the wall as he hurried forth.

'Fancy his doing what you told him!' goggled Mrs Muffin, full of admiration.

They had partially undressed Mrs Rotherham as she lay on the couch; and in awed obedience to a whisper Mrs Muffin rustled off to heat water for bottles and bring blankets from Constance's bedroom. While she was away, Constance knelt close, taking both cold hands within her own warm ones, and gently chafing them. The retching had not returned. Mrs Rotherham, shivering and exhausted, sought with unearthly eyes for signs of disgust or impatience in her daughter's face. Finding none, and un-suspicious of a power of disguise surpassing anything at her own innocent command, she sighed deeply and closed her eyes. Only after several minutes of endurance did she feebly murmur:

'You're such a good girl, Connie. Always so good to me.'

Constance, feeling sick, could hardly repress vehement denial. Self-reproach was a new sensation; and it was now confused by detestation of her mother's humility. Such humility was criminal. It was a complete travesty of truth. It had made the rest of the family, Father, Pen, and herself, belittle and feed upon a nature altogether virtuous. In passionate reaction, she would have withdrawn her hands and forsaken the invalid. Since that was impossible, she turned all her wrath upon the one who had thankfully escaped.

'That silly old man!' she thought, with the hardness of youth. 'He leaves everything to others. He's done it all his life; and made her a slave. Now he'll try to do it with me, shamming helplessness. He shan't! I shall be sick if I have much more of this awful strain!'

The wildness showed that she knew herself to be trapped by circumstance. Looking desperately for some support, she could think of none. There were no aunts or cousins on either side of the family. Her only uncle, of whose naughtiness she was ignorant, was dead; somebody who had once existed, like Pre-historic Man, but had never been seen. She would die rather than appeal to Mrs Smith; and the other ladies in Wilmerton could only think in terms of soup and charity and gossip and pious platitude. She hated them. Mrs Muffin had neither brains nor skill. Pen was too young—barely twelve—to do more than dust and lay tables out of school hours; and even these tasks she would dodge with the sweetest face in the world.

'I won't! I won't!' thought Constance, knowing that she would have to do anything that was done. She listened for her father's footsteps. Mrs Rotherham's cold hands were a little warmer; but there was no strength in their clasp. 'That silly, fraudulent old man!'

## 2

The days passed. The doctor, a brusque and disappointed fellow named Purvis, whose practice, in so healthy a town as Wilmerton, hardly supported himself and his family of hungry children, called daily; but he knew he could not save Mrs Rotherham, and he was too conscientious to think of running the Rector into debt. Mrs Smith, who never now mentioned her niece Blanche, made one perfunctory visit, saw no prospect of advantage to herself, and stayed away, pretending that she was one who never pressed unwelcome attentions. Other ladies, rebuffed by Constance, who preferred to make her own mistakes and to conceal them from busybodies, thought the Rector's daughter headstrong and unmannerly. Neither doctor nor really good-hearted callers guessed how deeply she needed love. The only person to do so was her mother.

Conversation with her mother, however, was difficult. Constance could not be always at the bedside, and her dashes upstairs from the kitchen, although frequent, allowed of only brief exchanges. Mrs Rotherham was lighter to lift at each encounter. Visibly fading, and with the power of concentration diminishing every day, she lay alone in silence. Only those great eyes, full of love, proved that she was conscious of what went on around her; and when she did speak her whispered words were, far too often for Constance's peace of mind, no more than acknowledgements of humble gratitude.

The acknowledgements could be silenced only by pretended remembrance of something left undone downstairs; but they were repeated at the next visit. They were never maudlin; they were clearly the consequence of physical inactivity and a ceaseless concern with the demands her illness was making upon a girl who was not used to the imprisonments of cooking and domestic work.

'You are getting out, darling? It's so important.'

'Yes, Mother. I always walk to Pickering's with Pen; and shop on the way back.'

'Father gives you . . . money?'

'I ask for it.' Constance laughed at the memory of her father's fumbling in his pockets and his habit of thrusting the money into her hands as if it burnt his fingers. 'You'd think he was a miser.'

'He's not that, dear. Not that.'

The defence was immediate. Mrs Rotherham tried several times to explain the qualities of her husband's character. It seemed to be her fear that Constance was judging him harshly; but even as she explained she fell breathlessly silent, unable to complete the sentences. The effect upon Constance, who dreaded the effort involved in all such struggles, was to give her extraordinary understanding of her mother and all persons excepting herself. Herself she did not recognise in Mrs Rotherham's ejaculations.

'Your father . . .'

'Yes, I must go, Mother. The saucepans will be boiling. I've got meat in the oven. I'll come back soon.'

'Yes, dear. You must go. Don't keep your father waiting.'

'I never do. He wanders in, you know.'

'I know.'

Fortunately Mr Rotherham was no *gourmet*. He ate underdone meat, watery cabbage, and venturesome puddings as he would have eaten ambrosia, with indifference; apparently lost in melancholy. As he did so, he sometimes stole a mystified glance at Constance; and as soon as he had finished his plateful he left her.

He would come stooping into his wife's bedroom like a man who had been pushed in by somebody outside, standing just within the doorway, and muttering 'How are you?' or 'How is she?' before turning tail and creeping out again. He usually left the door wide open, a habit which made Constance long to slam it. He was like an antediluvian Hamlet, apostrophising Yorick's skull or pondering the question of his sullied flesh.

Did he ever hear what they told him about Mother's health? It was never the truth.

His eyes sank deeper into his head, leaving the unclipped eyebrows as prominent as a pair of strayed moustaches. When, as often happened, he had forgotten to shave, the white stubble on his chin reminded Constance of the old beggar who hung about the Wilmerton railway station as a fake extra porter. Mr Rotherham was as useless as that old ruffian, and far more dismal. Only at sight of Pen, when she came home to tea, did his air of troubled bewilderment give way to a distorting grin. He had abandoned his old effort to treat both his daughters alike. Pen was his darling.

'Wretched little thing! But at least she keeps him away from Mother. Meanwhile, I do everything; and he gives me no credit for it. Damn! I wonder what he'd think if he heard me say "damn"?'

Constance did not cry. She suffered; and learned.

'Your father . . .' said Mrs Rotherham, hardly visible and audible in the darkened room. One saw her face half-buried in the white pillow, a small patch of cream in a sea of milk. She was so much wasted that the bed looked as if nobody were in it; and her cough hardly stirred the counterpane. It was a dry cough, unsatisfying, perpetually recurrent. The room itself was invisible to her; merely a grey cloud in which she could see none of the furniture which had been there ever since the Rotherhams came to Wilmerton. Yet it was in this room, in this very bed, that Constance had been born. 'Your father . . .'

Oh! Good heavens! Was there to be another struggle to defend one who had become her nurse's bane? Constance set her teeth.

'Yes, Mother?' she answered, with conscious martyrdom.

'He . . . can't bear . . . to see me like this. It wounds . . . him. He's troubled.'

'Yes, well, we all are,' retorted Constance. 'Even Pen.'

'Even Pen.' It was a relief to use that word 'even'. It gratified her sense of injury. But her mother did not notice the dryness. She was musing.

'Pen? Dear child! She's . . . too young . . . too young . . . to understand . . . so much that you understand. I forget . . .'

'She's twelve.' Constance did not mean to criticise Pen's reluctance to stay in the sickroom. She reminded her mother of a fact.

'It seems . . . unbelievable.' Mrs Rotherham ceased to speak. Her mind had wandered to the past. Presently she resumed: 'Pen. I think of her as . . . a baby. Such a tiny baby; always.'

'She's quite a large baby, now.'

'But still . . . a baby. She was never any trouble to me.'

'Unlike me.' Constance was half defiant, half rueful.

'You were born in a time . . . of great tribulation. I regret it very much. Very. Your father's never . . . been the same since . . . his vision, you know.'

Her attention caught, Constance asked sharply:

'What vision was that? I didn't know he'd ever had a vision.'

'Didn't you? I thought . . . you knew.' The sigh was one of exhaustion. It was frightening.

'Don't talk now, Mother. It tires you.'

'I'm very tired. But I want . . . to talk to you . . . while I can. Sometimes I'm afraid . . .' The white face turned in the pillow. Tears of weakness glistened in the swelling eyes. Mrs Rotherham had not the strength to wipe them away; and when they overflowed it was Constance, almost weeping in her turn, who dried the sunken cheeks. Speech became impossible; but at last the murmur continued: 'There's . . . so much I want to . . . tell you, darling. So . . . that you understand. I think of it . . . all the time. When you're . . . not here. And when you're here . . . I can't remember . . .'

Detesting her own impatience, wearied by the ordeal of having to listen so closely to what was spoken with such effort, and struggling to conceal her emotion, Constance pretended that her attention had been caught by a noise outside the house. She moved away from the bed, slightly parting the heavy curtains and looking down into the street. Spring sunshine flashed through flying clouds; raindrops lingered upon the pane; a draughty wind searched newly-leafed trees near at hand. She wished she could escape.

There was no escape. The feeble voice from the bed reached her, and she was forced to return. 'Your father . . .' It was like a summons to prayer, while the sunshine called and the outer air promised everything that youth could desire. 'Your father . . .'

'Damn Father!' exclaimed her thought. She returned to the bedside.

It was in this mood that she first heard, with complete scepticism, the briefly—and gaspingly—told story of her father's vision, illness, and return from death. It would in any case have been hard to grasp; when extricated from her mother's broken whispering it became grotesque.

'You don't really think he saw anything?' she demanded.

Mrs Rotherham's faint smile was so exactly like Pen's when Pen felt mischievous that Constance received an extraordinary shock. It was clear that she had never known her mother. She had assumed her to be what she seemed, quiet, timid, patient, a little dull. But if she could look like Pen, even for a moment, now, when she was so ill, she must at some time have had Pen's spirited relish for absurdity. Damn Father! He had smothered her!

'We . . . none of us . . . see what the . . . other person sees, dearest. Even . . . now, in our . . . daily life. We ought not to doubt, Connie.'

'But we do. You did.'

Mischief had gone. It was replaced by angelic calm. Her mother was a good woman, loyal to her husband, who believed it a duty not alone to control the tongue but to discipline thought in case it passed into sacrilege.

'I'm sure he had a vision, darling. I think his trouble . . . ever since . . . has been that . . . he can't prove . . . to himself that he had it. He doubts himself. You see him . . . doing it, don't you?'

'I see him worrying about something. I thought it was you. It ought to be you.'

'No; the vision. Wondering how he . . . came to . . . forget. For him, it was like . . . falling deeply in love, and then . . .'

Stirred by the unexpected reference to falling in love, which was a phrase to quicken the pulse, Constance cried eagerly:

'Then what?'

'What, dear? Oh, out of it.'

'How do you know? Is that what you did?'

'I? Oh, I was . . . talking about your father.'

'Yes; but what about you? Did you once have a vision? Did you fall out of love?'

Mrs Rotherham did not answer. Perhaps her thoughts wandered in the forests of memory and lost themselves. When she next spoke it was to gasp once again her gratitude for patience.

'I wish . . . I wish I could tell you how much . . . your goodness to me . . . Dearest; forgive me.'

In great pain, and in great disappointment at what could have been an evasion, Constance was ruthless.

'I'm not at all good to you, Mother. I'm not, like you, good by nature.'

The smile actually returned. It lighted the ghastly pallor into beauty.

'So much . . . better . . . than you think, darling. I understand. I've always . . . understood and appreciated you . . . better than you . . . realised.'

Consternation filled her daughter's heart.

'You never heard from Blanche, did you?'

Again Constance was startled. The blood warmed her cheeks. How had her mother reached this topic?

'No, not a word.'

'She went away at once, you know.'

'I didn't know.'

'Mrs Smith didn't say . . . why. Just . . . that she had gone. I suppose Wilmerton was . . . too quiet for her.'

'I expect it was. It's too quiet for me.'

'I . . . know. She didn't . . . behave very well that . . . Sunday, did she?' It was a question which Constance would not answer. 'I guessed. Something Pen said. I never . . . asked you before.'

'You mean, what happened? Nothing. Mother, you're talking too much. It's bad for you.'

'I . . . knew you were . . . too proud.'

'Too proud for what?' Constance, from breathlessness, could hardly pronounce the haughty words. Her mother's tribute had gone deep into her heart. It was the praise she had always needed; and it had been withheld through timidity.

'To show . . . pain. Your father, too, is a . . . stoic. He's afraid you think him . . .'

'Think him what?'

'I don't know.'

'What I think is that he's always found me a noisy bore.'

'Oh, no!' The cry was quite loud. 'Isn't that . . . strange. The misunderstandings, I mean. We're all so . . . defensive. I think he's . . . afraid of your judgment.'

'He afraid of me? It's ridiculous!' Her heart was beating fast. She looked sharply to see if the mischievous smile had reappeared on her mother's face. It had not done so. Mrs Rotherham said:

'We never know . . . our own power, darling. It's left to . . . others.'

The silence was longer. Constance, thinking her mother had fallen asleep, was about to tiptoe from the room, thankful to escape, when the faint voice resumed:

'I didn't really like her, you know. She's too much . . . like her mother.'

'Oh? I didn't know you knew her mother.'

'Mrs Smith.'

'But she's Mrs Smith's niece.'

'No, darling. The same . . . eyes. Didn't you notice?'

This must be delusion! Yet Mrs Rotherham's appearance was unchanged. She was as quiet as ever. Could she be wandering?

'But eyes don't mean . . .'

The weary tone was the same.

'To me, everything. She's exactly . . . what Mrs Smith must have been . . . at her age . . . With that . . . complexion the bloom soon passes . . . It will be . . . the same with Blanche.'

Constance stirred in discomfort.

'Mother! I'm surprised you should be so . . .'

'Uncharitable? I'm sorry . . . darling. I couldn't help noticing that Blanche, like her . . . mother, was cruel.'

The horses! The dogs! Constance could not dismiss the memory; nor that of Pen's burlesque. Wasn't Pen cruel? Wasn't she cruel herself? Or wouldn't she be so if she had the courage?

Although she had not spoken them, her thoughts must have been read.

'You've never been cruel, my dearest. Even . . . in childhood, when you might . . . thoughtlessly . . . You've never looked . . . at me as . . . Blanche did.'

'I didn't see her look at you at all. Yes, I did. She looked everywhere. But not cruelly.'

'She was too clever to . . . understand that . . . the simple . . . aren't deceived.' That wound must have gone deep; there could be no retort. Mrs Rotherham continued: 'You've never been as unkind . . . Even . . . when you were angry and impatient . . . with me.'

Constance could bear no more. This penetration passed her understanding. She went to the window again, to hide uncontrollable tears.

They had no such conversation in the ensuing days. Only at the last, when life was nearly gone, did Mrs Rotherham return in speech to her continuous preoccupation. She had been dwelling upon the whole of her married life, picturing days of past happiness or sorrow, gravely remembering her husband as he had been in youth, before their several disasters. No evasions distorted the picture; she knew every weakness in a nature to which Constance was inexorable in criticism. But she also knew that in spite of his limitations John Rotherham was an upright man, the truest and most considerate she had ever known. With what was almost her last breath, she gasped:

'Connie, my darling. Be kind. Always. To everybody. But especially . . . to him. He'll need it . . . more than ever. You do . . . understand, don't you? You know I'm dying . . . Never think . . . we . . . he, I, ever . . . *ever* . . . undervalued you. My pride, my love . . . God bless you. My . . . dear . . . dear child. Goodbye.'

## The Lights Call

I

ALTHOUGH she had seen the theatre often enough from circle or gallery, her knowledge of it went no farther. It was with a throbbing heart that she ventured at last into the dark cavity described, on a dingy lantern, as 'STAGE DOOR'. This cavity might have led to Dis itself, so black and complete was its silence. Nobody barred her way. No hoarse shout demanded to know her business. If such a shout had echoed, she must have screamed and run out again into the street—perhaps for ever.

The venture was culmination to a year of misery in Constance's life. She was eighteen, penniless, inexperienced, but already beautiful and vehemently ambitious. She had no mother. Her father, bereft of his wife, was a shadow who, when she spoke to him, averted his eyes and ignored her words. Unless Pen was at home, warming his heart with her grace and mischief, he sat blinking like an ancient and deserted dog.

The Rectory was thus a penitentiary. Mrs Muffin, worn out, and indignant with thanklessness, had withdrawn to her own cottage. Her place was taken by Mrs Randall, a sparse, religious, colourless woman, self-enslaved to one whom she considered half a saint. She rarely ventured beyond the kitchen; and when she left it she was on her way to bed after the supper dishes had been washed and put away. Pen's imitations of her humility were irresistible; Constance's, being charged with suppressed dislike, went deeper into character. She saw fundamental resemblances to her *bête noire*, Mrs Smith.

She would have been wholly wretched if the passion for acting had not sustained her. It was a light, a fire, a dream. She crept to the small theatre in Wilmerton whenever possible, sometimes taking Pen, and sitting rapt in the half-empty sixpenny gallery, watching stage and actors with delight, repeating what she remembered of their parts, and inventing parts of her own, until the world of unreality became her solace. On dark or thundery days, re-living the sensations of her mother's last weeks, she developed a febrile loyalty to that patient woman which caused her to cry a little. She loved her mother as never before.

Pen, on the contrary, seemed unaffected by their loss. She went blithely to school in the mornings, and returned in the afternoons, quietly indeed, but with no sign of feeling. When they went to the theatre together she chatted in the intervals and skipped on the way home, derisively mocking plays and players as if she saw them as follies in action. She was the heartless fairy of legend.

Only for Constance was the little theatre in Middle Street a shrine. She was enraptured by it, and hunted for plays among her mother's books or in Wilmerton's primitive lending library and secondhand bookshop. In this way she became possessed of such classic comedies as *The School for Scandal, She Stoops to Conquer*, and *The Clandestine Marriage*, together with a shabby volume of Dicks's *British Drama* with its glorious mixture of old-time favourites, from *Arden of Faversham* to *George Barnwell* and *The Road to Ruin*.

All were added to her one-volume edition of Shakespeare. She impersonated Perdita, Miranda, Lady Teazle, and the shrewish Katharina; and proceeded less confidently to the heroines of Rowe, Lillo, and Mrs Centilivre. When very bold, she essayed Hamlet himself, whispering the great speeches as she reluctantly swept the stairs or made the beds. Sometimes she rose with the daylight on mornings of gale, ran to the shore, and defied winds and breakers as she had done long ago. These were the best moments of all. They charged her imagination, filled her lungs, and gave her priceless hope.

At last, on this murky October day, after her father, hastening blindly to his study, had almost knocked her down without any knowledge of his act, she rushed from the house. Her fists were clenched.

'I will!' she had exclaimed, flying from disregard. 'I will!'

She never forgot that day. A mist obscured the sea; the pavements were wet and the air heavy with damp; the darkness was like that of a northern city in winter. She knew exactly what she was going to do. Erasmus Hurd's company of Strollers was paying a return visit to the Theatre Royal. She had seen it while still at school, in two Shakespearian comedies, and, last night, in a German play which she had only pretended to understand. She was convinced that she was a better actress than either of the young girls who played minor parts in the German play. And this was her chance, desperately taken as a retort to her father's insensitiveness.

Now that she was in the unlit theatre, cold fear, increased by the repellent grime of a stone staircase and unplastered brick walls of a sixty-year-old building, made her teeth chatter. Quaking, she forced herself to scramble up the stairs, stopping to listen, ready to fly, but repeating the words 'I will!' for bravery's sake. And at last she heard voices.

She had reached a landing, on which were strewn boxes of various sizes; and above her head loomed structures which she assumed to be pieces of scenery. They were battered and jagged, so that she caught her arm against a broken bar. The smell was of mouldering wood and the dust of ages. She peeped towards a single patch of light, about which were grouped a number of people who wore overcoats or woollen jerseys to protect themselves against draughts which might have come from an undercliff cave untouched by the sun.

As far as she could tell, the shrouded figures were those of men and women; but they could have been troglodytes. Only as her eyes became used to the spectral scene could she distinguish between members of this motley crew, of which the males were blue-chinned and unshaven, while the females were gracelessly bundled into clothes that made them look like prisoners newly discharged from gaol.

'Good heavens!' thought Constance. '"Here's sorry cheer!"' Her heart sank.

Two dejected figures stood apart from the rest. They were close together; and they faced a small man who wore a dark grey jersey and a pair of baggy brown trousers. This man held a book or sheaf of papers in his left hand, while with his right he stabbed the air to emphasise what he was screeching—there was no other word to describe the discordant noises which she had first supposed to be the cries of several people—at his victims.

She was struck with incredulous disappointment. Could this undignified little creature really be Erasmus Hurd? In costume, long ago, as Othello he had looked magnificent; and his voice had rolled magnificently—'Most potent, grave, and reverend seigneurs'—in a way to stir the blood. Even last night, in modern dress, he had still been impressive. His photograph in the part of Hamlet had stood on her dressing-table for a year past, as that of the finest actor she had ever seen.

On this empty stage, amid unidentifiable sheet-covered objects that might have been treacherous rocks, he had no magic, no grandeur. He was as insignificant as the cheeky little grocer in Elm Street who always facetiously addressed her as 'Madam'. She could imagine him slapping packets of tea or lard or biscuits on to the counter and crying 'Anything else—Madam?'

'Madam . . . Madam . . . Madam'; the recurring humiliation of that familiar impudence seemed to echo in her ears. For a moment she could not attend to what was taking place.

When she did so, the first shock was over. The old intoxication with whatever belonged to the theatre crept back as blood returns to numbed fingers after escape from a bitter wind. She watched the scene before her with excitement. Here was a real rehearsal. Here were real actors practising their craft. What they wore was of no account. Everything would be different when costumes were donned and the footlights glittered, when the stalls—now a dismal mass of shadow—were filled with eager audiences. She was seeing what ignorant people would call the seamy side of an art. It was her privilege to do so.

Erasmus Hurd waved the hand holding the papers, and spoke peremptorily, as if he played the part of Napoleon for laughs. But nobody laughed. What were they doing? One woman, standing by herself at the back of the stage, watched almost furtively with her head down. She had a broad brow, and her eyes were half-closed. She was very pale. Did she imagine herself invisible? Was she jealous? She did not move at all. She was like a cat at a mousehole. Constance gradually remembered having seen her last night, when her part had been that of a subdued wife who turned the tables on a more brilliant rival.

Where was the rival? She must be among those who ignored what was being said by Mr Hurd. They were talking among themselves in low tones, obviously bored or cynical. One man was telling some story to a couple of the others, much of it in clever dumb show; the girls were tittering together; the common trait being that of disrespect for the shouting producer.

She looked again at Erasmus Hurd, trying to discover in his diminutive figure the splendid performer she admired so much. It was impossible to do so. He threw his shoulders from side to side in ridiculous shrugs; his walk was a strut; owing to the way he cocked his head, the chin always ludicrously projected, as Punch's does, beyond the tip of his nose; the effect was grotesque. The whole impression was of caricature.

His attention was concentrated upon the two who stood mutely before him, listening, in the centre of the stage. They were a tall, very slim youth and a shorter woman whose hair was greying.

'Good God, Masefield!' he was bawling. 'You're supposed to be beside yourself with love for a whimsical gairl! Go at her as if you meant to bite, strangle, rape her. Not treat her as your grandmother!' At a slight titter from two girls, hardly two or three years older than Constance, he glared melodramatically, and stamped his foot. 'No laughing, ladies; your turn—none too pleasant—will come. Remember, we play this tonight. The audience, if we get an audience for another modern play after last night's fiasco, will report to their friends. Empty houses for the rest of the week! Bankruptcy! Finish! Here's your last chance to put life into the show. Tonight. Tonight. Understand? Now . . .' He went back to the supposed lovers. 'Try again: "This is the reward I get for years of devotion . . ."'

There was no doubt of it: Masefield had a cold and a lisp. He was very handsome, with a sweep of blond hair back from a noble forehead; and he had a voice as different from his mentor's as a violin's tone is different from a chorus of frogs. Constance immediately fell in love with his looks and his golden tenor. But he could not simulate tumultuous passion for a woman old enough to be his mother. Constance imagined him equal to Lorenzo's speech beginning 'How sweet the moonlight sleeps upon this bank' or the 'Ode to a Nightingale'. Here he was mis-cast. Couldn't Mr Hurd recognise that? He must be crass not to do so.

Her teeth no longer chattered. She forgot the chill of the damp theatre and the dirt of the bare boards; and was absorbed in her criticism of a tyrannical little man. This little man was quite unlike the Othello she remembered and the Hamlet of her treasured photograph. His face was so thin that she likened it to a slice of bread. His heavily-lidded eyes were lost beneath almost invisible eyebrows. His mouth, when not stretched wide in rant, was sealed in a line of complacent cunning. Only when, thrusting Masefield aside in contempt, he took his place and spoke the words with harsh but vehement ardour, did he reveal stupendous energy and give life to what had previously been mechanical.

Carried away by his own enthusiasm, he came near to battering an actress who was newly inspired to play the wanton. The middle-aged woman became a Beatrice, proud, mocking, and flirtatious; while Hurd, miming, raising the harsh voice, dropping it to a whisper which all could hear, using hands, shoulders, and innumerable bird-like turns of the head, wooed like an amorous cat.

'You see?' he cried, abandoning the performance and turning again to Masefield. 'You see? Now, then!'

Constance was fascinated by the brilliance of his impersonation; still more fascinated by the sudden change of mood. She had seen something new and wonderful. It was impossible to like the man—his conceited strut was again ridiculous; but his magic had stopped all tittering and boredom among the rest of the company and filled her with admiration.

Masefield's attempt to imitate was pathetic. He was dismissed. The others in turn were summoned and drilled in a play full of brittle speeches which had to be delivered at high speed in order to make them seem witty. All the characters were shallow and conscienceless, all existed only to score off each other and be discountenanced. Unless they were made quick and smart they would be merely puppets.

This explained many of Hurd's abrupt changes of address. He was trying, obviously, to galvanise his cast into vivacity; and his cast, not understanding his aim, continued to be as heavy as dough. He was exasperated. He shouted. He flung down his papers, emitted scathing insults, treated everybody as incompetent, and at last shook his fist at them all.

'I give up!' he cried, in a terrible voice. And, a moment afterwards, throwing despair aside, he said almost mildly: 'Let's try again, shall we?'

So engrossed was Constance in the extraordinary exhibition that it was some time before she discovered that some, at least, of the company had seen her and were remarking upon her among themselves. They were impervious to Hurd's tantrums, which were too familiar to be frightening; and while he railed they stared at a stranger as animals stare at one of their own species before attacking it.

The stare was so concentrated upon clothes which they found amusing that the little man stopped in the middle of a tirade.

'You're not attending, ladies. If you want to learn, you must attend. Listen. What?' He wheeled unexpectedly, saw Constance, and joined in the general cruelty. 'What's this?' he demanded. 'Who are you? Go away!'

Constance, crimsoning before the unexpected attack, did not move. She had unconsciously assumed a pose which gave her blonde good looks a quality suited to Desdemona. Even the little man was arrested.

'What do you want?' he cried, with blunted sharpness.

Constance refused to be afraid. Her voice, having defied the breakers of the English Channel, was richer than any she had heard that morning.

'I want to be an actress,' she replied.

There was a stir of laughter among the watchers. An older man made some remark which convulsed his two neighbours. Even the badgered Masefield, who had recovered from the harassment he had endured, allowed a cold smile to cross his proud face. He, like the rest, awaited with malice the inevitable crushing retort.

'So do twenty thousand other fools!' snapped Hurd.

'They can't act,' shouted Constance. 'I can!'

Indeed, her acting at this moment was superb. She was the very Portia whose part she had often rehearsed before the mirror. Had she cried aloud Portia's command—

> 'If thou dost shed
> One drop of Christian blood, thy lands and goods
> Are by the laws of Venice confiscate
> Unto the state of Venice—'

the others could not have been more surprised. A second murmur of laughter caught her ears. She knew that the elderly man must have made a further comment to his neighbours; and that the girls were murdering her with spiteful glances. She was not disconcerted. Her temper was high.

'Go away,' cried Hurd. 'Go home to your mother.'

'I haven't got one.' Her defiance was magnificent.

'Your nurse, then!'

'I'm going to be an actress. The best actress in England.'

The laughter was no longer a titter. It was a baying chorus. Something in her air—perhaps merely her beauty, which had been heightened by resentment of the laughter—softened Hurd's impatience, however. It also had its effect on the greying woman who had not moved the statuesque Masefield to passion. She touched Hurd quickly upon the wrist, and spoke to him in an undertone.

The words were inaudible to everybody else; but they made him glance sharply, first at her, and then, with a curious glitter which in after days she came to know well, at Constance. It was the glitter, she found, of scheme; swift, secret, evil. He then stared at his feet as if they were shod with gold.

Constance saw that one whom she had at first taken for an insensitive hag was not only capable of playing the wanton but was as alert as herself. Though robbed of brilliance by the lack of paint and footlights, and, possibly, of a wig, she became recognisably the company's leading lady, Ellis Rooke—Portia, Ophelia, Imogen—whose performance as Juliet, two years earlier, had seemed to a schoolgirl the most beautiful piece of acting imaginable. Every tone, every gesture, had been that of an innocent. Wonderful!

How deceptive the theatre was! Miss Rooke had no beauty. Her upper lip was too long, her chin too short, and her mouth, from much speaking, was too loose for sweetness. Yet there was something extraordinarily attractive in her natural melancholy. Care, until she cast it away for an assumed character, was her lot. It revealed a new truth to Constance, who thought:

'Even leading ladies can be unhappy. I shan't be like that!'

Hurd whipped round, quelling the merrymakers with a scowl, and concentrating upon herself a lion's sombre ferocity.

'Wait there,' he commanded.

It was a triumph. Her perceptions, ordinarily very quick, were given lightning speed. She understood at once that Miss Rooke had spoken in her favour, with some particular part, it might be, in mind. The whisper might have been 'Perdita'. She also caught the impression that Hurd, taking pride in abrupt decisions, and subject to vehement changes of mood, felt respect for Miss Rooke's judgment. It fired his more vivid imagination.

Were his changes serious, or only mocking? Constance could not tell; and in fact never discovered. The man was a mixture of genius and charlatan, scheme and impulse. She thought at this moment that he could be diabolically cruel. She found that he could be both mean and vengeful, obtuse and penetrating. Never honest.

Was Miss Rooke his wife? Was that why he accepted her judgment?

Excitement became intense. When a chilling draught from behind penetrated her clothing, she felt her teeth chattering again. Drawing back, half realising that her grace had won the interest of this strange pair, she tried to remain perfectly still while the rehearsal continued. It was almost impossible to do so; for cold, anxiety, and excitement were attacking self-control as never before. With a great effort, she concentrated attention upon what was happening.

In spite of ignorance of stage business and the need for changes of posture in any dramatic scene, she could tell that Hurd was a master of technique. He shouted instructions in that harsh voice, and was obeyed. If the effect he wanted was not instantly obtained, he flew into a rage, stopped everything, and forced his cast to try again and again until he was satisfied. The power wielded by one small man was astonishing.

The play, being modern, held no poetry. Speeches were staccato; often bitter; and to a listener unacquainted with what was still to come they were sometimes incomprehensible. This did not matter. She was enthralled. To the end of her life she remembered this occasion; and with much experience thereafter of other producers she held the view that he had more sense of the stage than any of them. If character had been among his virtues he would have been a great man.

Miss Rooke, rousing herself, recovered youth. She developed from the early flirt, who sported with a lover as young as herself, into a woman infatuated with a cynical man of middle age—played by the saturnine joker who had ridiculed Constance to

his fellows—and gave power to scenes in which regret for the
past and despair at betrayal carried the play to its climax. She
was constantly interrupted by Hurd, in order that some gesture
or intonation might be discussed; and she was apparently never
resentful of the interruption. That was another lesson for
Constance, who was by nature wilful.

It was evident that Miss Rooke knew a great deal about the
stage, and about life. She must have been aware of all the
jealousies emanating from those who watched and wished that
she could be humiliated. She knew that they all sneered at young
Masefield; and that the man whom she was supposed to love
sneered at her as an actress. She knew, too, that the titters at
Constance had begun in disdain and would attain to venom.
No sign of awareness escaped her.

There was one youth in particular whose hostility was un-
hidden. Constance read his contempts, for Masefield, herself,
Hurd, and Miss Rooke. He was dark and slight, already bitter,
not with a sense of failure, but because he was naturally splenetic.
He felt—and showed—particular contempt for Masefield, as if
he felt how much better he could have played that part. Was it
true? Was he the superior actor?

Constance supposed Masefield had been given the part because of his looks. He was the schoolgirl's dream hero. But he
was stiff, too conscious of himself and his beauty, unable to
imagine the relation with Miss Rooke in her stage part. Constance
thought: 'If he were playing the part with me, he'd be better.'
One day he should play that scene, on the stage or in real life,
with her. The fancy quickened her breathing.

Hurd at last said:

'It's a bloody mess. Enough to break a man's heart. Schoolgirls would do it better.' He considered. 'But I'm tired. We'll
come back to it this afternoon. Three o'clock, sharp. All right.'

There was a general movement among those who had been
stormed at for the past hour. They were like children dismissed
by a disgusted form-mistress, so that they reminded Constance
of Pickering's, where she had been the only subtly defiant

culprit. Possibly from relief, they ceased to torment her with their stares. She was forgotten.

But not by Hurd. He gave her a glowering look, intended to lower her crest. It made her quail; but with a great effort she stayed where she was, allowing the others to jostle past and out on to the stone stairs up which she had toiled a lifetime ago. They were all murmuring; but whether in complaint of a slave-driver or in promises of recovered strength from coffee in the town she could not gather. Hurd and Miss Rooke remained in the centre of the stage, their heads close together.

What did it mean? What were they saying? Miss Rooke appeared to urge something, while Hurd, at first nothing but a frown which seemed to embrace his whole body, listened, objected, made his violent gestures of impatience. Miss Rooke persisted, using no gestures at all. What did Miss Rooke really think of him? Were all his ways familiar to her, and to be borne resignedly? She was not really resigned; she was patient, as Mother had been patient with Father; but she could insist, which Mother had never done.

The conversation was all-important. If it ended with one final shake of the head, or a bawled 'No!' everything would be at an end. The Rectory would be a prison. She could not bear it! She would have to run away, go to London—and then, what?

He did not bawl. He did not shake his head. He gave a quick nod of decision. Then, to Constance's astonishment, he turned, and without a further glance at herself, walked to the opposite wings and disappeared. She was aghast. What had happened? What was to follow?

2

What followed was crucial. Miss Rooke, now alone on the stage, beckoned; and they stood face to face, Constance the taller but with lost self-confidence, a child dreading dismissal.

Miss Rooke must have known this; for there was only kindness in her manner. Her voice, as gentle as Mrs Rotherham's had been, was like a quiet caress.

'I don't think you could stand this, could you?' she asked. 'It goes on day after day, week after week.'

Tears of relief started to Constance's eyes.

'I could try,' she earnestly replied. 'All I want is a chance. I don't ask for anything more.'

Miss Rooke's weariness was evident; but she smiled.

'I wonder if you believe that. Most beginners blind themselves to the drudgery . . .'

'I don't.'

'. . . the discomforts, the humiliations . . .'

'I'm used to humiliations,' said Constance, thinking of many she had received.

'Really? With your looks?'

'My father doesn't notice them. He's a splendid man; but he's old. He lives in a dream. He loves my young sister. He's bored with me. I used to be the noisy one.'

'And you aren't now? Isn't it possible that you imagine that? It's a phase with some girls. They want to leave home for excitement.'

'I only want to act. I've wanted it all my life.'

'That sounds like the real thing. I was like that, long ago.'

'You wouldn't have done anything else.'

'One learns.' Miss Rooke's face was drawn. She, too, had humiliations to remember. 'I mean, one learns that ambition's a deceiver. Well, now, come and sit down. Tell me about yourself.'

Constance, following to a small settee which had been covered with a dust-sheet, was at her best. She told that most fascinating of all stories (to the narrator), her own history.

It did not take long. It embraced everything; school, parents, Pen, and her own ardour. She was heard without interruption by a woman whose interest was conveyed by attentive immobility. There were no exclamations, no protests; the hearer's head was not once shaken, although her dark brown eyes moved at times, almost imperceptibly, to note Constance's lips, hands, ears, and beautiful neck. Each of those items was inventoried.

Constance was too clever to appeal for sympathy. In speaking of Pen she showed no resentment of her father's preference. She had the extraordinary sensitiveness to response from an audience which separates a virtuoso from labourers in any craft. As if with the antennae of a butterfly, she judged what would arouse the lady's sympathy, and ascertained the degree of her success.

When the story ended—as it did with the laughing words 'I think that's the whole story'—she felt a return of dread; but she knew she had done well. Miss Rooke was far more experienced than herself; valuing pauses and tones and omissions, not merely as the little cheats of story-telling, but as proof of character.

The pause was short.

'What you tell me is extremely interesting. I must think it over; discuss it with my husband. Would you mind if I saw your father? You're only eighteen, you say; that's a great problem. Also, of course, we should have to hear you in action.' Her smile was mischievous; a revelation of inner spirit which quickened Constance's affection. 'Then we'll see. But you must steel yourself against disappointment. My husband is very severe.'

'I know,' answered Constance, with a smile equally mischievous.

'You're a darling,' said Miss Rooke.

The further ordeal, of speaking lines to a scowling Hurd, was greater. It was undergone in a small room above the stage which contained as furniture little more than a table bearing a large and battered mirror. Beside the mirror was a big shabby enamelled tin box full of coloured sticks which she recognised as those used for make-up; and beside this lay a dish like an upturned saucepan lid full of ash and the stumps of blackened cigars. They had been blackened by nicotine and saliva.

On the walls were pinned two or three old playbills, some lists of unreadable names and dates, and a series of photographs of Hurd in various parts, some of them brown with age and perceptibly flyblown. The atmosphere was stale with cigar smoke and the smell of grease-paint, while daylight struggled through a dirt-encrusted window. The only warmth came from an old oil stove. Nothing could have been more miserable as a setting for what she afterwards came to know as an audition.

Nor was her nearness to Hurd more reassuring. He had turned the chair in front of the dressing-table so that he faced her; and she, separated from him by little more than a couple of yards, had behind her the room's grimy door, which she could not bear to touch. Hurd himself was pitilessly bored, and yet at the same time sharp-eyed to discover every hidden tremor.

His strong cigar—she found that off stage he smoked almost incessantly, looking meanwhile as raffish as a bookmaker—was gripped by yellow teeth at one side of his mouth and constantly chewed to the accompaniment of grimace. A small grey cloud from it hovered overhead, while lesser drifts made Constance's eyes prickle in discomfort. Another girl, similarly affected, and embarrassed by his nearness, would have stammered, coughed, been silenced; but she, seeing that all was being done to test her nerve, resolved that she would foil a malicious little devil as he should always be foiled.

He probably expected her to pant a schoolgirl's recitation of Portia's great speech, or a sepulchral version of 'To be, or not to be'. She would do neither. He should hear, instead, Perdita's delicious lines,

'Here's flowers for you;
Hot lavender, mints, savory marjoram;
The marigold, that goes to bed with the sun . . .'

and that last speech of Katharina's, in *The Taming of the Shrew*, which ends proudly with the advice to women to

'place your hands below your husband's foot;

In token of which duty, if he please,
My hand is ready; may it do him ease.'

She did not recite; but delivered both, with a little faltering, as she had said them to herself a thousand times.

There was a terrible silence. Hurd chewed his cigar, from which smoke had ceased to float aloft.

'Why bowdlerise?' he barked.

'I kept to the speech,' she defiantly answered.

Another silence. Then:

'Who taught you?'

'I taught myself.'

'And chose those speeches? Why?'

'I thought you might like them.'

'You'll never be an actress, you know.'

It was crushing; but Constance, knowing that he meant to frighten her, smiled without protest. She began to pull on her woollen gloves.

'What? Where are you going?'

'Home.' She turned away, a queen.

'Just a minute.' Hurd stared at her fixedly, chewing the dead cigar and jerking the corner of his mouth. Reaching behind him to the dressing-table, he picked up one of several typewritten sheets which lay there. 'Read that.'

Gloved still, she took the sheet and saw that it came from a play unknown to her, and that it was in prose. Several names appeared; but she read from the top line.

'"Well, like all stout women she looks the very picture of happiness, as no doubt you noticed. But there are many tragedies in her family, besides this affair of the curate. Her own sister, Mrs Jekyll, had a most unhappy life; through no fault of her own, I am sorry to say . . ."'

'That's enough. You obviously don't know what it's about. Nor do I. The play's by Oscar Wilde. I'm not putting it into our repertoire. His name stinks, for one thing; but after last night's fiasco and tonight's probable ditto-ditto I'm doing no more modern plays—unless I change my mind. That could happen. Fluid, you see. It's a sign of genius. Consistency is the hobgoblin of little minds. But I think I shall stick to Shakespeare and Sheridan. No royalties. Were you in the theatre last night?'

'Yes,' answered Constance.

'Like it?'

'Not much.'

She saw him look deliberately straight into her eyes; saw that in his own there was a glitter of evil. Instinctively she remembered that the door was close and its handle to her right hand. Was this expression mesmeric? It had a strange confusing effect upon her, almost that of paralysis. Yes, he was like a stoat. She understood why rabbits let themselves be murdered. Rabbits and women. But she was no rabbit; and nothing . . . All the same, it was the first time she had felt such apprehensiveness under the gaze of a man.

Whether Hurd read her feeling or not she had no means of guessing; for as it became intense his expression changed. He gave a short laugh of good humour.

'Hm, it was by Sudermann. German. Much admired by the *ton*, who think anything foreign's bound to be good. The rage lasts for a year or two. Then it drops. You're too green to understand what that means. Not innocent; green. There's a difference. However, you were honest enough to admit you didn't care for it. I could teach you a lot, if I had time—and inclination. No time, though. I'm a slave, as it is, to the mediocrity of others. You remind me of Mary Anderson. Does that name mean anything to you? She was an actress—of sorts. Is, I should say. You'll never be her equal . . . Well, I don't know. The stage is a chancy business. You'll probably pick up a few ideas before you're forgotten . . .'

This alternation between familiarity, harshness, and discouragement, she later found, was characteristic of the man. It was known to his company as 'Hurd's cat-and-mouse trick'; and caused him to be as much hated as he was admired and despised. Masefield, especially, was maddened by it; but Hurd, being jealous of Masefield's height and good looks, was continually vindictive towards Masefield. He called the young man 'Vox and praeterea nihil', or 'the profile', and took every opportunity of insulting him before the others.

As yet unversed in the trick, and assuming herself to be dismissed as a bore, Constance turned again to go. Her glove was in contact with the door-handle when she was recalled by muttered soliloquy.

'Why Ellis should want to see your father, I'm damned if I know. Well, there it is; good old female obstinacy—known as intuition. No good at all. Eh?' Grimacing, as if in disgust, he again subjected Constance to that paralysing stare, which was full of lechery. 'We'll hear what she says. Meanwhile, come to the front of the house tomorrow night. Not tonight; tomorrow. I'll tell them to give you a seat. I'm playing Shylock; it's worth seeing. All right; go home!'

Out in the street at last, and caught by a dank air from the sea, Constance was choking. She had passed headlong from cold to suffocation, depression, and excited hope. Hurd's baffling mixture of encouragement and derision had had its effect. She was fascinated. His stare, which in later life, when sophisticated humour had developed, was recalled with contemptuous merriment as a seducer's artifice, had quickened her pulse. She ran home to the Rectory. If she had been less infatuated with the theatre she would have stayed there in security for as long as her father lived.

Such security was impossible to her. Nevertheless the sense of guilt was oppressive. She crept about the house, and up to her bedroom, listening for the fatal ring at the doorbell, and, when it came, left the answering to Mrs Randall. Then indeed she opened her door and strained her ears, catching a murmur of voices, a rustle, and footsteps below. Silence followed.

It seemed to last as long as a Winter night, while with fists clenched she endured torturing suspense. Would she be called? If so, what could she say? Speeches formed in her mind, speeches which alternated between those of cold obstinacy and hysterical protest; and all were dismissed as useless. Father would never let her go. He would listen to what Miss Rooke said, his head lowered and that gloomy frown upon his forehead. Then he would say 'No', and every hope would be shattered.

'I won't!' she muttered—again and again. 'It's my chance. I *must* take it.'

The door of the study was opened. The sound of voices rose and faded. The front door was shut. Her father returned to his study. She was not sent for. That was worse than death.

Later she heard Pen arrive home from school and rush upstairs to her own room, singing. But before Pen could see her she had retreated. It would be terrible to be seen while she was so much disturbed; and the silly little thing would tease her with questions which she could not answer. The singing stopped. Pen came out again and went downstairs, where it seemed that she marched confidently, as Constance could never do, into the study. No sound followed. Was Father telling Pen what had happened? Was he smiling at Pen as he always did? Was he sitting with his arm about his pet, while Pen ruffled his hair, confident that her every action would be allowed, and welcomed?

At last it was teatime, and Pen called her. She forced herself to enter the drawing-room with proud dignity, seeing Pen, irresistibly pretty, still in her school uniform, but with eyes brightened by recent tears. Father then shuffled gravely into the room, glanced at a point above her head, and seated himself as he did in church, with an expression suggesting doom to all evil-doers, including himself.

Only at the end of five minutes did he show any sign of acknowledging her presence. The weary, bloodhoundlike eyes were painfully focused.

'Well, Connie; so you want to leave us.'

All speeches were impossible.

'Yes, Father,' she answered.

What would happen? She knew he would not shout or scold;

but he might reproach her in the tones of Hamlet's ghostly father. He would be justified in doing so. Oh, it was agony. He was cruel. He didn't mean to be cruel; he never meant to be cruel; but silence could be the greatest cruelty of all. She heard him sigh.

'I knew this was bound to happen,' he said. 'I feel I ought not to stand in your way.'

'No, Father.' She was choking again. The blood burned her cheeks. She could not look at him. 'Thank you.'

There was a long pause.

'I've promised to let you go, on trial, for three months.'

'It's very good of you,' Constance whispered. Although her rebellious heart asserted that he would be glad to be rid of her she meant no irony.

This was all. Pushing aside his teacup, Mr Rotherham rose to his full height, looked down at her long and earnestly, and went away. He had indicated that she must descend into Hell in her own wicked way. Wasn't that the meaning of his speeches, of his silence? As she sat at the table, joyless and conscience-stricken, she was shaken by one great sob.

The sob, so rare a betrayal of feeling, caused Pen to jump up and put her arms round Connie's neck, pressing her cheek close. The cheek was wet, because Pen had been quietly crying.

'Poor Con! Poor Daddy too! You won't forget us, will you!'

'Never,' said Constance. 'Never!' She was newly horrified by realisation that she was deserting the one person, tiresome, lovable, puzzling, who cared for her. 'I feel awful. Selfish, wicked—that's what he means me to feel. But unless I do this . . .'

'I know. Of course you must. But I don't know what we're going to do without you.'

'You'll have Father to yourself.' It was the solitary bitterness of speech Constance allowed herself. 'He'll be happier when I'm gone.'

'No, he won't. That's quite wrong.'

'I'm sure of it.'

'You can be sure—and wrong. He just can't show his feelings, poor old man.'

'He does to you. He could have said he was sorry.'

Pen withdrew her cheek; but continued to press Constance in her thin little arms.

'Could you do that?' she asked. There was significance in her question; but she hurried on: 'There! I've made your cheek wet.' Uncontrollably mischievous in spite of tears, she dried the cheek, polishing it with her handkerchief. 'Now you'll shine like a ruby! We shall be able to see you in the dark. "A good deed in a naughty world."'

'Yes, in the dark.' Constance pushed away Pen's handkerchief. 'That's where Father thinks I'm going. The Abyss.'

Pen would not repeat her contradiction. She said, still nonsensically:

'And however far away you are!'

'However far,' Constance agreed, lost in her own thoughts.

'And you'll write to me. And you'll come back very soon.'

'Yes, I'll write to you.'

'And I'll write back. Some of my writing's been put in a case at Picky's—an example to the school.'

'Little demon! You'll always be held up as an example. I shan't.'

'It will be as if you were still here. Well, you *will* still be here, of course. I shall think of you all the time.'

'You won't.'

'Quite often.' Pen was laughing and crying at the same time, as she often did. She was a fairy; she was Robin Goodfellow; she was compact of sweetness. Feeling shamed by such charm, Constance did what she had never done before. She kissed the wet cheek.

'And now,' said she, chasing Pen's lightness of heart, 'I'll tell you the story of my theatrical life.'

# First Love

I

IN retrospect, nearly sixty years later, she could laugh at those days.

'Green,' she thought. 'The *mot juste*. And yet not quite so green as that old scoundrel supposed.'

She had a gift for seeing herself, not defensively, but with sportive approval. Also, the Hurd episode, painful as some of it was, and ludicrous in its conclusion, unquestionably held the germs of later·success. She dwelt upon it with amusement, employing her lifelong gift for vignette. The elaboration of detail might be suspect; but the sharp outline, and a memory for words spoken, were always there. •

'Near enough. Near enough,' she would say with smug relish, if qualms of honesty insinuated a doubt. 'In any case, they're all dead and done for; so there's nobody to contradict. I shouldn't mind if they did. The only one is Pen; and Pen wasn't there. Too young. What she found out later can't be helped. I wonder how much? Pretty nearly everything, I expect; the little witch.'

Wasn't 'bitch' the more appropriate word?

'Dog doesn't eat dog,' she announced airily; and leaning back, gave an old woman's cackling laugh.

With a return to those days of immunity from Pen's devilry, she opened the book of memory at a poignant chapter. It related to a time when she had become a settled member of the Hurd strolling company. She was then, nominally, 'Assistant

Stage Manager', and really a drudge who waited upon everybody else and saw that all was in order on the stage before the
curtain rose. Her work began in the morning, and continued
until the show was over at night. She did not act; but studied
minor parts in case one of the others could not go on, and as an
extra lady in crowd scenes—the crowds were very meagre—
wore ancient clothes fitting where they touched and held
together with safety-pins.

Nevertheless she was still gloriously happy. She knew that
her chance of greatness would come. She watched the principals,
absorbed tones and movements, noted unexpected omissions,
or chance slips in texts familiar to her, and gave particu.ar heed
to the savage cuts made in the prompt copies. Some of these
were wanton, more were made necessary by the smallness of the
company; but all added to her knowledge. She still rejoiced in
the accidents, wild haste, and improvisations of theatrical life,
for which she felt she had been born.

It was not long before she decided which of her fellow-
travellers could be trusted and which not. The men were generally full of mock-deference to one whom they recognised as a
lovely baby; the women were never guilty of the spitefulness she
had scorned at Pickering's. They all helped her. She was fascinated when she watched their performances on and off the stage,
and when she heard their dropped comments on each other.
And although at first she was excited by flattery—she never lost
her love of that—she was never long a victim of it. Charm was
often used for selfish purposes, she found; once it was withdrawn
she had learned one more lesson. Furthermore, her own ability
to charm was enhanced.

Outwardly, Hurd's Strollers were a happy-go-lucky band of
troupers. They met bitter railway journeys in unheated carriages
with stoicism, and the incidence of lost or delayed baggage with
rueful merriment, the older men telling tales of previous misfortunes and the imaginary remarks of fabulous landladies.
Landladies, indeed, and Hurd himself, were the subject of constant and astonishing ribaldry. On the other hand all expressed

warm affection for Ellis Rooke, speaking of her in a chorus of praise which swelled into slightly overemphatic adulation.

This was deeply interesting to a beginner. So was the fact that each man and woman unconsciously revealed a concentration of egotism which enabled him or her to enjoy fancied superiority to everybody else in the world. All punctuated their exchanges with endearments; the words 'dearest' and 'darling' being constantly used. All noticed every slight to themselves, and resented it with the artist's suppressed hysteria. Constance noted all these things.

She might have taken herself with equal seriousness if the blood which made her Uncle Terence impenitent in disaster had not run freely in her veins.

She was thrown more into contact with one of the other girls, Maude Marsh, than with the rest. She and Maude shared a room, sometimes a bed, in most of the lodgings which they were found or found for themselves. Maude was large-mouthed, looked kind and good-humoured, and was an untrustworthy confidante. She played hoydens, or such rustics as Audrey, in *As You Like It*, with spirit, laughed at everything, and, as a room-mate, showed great inquisitiveness. Having questioned Constance from the first, she produced sharp criticisms which she thought necessary, and repeated to others what she had been told. Constance came to regard her as a friend, but a dangerous friend.

Another certainty was that the elder and darker of the sisters Dodd, Roberta, was motherly under a mask of ugliness, while the younger, Gwen, whose hair was almost as golden as her own, was both curious and given to secret ridicule. Her *gamine* smile had resemblances to Pen's; but she had not Pen's—what was the word? Could it be 'quality'? 'Genius' was much too strong. Pen's gift was for mischievous impersonation; a flying talent for mimicry which Gwen lacked. In spite of sisterly belittlement of somebody whom she knew too well for comfort, Constance could not deny that Pen was exceptional. It was by comparison of talents that one estimated true values.

The girl who could look statuesque in serious parts was Doris James, a solicitor's daughter from Weston-super-Mare. She made no effort to be friendly; but she was never either coarse or heartless, as Maude Marsh became when crossed. Constance formed a secret admiration for her, and for a while imitated her in good faith; but finally concluded that her reserve was due to stupidity. Imitation then ceased.

The oldest member of the company, apart from Miss Rooke, called herself Rachel Delmaine. She was gifted, looked sad rather than contemptuous of her juniors, had fits of deep melancholy and spoke in a deep voice with an air of weary disillusion. Constance at first longed to know her history, which, when she heard it from Maude, filled her with distaste.

As to the men, the older ones—Moore, Simon, and Caldicott—teased and tried jovially to test female prudishness with comic stories which, having originated on the Stock Exchange, where invention is rife, had blunted on their way to theatrical dressing-rooms. The younger ones had no true joviality. Masefield looked haughtily over her head; Devlin, a neurotic flirt, winked, and kissed or tried to kiss all the girls, and in spite of great acting ability enjoyed no respect. Stockhouse, the swarthy and physically adroit cynic who pungently satirised Hurd, was mystifying. With much padding and a crimsoned face he made a rollicking Sir Toby Belch; and without padding he shone as either Cassio in *Othello*, or Laertes in *Hamlet*, or an exuberant Lorenzo in *The Merchant of Venice*. His doubling and trebling of minor parts in other plays showed marvellous versatility.

Another thing she noticed was that while Devlin was terrified of Stockhouse, giggling self-consciously before the critical grey eyes, and Masefield betrayed fear of Hurd by a paler hauteur and uncontrollable trembling of sensitive lips, Stockhouse was cruel to both Devlin and Masefield and impudently unafraid of Hurd. The other girls were wary of Stockhouse, and at first Constance was similarly uneasy; but this feeling passed when he made no attempt upon herself. He scrutinised her person with meaningful assessment; but always looked away when she returned his glance. For this reason her curiosity about him was stimulated. It was not yet overwhelming.

The other men, pretending that they did but fill in time between London engagements or much nobler tours, bought two theatrical papers every week, *The Era* and *The Stage*, and with consuming interest studied the 'Wanted' advertisements. She did not know whether they found anything of value there; but if a letter arrived for one of them it was eagerly opened with some furtiveness and read to an accompaniment of whispers and sometimes of resigned shruggings. What could the letter contain? It was long before she was able to imagine.

Snatches of talk convinced her at last that, to a man, they dreamed of escape from Hurd into realms of magnificence.

'Laddie,' they said; 'five pounds a week! You could *live* at the Bodega in Bedford Street on such a salary!'

'Aye,' would be the response. 'Aye. And for ten—let us be ambitious—you could eat caviare, drink brandy, smoke Havanas. "Very heaven" indeed!'

Long sighs followed; and much sugar was added to their cups of tea.

This feast of caviare, brandy, and cigars seemed to be a point beyond which imagination could not fly. Constance, reared in abstinence, thought it a very gross view of Paradise.

When she found that Rachel Delmaine showed equal, and even more surreptitious, interest in the advertisements, she marvelled. Was not Miss Delmaine, who played all the secondary principals, not satisfied? No doubt she was a little old to enjoy touring; but surely she was rewarded by her work and by her association with so happy a troupe? How strange men and women were! They were never satisfied. But what did the advertisements offer? She began imitatively to read them herself, only to find that large numbers of them had been inserted by actors enjoying periods of rest.

She became used to shivering journeys after nights of perhaps four hours' sleep, to hurried rushes at Miss Rooke's side through the streets of blackened towns, in search of lodgings, to anxious glances at walls and ceilings in the bedrooms she shared with Maude Marsh, lest they should bear signs of resident vermin, to dirty lavatories, cracked crockery, and cruets green with verdigris; and she no longer screamed in panic when cockroaches took to their heels by candlelight in kitchens or musty theatres. Maude, indeed, enjoyed forays with the cockroaches as much as she enjoyed battles with landladies who chatted too long, asked too many questions, or added too many items to their charges. She was a warrior.

The forays and battles revealed much to Constance about her room-mate's character and about human conflict. Knowing nothing of money, she was relieved by her freedom from the chattering that sometimes preceded a booking. Maude saw to it all.

'What you'd do without me, I don't know,' she said. 'I beat that old hag down from twelve bob to eleven. That saves you sixpence. She was trying it on because we were two gels. You heard her say "No gentlemen visitors", didn't you? Sauce!'

The small provincial towns to which Hurd's itinerary took the Strollers taught the beginner, also, something of English squalor. The dilapidated theatres which in later life she shunned as plague-spots were still irradiated by the vision she had of play-acting. Only later did she understand that the company was too small, unequal to its intellectual pretensions, and always on the verge of bankruptcy.

It was run by Hurd in his own interest; and Hurd saw himself as a Koh-i-noor among glass beads, a man so brilliant that he illumined every setting.

'I am Hurd. I am Hurd. The Great Hurd. Head and shoulders above the Common Herd,' was what Stockhouse made him say. Wicked Stockhouse! And yet . . . And yet . . . Her own gift for mimicry was dormant; but she was reluctantly delighted with Stockhouse's malicious performance, and her admiration for Hurd was weakened. Ridicule is the most potent weapon in the world.

Still clinging to belief in his genius, she tried to find out whether Hurd really adorned the London stage at proper seasons, as his radiant billings claimed, or whether he planned to open at some future time in Shaftesbury Avenue, or whether he disinterestedly preferred to take great drama and great acting to benighted regions of England. Any one of these facts would do him credit; and she wished him to enjoy that credit.

Why, then, did he pack up in the darkness of every Sunday morning, and pass from one drab provincial town to another? Nobody would provide a satisfying answer. When she put her three questions to the girls, beginning with Maude, they looked suspicious, twinkled, and at length laughed. Constance, aware that she was being ridiculed for simplicity, flushed, at which they laughed anew. Maude said: 'Ask Hurd. Go straight into the lion's mouth! He'd love it!'

When she turned to the blue-chinned older men, they smiled, patted her hand or her shoulder, and muttered: 'These are mysteries indeed, my darling. We're all in the lap of the gods, even Mr Hurd.' Shunning Masefield, whose fine appearance continued to ravish her senses, but whose embarrassment at her approach showed itself in redoubled hauteur, she decided that any other application would be vain; and for a time was quite baffled.

There remained, however, the enigmatic Stockhouse.

He was not handsome. His eyes, which immediately caught the attention, were both dull and secret. His ears were too large; his nose too short and thick, so the lip above the irregular teeth was over-long. His hair, of which two or three thin strands had always escaped the brush, was lustreless and as straight as that of an Indian brave. And yet he inspired curiosity.

What was he really like? Constance received an impression of intense, egotistic quickness of mind. He had something biting to say of, and frequently to, every member of the company. He dismissed as worthless every town they visited, every dramatist who had written for the stage, every actor and actress in the

public eye, every novelist, every historian, and every English
painter from Reynolds to Millais. He did not believe in God, the
Church, the State, or British virtue, which he dismissed as
materialistic hypocrisy.

'We're a nation of burglars and bullies,' she heard him declare.
'No principles anywhere. We can't paint, write, or sing. We're
the braggarts of the modern world. My God, look at those
back-to-back houses. If there were any angels, they'd weep.'

'Aye, laddie; you've got strong views,' mumbled Old Moore,
who had listened to the tirade without understanding a word
of it!

Constance had already made up her mind to avoid putting
herself at the mercy of that tongue when Stockhouse one day
lingered beside her after a rehearsal, smiling like a cat which has
just caught a long-elusive mouse. He did more than smile. He
helped her to move a large jar which somebody had dumped in
the middle of the stage.

'I'll do that for you,' he said abruptly. 'Where do you want it?'

Every lovely girl knows when she should accept assistance
from a male. Constance watched him roll the jar to the wings,
clap his hands together to free them from dust, and turn to her
with complacency. Moved by sudden impulse, and finding that
they were alone, she put her question.

'Mr Stockhouse, can you tell me why Mr Hurd never plays
Shylock, or Othello, in London?'

Stockhouse, continuing to smile very mysteriously, at once
answered:

'That means you can't wait to get there yourself.'

'Quite wrong,' she retorted. 'I'm simply curious about Mr
Hurd.'

'He's unworthy of your curiosity. But I'll satisfy it. The plain
reason is that they wouldn't look at him there.'

She persisted.

'But why not? He's a great actor, isn't he? A famous London
favourite?'

As she had expected, Stockhouse's smile became that of a

mischievous elf, as it did when he caused laughter by his mimicry of Hurd. She thought it a sign of conceit.

'Famous? They've never heard of him.'

'But on the bills: "the great metropolitan tragedian . . .".'

'A lie, to deceive the locals. Have you ever seen a great actor?'

'Apart from yourself,' said Constance, with irony, 'only Mr Hurd.'

'As to me, you're right. As to Hurd, he's the faint, faint copy of all the terrible actors that ever "strutted and fretted his hour upon the stage".'

Constance grew warm at his mockery.

'Are you jealous of him? I don't understand you.'

Cruelty darkened the secretive eyes.

'I didn't expect you to understand me. The suggestion of jealousy is ridiculous. But, in return for your compliment, I'll tell you. Old humbugs like Garrick, Macready, Kean, Irving were all ranters.' He assumed a pompous air, adding a few unintelligible words in a hollow tone, drawing his mouth down as Hurd did in acting Malvolio, and beating the air slowly with what she noted as exceptionally slim, pale hands. 'Like that, you see. All solemn humbug. "The sta-a-age." In fact, stagey. I never saw them; but I know . . .'

'I was wondering about that,' interpolated Constance.

'Oh, yes; I've seen Hurd, who's their ghost. Well, now, they left their rags and props and fusty declamation in the slop shops. Hurd, the old scoundrel, picked them up at fifth hand. Every one. All the rubbish of the old school. It was his chance. He was playing small parts in drama—*Ticket of Leave Man*, *East Lynne*; that sort of thing—on tour. Ten years of it. Then he met Ellis, who really can act. She'd come into a little money. That was her misfortune. He wooed the girl. He won her. And when he'd got his dirty little paws on her money—I expect you've seen they're like a monkey's—he made up his mind to be "the great metropolitan tragedian". So he hunted up two or three old hacks like Moore, some seedy out-of-works like Simon, fools like Masefield, and dear little nurselings like you; and took the road like Barnum's Circus.'

'How cynical you are!' protested Constance, hurt by the word 'nurselings'. 'I don't believe a word of it.'

'You asked me to tell you. I've told you. Moore can't get out, and knows it. The others send vain telegrams every week to the managers who advertise in *The Era*; they never get anything. And you're a lamb ripe for slaughter. Get out as soon as you can. You imagine Hurd's good, because you've never seen anybody else. He's not good. He's thoroughly bad. Nobody with any knowledge thinks anything of him at all—not even Moore, who's his toady. Moore's talked to me after a couple of whiskies. So there you are. Bear my simple words in mind!'

So saying, Stockhouse gave his jeering glance, and turned away, leaving her, shocked and angry, to think harshly of him and to conserve her defiant admiration for Hurd as she could. Of course Stockhouse was envious. He was conceited. But also he was brilliant. What was the truth?

Something worse—or better—followed.

'By the way!' This was Maude's conversational gambit. It preceded every item of news, every comment on dress, the cast, the towns they were in, and whatever Constance had done wrong in the past twenty-four hours. 'By the way . . .'

They had run through sleet to their lodging after the show, and were preparing by candle-light to go to bed. The room was very small, at the back of an ugly little house in a side street of what Maude insisted upon calling 'Muckbottom'! The walls of the room were covered with soiled bronze-coloured paper, and their beds were of iron, enamelled black, and much scratched by previous theatrical lodgers. An unusually large mirror stood on an ordinary kitchen table draped in patterned cotton so ragged that shabby unpainted legs showed in a dozen places. Two or three photographs had been pinned to the bronze walls, presumably those of earlier occupants. They were inscribed with scrawling signatures.

This room was as cheerless as a cell. It was like a number of similar rooms which they had shared in recent weeks; and only familiarity with the others prevented Constance from shuddering with disgust at the conditions in which young actresses were expected to sleep.

Both girls were yawning. Maude, as she spoke, was sitting on the edge of her bed, wearing only a white-frilled chemise and drawers, over which she had draped a monstrous grey woollen shawl, and wiggling her toes. In her hands were some wet stockings, which had been splashed during the late scamper, and which she proposed to rinse before sleeping.

She discarded her gambit, for repetition later.

'Gosh! I'd like to soak my feet in boiling water. They're frozen. I wonder if we've both caught colds? I shouldn't wonder. That would please dear Erasmus; so fatherly, so careful of his little doves!' The name reminded her of what she had been going to say. 'By the way, a word of warning, darling. Never let yourself be alone with Erasmus in a room with a sofa. It's not safe.'

Constance, splashing her face at a basin on the marble-topped washstand—this splashing was a nightly habit very annoying to Maude, who disliked cold water—paused in bewilderment. She had been remembering a multitude of things—the dark streets, a half-empty great theatre, Stockhouse's conceit, Stockhouse's contemptuous account of Hurd's career—and was unprepared for any fresh attack upon peace of mind. Being afraid to turn round, in case she sprinkled the strip of ragged carpet, she looked sideways towards the mirror, which presented an almost full-length picture of the shrouded Maude; and as Maude was also making use of the mirror for the purpose of less charitable observation of Constance's maturing beauty their glances met.

'Why, what would he do?' asked Constance, innocently.

'As if you didn't know! Well, as much as you'd let him. And a bit more.'

Constance flushed. She could not misunderstand.

'But surely,' she objected, 'he's not that sort of man at all.

Mr Stockhouse says he's an antediluvian actor; but to the company . . .'

'Like a father, you think?'

'No, more of a censor; a drill-sergeant; a dragoon.'

'What words you use!' laughed Maude. 'They're like swearing!'

Constance looked at the immense shawl. Beneath it, she knew, were beautiful white shoulders and plump breasts; but only a lovely neck was visible. She lifted her eyes to the laughing—and yet sharply watchful—face above.

'Has he ever behaved like that to you?'

'"Like that"! Innocent doxy! Afraid to use the word. It's Rape. Rape. Never mind about me. I'm warning *you*.' The big mouth was stretched in an amiable grin which deepened into something more ominous. Shadows heightened by the candle's occasional flicker revealed Maude's capacity for malignance.

'I thought he was devoted to Miss Rooke,' said Constance.

'Did you, though!'

'Isn't he? Isn't it a happy marriage?'

'Who says they're married? In any case, that's got nothing to do with it.'

Shocked and excited by the innuendo, Constance was glad to conceal her cheeks with the rough little towel. Maude had never before spoken with such open coarseness . . .

'But he's quite an old man. Surely it's only young men! . . .

'Don't be a fool! My God, the old men are the worst. Hurry up with that basin. I must wash these things; and my teeth are beginning to chatter.'

'So are mine. I'm finished. What I was going to say was that I'd never felt nervous of him—not in that way.'

There was an exasperated sigh.

'All right. All right. That's what I get for Christian charity! Don't you see, it's exactly what he wants. Starry-eyed trustfulness. Adoration. Then a little private rehearsal: "We must get this right, my pet." Ellis won't be there, so she can't see a thing. So he says: "Sit down beside me. Closer. Closer. Now the hands; lean back. I'm not going to hurt you. Just a little lesson . . ." And so then what?'

Having spoken, in the part of Erasmus, very caressingly, Maude made her demand in a voice of savage warning. It caused the blood to rush to Constance's face and neck, staining them crimson. She knew Maude must see this with relish as a tribute to her performance; and breathlessly, but with an effort at recovery, she retorted:

'Was that how it was with you?'

'Ah, naughty! Mustn't slap! In any case, I didn't come straight from the nursery, like you. The old man's technique doesn't vary much. It worked with Ellis. It worked with Betty Brown. There must have been others, poor dears.'

Constance, choking, at last managed to say:

'Who was Betty Brown?'

'Our Rachel.'

'What, Miss Delmaine?'

'Miss Delmaine. *Née* Betty Brown. What's in a name? Erasmus played her like a fish. Praised that broad forehead—a sign of intellect. And her beautiful grey eyes—an inspiration to him. And so on; when all he wanted was to see what she was like in bed, the nasty wretch! He was younger in Ellis's day. Younger; and he may have been attractive, which he certainly is not now. He tempted Ellis by promising her love, leads, and London. That's how it will be with you. London: wonderful place! A magnet to every girl in the profession. She'd give anything to get there. She doesn't, as a rule; but if she does . . .'

'What?' Constance was still suffocating.

'You think *you* will, don't you?'

'Yes. In ten years.'

'Poor mite! Three months in the smalls; and she thinks she's ripe and ready. All right; you do go to London; but it's in search of an engagement. You traipse up and down Charing Cross Road and Maiden Lane; hang about the agents; pawn your treasures; and wear out your shoes. Either you slink home or you go on the streets. I've hung on, myself: but then I'm tough.

You're not. Of course, being Goldilocks, you may get into the chorus of a musical comedy, on tour, when you're thirty.'

'This is awful!' ejaculated Constance. 'Is this what you see for yourself?'

'Just about. I see myself playing parlourmaids all my life—also on tour. With luck, parlourmaids in farce, where they drop trays and open the wrong doors. Gosh, I'm giving myself the hump by looking into the crystal. Meanwhile, I'm freezing to death!'

'You're as cynical as Mr Stockhouse,' said Constance, more horrified by the crystal-gazing than by the prospect of danger from Hurd, which had its thrilling aspect. 'This is what he says. You must be copying him.'

'Oh, no; I copy nobody. I've had eight years of these blasted digs; and I'm not the girl I used to be.' Maude rose from her bed, threw off the shawl, and looked at her figure in the mirror. It was a good figure, at sight of which her expression composed once more into one of complacency. 'There! You see how kind I am!'

'Yes, you do look kind—when you want to,' admitted Constance. 'And you've got a lovely figure.'

'Meaning, I'm not, and I haven't. Well, some girls would be jealous of *your* looks.'

'There's no need for you to be.'

'Thanks. I'm not. But I warn you; the better the looks, the greater the risks. The risks and the disillusion. You'll take disillusion hard. That's what Betty did. The bottle followed.'

'The bottle?' Constance stopped, aghast, in the act of slipping off her skirt. Maude was already at the vacated washstand.

'Didn't you guess? That mouth? The puffy eyes? Her breath? Not smelt it before she goes on? I know you haven't seen her drunk. I used to share digs with her; and I have. Oh, my God, the weepings at night and the wallowings in the morning. She tried to get me to drink with her. They do, you know. I told her I'd promised Mother; so in the end she gave up trying. I don't know; I suppose they think if somebody's as bad as they are they won't feel so repentant. You'd hardly believe Betty was once a beauty; lovely ivory skin . . .'

'I do believe. She's still beautiful.'

'A bit *passée*. Going downhill. Erasmus again. And the worst of it is, after all he's done to her, she's still besotted with the old rake. She wails "Oh, if he'd only be kind! Be like he was!" Erasmus knows all about it; he plays on her feelings—cat and mouse, cat and mouse. The brute! She'll get worse and worse, till she ends in the gutter.'

Constance shivered with more than the room's chill.

'If you think all this,' she cried breathlessly, 'I can't understand why you stay.'

The broad smile returned to Maude's thick lips.

'With Erasmus, d'you mean? Oho, that's easy; I'm waiting to see what happens,' she answered.

'To me?'

'Little egotist! As if I cared what happens to you. I should be amused if you skidded. It would wake you up. Cool your virgin blood, which is as hot as hell. Isn't it? Isn't it?' Cruelty was suddenly rampant. 'No; what I want to see is Erasmus on the run. It's coming, you know.'

Incomprehensible words! Constance put a knee on her bed, causing the long metal bands supporting the mattress to crack and whang in protest. Once between the sheets she pulled all the insufficient bedclothes up until they covered her eyes. This conversation, like the one which preceded it, had suggested so many unfamiliar notions that her head felt too small to hold them. It had begun to ache.

She was trembling with cold and excitement. Having been irritated by Stockhouse's scornful denunciation of Hurd as an actor, she had now been forced by Maude to see the man as a professional seducer; and she was deeply affected by both arraignments. Maude's warning, and Maude's almost triumphant pessimism, coming on top of Stockhouse's contempt, a long day's hard work, the disappointment of an echoing, half-empty theatre, and the night of sleet were overwhelming.

Warmth came slowly. It spread to her hands and feet; and brought revived confidence in her star. She knew that, somehow, she would get to London and make a great reputation there. She was determined to do so. And as she reconsidered Maude's ludicrous but exciting description of the way Hurd would lead up to his assured physical attack she passed to speculation as to Maude's own chastity. How had Maude come by her knowledge? How had Maude dealt with the would-be-lover, with any would-be-lover?

This in itself added to her excitement. Warmer still, and heated from within by temptation, she began to anticipate the coming risk. How would Hurd begin? What would he say? How could she parry his attack? Speeches flew through her mind. Actions could be imagined. And as the situation grew ever more risky and thrilling, it became at last irresistibly comic. Lying curled into the shape of a question-mark, she began suddenly and surely to giggle.

2

Neither Maude nor Constance foresaw the sequel to those historic conversations, nor the event which had momentous consequences for Hurd's Strollers.

The event was that Ellis Rooke, assailed that night by the freezing sleet, and already unwell as a result of unceasing strain, caught cold. Hurrying as the others had done to her separate lodging, she ignored sharp pains in her back and breast, sneezed many times, and, because she knew that her landlady must be in bed and fast asleep, took no steps to check the mischief. As a consequence she had a broken night, and by next morning was so ill that she could hardly rise.

Erasmus, in another and more comfortable lodging which Ellis had secured for him, threw off a wet overcoat, sat before a banked fire, drank frequently from a silver flask which (he was told) had belonged to Irving, and, until he fell asleep, thought with resentment of the miserable audience which had failed to respond to his masterly Hamlet. He awoke, chilled, in the darkness, looking like the ghost of Hamlet's father, and did not sleep again.

The rest of the Players, waiting upon a gale-swept platform, watched in silence as Hurd appeared, but raised a cheer at sight of Ellis. She was late, and very haggard. Hurd, they saw, did no more than glower at her, with a sharp nod at the station clock; and this led the girls to observe her closely. They realised at once that she was ill. Maude took her arm; Constance seized her suitcase; but there was no time for more, because the train came rumbling in at that moment and there was a scramble for seats, in the course of which Maude and Constance were separated from the others.

'Did you see her?' Maude said. 'She could hardly walk. Now we've got this long journey in a train that's not fit for cattle. Cattle have a value for dealers and drovers. We haven't. Our old drover has no heart. The way he looked at Ellis was disgusting.'

All, it appeared, were disgusted. But they could not help Ellis. She was too ill.

At the end of the journey, finding her collapsed and almost fainting, the girls looked round for Hurd, to find that he had been greeted by a stranger with whom he was walking away. Seriously frightened, they ran to Moore, who came at once to Elis's side.

'She must have a doctor,' insisted Maude.

'Aye. Aye. But where's he to be found? That's the question.' The old man had the gestures of a courtier, but no capacity for decision. He hung back, supporting Ellis, while Maude interrogated the porter, found the address she wanted, and set off, with Constance at her side, to find the doctor. It was mid-afternoon; at first he refused to see a patient; but when he did so he insisted that Ellis should go at once to the local hospital. A sad little procession therefore took her to a shabby building where she was handed over to nurses.

Maude and Constance, warmest-hearted of the Strollers, stayed in the waiting-room for an hour, when they were dismissed.

'You can do nothing,' said the nurse who found them. 'She's very ill. Come back this evening.'

Very ill. Very ill. 'You can do nothing.' Convinced that Ellis was dying, they ran to the theatre, where, unable to check their tears, they communicated alarm to the whole company.

'Ellis?' exclaimed the others, incredulously. 'Ellis?' It had not occurred to any of them that Ellis would ever be ill. 'Oh, dear, dear, dear!' They gathered together with long faces. 'What on earth's to be done?'

Hurd was equally incredulous, learning the news while he rated the baggage-man.

'What's that?' he cried. 'Why didn't she tell me? Where have they taken her?' When invited to visit the hospital and hear a report at first-hand, he refused. 'Certainly not. I'm too busy. Besides, those places smell of death. Upset my nerves. Damn! Damn! Why didn't the bloody woman tell me? Just like her! Damned obstinate fool!'

He continued to storm, making ugly mouths, shrugging, bawling at Masefield, and at last haranguing the bristly, sandy theatre manager, who tried to pacify him by saying: 'Nay, nay, Mr Hurd; you'll be ill yourself if you don't calm down. And then what would happen? Just be quiet for a bit. We're all very sorry for you . . .'

'You need to be!' shouted Hurd. 'My best actress. Left me in the lurch!'

'You go and see her, sir. Perhaps it's not as bad as the young ladies think. They've had a shock. Young ladies sometimes exaggerate. You go and see for yourself.'

'I won't, Harringay! I won't. Don't you understand that if I go, catch her complaint, whatever it is, and am driven to me bed . . .'

'Oh, we can't have that, Mr Hurd. I've got bills all over the town. "Personal visit of Erasmus Hurd." All over the town. They'd lynch me!'

'Yes, that's true. That's true. They want to see me.'

'They certainly want to see you, Mr Hurd.'

'I've never yet let the public down. *The show must go on!*'

This tag relieved him. It provided an excuse for staying away from a place of evil omen. The others, however, saw that he trembled; and the sharp glance he flung round upon them showed that besides fearing criticism he was deeply agitated. He knew, as well as they did, that Ellis held the company together.

She was not only its leading actress; she thought of everything, decided on female costumes, quietened Hurd, was mother to the girls and comprehending sister to their elders. She never lost her temper; she was never obtrusive; they relied upon her to an extraordinary degree. 'Ask Miss Rooke.' 'Miss Rooke will tell you.' 'Miss Rooke . . . Miss Rooke . . .' The name echoed through all their trials, and gave them solace. Now they might not see her again. Woe! Woe!

'Aye,' said the deep-voiced Moore, delivering an oration over one already dead. 'Aye. Aye. She's booked for a higher stage than ours. A great actress. A great woman.'

'It's like losing a finger,' added Gwen Dodd. 'You didn't know until then that you used it all the time. A forefinger!' She was pleased with the apt comparison.

'More like an eye!' declaimed her sister. 'What's worse than blindness?'

'Oh, for God's sake be reasonable!' protested Stockhouse. 'She's not the queen of the fairies.'

'No, she's better than that!' cried Constance, with the greatest spirit. 'She's real! She's our dear, good, kind friend. We love her. And if she dies . . .'

There was a general groan of sorrowful assent. Stockhouse, as if struck by the first sign of passion he had noticed in this immature golden-haired beauty, looked inquiringly at her from under dropped lids. His lips smiled in irony; but she had aroused his attention.

Hurd himself spoke no word of regret. He brooded.

It was some time before he would believe, or admit to believing, that Ellis was really ill. They thought he tried to persuade himself that her withdrawal was due to shame at a bad performance on the Saturday night, or a wish to revenge herself upon him for an imagined slight. When at last assured by the doctor in person that she was delirious and in great danger, and that it would probably be several weeks before she could act again, he showed his alarm by acts of tyranny against the entire company.

Rehearsals were endless, full of interruption, and punctuated with fits of pretended despair. Miss Delmaine was taken again and again through her speeches, damned for faulty phrasing and intonation, seized by the elbow to correct movements, and exhorted to show animation. 'Animation . . . Animation . . . She's a spirited young woman; not a walking corpse.' Constance marvelled at Miss Delmaine's patience, and felt wretched at the suffering it must hide. Maude said: 'If he did that to me, I'd smack his face!'

Masefield, who was a particular butt, grew colder and colder under insult; even Moore drew himself up on occasion, from mortified vanity. Others were found fault with for doing what Hurd had just told them to do; and during performances reverted to their old ways without rebuke. What was worst of all was that Hurd, through mental disturbance, forgot his own lines in face of the audience. However clearly prompted, he was unable to catch the words, faltered, staggered about the stage; and afterwards, in paroxysms of anger, screamed like a frightened parrot.

'You fools! You fools!' he shouted, snatching the promptbook and hurling it to a distance. 'You mumble, mumble, mumble!' Then he rushed to his dressing-room as if insane.

'It's intolerable!' exclaimed the quivering, white-faced Masefield, after one such fit of hysteria. 'I shall walk out on him!'

'Capital!' sneered Stockhouse. 'He'd miss you. Damned if I don't do the same!'

'Careful, laddies; careful!' was Moore's warning. Moore, who took everything seriously, could not distinguish between petulance and derision. 'You don't want to be resting in Winter on an empty belly.'

'Old Moore's Almanac!' Stockhouse was impenitent. 'He prophesies dearth in February.'

'There are limits to endurance.' Masefield, alarmed by the prophecy, and smarting anew at Stockhouse's ridicule, flushed a disagreeable salmon-pink which destroyed his alabaster beauty. His gestures, always stiff, were desperately unexpressive. His Adam's apple worked up and down.

Stockhouse, merciless to ineptitude, gibed again.

'Our dear Masefield would live on his divine afflatus.'

'Hm. That's windy food.' Moore sententiously elongated his blue chin.

'Alternatively, he could go on the streets,' said Stockhouse. 'I understand these things are done.'

Constance did not understand why Masefield flung away, his face again flushed and distorted with anger. She hardly noticed his going. Chilled to the heart, she imagined her own return, crestfallen, to the Rectory, and Wilmerton at its bleakest. Absorbed in the vision, she was unaware of Stockhouse's approach until he whispered in her ear.

'Troubled?' he asked.

'Reading the Almanac,' she answered.

'Take my advice. Follow your own stars. They're radiant.'

She observed how dark, like plovers' eggs, the whites of his eyes were, and how one thin slip of them was visible under each iris. His brow was solid; the ever-present smile upon his lips seemed for once to be free of malice.

'I mean to,' she said. 'It happens at the moment to be behind a cloud.'

'We must talk about this. I'm interested.' His smile deepened, becoming deliberately enigmatic.

'That would be lovely,' replied Constance, with deliberate naïveté. She had understood his provocative meaning, and was equal to it.

Altogether deafened and confused by Hurd's bullying, the company adjusted itself in haste to new parts and rearranged performances.

'Good God!' snarled Hurd, in a passion over some fumbling in *Othello*. 'What incompetence! They'd laugh us off the stage! We'll have to stick to the *Merchant*. I carry that on my shoulders!'

'Sauce!' stormed Maude in a whisper, when he had marched, shrugging, from a bad rehearsal. 'As if he'd got any shoulders! Puny midget!' She had a great eye for physical strength, however dumb its possessor. 'If we had a man in the company, he'd wring the devil's neck!'

'Turning him into Richard Crookback?' inquired Stockhouse, with irony. 'I must suggest we dig out the history plays.'

'You daren't! In any case it's his soul that's cracked. "Not on thy sole, but ont hy soul, harsh Jew," I wonder he doesn't play Iago himself. It would suit him better than old black-face.'

Stockhouse smiled, saying between his teeth:

'I wish he'd pass Iago to me. I was born for the part.'

'For all parts, of course. Nothing like having a good opinion of yourself.'

'Hurd doesn't seem to think much of your Emilia, my dear.'

'Who cares? If he was any good he'd go back and see Ellis. What's fifty miles? Old Moore could play Shylock for a night or two.'

'Oh, heavens! Spare us that!'

'Well, I know. But Hurd could still be billed. That's what he's doing with Ellis. We'd put a slip in the programme—"owing to indisposition". No money returned, of course.'

'And none coming in, they say.'

'Naturally. It's got round that Ellis is ill. It's she that's the draw.'

'If Hurd went, our drawers would all be down.'

'Shut up! We don't want any bawdy from *you*!'

Maude, who had been scolded for clumsiness in Emilia's challenge to Iago, and had fallen awkwardly when stabbed, was so angry that she shouted at Stockhouse as if he had been Hurd. But, not being Hurd, Stockhouse merely gave his tantalising smile and waltzed away with a soubrette's backward kick, leaving Maude to continue with abuse of Hurd. Constance was fascinated by the gesture.

Stockhouse was lucky. He was not one of those who had to learn a new part; and for some reason, which Constance assumed to be his invaluable versatility, he was never insulted by Hurd, but only subjected to occasional darting glances of hostility. After this scene, she remarked the fact to Maude.

'Have you noticed it?' she asked.

'Of course,' was the reply. 'The reason is that Hurd's afraid of him. Hurd's a thorough coward; and Stockie's got a *look*. Have *you* noticed *that*?' She screwed up her eyes in imitation of Stockhouse. 'Hurd's afraid he knows all. It might be true, too; the clever devil. A bit too clever, sometimes.'

'Yes, he is clever. Extraordinarily clever. Don't you think that "look" is put on, to impress?'

'Always. Stockie's a mass of vanity. But then all actors are vain.'

'What about actresses?'

'Don't you start! I've had all I can stand from Hurd and Stockie. A pair of—I won't say what they are; you'd be shocked. And come and run through Nerissa with me. I've never played her before.'

'You'll be wonderful!' said Constance, with real admiration.

'Ph!' scoffed Maude, suspiciously. 'To Betty's Portia? She'd cast a blight on anybody!'

Maude thus condemned one detail of the reorganisation; for in Ellis Rooke's absence Rachel Delmaine stepped into the part of Portia, with Doris James (a previous Nerissa) as her understudy, Simon as a humdrum Bassanio, and Masefield a frigid Antonio. Caldicott kept his rôle as the noisy Gratiano; and to everybody's surprise Constance was given her first speaking part, that of Shylock's lovely daughter, Jessica.

'You'll probably make a mess of her,' said Hurd, rudely. 'I'll have to coach you.'

'Careful!' whispered Maude in Constance's ear. 'Coach; not couch!'

'What's that? What's that?' Hurd scented ribaldry. 'Pay attention! Where's Lorenzo? Oh, there you are, Stockhouse. See she learns her lines, will you?'

'Not only her lines, I hope,' answered Stockhouse, under his breath.

So, as was fated, Constance was wooed by Lorenzo.

### 3

He smiled at her; but he was patient. The rehearsals between them were always amusing. He instructed her in the art of walking and turning, encouraged her to release her hitherto restrained charm, and made her, if not a credible Jessica, at least a young beauty in love. The experience was a revelation.

She assimilated more ready knowledge from Stockhouse in a week than she had gained from others in nineteen years. He seemed to understand more of everything than anybody she had ever met; and he told her so little, seriously, about himself that she was left to guess at the heart and brain behind his mask of omniscient scorn. From a slight dread of him she came to have a kind of laughing terror, feeling that he must find her ridiculously childish. She did not wish to be found childish.

At the same time he encouraged her egotism, speaking in ventriloquial asides, and making comments which put all their companions in a ridiculous light. In this way he flatteringly suggested that she alone followed the intricacies of his judgment. She thought she caught momentary glimpses of admiration, even of affection, in those dead eyes; but as his manner always suggested indulgence she began to wonder very often about his real opinion of her. Curiosity grew. She was more and more fascinated by him.

Fascination led to other flights. She believed that for such a lover as Lorenzo she would do as Jessica did in the play, and steal her father's possessions. This in turn caused her to compare Shylock's wealth from usury to John Rotherham's poverty from dreamy service to his parishioners. There were no jewels, and no ducats, at the Rectory; only aged furniture and shelves crowded with musty books the bindings of which were being rotted by Wilmerton's salt air.

'Poor Father!' she one day exclaimed to herself. 'Alone in that dreary house! And he can't even read his old books any longer!' She had an instant's longing to run home and fulfil her mother's entreaty that she would guard him; but there came at once the flying counter-thought: 'He doesn't want me. He never cared for me. He's got Pen. Always Pen. I wonder how she is. I must write to her!'

These, in spite of anxiety about Ellis, poor houses, and cold lodgings and theatres, were the happiest days she had ever known. Feeling happy, she looked radiant. Every mirror gave the assurance that her looks improved daily; and she saw that the men in the company, especially Devlin, who was a born flirt, took great notice of her. 'Our Connie,' they said, with amused pride. 'How are you this morning, darling? You're like a glimpse of April!' Devlin, with his arm about her shoulders, whispered the title of a once-popular song, '"You're Queen of my heart!"' Old Moore, sticking to Shakespeare, declaimed in tremendous style:

'"Shall I compare thee to a summer's day?
Thou art more lovely and more temperate!"'

Maude alone pronounced deprecating words.

'Smirking at yourself in the glass!' she jeered. 'You're as bad as the men. Even Erasmus is grinning. Also Stockie, which is unusual for him. Take care, my pet; "trust them not; they are fooling thee".'

Such remarks deepened what Maude called the smirk. It was not a smirk, but the light of joy at being for the first time admired without a grudge, and by men. Her father's abstracted disapproval, and the embarrassed flight of the stupid boy Tom, had left deep wounds. So had the efforts of mistresses to curb an exuberant rebel. How far away, now, were the ever-hated disciplines of Pickering's!

'Thank heaven! No scowls, no snubs, no bad reports! Father can't look cut to the heart! Yes, and I wonder what happened to Blanche? Conceited prude, with her horse-riding and her mincing accent! Giving me the slip! And so terribly condescending! She wouldn't recognise me now. *Jessica!*'

She was Jessica! Jessica before them all! She and Stockhouse, playing together as young married folk in the moonlight, were speaking beautiful lines as they should always be spoken! It was evident that Stockhouse had been astonished by her, especially in the laughing scene of protestation about the night. His delivery was quick with relish; his grace increased; his response was altogether gallant:

> '"On such a night" (it was a caress)
> Did pretty Jessica, like a little shrew,
> Slander her love, and he forgave it her."'

Hurd, passing by, stayed to listen, and, having listened, gave his sharp nod.

'I'll take our scene this afternoon, Constance,' he said. 'See she knows it, Stockhouse.'

When Hurd had gone, Stockhouse murmured under his breath:

'He sees ducats in you, darling. I know the tone. Cupidity as well as concupiscence. There's a man for you! Sex and shekels. On his next tour he'll want you for Ophelia. But you won't be here, I hope.'

'Where shall I be?' asked Constance, archly.

'I know where I should like you to be,' said Stockhouse.

The days followed, every one of them full of preparation; and the Strollers moved southward and westward, out of the smoke of the Midlands but not into longer daylight. At last, on the Sunday evening, they reached a town larger than some of the others Constance had seen. She saw wider streets and a large market-place, no longer the grimy rows of small houses, but a mixture of ancient buildings and Victorian villas. No sooty rain was falling; but the scent of wood fires suggested a slow emergence of trade from agriculture and what she thought might be a milder climate of appreciation.

'My spirits are up,' she told Maude.

'Poor innocent!' was the reply. 'In the north, minds are brighter. Here, they're stagnant. We shall have a slow-witted lot, hard to move.'

'You're trying to frighten me!'

'Yes, I mustn't do that, must I?'

Early next morning she saw, with delicious sensations, the first copies of the programme for that night's opening performance. She secretly appropriated one of these programmes and sought her own name. It was there! JESSICA . . . CONSTANCE ROTHERHAM. Wonderful moment! Wonderful, wonderful moment! Nearly sixty years afterwards, when a hundred and fifty other programmes were added to her collection, she regarded this one as jejune; but at a first encounter it had miraculous quality. JESSICA . . . CONSTANCE ROTHERHAM. The name would mean nothing to those who attended the show; but to herself it represented triumph. She was tempted to send a copy to her arch-enemy at Pickering's, Miss Thomas.

'No. No, I won't. Too much as if I cared what she thought. Which I do not!'

She did, however, enclose one in a hasty note to Pen. Then, with increasing excitement, she awaited the evening.

It came. There was the usual panic, when it seemed that any intelligible performance would be impossible. Hurd stamped about the stage, cursing, demanding to know what fool had

neglected essential props, bawling at the scene-shifters, scolding
the new Portia for looking like a tart in her dress for the caskets
scenes, snubbing Launcelot Gobbo and his father, whose duo-
logue, he said, went as slowly as a funeral service, and at last,
having put everybody on edge, disappearing.

'Lost without Ellis,' was Maude's sharp comment to Constance. 'She's always pulled him through the trial scene. He
knows Betty won't. I think he's had a wire about Ellis; but what
it says I don't know. He crushed it into his pocket . . . You
look splendid, dear; they'll all love you. But they won't show it.
I know this place. I used to stay here with an auntie when I was
a kid. All they know about is cattle.'

She whisked away on ploys of her own, leaving Constance,
shaken by the confusion and the would-be reassuring remarks of
the older men, with chattering teeth.

'Golly, I wish I was dead,' she thought. 'What if I break
down? Stockie's keeping away on purpose. Sniggering because
I'm in a dither.'

Distrust of her partner was interrupted.

'Keep up your spirits, darling.' It was Stockhouse's most
ventriloquial voice. 'We're going to have a great success, you
and I.'

She saw, behind the make-up which gave flame to his cheeks
and lips, and gleaming unreadableness to his eyes, what she
prayed might be true kindness.

'You'll help me, won't you?' she entreated.

'And you me. Let's run through for the last time.'

Beyond the curtain was the sound of an assembling audience;
presently the scratching of a local band, accompanied by many
ugly coughs. Old Moore peeped through a hole in the curtain,
turning from it with a solemn grimace.

'Half a house!' he muttered. 'There's an epitemic of influenza
in the town. Erasmus hass the pip. Ant I ton't trust this stache,
for try rot! Got, what a profession!'

Constance, busy gabbling her own lines in one last effort to
fix them in her mind, saw figures gathering and dispersing, and

Masefield, already on the stage, 'acting' to himself, presumably to induce the proper mood. His gestures were meant to be easy, and were not easy, since his notions of dignity restricted every movement. Antonio, in a sense, was his best part, demanding little but carriage and elocution; but he recited it so elaborately that he seemed merely to be listening to his own sonorousness. Constance could not ridicule, as Maude did; he was too handsome to be scorned. She would have felt pity, if she had been able to spare pity for anybody but herself.

There came a scurry as the band scratched to a discordant close.

'Curtain up in two minutes. One minute. Up!'

'"In sooth,"' she heard Masefield intone as he and two others strolled warily upon the suspect boards, 'I know not why I am so sad. It wearies me; you say it wearies you . . ."'

Coughs, always a bad sign, suggested a difficult house. Lights in the auditorium were still popping down as he spoke. Latecomers were squeezing into their seats. Somebody struck a match in order to read or recover a programme . . .

'Every blasted feature of the perfect show!' Stockhouse was again at her side. 'That poor eunuch frozen with panic. He'll fluff badly within the next ten lines. There! He's in a tangle with "want-wit". Did he say "wit-want" or "Wint-wat"?'

'Sh! Sh! I hope I do no worse!'

'Impossible! If you fluff, I scream. That will distract the mutton-heads.'

'Also Mr Hurd, I think.'

The scenes in which Antonio appeared were safely over. There followed Miss Delmaine's agonising attempt to be a radiant Portia at home in Belmont with Nerissa. The poor woman, demoralised by Hurd's attack on her costume, was struggling with tears, sniffing loudly in the midst of stage merriment, and pausing often to collect fading strength. Constance, professionally aware of flatness in another, was moved to pity.

'Poor thing!' she whispered to Stockhouse. His humming reply was unkind.

'Yes, she's a poor thing. Relying on Dutch courage. Never sink to that, my pet.'

'I'll never sink to that,' responded Constance, bravely. 'I'm teetotal.'

'Hurd's fault. He snarls at her as one bitch to another. Why give her the part at all?'

Hurd himself was on, more Hebraic than any Jew off the stage had ever been, gesticulating, fawning, exulting in the prospect of his 'merry sport' with Antonio's flesh. The Gobbos came and went, to the titters of an audience half-stupefied by boredom with a stale plot and a laboured performance, and accordingly thankful for even strained jesting. They waited for the trial scene, which they would follow with moving lips.

Meanwhile the terrifying moment approached. Constance was taut.

"'Hear thee, Gratiano; thou art too wild . . .'"
    "Hood mine eyes, . . . and say 'amen' . . . never trust
    me more . . . *And I must to Lorenzo and the rest—*"'

'Where are you, Jessica? Come on! Look sharp!'

It was Launcelot, back again, sweeping her into action. She was dazzled by the footlights, her legs stiff with the late rigidity of suspense; and words were coming from her lips with what, thinking her tone muffled, she did not know to be startling beauty.

"'O Lorenzo,
    If thou keep promise I shall end this strife,
    Become a Christian and thy loving wife.'"

The words, spoken when she was alone on the stage, but ardently addressed to the absent Lorenzo-Stockhouse, came straight from her heart.

No word of praise from Hurd; none from Stockhouse. Only Launcelot's careless 'Good girl; keep it up,' saved her from being crestfallen. But a surge of determination came to her aid; and when the lovely scene with Lorenzo was in progress she did not once falter. Stockhouse was at his best, supple, musical, and adorably considerate.

'Splendid!' he kissed her quickly before the words 'How sweet the moonlight sleeps upon this bank' and, while the local musicians scratched what they supposed to be an Elizabethan air, he whispered again, as if in ecstasy, that she was the delight of his life, a perfect being.

Play-acting! Play-acting!

'I am never merry,' sighed Jessica, 'when I hear sweet music.'

'*Abominable din*, you mean. The reason is, your spirits are attentive . . .'

The rest, a long-drawn anti-climax for Constance, followed, Portia and Nerissa returned to Belmont. Their husbands, arriving later, were mocked. Lorenzo had his last words. Gratiano ended the play. Hurd was back again for the call, surrounded by his cast, holding Portia gallantly by one hand, Nerissa by the other. A waking audience clapped in dutiful acknowledgment; the curtain rose a second time on the cast, all members of which bowed low, concealing their thoughts, before scampering to the wings so that Hurd might take the final call alone. It did not come. The clapping died away; there were omnibuses to catch.

'No, no, no!' shouted Hurd, as the curtain's tail frisked. 'Stop that! They're going. The bastards!'

He strode from the stage in fury, while the band struggled with half-a-dozen bars of 'God Save the King', and Stockhouse, his arm remaining about Constance, kissed her again.

# 4

To the excitement of the occasion was added the excitement of a man's kiss, the second of the evening, and an extraordinary new experience. Had he meant more than an exercise in privileged opportunity? What were his real feelings? Had he guessed that she was on fire?

When, feeling the light clasp of her body relax, she freed herself and looked straight at his eyes, she learned nothing. He was already turning away, waving a hand in uncommitted farewell. A moment later he had disappeared. Her joy collapsed.

'Well, pravo our little Connie!' acclaimed Old Moore. 'A princess inteet!'

Maude said: 'Very good, darling. I'm madly jealous!'

She was laughing; but there was calculation in her eye. She had noted the kiss, Stockhouse's departure, and the involuntary revelation of Constance's disappointment.

This made all the more generous her tribute to a performance which might have aroused envy. Constance, greatly disturbed, heard nothing but an unsentimental voice showing no understanding of her pain. There echoed in her ears lines recently delivered by herself with such beauty that those listening in the wings sighed in admiration:

> '"In such a night
> Did young Lorenzo swear he loved her well,
> Stealing her soul with many vows of faith,
> And ne'er a true one—"'

Her heart seemed to turn to water. There had been no vows of faith. She had seen only the lip-smile of a cynic to whom instinctive response to a kiss was one more droll illustration of female seriousness. He was indifferent to her. The amorousness of his part had been wholly assumed.

Bewilderment was succeeded by resentment. Before she slept that night pride was already in control. Her last waking words, spoken between clenched teeth in the true Stockhouse manner, were:

'All right, Carl Stockhouse; *we'll see*!'

It was a promise to herself, and a threat to prized immunity in another.

The weeks passed. Winter was upon them. Sunday brought a long journey to the West of England. Unknown to Constance, Hurd's news was darker than ever. Two bookings for future weeks were abruptly cancelled; others had not been confirmed; in the North, Ellis Rooke, worn out, lay at the point of death. Older members of the company read the signs as Constance could not do. There were whispered talks, tears, and ever more anxious studying of *The Stage* and *The Era*. Everything was in disarray. If she herself was blind, it was because, back in the drudgery of her first employment as Assistant Stage Manager, she basked in dreams of love and success, achieved and expected. There came also an ardent letter from Pen, written in the scrupulously neat hand approved by Miss Pickering, which Constance had never been persuaded to use. Hers was flamboyant, a declaration of optimism and rebellion; it had brought galling reproofs and extra homework, which she would never forgive.

The letter, after expressing joy in a sister's triumph, carried other intimations of the utmost value. The programme had been shown to other girls, who were thrilled. Better still, it had been shown to Miss Gosling; and Miss Gosling had asked if she might borrow it for a day.

'Not bad. Not bad,' thought the gratified reader, smirking once more, without a glance at the mirror. She imagined Miss Gosling carrying the programme as far as Picky herself; and pictured the cross face of Miss Thomas. Jealousy, of course; the old vinegar-bottle.

Absorbed in delight, Constance did not at first notice a postscript written upon the letter's fourth page. This was less welcome.

*I haven't wanted to tell you,* Pen wrote; *but I think I must. Daddy hasn't been too well lately, and I've been rather frightened. He's talking to himself more than ever, and behaving strangely, going out in the dark and coming back soaked to the skin and quite worn out. He's left off shaving, and when I asked him about it he*

*said it was because he was afraid. I don't like to talk about it to
Mrs Randall, because she has gone all religious, and keeps on saying
things like 'it's God's will,' and hinting that she must look after
herself. And I can't ask Miss Pickering anything, in case she says
he ought to be taken away. Do tell me what you think I ought to do.*

This was alarming. It was impossible to run home, even for a
day; yet Pen was evidently as uneasy as possible. Their father's
fear of shaving could mean only that he had been tempted to
use the razor to end his life. He must be very ill indeed. But
what was to be done? If Ellis were here, she would know, would
advise, would arrange something. Nobody else was capable of
giving any help at all. They would all shake their heads, shrug
their shoulders, say a few words of common sympathy—and
do nothing.

'I suppose I could ask Mr Hurd,' thought Constance, doubt-
fully. 'He wouldn't understand. He'd storm. He'd tell me to go,
and never come back. I couldn't bear that. Carl? No! He's not
interested in other people; only himself, and a little in me.
Maude? She'd give plenty of advice that I couldn't take. I must
write to Pen; tell her if things get really serious to send me a
telegram. But I shouldn't really know what to do if she did . . .'

'Who's that from?' demanded keen-eyed Maude. 'Oh, you've
got a sister, have you? Something I didn't know. Can't imagine
it, somehow. I should like to see her. Is she another blonde?'

'Oh, no.' Constance had a vision of the little imp who
charmed everybody by her false air of innocence. 'Dark as an
Indian. Very small. Rather clever, in a way.'

'Fancy! Your sister and clever! Very odd! She writes a pretty
little hand. You sound as if you were fond of her.'

'Do I! Well, she's five years younger than I am. Quite a kid.'

'Is she fond of you?'

What strange jealous questions Maude asked! Constance
heard that pursuing voice of long ago—'Con-nee! Con-nee!'

'I never thought about it,' she confessed. 'I suppose so. Being
a sister, I mean.'

'It doesn't follow. I should rather like to have a young sister. I've only got a brother, who's a bit of a bore. What's her name?'

'Pen. Penelope.'

'Hm. Too short, and too long. Is she stage-struck, too?'

Two other memories swept back upon Constance. One was of the comments overheard after the school play. 'Exquisite! A born actress! In the West End in twenty years!' That was unwelcome. The other was of Pen's impersonation of Blanche. It had been devilish; and a charge against herself of gullibility in face of pretentiousness. Pen had seen through it at once. Bother the child!

'She's still at school. Besides, she's looking after Father. He's ill, she says.'

'What's the matter with him?'

That was unanswerable.

'I only know she's worried about him. He adores her.'

'You mean he doesn't adore you, I suppose.'

'He never did. She pets him. I can't do that.'

'Too busy thinking about yourself.'

The words, as they were meant to do, chilled the new self-complacency. They lingered when the candid speaker had forgotten them; and continued to disturb Constance from time to time. So did Pen's entreaty for advice. 'Maude means I'm selfish. She doesn't understand what it was like. Yes; it sounds as if he's half-mad. I don't like that. Perhaps Pen exaggerates. She's all alone; worse off than I was. Poor kid! But what am I to do? Hundreds of miles away. I know what I ought to do; but I can't do it. If anything happens . . . No, I really can't! I'll tell her to write, wire . . . I'm dodging . . . Oh, well, that's what life is!'

The phrase was one she had quickly learnt from Stockhouse, who was now, to her, 'Carl'. He used it when he was bored, without reference to event or opinion. Its meaning was 'that's enough of that'. At this point he always looked away, frowning; and sometimes moved away also. That was a further tantalisation. She feared it might indicate impatience with her own slower wits. To appear less stupid, therefore, she adopted his fatalism.

Other striking phrases were 'Moribund's Mummers', to describe Hurd's Strollers; 'City of Dreadful Night', for Manchester in particular but any other northern town where darkness was day-long; 'Men are all fools; and women are . . .' He never finished his sentence; but looked sideways with the dead eyes and bitterly smiling lips.

She guessed that the unspoken word was 'wantons'.

They more than once walked together if the afternoon was dry. Maude at first made a third but her argumentative spirit led to quarrels, and, being no walker, she found Stockhouse's erratic pace an exasperation.

'That boy's a bore,' she told Constance. 'He can't walk straight. And he either dawdles or sprints. It's a bad sign. Means he can't be relied on.'

'Maude's high heels are ridiculous,' said Stockhouse, when he and Constance were alone. 'Knowing she's short she wears them to pretend otherwise. She'll end up as a cripple.'

Constance, thinking 'You're none so tall yourself,' laughed in safety. She was of the same height as Stockhouse, and needed no high heels to raise her to his level. The equality was delicious to her. Also, she preferred to listen to one dogmatist at a time. His lectures were delivered with the authority of a twenty-six-year-old Solon, and greatly impressed her by their assurance. His favourite conversational opening was 'What you ought to do . . .'

On one exquisitely dusky day, when the sun was a crimson ball in the sky, they had climbed a hill and were looking down upon trees and church towers emerging from wintry mist. Both were silent; Constance tender, Stockhouse remote.

'What you ought to do,' he suddenly exclaimed, 'is, give up all this Shakespearean twaddle. It leads nowhere. You ought to go into modern plays. I don't mean the trash bowdlerised from the French. That's disgusting. I mean plays by people like Ibsen.

The Old Man's afraid of Ibsen, Ibsen needs acting, not rant. You've never seen an Ibsen play; so you don't understand what I mean. I'll lend you one or two . . .'

'Aren't they Norwegian, or something?' asked Constance, intelligently.

'Ah, they're translated—very badly. If I knew Norwegian, I'd do them better.'

'Couldn't you learn Norwegian?'

'Oh, yes, if I had time. Well, I might do it. Yes, it's an idea. It wouldn't take me long. They're about real problems—hereditary disease, parochial hypocrisy, bad drains, female emancipation . . .'

Constance archly seized upon his last words.

'You believe in female emancipation, do you?'

'Up to a point, yes.'

'I thought you despised women.'

'Their dishonesty. It's more or less forced upon them.'

She was enchanted. This subject, beginning with the general, led directly to the personal. That would be lovely! Very innocently, she inquired:

'Why "forced"?'

'Oh, people like Ibsen go to the root causes of it.' Stockhouse hurriedly resumed his discourse on the drama. 'So does the Irishman, Bernard Shaw. I've seen a touring company in one of his plays; but others have been done in London. A thing called the Stage Society does them on Sunday nights for progressive people. Or there's Oscar Wilde, another Irishman.'

Constance substituted knowledge for innocence. She felt extraordinarily adroit. She said:

'Mr Hurd says he's no good.'

Stockhouse uttered a scornful sound.

'Huh! You know why, don't you?' There was another side-long glance; but no explanation. He continued: 'Shakespeare, apart from old-fashioned murders, which they call "tragedy", when the real tragedy is failure, is static. Beautiful words, noble phrases for anaemics like Ted Masefield; but out of date.'

Constance indignantly protested.

'I don't think he's out of date . . .'

'That's because you know nothing about modern plays. Shakespeare's dead. He's been deified by the Victorians; but it's really all conventional stuff, like the sonnets all the Elizabethans wrote to imaginary women—Julia, Idea, Anthea—not real women at all. Poets just thought of some pretty name, and stuck it on like a stamp. You may not know it, but all the Shakespearean heroines, including darling Jessica, were dressed-up boys.'

Constance, astonished by his erudition, and reaching after wisdoms which she had not learned at Pickering's, hoped that she appeared, at least, to understand what he meant.

As if tired of both Elizabethans and Edwardians, he began to talk about himself. His father, he said, was an artist—not a story-telling Academician painting rubbish in gilt frames, but a man who illustrated really modern books and magazines. He was a very good artist, and a fascinating man, with broad shoulders and a piratical beard. Foreign-looking—well, *his* father had come to England from Westphalia—and very distinguished. He often went away—Spain, Germany, Italy—for weeks at a time; and finally stayed away altogether.

'So you didn't see much of him?' suggested Constance.

'Not a lot. When he was at home he was working—or out at the pubs. When he came home he swore a good deal, and threw things about. Well, I don't blame him. My mother is—or was— I don't know if she's still alive—a thoroughly conventional woman; church-going, but not religious; "what will the neighbours think?" that sort of thing. She was always upset when he got tipsy, and tried to shut him up. "Sh, sh! They'll hear you!" He'd say "To Hell with them! And you, too!" In the end he told her to go to Hell altogether.'

Constance had one of her visions; this time of eternal domestic din, which she did not approve. How different from her own home; and how different from her own father, who never got tipsy, but had visions, and was now frightening young Pen by hints of suicide. Poor kid! . . . She said nothing.

'Naturally,' continued Stockhouse, 'when he said he wasn't coming back, she thought how the neighbours would despise her. That was her first thought. Shows you the kind of woman . . . After he'd gone, and she'd told lies about his having a commission to do pictures of Europe, she clung to me like a leech.' He spoke these words between his teeth, in a conspiratorial tone. 'It was Hell. Nothing about this to Maude, by the way. She's a hard-minded fool who only thinks of her twenty-five bob a week. God, she makes me sick! Like my mother! Not the same type; but you know what I mean—a bore. Well, I stood it for two or three months, and then I cleared out—without saying a word. I knew there'd be a terrific fuss. Sixteen, I was . . .'

Constance thought: 'I was eighteen; we're alike!' She said:

'What on earth did you do?'

'Oh, all sorts of things. Clerk; served in a shop; addressed envelopes. At last I threw it all up and went on the road. I knew I could act; and I've proved it. I was two years in a travelling melodrama, *Lightning's Flash*; but I got tired of it. The company broke up. Then I was in a musical show.'

'Wonderful!' She was amused. 'Did you sing?'

'Oh, yes; I'd been in the choir. I was only on the one tour; seaside shows in the Summer. Then I came across Erasmus. He told me the tale; said he'd carry me to the heights. That was two years ago. Such heights!'

'I wonder you've stayed so long.' She feared he would notice the catch in her voice, which betrayed her fear of losing him. Evidently he did not notice.

'Experience. That's the main thing. Variety of parts; variety of audiences.'

'It's extraordinary how unlike audiences are, isn't it? I hadn't realised that.'

'Every one. You have to dominate them.'

'What about repertory?' She had picked up the word from

Maude, who despised repertory companies as a scuffle of amateurs pretending to be professional.

He shook his head with decision.

'I'm a slow study. Got too much in my head. Ideas; art; perfection. Repertory's just a rush. I must have time for thinking. I think a lot. Deeply, I mean. As far as that goes, Hurd's is a sort of repertory. At his whim, which is got by panic out of egotism. I admit he knows the game; but he's now crazy for want of Ellis. She's the real brains. And she's not coming back.'

'Do you really think that?' Constance took fright. 'It sounds terrible. I shouldn't be here but for her. She came to see my father.'

'Yes, she got fifty pounds from him. Did you know that? She could persuade a banker to lend money.'

'From Father? I can't believe it.'

'I happen to know. I have means of knowing.'

'But Father? You're sure? It must have been because he wanted to get rid of me.' She was aghast; almost bitter against her father; instantly resolved that she would not, after all, hurry to his side. He had wanted to get rid of her, to be alone with his darling Pen! It was shameful!

'My God, you were lucky! I still feel furious when I think of my mother's adhesiveness. No peace. No freedom. "What are you doing tonight?" "I shall be all alone then." God, it was awful. I haven't seen her, haven't written to her, since I left home. My revenge! And I'm definitely making a career for myself.'

'You are indeed!' Constance was distracted from personal resentment by that boast. She had no pity to spare for a twice-deserted woman. She herself had been sold for the sake of peace. 'We all think tremendously highly of you. Moore says you'll get right to the top.'

'Yes, I shall.' He spoke with conviction, as a zealot speaks of Paradise, adding between his teeth, very emphatically, 'Yes. Yes. *Yes*.' She thought the grim repetition a proof of confidence. 'So will you.'

Surprised by this unexpected graciousness, she gratefully acknowledged it.

'Do you think so? Of course, I mean to; but every now and then . . . It was because I was so bent on it that I went to see Mr Hurd. I simply screwed up my courage.'

He did not respond. Suddenly he exclaimed:

'We must move quickly, you know.'

'We?' she asked, with quickened heartbeat. She listened eagerly for his answer.

'Seize the future. A great future. We must plan. Scheme. That's essential.'

His gaze was directed to the emergent trees and towers. She, in emulation, saw them as symbols of united achievement, and was exalted. She turned, expectant of a smile, an outstretched hand, words of love; and ready for the inevitable kiss.

Neither gesture nor kiss followed. He had reassumed his normal detachment. A quick nod, acknowledging some inner call to ambition or campaign, was the only sign he gave of warmth. 'Yes, yes!' he seemed to be saying. But it was to himself alone; not to her. Immediately afterwards he began to descend the hill, confident that she would obediently follow.

The return journey was made in silence. Constance, alert for any proof of concern for her, and finding none, felt the blood rise to her cheeks. In the midst of shame and disappointment she was thankful that her emotion seemed to have passed unseen. He was absorbed in planning his own career.

At parting, Stockhouse smiled at last, but without affection. He said abruptly:

'That was a good walk, wasn't it?'

'Lovely,' answered Constance, with the irony of chagrin.

Only when alone did she relapse into temper, finding it an outrage that a young man should indifferently mock such a companion as she knew herself to be. He was as indifferent to her as her father had been. She would never walk with him again; but would behave with comparable disregard. Men were all selfish; all horrible.

To temper succeeded melancholy. She was not wanted. The afternoon represented, for her, a failure in charm. Father, Tom, Carl; all had shown the same distaste. And yet . . . And yet he had said 'we'. Didn't that mean attraction? Had she said something to arouse dislike? What ought she to have said or done? What did one do or say when one was in love with an enigma?

# *Flight*

I

WITHIN twenty-four hours of this exasperating walk a series of happenings occurred which—ever-ready to dramatise her own life—she saw in retrospect as the climax to Act I.

The day began in one more shabby bedroom, on the wall of which hung a large and impressive picture. This portrayed the artist's vision of an ascending angel, clad in white, whose equally white hands clasped a small bird of the pigeon species. Both angel and dove wore expressions of piety; and the barefooted angel was supported by rolling white clouds.

Overnight Maude had spoken disparagingly of the picture, pointing out that the angel's wings were furled and the clouds too insubstantial to support her body; but Maude was not in general a religious person, and only believed in moments of peril.

'I suppose that's how you see yourself?' she suggested.

'Just about,' pertly answered Constance.

'Little hypocrite!' One would have thought Maude a giantess, whereas she was fully two inches shorter than Constance. Her words, however, were intended as a compliment.

By morning light the picture had become ethereal, the angel a wraith, and the clouds a mere background to miserable thoughts of Stockhouse. How humiliating his attitude to her was! She directed her attention to Maude, who sprawled in the other bed like a beauty on the cover of *La Vie Parisienne*. No perplexities ever affected Maude. She was never troubled by unrequited love. She was ineffably self-satisfied, cheerful, mundane; the last person in whom one could confide.

Their breakfast of half-cold bacon and eggs, eaten from chipped plates, and washed down with lukewarm coffee, was revolting. Constance, feeling sick, became deliberately an actress, hiding all emotion, setting her plate aside with exaggerated disgust, and pouring another cup of the disastrous liquid as if it were hemlock. In doing this she glanced at Maude, and was disconcerted to find that the shrewd eyes were busy in close concentration.

'Are you all right?' asked Maude.

'Oh, yes.' Constance was alarmed by the direct question. 'Why?'

'I only asked, didn't I?'

'I was wondering if this coffee was poison.'

'It is. But you thrive on poison. I don't.' She left her coffee. 'I'd like to make the old girl drink the stuff herself—quarts of it —and die in agony. I bet I'll write something rude in her visitors' book when we go.'

'You'll say "Just like home", as you always do,' retorted Constance.

'What I write is "Just like Hell", corrected Maude. 'But I smudge it, in case we come again. Otherwise she might add a drop of strychnine.'

'Do you think we ever shall come again?' Constance's melancholy rose in flood.

'That depends on Erasmus,' said Maude. 'He's capable of anything. Did you know his real name is Tom? I heard Betty call him that. It seems the "Erasmus" is something he found in a book, the brute.'

'How horrible! He might have found a sweeter name— Clarence, or Duncan.'

'He wouldn't be able to think of it.'

'I wonder Ellis didn't choose something better.'

'Poor Ellis!'

'Oh, poor Ellis!'

Both relapsed into depression.

Still concerned for Ellis, they walked together to the theatre, past the neighbouring small houses until they reached High Street and the shops where Christmas toys were displayed. Some of the toys had been tied to scrubby Christmas trees, and were draped with little festoons of tinsel.

'Gosh! how loathsome!' muttered Maude. 'Always the same. Always tawdry. I shouldn't be surprised if this tinsel—tarnished, they use it again, year after year—is what I saw when I was a kid. I used to rub my nose against the window then. I didn't know what I know now. See those kids just ahead? They're doing what I did, poor mites!'

It was true. Two little girls in ugly overcoats and crimson mufflers were marvelling at half-a-dozen golden-haired dolls. They were arguing about their preference—'No, she's better!' 'No, she's not. The other's the nicest!'

'Silly kids!' complained Maude. 'You can tell they'll quarrel all their lives. Sisters. Twins, by the look of it. The dolls are just like you.'

'Oh, I hope not!' The word 'sisters' had disturbed Constance, making her think of Pen, in the Rectory; and from Pen she went on to remember how Carl Stockhouse, with self-absorbed face, had nodded to his complacent ambition. 'I'm like the kids,' she thought; 'looking in the shop-window, and . . .' 'What did you say, dear?'

'That was long ago,' replied Maude. 'My auntie must have been dead for a couple of years. More. She wasn't a bad sort. I was fond of her. A bit strict, though. She'd been governess in a "county" family; so she was a snob. Also, no children of her own; so I had to suffer for that. Still, she was kind. Funny how you look back on your childhood as a cosy, sunny time.'

'I don't,' said Constance. 'I was always trying to get away from Pen, and the house. Wanting to be an actress.'

'And now you've had your wish, you don't like it.'

'I love it. But it's not quite what I expected.'

'You were taken in by the lights. We all are. Those kids are taken in by the Christmas trees. They'll go to the panto. Same thing . . .'

For a little while neither spoke; but Maude was evidently continuing to ponder on disillusions of age and experience, for she said abruptly:

'Look along there at the theatre. On a drab morning like this it's more like a hospital. Gosh, I wish I hadn't said that. It's made me think of poor old Ellis, all alone . . .'

'All alone.' Constance was reminded, also, of her father.

'I dreamt about her last night. Woke up grizzling, and couldn't get off again for ever so long. You, of course, were lost in girlish dreams of love.'

Constance started at the charge.

'I was awake. I didn't hear you grizzling.'

'I wonder how she is.' Maude had not heard the muffled protest. 'That devil doesn't care what happens to her, the miserable dwarf. Too wrapped up in his own grandeur. There he is, by the way; looking like a mute. Oh, what an actor! All trappings; but in his weasel heart . . .'

Hurd, wearing his big black theatrical cloak and black sombrero, and carrying an ebony stave, crossed the street a hundred yards ahead. He was unsteady, a man groping blindly through a fog of sorrow. As he disappeared into the side street leading to the stage door, Maude clutched Constance's arm.

'He's seen us. Don't let's go in for a minute,' she entreated. 'He's going to break the news that she's gone. I know it. If he acts the bereaved husband I shall spit in his face. Then he'll be pained. Quite shocked. Injured. He'll expect me to apologise for unmaidenly conduct. Has it ever struck you that he's another hypocrite, darling?'

Both reached the theatre half-weeping. Hurd was nowhere to be seen; but as they met the others, grouped in the dusty wings like mourners at a graveside, they knew Maude's belief was true.

'It's my dream,' she whispered, crying, and bowing her head.

'Ay, ay, ay,' groaned Moore, in his sepulchral voice. 'A plack tay. A plack tay.'

The Dodd sisters were sobbing. Rachel Delmaine, more

haggard than ever, stood with a strained face of grief, not tearful, but a picture of sorrow. Only Stockhouse, looking completely cynical as he glanced from one to another, appeared unmoved.

'Well?' he asked Maude. 'This is what we anticipated, isn't it? In their hearts, all these girls are thinking what leads they'll get now she's gone.'

'You're nothing but a cad, Stockhouse!' cried Maude, violently.

When she saw Hurd later, Constance was shocked to perceive that he, too, had been crying. Her heart immediately softened to him; and she impulsively put out her hand. He did not take it, but gripped her elbow, speaking in a broken voice.

'Child, child,' he groaned. 'This is a very grievous blow. For me, it's the end; utterly the end.'

They were alone upon a stone landing from which dressing-rooms opened. Through an open doorway she heard voices of lament, and knew that her companions were gathered within, heightening the general trouble by exclamations of grief. She brushed aside memory of Stockhouse's outrageous sarcasm, which returned persistently; but she believed in the sincerity of Hurd's ejaculation because she felt it to be true. Without Ellis he would be lost, as they all were. Tears filled her eyes. When he pressed his cheek to her shoulder, tightening the grip upon her elbow, she did not shrink, but braced herself to support his momentary collapse.

'We all know . . . understand,' she whispered. 'You see them; hear them.'

'Yes.' His voice was deep, solemn. 'But you, Constance; you have true feelings.' He looked earnestly into her eyes.

Somebody, she thought it was Maude, appeared in the doorway. Hurd released his grip, stood for a moment with bowed shoulders, and went back into his own dressing-room. Their brief colloquy was at an end.

Subsequently he addressed the entire company, which had gathered at his request on the stage.

'Ladies and gentlemen,' he said, with measured gravity. 'We shall act tonight as arranged. I shall be with you. I can do nothing—up there. Arrangements will be made. *She . . .*' his voice deepened. '*She* will be brought down to us here or elsewhere for burial, for mourning; but we are the servants of the public, and we are under contract to perform until the end of the week. I shall see you all again tonight. Meanwhile, I beg that you will concentrate your attention upon one thing only—the show. Mr Moore will give you . . . his assistance . . . in my place. Thank you.'

He made his exit with a gesture familiar to them all as that which in taking the curtain he modestly shared applause with the entire cast. Constance, who had been dreaming, half expected her companions to cheer. Instead, they shuffled and were silent. She instinctively looked for Stockhouse's smile of irony, which was not absent.

The play that night was again *The Merchant of Venice*. Because they were actors and actresses, to whom private concerns must yield to art, they played as if unstunned by disaster. Gratiano was as boisterous as ever, the Gobbos as droll, and Portia, although never approaching the Portia they remembered, pronounced her legal challenge with such effect that the audience was evidently stirred. Shylock himself was richly villainous; and his reception when, in Miss Delmaine's company, he took the final call, was everything a star could ask. It was, indeed, so cordial that Moore, as the eldest Stroller, ventured a congratulation. Hurd's simple reply, made, sighing, with mournful dignity, was: 'She would have wished it.'

He backed from the curtain, still bowed, and made a slow progress to the wings. There, catching sight of Constance, he paused, bestowing again the earnest look with which he had acknowledged her sympathy.

'You gave an admirable performance, Connie,' he murmured. 'Admirable. I have plans for you. Tomorrow.'

So promising, he continued upon his stricken way; while

Maude, who had been standing a yard from them, whispered with urgent inquisitiveness:

'What did he say?'

Stockhouse, also near enough to have heard the words, lightly pressed his Jessica's waist, adding:

'My guess is Rosalind. Or could it be Juliet?'

'With him as Romeo? Oh, Gawd!'

Constance was not dismayed. On the contrary, her spirits mounted. Both Maude and Carl had betrayed jealousy, the one of herself, the other of Hurd. Were not these favourable signs? For a while her grief for the loss of Ellis was assuaged.

2

It returned, inevitably, in the darkness of the night; but only as one item in a tangle of curiosity, ambition, hope, and disagreeable memories. The memories carried her to the Rectory at Wilmerton, her mother's assurance that she had always been dearly loved, and now the fear that her father was dying. If he died, what then? *What then?* She would have to go home, make decisions, lose Carl . . .

The terror produced more poignant agitation, which grew stronger as the night lengthened. She could not sleep. Her head seemed about to burst. What would Mr Hurd say? What was really happening at home? Would she receive a telegram from Pen? If a telegram came, the news would be bad. She ought not to have left Pen to face everything alone. If Carl was jealous, his indifference must be a sham; and in that case what would he do next? How strange that Maude should be angry because she had received no compliment from a man she despised! Oh, if only Ellis was still alive to help with understanding and advice!

So the torment continued. She had a hideous vision of a curtained bed many miles away, where Ellis lay as Mother had done, pale and without sensation. Could the loyal spirit be hovering near? Mother's had given no sign; and Constance had too clearly perceived her father's fundamental agnosticism to believe that Ellis would come again. She pictured a coffin, a grave, tears, and, apart from fading memory, no more.

How kind Ellis had been. She had been the one to detect quality in an aspirant; to hear without interruption the blurted story of hope; to persuade Father into giving his consent. Had she truly, as Carl claimed, coaxed fifty pounds out of that reluctant pocket? For what? As a bribe to Mr Hurd? Was she really Mr Hurd's wife? What was the truth about him? What were his 'plans'? When would she learn them? Would Pen telegraph? What would Carl say and do when they met? What a mixture he was of kindness and cruelty! Maude could be thoughtlessly, maliciously cruel; but his cruelty held deliberation . . .

At last heavy sleep came.

She was dreaming unhappily when cold fingers walking over her forehead brought sudden awakening to the dreariness of another dark day. Maude, half-dressed, was standing at her side, preparing for a second attack, looking down with an expression in which mischief and hatred were combined.

'Wake up, little girlie!' said Maude. 'You've got to face your future, you know.'

'What is my future?' Constance asked, staring up in confusion.

'God knows,' was the reply. 'What's anybody's future? What's the good of all the work and worry we put into the present? I tell you, Ellis's fate is our own. "In the midst of life we are in death." Have those words ever meant anything to you until now? Did your father, being a clergyman, sing them to you in your cradle?'

'My father never sang to me. I don't think he ever sang at all.'

'Mine was a singing-bird. He used to sing me whole operas. Vain of his tenor voice. But those words have been running in my head all night, giving me the pip. I've still got it. And it's time for you to get up. Don't forget it's today that Erasmus is going to tell you the old, old story.'

'I shall always think of him now as "Tom" because you told me that was his real name.'

'Whatever his name is, he'll tell the same story. But remember: *don't believe a word of it!*'

There was no smile now; only an expression of mingled severity and resentment. Thinking at first that it revealed dislike of herself, Constance was wounded. Then, perceptively, she guessed that during the night, when she seemed to be asleep, Maude had been thinking of Ellis, and of more than Ellis. She realised, without warning, that she did not understand Maude. She was used to alternations of sentimentality and ruthlessness; but this was something different. Maude suffered as other people suffered. Although she behaved as if she had neither troubles of her own nor concern for the troubles of friends, she had foreseen Ellis's death, had shrunk from entry to a theatre where fore-knowledge would be confirmed, and now showed hateful scorn of the man who, in her opinion, had ruined his wife's happiness. What did she know? And what, in her twenty-six years, had she lived through?

'I don't want to get up,' groaned Constance, after these speculations.

Maude was ready.

'Can't face it, eh? I feel like that every morning.'

'You don't show it.'

'What would be the use? I should get no sympathy from you. Or anybody else.'

Constance thought: 'She doesn't trust me. She's always play-ing a part; but not, like Antonio's, a sad one. Once an actress, always and everywhere an actress. That's why *I* don't trust *her*.'

Grief, curiosity, and ambition were drowned. Involuntary comparison with Maude was accompanied by physical sensations, from headache to uneasiness in the shoulder on which she had lain. She sat up in bed, saying:

'I think you're really rather brave, Maude. Under the show.'

'Oh, I am,' answered Maude. 'I can even bear the stinking fish we're getting for breakfast. Do you get the whiff of it?'

Constance, again baffled, revised her view. She decided that Maude had a tough skin, with flesh and heart of even greater toughness. These made her as *blasé* as Carl; and as little candid.

Carl: uncandid, impenetrable. Another masked personality. But jealous. How significant! How exciting! Excitement must be concealed from Maude, who would jump to its cause and show no mercy; and from Carl, who, feeling embittered triumph, would withdraw from danger as a tortoise withdraws its head from an enemy. The need for the exercise of her natural reserve was greater than ever. She, too, was an actress; she, too, must wear a mask, now and for ever.

They again assembled in the dark theatre, lamentation silent under a return to everyday gossip. When Constance first heard the murmur and an occasional titter she was censorious. How facile they were! There was nothing under the masks. But was she herself any better? Already, because nothing remained of yesterday's shock, Carl's scathing irony had been confirmed.

Where, amid the chatter, was Carl? He could not be seen. He must have overslept, or gone for a walk—could it have been with one of the other girls? No, all were present. He must have gone alone. He had no need of companionship. Certainly not of hers.

Spirits plunged. They were still low when Hurd arrived. His mood also had changed overnight. He was preoccupied; not the bowed figure of grief they had seen on the previous day, but a very commander. Carl had told her that when a man died every friend thought: 'Thank God I am done with him!' At the time it had seemed the acme of cynicism. Now, viewing the faces around, she wondered whether he had not spoken truly.

Hurd did not refer to Ellis. He was brief, businesslike.

'*Othello* tonight, ladies and gentlemen,' he said, peremptorily.

'You, Emilia, must practise that fall. Where are you, Iago? And where's Cassio?'

There was a rustle, as if all had started with fear lest Stockhouse, being absent, should doom them to an outburst of rage; and when he sauntered on to the stage another rustle, accompanied by murmurs of 'Here he is! Here he is!' showed their relief. Feeling blood rise to her cheeks, Constance saw him as a hero, and the company as men and women who, like herself, were on edge, dreading any loud noise. Yesterday they had pretended to be a stricken host; today they were pretending that nothing had happened. All was pretence. Quick tempers, perhaps hysteria, would leap out if the rehearsal was bad.

'There you are at last, Cassio,' cried Hurd.

'I was detained.' Stockhouse neither apologised nor explained. He met Hurd's stare with an insolence defying further reproof. No other member of the Strollers would have escaped; and Constance did not need Maude's meaningful grimace to remind her of the explanation. Her pride in Carl was heightened. He had obvious distinction. He was the noblest Roman of them all, darkly scheming his way to London. *Their* way! Did he remember?

No greeting passed. Stockhouse crossed the stage to Moore, who was already assuming the dignity proper to a Duke of Venice. They spoke awhile. The rehearsal proceeded.

At the end of it—and this morning mercy was shown to all by an Othello content merely to mutter a few of his own lines and supervise inferiors with particular warnings—a friendly discussion arose in which Emilia compared views with Iago on his murder of her. This occupied Maude's whole attention; and Hurd must have noticed the fact, for without appearing to single her out in any way he spoke to Constance in an undertone as he passed.

'I want to talk to you, Jessica. About my plans. About *her*. Stay behind the others. Say nothing. Just stay. You understand?'

He might have been giving her some trifling instruction about properties; for, with a grave smile, he passed on his way without a backward glance. Constance, struck by his confidential tone and the strangeness of his command, felt her pulse quicken. She was doubly confused when she observed Miss Delmaine standing alone at the other side of the stage, face averted and shoulders rigid, as if she had at that moment turned her back.

'Well, little one; were you interested to see two strong men stand face to face?' demanded Maude, when her colloquy with Iago was ended. 'I thought it was as good as a play.' She laughed. 'I'm always expecting Master Erasmus—my Emilian mind runs on daggers, you see—to plunge his poignard into Stockie's bosom. And, speaking of the Devil . . .' She became aware that Stockhouse had approached. 'Where had you been, Stockie?'

'Flowers,' he murmured, conspiratorially. 'For Ellis. I was finding a florist's.'

'You won't do that, laddie. I know the place.' But Maude's attention had returned to the fact. 'It was a nice thought, Stockie. Does you credit.'

'I found one.'

'Really? Can you show me? What's the good, though. She won't be here for days.'

'She'll be here by Saturday. The man spent a lot of money yesterday in telephoning. So did I.'

'But you haven't got any money! None of us have got any money. Hurd sees to it.'

Stockhouse favoured Maude with his most sarcastic smile, and Maude retorted with one of equal sarcasm.

'Can we all buy flowers?' asked Constance. 'I haven't got much money; but . . .'

'I've ordered some for you, too,' said Stockhouse.

'Dammit, the man's got a Savings Bank account!' cried Maude. 'I always thought you were a dark horse, Stockie.'

'I'm a very dark horse indeed,' announced Stockhouse. 'So dark, I can't be seen.'

He would have left them upon this note of gratification; but Maude ran after him. Constance, divining his pride in scheme, but remembering Hurd's instructions, slipped into the darkness; and from a place of concealment watched them go off together. The others had already crowded towards the staircase. She was alone.

It was several minutes before a pad of soft steps revealed Hurd's presence. He advanced a pace from the wings, looked about him, saw nobody, and muttered something to himself. Evidently he assumed that she was not there; for Constance caught the words: 'Damn the little bitch!' She hesitated. There was time to remain undiscovered until he had gone again; and if she was no more than a 'little bitch' she would be justified in changing her mind. Yes? No? Why be afraid?

'I'm as brave as a female bulldog!' she told the Fates, who approved; and, so saying, she called out: 'Mr Hurd!'

'Ah, there you are, my dear!' he cried, sweeping his arm upward and backward in a familiar grand gesture of welcome. 'You're there. Good girl! I couldn't . . .' He pretended to be blind. 'The darkness here and on the stairs. Prodigious! Keep close to me. We'll go to my dressing-room. We shan't be . . . disturbed there.'

What a curious melodramatic way he had. It was conspiratorial; but at the same time it was natural to him. He could only forget he was an actor when he was in a fury. He was not now in a fury; he was seeing himself as a kind godfather with some wonderful plan for the youngest member of his company. This was emphasised by the courteous bow with which he ushered her into the dressing-room.

It was the only room in the theatre to be occupied by a single actor. The women, including Miss Delmaine, shared one with a cracked, dirt-encrusted window; and the men scattered about in what Carl Stockhouse called 'hog-pens', cupboard-like cubicles lighted by wire-covered gas-brackets. Thus it had been in every theatre Constance had visited. Well, it was a poor enough place, unheated, and with crumbling walls. She saw Hurd's triple mirror on a dressing-table littered with grease-paints, costumes hanging without order on great nails, and a low divan covered with the travelling-rug he used on their Sunday journeys.

'Don't be afraid,' urged Hurd, in a tone of mellow reassurance.

Maude's warning! The very words! She would have been amused if another thought had not followed the memory. They were alone in the theatre. Unless some stage hand should tramp this way that could be dangerous. Not yet frightening; but, once stimulated, doubts multiplied.

'I'm not at all afraid,' she answered, pleasantly.

Hurd gave a short laugh.

'That's good. That's good. Why should you be? We're in accord; close accord, I'm sure. Well, let me begin. I mustn't waste time; though I hardly think anybody is likely to disturb our little . . . discussion. I know you must be feeling the grievous loss we've suffered. That's natural. She was a good friend to you. Do you remember? That day at—what was the name of the place?'

Wilmerton. 'The Theatre Royal.' Memory of her fears, the cold, Hurd's rough manner, and above all of Ellis's thoughtful kindness, was so strong that, coupled with returning sense of loss, Constance felt tears rising. How different Hurd was today from the martinet of Wilmerton! He was sweet, benevolent. Could Carl and Maude have been wrong about him? 'She was wonderfully considerate then—and always. A wonderful woman.'

'Quite. Quite. That fateful day! I see it moves you.' His voice deepened. 'Ah, the wonder of life! A first contact with the profession you're destined to adorn. It is natural that you, with your sensitive nature . . . I understand. I hope I shall always understand. My loss . . . even greater. Oh, much greater. Irreparable. For seven years she was my loyal assistant; first among my Strollers, and devoted to me.' Sighing, he paused. When he spoke again, his voice was broken. 'I'm a lonely man, Jessica. Lonely and unhappy. I need all the sympathy your warm heart can spare. All the kindness, tenderness, sweetness . . . I value these qualities in you. They're real, you see. They mean . . .

everything to me. The rest? Oh, "they have their exits and their entrances", but they have no hearts; no real comprehension of what a man needs from a woman—a beautiful woman . . . Won't you sit down?'

'Thank you.' Constance turned the chair standing before the dressing-table.

'No, no; you'll find the divan . . . Not?' He seemed to be amused that she should prefer the chair.

'Thank you, this chair has a back; and mine's rather weak,' explained Constance with a smile which did not indicate all her feelings.

'I could support you, if need be, with my arm,' said Hurd indulgently. She saw his big teeth as he smiled, was made to think of *Red Riding Hood*, and felt apprehensive. 'You looked bewitching when you said that. Quite bewitching. I have high hopes of you—as an actress, of course; as an actress. You show great promise; greater, I must admit, than I should have expected from your . . . quite remarkable . . . beauty. It's rare indeed to find so much talent allied to such beauty.'

He looked intently at her, with an air of profound admiration. Knowing that he was adapting his compliment to her simplicity, she instinctively stiffened, straining her ears to catch any sound in the theatre. There was no sound. She was led, like an experienced flirt, to play the *ingénue*.

'I hoped you might be pleased with your new Jessica.'

'Pleased? I was entranced. I was—and am—so deeply pleased that I . . .' He took two or three steps, as she had seen him do on the stage, particularly in the part of Hamlet, where they accented the soliloquies. He turned back, coming nearer, bending over her with a hand on the back of the chair. His next words were spoken in the penetrating whisper he used at the crisis in *Othello*—'My wife! I have no wife! . . . I hope you will be gratified . . . by what I shall do . . .' The whisper ceased. In a more normal voice, but one which still caressed, he asked: 'Are you familiar with the *Dream? A Midsummer Night's Dream?*'

'We did it two years ago as a school play,' answered Constance, looking at his hand, which had made contact with her shoulder.

The effect was startling. His hand was withdrawn. He stood erect, hissing like an angry cat.

'Sh! Sh! Oh, dear, dear; not a school! Let us forget that, shall we? You're grown up now, you know. A woman. A lovely woman; young, tender, full of grace and charm. You only need a little—if I may say so—a little coaching—shall we say in the art, the delights, of love . . .'

How Maude's mischievous voice echoed in her ears! She felt her heart beat very fast. In following her into the dressing-room he had closed the door. There was no escape that way. He had again approached very near. His expression, although he smiled, did not conceal purpose.

'I wonder what you mean, Mr Hurd?'

'Don't be afraid,' he repeated in a low tone. 'Surely you trust me?'

She had no doubt of his meaning; and was now really frightened. But she was not a fool, and even in danger commanded both voice and mind.

'I shouldn't be here if I hadn't trusted you, Mr Hurd. I'm sure all the Strollers trust you. They look on you as a father.'

'A father?' He was disconcerted. 'You mistake me. I am a man!'

'Of course you are a man. But my own father's very little older than you . . .'

'Father? Your *father*!'

'He's very ill. I may be sent for . . .'

'Father?' he repeated. 'That has nothing whatever . . . I thought you understood I spoke to you as a man . . .'

'I understood you to speak of the *Dream*,' she said. 'What were you going to say about that?'

'Going to say?' He recovered from astonishment; purpose had revived. She knew it; she was alert; but she knew that no help was at hand. 'I was going to say—Titania. But the living creature, no fairy, no saint I am sure, puts thoughts of plays, even Shakespeare's plays, out of my head. This isn't midsummer; this is here and now, you and me, alone together, without . . . You're beautiful, warm, endearing, delicious . . .'

He was upon her. His strong grip was about her shoulders. He was dragging her to her feet. She had a terrible temptation to submit, yielding to a fury that made Stockhouse's charming kisses insipid.

'Mr Hurd! Mr Hurd!'

'You darling! You irresistible darling!'

The strength opposing, dominating her own, was superhuman. She struggled, but did not scream, tearing at the hand which violently clasped her breast, savagely thrusting her elbow under his chin and with tremendous effort thwarting his effort to throw her down upon the fatal divan. He was panting, laughing hoarsely as wrestlers do. His hand had gone involuntarily to the bruised chin, which had reddened from her blow. She saw him as a maniac, a grotesque; and in that moment, she, too, laughed. The laugh was hysterical; but it was full of contemptuous defiance.

'What!' screamed Hurd, to whom the sound was a taunt. 'What!' He struck her.

Laughter became reckless scorn. No man living should dare to strike her.

'Rape, Mr Hurd! Rape! Your . . . speciality! With Betty Brown! With Ellis! Never with me! Never!' She brought her hand stingingly across his cheek.

He was astounded. His teeth were savagely bared, like the fangs of a frightened animal.

'What do you mean? I say what do you mean, you bitch?' Anger roused him to an extremity of lust. Determined to punish resistance, contempt, and incredible knowledge of the past, he was ready to kill her.

There was a slight noise. The door was slowly opened, revealing the face of a woman, so white that she might have been dead.

## 3

Hurd, whose back was to the door, was as quick as Constance to hear the sound. He wheeled about, panting, dropping his arms. He might have been Macbeth facing the ghost of Banquo; but he was not acting; his consternation was genuine. Miss Delmaine did indeed look spectral, a figure of anguished reproach; and in the following silence she did not move.

Constance reached for the back of the chair from which she had been dragged. Her knees were unsteady, and her eyes were half-closed; but she knew nothing of the signs of weakness. Her sensations were dominated by thankfulness for salvation. Always previously she had been repelled by this woman's coldness; now she could have kissed her hands in gratitude.

But the situation was not ended. Hurd, recovering, and identifying Miss Delmaine, drew himself up as Lear does in defying the storm. His words were not Lear's.

'What do you want?' he cried. 'Go away!'

The shout roused Constance from dream. She had instant memory of having seen her present deliverer immediately after Hurd's whisper to herself in the wings. Miss Delmaine's back was then turned. Therefore she had watched the exchange with the jealousy of a discarded mistress. Jealousy had led to suspicion, concealment in the theatre, eavesdropping, and—this. So much was certain.

'I heard my name.' The words were pronounced in a mournful tone of tragedy.

'Rubbish!' Hurd's fury with Constance was transferred. He was still not master of himself; being trapped, he snarled.

'I heard my name. *She* called me.'

'She did nothing of the kind.' He passed to a blustering lie. 'A private rehearsal. You've got no right to interrupt. You'd know that, if you weren't a bloody fool!'

'Rehearsal.' Miss Delmaine did not look directly at him; but as if in a trance, stared wearily at Constance. In doing this she swayed a little, for a reason which Hurd at once saw and proclaimed.

'You're drunk again, you sot! No, no; stay here, Constance. I'll soon get rid of her.'

As he stepped threateningly towards Miss Delmaine, intending to drive her from the room, Constance followed close behind. When he would have intercepted her flight she struck hard with a clenched fist at his outstretched arm, paralysing it, and pushed to Miss Delmaine's side. There, with an instinctive effort to draw the bodice across her exposed breast, she whispered urgently:

'You heard your name, you did—spoken loud—by me! He knows why.'

'Liar! Both liars!' cried Hurd. 'God damn it! If I had a whip . . .'

Constance laughed breathlessly with renewed courage.

'Yes, a whip!' she taunted. 'A ring-master, Mr Hurd. But we both know you. Remember that! Come on, Miss Delmaine! Let him dream of whips!'

'Tom!' It was a broken cry of entreaty, addressed not to Constance but to Hurd. 'You promised me! You promised me!' Great tears rolled from Miss Delmaine's eyes.

'Shut up! Constance! God damn! God damn you both!' He was ready to strike Miss Delmaine, ready passionately to throw Constance to the floor.

This was the last second for escape from a maniac. Constance touched Miss Delmaine's arm.

'Come!' she whispered. 'Now! At once!'

It was useless. The poor woman was like a sleep-walker. She would not—she could not—move. She could only stare piteously at the man she loved. Without a glance at Hurd, therefore, Constance shouldered her way through the doorway, stumbling over an extended foot, and, recovering her balance, ran blindly down the stone stairs. She was shaken by hysterical sobs; and in this condition reached the street, heedless of cold and the passers-by.

Her moods changed quickly as she ran. At first she looked apprehensively over her shoulder in case Hurd should be mad enough to pursue. She then found that she could run no more. At one point, still unconscious of inquisitive eyes, she stopped altogether, to laugh excitedly at her escape, and to ejaculate abuse of Hurd.

'Disgusting monster! Monster!'

Some muttered incoherencies followed, of which she after-wards remembered nothing. They welled from released know-ledge of evil, and had no place in her normal thoughts. She shook her fists, clenching her teeth in anger and hatred.

When next capable of seeing anything at all, she noticed that a man stared at her; and after she had hurried past him was prompted to consider her reflection in a shop-window. That was horrifying. Her hair was down, her cheeks swollen, blood trickled from the corner of her mouth.

'How terrible if Carl saw me! Wanton indeed!'

Thereafter she walked sedately, with one hand at her throat to hide her torn bodice.

She knew she had escaped by good fortune. She suppressed, as far as she could, shamed belief that for one moment, so unruly had been her physical response to Hurd's purpose, she had been tempted to yield. That must never be admitted. Instead, she praised herself for triumphant resistance, felt contemptuous pity for Miss Delmaine—a former victim who continued to cherish infatuation for her seducer—and spared trifling gratitude to Maude for warning her in advance of the very phrases Hurd would use.

He had used them. Following a stale formula, he had flattered and wooed one whom he took to be a green goose. Thank God she had known what he would say and do! Thank God his repetition of the familiar had enabled her to laugh! Maude's imitation had been perfect. Well done, Maude!

Well done! Yes, but how had Maude been able to prophesy so exactly? Deep distrust of Maude was born. Was she unchaste?

Her mind went back to Hurd. She was now walking at an

even pace, although her legs trembled, in what she believed to be the direction of their lodging. No vision of his distorted face and the bristle upon his chin was possible in the street; but her head was crowded with memory.

'What a brute! What a horror! And so inept! Using his old tags on somebody like me! And he could only rage and curse, clamour for a whip . . . Ridiculous! That poor creature! She should have come with me. I tried. She'd been drinking—for courage. What's happened now? Has he killed her? He'd have killed me if I hadn't run. He tried to trip. He's mad! What's to happen now? From now?'

The question came as such a shock that she was forced to put her hand to the wall of a house. She had been so preoccupied with immediate sensations that she had not imagined anything beyond the immediate moment. Yet the theatre was still there; the seats in it were still to be filled that night; a performance had still to be given.

'He won't be able to manage it!' she thought. 'Nor will she!' And then: 'How can we meet as if nothing had happened? I can't do it. I won't be alone with him again. I've only got Maude to help me; and I don't trust Maude. I can't tell her a thing. She'd laugh. She's insensitive. No help at all.'

Now the lodging was close at hand. She prayed that Maude would not be there to see her disorder, guess at its cause, exult in her ignominy.

She tiptoed into the dingy hall, listening intently for any sound. There was no sound. She ran quickly up to the bedroom, to find it empty, with the beds made and the two nightdresses neatly folded on the coverlets. Then she again surveyed herself, this time in the big mirror, and with increased dismay.

'Shocking!' she ejaculated, hastily throwing off the torn dress, catching sight of a reddened patch on her breast which would soon be a purple bruise. That must be covered instantly. But her hands shook so much that she could hardly bring the substitute dress over her head and shoulders. This was partly because she was in haste to conceal from Maude's eyes every sign of the struggle, and partly because reaction had produced a fit of uncontrollable shivering. Once the dress was on, however, she carefully sponged blood from her lips and cheek, bathed her eyes, and used a hair-brush. If she could present an appearance of calm, even if the lip should be swollen, she would be in a state to endure scrutiny.

Brushing the long golden hair, she found steadiness returning to her hands; and although she still exclaimed she knew that she was recovering. Her mind darted from thought to thought with the old speed and the old confidence. She was mistress of herself. If she could mend the dress quickly enough then nobody except Hurd and Miss Delmaine would dream that within the hour she had been struggling desperately with one whose strength was at least twice her own.

'A gorilla!' she exclaimed. Now she could see the distorted face quite clearly, feel the hot breath and the almost irresistible arms. She told herself that she had never been tempted to submit. She was quite convincing in her assurance. Other women might have been overwhelmed. She had thrown him off. She had slapped his face. She had taunted him. She had escaped. She was Constance Rotherham, untamed, immaculate, triumphant.

And all the time, under bravado, she was quaking at the prospect of meeting Hurd in the theatre, and wondering how she was to evade any possible contact with him. Shivering returned. She sat on the edge of the bed, examining her discarded dress, smoothing it, planning its repair, and listening. If he dared to come here she must be ready to summon help. She wished that Maude would slam the front door as she always did. She wished she could be transported home by the magic of dream. She wished . . .

What was that? A knock at the front door? Hurd! If so, the devil must be repelled! She ran to the door, opening it, waiting with strained ears for the sound of his voice.

There was a voice; but it was not Hurd's. Poised to drag her bed across the floor as a barricade, she listened. She thought she heard her own name. 'Like Miss Delmaine!' she thought. 'She heard *her* name, poor thing!' Then the front door was shut, and she knew that her name was indeed being called from below.

'Miss Rotherham! Are you upstairs, Miss Rotherham?' Mrs Ransom was alone in the hall, holding an envelope in her hand. An orange-coloured envelope.

'Yes, Mrs Ransom. I was just coming.'

'There's a telegram for you. Shall I bring it up?'

She bounded downstairs, almost colliding with the landlady, who had begun the ascent; a small grey-faced pinafored woman smelling as musty as her own house. The telegram was seized, torn open in haste, and its brief contents mastered.

*Daddy dying. Please come. Pen.*

She could not tell whether shock or relief came first, so rapidly did they merge into a single emotion. Sorrow was not involved; but her heart certainly plunged at this contact with something that linked her with childhood, revived guilt for desertion, aroused dread of responsibility, and was transcended by loyalty to Pen. The relief was otherwise. She would not need to see Hurd again. Furthermore, any agitation detected by Maude would seem to have been caused by bad news. She must leave at once, whenever there was a train. Decision was followed by a pang. This meant a parting from Carl. He would forget her. She would never see him again. Her heart would break.

'Is it bad news?' asked Mrs Ransom, with quickened relish. Telegrams, in her experience, always meant bad news; and bad news was drama. Never had the little black eyes been more inquisitive, nor the toothless mouth more avid.

'My father. Dying. Miss Marsh . . .'

As the name was spoken, the front door was energetically thrust open.

'Who calls?' cried Maude, with mock drama. ' "She who robs me of my good name . . ." ' She was in high spirits, having made a magnificent entry upon her cue.

'Maude, thank goodness !' Constance raised the telegram.

She had reason to bless her friend's resourcefulness; for Maude grasped the situation at once.

'Trains. London,' she said to Mrs Ransom. 'Got a time-table, Ma? What, two-thirty? Splendid. Now don't fuss, Connie. You've got time for a snack; I'll help you with your case. Where's that fellow Stockie? He's probably still hanging about. I said we'd take a bite with him as he's rich. He must have robbed the bank. Just a tick !'

She turned back to the door, disappeared, and returned frowning.

'Gone !' she announced. 'Repented. Thought he'd been trapped, the loon. Never mind; we'll show our independence. Out of the way, Ma !'

As soon as they reached the bedroom she pounced upon Constance's discarded dress, held it up, and noticed the torn bodice, which was split almost to the waist.

'Hello, what's happened here?' she demanded. 'And where did you get to when we all came out? Up to some mischief, I suppose.' Her eyes roved. Fortunately Mrs Ransom, thinking of her rent, had followed them upstairs. 'Oh, it's all right, Ma; I'll settle with you. Miss Rotherham's no bilk. She's had bad news. She can't be bothered with you now. Hurry off. I can smell your dinner's burning !' And when Mrs Ransom had crept away in her slippers, said 'Now, then, Connie, I'll break the news to Erasmus. Aren't I kind ! And I'll kiss Stockie for you. He'll like that. I'd love to see his face. He won't be able to cuddle his Jessica for a little while. You'll come back, I suppose? He and I have been for a walk to the florist's. I tried to get him to talk about you; but he wouldn't, the little prig ! Now, where do these go? Don't forget your nightie, though I expect you've got dozens more at home.'

Constance, thankful for the spate of words, which suggested, falsely enough, that Maude had drawn no conclusions from the torn dress and its owner's flinching under questions, began to fold garments preparatory to packing her case. She hoped there would be no return to suspicious inquiry. She prayed that there would be a chance to say goodbye to Carl. She was thankful that Maude had made that kind promise to explain her departure to Hurd. Indeed she was stricken with remorse for recent condemnations of Maude, and was able to laugh in reality as the flow of chatter continued.

'I ought to have been a lady's maid,' declared Maude. 'By the way, where's your hat? Where's your overcoat? Why on earth did you leave them at the theatre? Connie!'

'I came away in rather a hurry.'

'Oh. Yes, I bet you did.'

Nothing more followed. Constance saw movement betokening thought in the shrewd eyes.

After a few minutes, when the packing was nearly done, Maude said:

'Well, one of us must run back to the theatre to get your outdoor things. Better be me.' She slipped on her coat and pinned the big hat at an angle suggesting piracy, and heightened the rakish effect with a tremendous wink. As she was closing the door, she added, over her shoulder: 'I should put some powder on that cheek, if I were you.'

Scanning the cheek, Constance saw that it was inflamed near the corner of her mouth. Evidently, therefore, the ruthless Maude had guessed everything, and was generous enough to put no further searching questions. It was a great relief; for Constance knew that circumstantial lying is quite useless if the liar is overwrought. Angelic Maude! She was a great woman.

Speculation continued. Would Maude, at the theatre, see Hurd? Would she find Miss Delmaine. What had happened to Carl? The worst imaginable sequel would be Hurd's arrival in Maude's company. She imagined it, her heart racing. What would he say? What could she do? At least she would not be alone with him. Maude was a legion. But there was another doubt. Should she not have braved all, and gone to the theatre herself?

'I'm a coward. I've lost my nerve.'

She did not believe either accusation. She did not regard herself, even for a moment, as a coward or one capable of losing her nerve. As well speak of chaining the wind. All the same, she was quiet as she shut the case. The period of waiting for Maude's return was an ordeal.

Fortunately it did not last long. Maude always moved quickly, and today she was in haste. Constance had hardly begun to straggle about the room in cramped impatience when she was back, breathless, flinging the lost hat and coat on to a bed.

'Whew! There you are! Couldn't be served quicker in a cook-shop, as my Mum says!'

'Did you see anybody?'

'Meaning Erasmus? No, I didn't. I flew up, and flew down again, like a dear little bird. Not a sound. Nobody. Oh, I did run into Stockie; but that was in the street, on the way back.'

'Yes?' Constance could not hide her eagerness to hear of Carl.

'He wanted to know what I was doing with your things. I told him you were going, and why. I think he'll come to the station to kiss you goodbye.'

'Did he seem troubled?'

Maude grimaced.

'It would be against his principles to show any worry, darling. Besides, he's got eyes like a fish; they can't express feeling. I might have been telling him I'd dropped a sixpence, which he'd have been pleased to hear. By the way, I haven't had a chance to say I'm sorry about your father. I really am sorry. I hope your young sister exaggerated.'

'She doesn't,' said Constance. 'If she says a thing, it's true. Thank you for your sympathy. I'm grateful to you for that, and for all the other kindness.'

'Fancy! I can't imagine you being grateful for anything.' But the insult was accompanied by Maude's broadest smile.

'Well, you see me now. And I've told you. And it's true. I suppose we'd better start.'

'High time. We don't want to get sentimental, do we? Come

on, dear. If that fellow Stockie had been any good he'd be here to carry your bag; but of course that would be *infra dig*. I expect he'll stroll on to the platform as the train moves out. A careless wave of the hand—"ta-ta".'

The way to the station took them past a number of shops, but away from the theatre; and as they walked Constance looked many times over her shoulder in fear that Hurd would come from behind, shouting. It reminded her of bad dreams in which she fled from a bear.

No such calamity occurred. The station, a long low building built a dozen years earlier and already shabby, lay at the centre of a crescent-shaped yard in which stood a couple of old growlers, their muffled drivers reading newspapers in shelters from the cold. These men roused the Tory in Maude.

'The British Working Man!' she scoffed. 'He's always been the same, and always will be. Began as a shepherd; and now he's a cabby. Look at those poor horses; full of sorrow. Not a porter about, of course. All at dinner. They'll wake up bawling in their own lingo when your train gets here. They don't like a draught; and as for carrying bags or helping young ladies, it's too much to expect. Have you got money for your fare; or must Auntie Maude . . .? I'm glad you're not quite feckless. I suppose your father's rich. Good; there's a flash of sunshine. Makes the rails look like quicksilver!'

They lunched in the buffet, which was one of the most dismal rooms in Christendom, with a barmaid behind the counter who looked them up and down as if they were spiders.

'Ghastly!' Maude wrinkled her nose over a moderately fresh pork pie. 'You'd better have a glass of port to pull you round. You look washed out, except for that bruise. I'll pay.'

'No, thank you. I've never tasted it; and I'd better not start.'

'Ah, it's gin that makes the tears flow. That's why funeral parties always drink gin. It looks good at the grave-side. But I suppose your tipple will be champagne.'

'Not at home, certainly.' Constance grew melancholy. 'Yes, I dread getting home.'

'Poor kid! I'd forgotten. I'm sorry. I was trying to be bright. Now what will you do when you step out at Paddington?'

'I haven't thought. I don't know anything about railways.'

'Gosh, you *are* innocent! Well, don't trust anybody except a policeman. Go up to the first bobby you see, put on your country-maiden expression, and make him look after you. For two pins I'd hop on the train myself, as a chaperon. That would be rather good, wouldn't it?'

'It would be wonderful. But the Strollers—'

'Yes, the Strollers. And dear Erasmus, of course. I'll give him your love.'

'On no account!' Constance was seized with desperation.

'I thought so. What did he do to you?'

The question jumped so suddenly from Maude's big mouth that Constance thought all the blood in her body must have rushed to her face.

'We had a rehearsal,' she answered.

'I see. Yes? Did it go off as planned?'

'Miss Delmaine joined us.' Constance could once again be demure.

'Golly! Erasmus pleased?'

'He dissembled,' said Constance.

'As you're doing.' Maude laughed; and, finding her laugh too loud for their surroundings, clapped a hand to her mouth. 'I wish I'd been there.'

'I wished you were,' replied Constance.

Their conversation was interrupted by hoarse shouts from the platform, where only a few other passengers awaited the train. To the west they could see two sets of silvery rails which wound through sidings and on towards what Maude said would ultimately be the Atlantic Ocean.

'That's what you'll cross when you go to America,' she said, cheerfully. 'Bear it in mind. I hope I'll see you again before then; but you never know.'

'Are you saying goodbye to me for ever?' asked Constance.

'We won't talk about that. I don't like goodbyes. And I'm really rather fond of you, you know, Connie. I don't know why. Propinquity, I suppose.'

'What does that mean?' Constance was touched by this unexpected admission. She was in a mood to return love with equally unexpected warmth.

'I don't know. It's a word. Are we on the right platform? We don't want to end up on the coast. There's the train; I see its smoke; I hear its little whistle. Now porters will totter out, wiping their mouths, and muttering.'

There was a great rumble as the train, whirling dust and grit, rushed past them and noisily came to a halt. 'Tsss! Tsss!' said the engine, celebrating its brief rest. An oily, coal-blackened man hung out, surveying the few waiting passengers. Constance looked in vain for Carl, feeling a child's misery at disappointment.

'You'll give my love to them all,' she said, quickly. 'Explain why I couldn't . . .'

'I won't miss anybody. I'll call a rehearsal. "Ladies and gentlemen . . ." Like old Erasmus. I know they'll all burst into tears.'

'They won't. I shall miss Ellis's funeral.'

'But Stockie will add your flowers. They'll be mostly from him.' Maude also, was looking towards the entrance. 'Don't forget the bobby. And don't let any handsome black-eyed man carry your bag. You'd never see it again.' Suddenly she exclaimed: 'Hullo, there he is, the little devil!'

Little devil: did she mean Hurd? No, it was Carl. And—it was exactly as the prophet Maude had anticipated—he had left his coming to the last minute, and was showing no signs of haste. His hat was carefully drawn down over one eye; he wore his most cynical expression of self-assurance.

'But he's carrying a bag!' cried Constance.

'Good lord! What's he doing that for? Is it Christmas toys for you? Father Christmas? Hurd's head?' Maude repeated her first question as Carl strolled up to them with the nonchalant air he cultivated. Constance could not bear to look at him; but she felt a throbbing in her throat. 'What's that bag for, Stockie?'

'I'm going, too,' answered Stockhouse, suavely. 'I thought it was time to emulate Dick Whittington.'

Constance was overwhelmed with emotion; Maude with whistling surprise.

'You mean it? But what about Hurd? What about your contract?'

'There's no contract, darling Maude; it's expired. He thought he was being clever. He wasn't. That's all. And I'm following my star.'

'Meaning Connie?' Maude looked from one face to the other, sharp to observe Constance's wet eyes, equally sharp to observe the curious pallor which betrayed Stockhouse's bridegroom-like agitation.

'That's as may be,' he said, coldly.

The guard blew his whistle; porters shouted their age-old chant of 'Stand away, there! Stand away, there!' Maude hustled both friends towards the open door of a compartment.

'You're both damned fools,' she said, roughly. 'Go on; get in.' She kissed Constance, with the words, in an undertone, 'not the damaged cheek, you notice.' And, to them both again, as they jointly occupied the window: 'My prophecy's coming true. Hurd's doomed. Serve him right. I shall be the next; he'll never recover. Goodbye, darlings. Goodbye. Goodbye. Don't forget to write!'

She waved a dry handkerchief as the train moved slowly out of the station towards London and its supposedly inextinguishable lights.

SCENE SIX

# *Home Again*

I

IN the flurry of saying goodbye to Maude, Constance hardly
realised that she had been pressed close against Carl at the
window; and as the train moved away over jolting points she
turned to find that they had been rushed into the midst of half-
a-dozen seated passengers. There were two old countryfolk with
lined cheeks, who sat hand-in-hand enjoying what for them must
have been a grand adventure; a schoolboy with a great bang of
flaxen·hair cocking his badged cap to the back of his head; and
three apparently unrelated men who would have been as bored
as caged animals if they had not cast disapproving eyes upon a
couple of interlopers. None of these people made any effort to
make room.

As a consequence Constance squeezed into a few inches of
space beside the old folk, while Carl managed to find room on
the opposite side of the compartment. Conversation between
the two was impossible. It was made the more unlikely when
Carl took a small book from his pocket and began to read.
Constance, with nothing to read, felt cold-shouldered by the
world, and was conscious of the fact that every smiling glance
at Carl, besides causing him annoyance, was causing the muscles
around her mouth to ache. She became grave.

The train was passing through attractive country, hedged,
and dotted with tall trees. In the distance rising ground suggested
a continuous variation of scene; and she began to imagine it as
a background to pastoral drama. As the day was clouded, there

were no highlights: therefore the drama was subdued. She and Carl were on stage together, he tormenting her with reticence, she preparing for a dénouement which was postponed until the observant mutes whom she regarded as extras without parts in the drama should have withdrawn with kicks and curtseys into unseen wings.

This was indeed high drama. She cherished the knowledge that her going had affected Carl to the point of abrupt desertion of the Strollers. Therefore he loved her. Therefore, once they were alone, he would declare himself. Only the presence of the mutes delayed what she longed for. His sullenness was provoked by suspense as great as her own. Was it? He was a strange, teasing man; but after this he could not possibly remain as uncommunicative as he had been. That was unthinkable.

No stop was made at a number of stations. The train roared past platforms on which local travellers, staring in admiration at an express, waited like sheep at a gate for their own more sober conveyances. All silent; all patient; merely little figures hunched against the afternoon's cold.

Why didn't Carl look at her? If he would only smile. If he would only show that they belonged to each other. He read his little book. Once he had lifted her case to the luggage rack he had ignored her presence. Very well, if he ignored her presence she would ignore his. She looked away from him. The boy produced an apple and began to eat it. The bovine men closed their eyes. She imitated them, busy thoughts continuing, and the morning's events becoming as distant as the details of a dream.

Every now and then she opened her eyes. Carl was still reading his little book. She believed that over the top of it he must have been observing her; but she could not be sure of this. Her excitement died down; she began to look forward to arrival in London, to a further journey, to arrival at Wilmerton. The final prospect made her heart feel like a stone in her breast.

Dusk began to creep over the landscape. A light in the ceiling

of the compartment suddenly brightened and besides creating
new shadows in the faces of the travellers, so that Carl's expression became that of a devil, intensified the darkness without.
Ever and anon there came a shrill whistle from the engine, and
the steady jolting was deepened to exaggeration as they passed
under bridges or plunged into tunnels. Those who slept remained as if petrified; those, such as the boy, who remained
awake, were visibly restless. Lights arose all about the track, at
first the illuminations of streets, and then of windows, window
crowding upon window, until it became clear that a great town
was all about the lines, threatening in its tall buildings, but
brought close to the train in the warmth of urban life.

These must be the outskirts of London. Soon the city itself
must engulf them all. And at last the slumbering men awakened,
coughed, pulled themselves erect, looked at their watches,
looked up at the luggage-racks, and took reluctant cognizance
of their fellows. Constance felt herself to be subjected to scrutiny.
She saw Carl close his book and put it away. And when he had
done this he looked at her, his lips twisted in a smile. Her heart,
no longer heavy, leapt. She returned the smile with gaiety. She
knew herself to be loved.

At last a great black roof shut out lights and sky. Immense
echoes filled the air. The train, which had been slowing down,
stopped altogether. They had arrived.

With great deliberation Carl waited in the carriage until all
the others, led by that impatient schoolboy, had left it. Obeying
a jerk of his head, Constance jumped down to the platform and
stood while he reached for their cases. She saw his arms stretched
to the racks, and was a little disappointed to see, as the sleeves
were drawn down by this action, how thin his wrists were. An
unpremeditated comparison with other, very muscular, wrists
the power of which had been almost irresistible but a few hours
earlier, told her that she would never again be so ferociously
embraced. She told herself that Carl was gentler, more considerate; yet a longing to be closely embraced touched her heart. The

perception was gone in a moment; it did no more than touch her love.

Then he was beside her, breathing a little fast from his exertion, and smiling more sweetly than he had ever done.

'Well?' he asked, setting down the second case. 'We're here.'

Men and women were crowding past, so bent upon their own purposes that they had no time to notice two young people who were equally blind to the rest of the world.

'And alone,' Constance prompted. She pressed against him; felt herself lightly caught and held, raised her face, and felt his first kiss upon her lips. It was an exquisite experience, too brief, too moth-like for the satisfaction of her own warmth; but in its very brevity something to be remembered with joy for the remaining hours of that thrilling day. She looked deep into his eyes and found them dark with undisguised emotion. It was an instant of perfect happiness.

'There!' said Carl, in the tone of one who says 'That's done.' He stooped and took up both cases, in spite of her effort to carry her own. 'No, this is for me. You must learn to obey.'

She wished for nothing better. She felt that this was what she had always wanted, the companionship of a passionate friend, who would command as he revered; a simultaneous exercise of love and service. Her step beside him was as light as the ecstasy of her heart. Just so might they walk together into Paradise.

'We'll get a taxicab,' he said with assurance. 'That's the latest thing, you know. But perhaps we'd better have some tea first. Look, I'll settle you in the refreshment room . . .'

'Don't leave me!' implored Constance, half-seriously. 'Maude said I wasn't to trust anybody but a policeman. I don't see any policemen.'

'Naturally,' Carl replied, with a return to lofty derision. 'The police are outside. I don't know what they're doing there.'

'Perhaps arresting thieves?' she gaily suggested. 'Maude seemed to think there would be hundreds.'

'Maude is a complete fool.' He dismissed Maude. 'What she says is totally unimportant.'

'Never under-rate her.' Constance recalled all that Maude had done that day. 'If she hadn't met you in the street, you wouldn't be here. With me.'

'I wonder what Hurd will say when he realises I'm gone.' He gave a short laugh—only two sounds, indicating conviction that Hurd would be paralysed by his absence—and lost himself in malicious reflection. His lips moved in unuttered taunts.

Constance said nothing. She was re-living the scene with Hurd, her flight, the appalling picture of dishevelment in the shop-window. Instinctively she pressed the back of her gloved hand to the lips smarting from their first kiss. Had he noticed the injury? He noticed everything. It had not affected him. He was far away, exulting in Hurd's ruin. Did he see what she saw? It was a picture of the others assembling in the theatre for tonight's performance. Their cries would be: 'Where's Stockie?' 'Where's Connie?' 'Good heavens! Good heavens!' Only Miss Delmaine would have any clue as to herself. The rest, with nothing but mysterious hints to guide them, would be baffled. Having extracted all possible pleasure from suspense, Maude would show Pen's telegram. 'Poor kid!' they would say; 'aye, aye; blood is thicker than water. But where's Stockie?'

Caught in mid-step by a discovery, Constance stumbled. When neither Carl nor she could be found it would be assumed that this was a prearranged elopement!

She was too much excited to eat more than a mouthful of cake; but the tea was refreshing. When they had emptied their cups, and Carl, with a careless gesture betokening superlative acquaintance with the great world, had put some coppers under his plate, the journey was resumed. To his obvious chagrin none of the new taxicabs was available; and they were forced to take an old horse-drawn four-wheeler which smelt as musty as a junk-shop and was driven by a very old man whose face could not be seen behind a huge red muffler. But the jog-trot drive through busy lighted streets was delicious. She leant against Carl, who kissed her again, and she rejoiced to feel his arm about her waist. In this state she watched, entranced, the constant changes of lights and shadows.

'It's wonderful!' she exclaimed. 'Really wonderful!'

'What is wonderful?' he indulgently asked; and when she cried 'The movement, the crowds, the traffic!' his arm slackened. She must have said the wrong thing.

'And being with you, of course. That's more than wonderful; it's a dream.'

Yes, she had done well to make the correction; for there was the tenderness of Lorenzo in his voice.

'A dream you often imagined?'

'No, no. A beautiful surprise dream. Beyond imagination. I never dared hope that we should be together—here—really in London—with the future glowing like a star!'

His arm tightened again. He kissed her cheek; and when she offered her lips he would have kissed them, too, if the cab had not, by jolting, spoiled his aim, so that he reached only her ear. Constance, amused by the mischance, laughed; not aloud, but secretly.

He did not miss that tremor of merriment.

'Why the laugh?'

'Happiness. Because everything's so lovely.'

That had been right; he sought no further explanation.

'I'll put you on your train for Wilmerton,' he announced. 'Then I must get in touch with the friend who always puts me up when I am in London. You'll want to get home to your father. When you can make plans we'll arrange to meet.'

So they were to part. Naturally that was inevitable, however unwelcome. He made the fact quite clear.

'Where can I write to you?'

'I'll write first, give you an address.'

'Your friend's?'

'I'll see!' It was cold. She had been too possessive.

Recognition of this led her to reflect: 'It's all so new. I mustn't expect him to tell me everything. Not until we're married. Then it will be different.' Here thought passed into sensation, with imaginings of a time of blissful intimacy. Her sigh was one of expectant happiness. The feelings aroused by Hurd quickened her wish for ardour in a true and honourable lover.

The cab stopped. There was a clamour of slamming doors and jingling bells as hansom cabs and motor-cars arrived or went away. A portico loomed overhead; there was a surge of porters whom Carl waved away. He helped her from the cab, and once more seized the cases, which he bore into an enormous booking-hall. She thought the cabby looked after them strangely; but she had no time for interpretation, since Carl, although laden, strode purposefully to a small window. He rapped with impatience, spoke to a face which appeared in the window, engaged in some argument, withdrew the glittering proffered sovereign, asked a further peremptory question, and received a short answer. The face disappeared.

Carl said something more, apparently in angry retort; and looked over his shoulder at herself. For once his pale cheeks were flushed. He hesitated, picked up the cases, and came towards her.

'Is something wrong?' she asked.

'They're all fools. No manners; no sense. This is the wrong place.'

'Oh, dear! Didn't you tell the cabman?'

'Of course I told him. He ought to have taken us to Fenchurch Street. These damned stations!'

'What a stupid man! I expect he's deaf. He was muffled to his ears,' she suggested.

There was no reply. Carl strode again to the crowded court-yard. As it happened, the same cabman was there, having been too slow, or too artful, she supposed, to drive away immediately, as he should have done. He peered over his crimson muffler like a Father Christmas whose white beard had fallen off.

'You've brought us wrong,' said Carl, sternly. 'We want Fenchurch Street.'

'Eh?' mumbled the old man. 'You said Victoria, sir. Victoria you said. That's where I've brought you.'

'Well, take us to Fenchurch Street.'

There was a growl in response; no apology but a hesitation, as though the cabman contemplated a refusal to take them any-where else. But Carl had already opened the cab door and put the cases within. His sign to Constance to follow them was curt. Elated at finding they were not to part yet, she heard him mutter something irritably to himself. The cab lurched; the horse's hooves scrabbled slightly; they were in motion, out again in a broad street, heading into the wonderful unknown.

'Isn't it exciting!' Constance cried, in delight. 'As if we were going to the North Pole. Or is it the South Pole? Something beautiful and mysterious.'

Carl, brooding over whatever had ruffled him, sat as far as possible from her. She saw his face only when the light of a street lamp intruded; and it was as pale as old parchment; mortally pale, as Miss Delmaine's had been. The derisive smile was absent. She had become a bore; and the happy nonsense of her exclamation was made to seem childish. Well, she would say no more. He must resolve his own problems, whatever they were.

But what were they? The cabby said he had been told to drive to Victoria. She hadn't heard the original direction; but the two men were at variance, and, although brusque, Carl had not scolded the man for stupidity. How strange that was! She forgot her surprise at an omission, because she had caught sight of a great building. Beyond that was another half-lighted mass, a tower with a huge clock; and as they approached the clock began to strike in deep tones stirring to the heart. Now came dark water; it must be a river, it must be the Thames, and the clock, whose notes were majestically clear above the sound of traffic, must be Big Ben! How wonderful! If she had been childish it was because she was indeed a child, enjoying new experience and rejoicing in it.

Lights shone upon the moving water; a dark boat, a barge,

moved slowly upon it. They were driving by the river's side, and the outlines of a bridge showed ahead. She craned to see the marvels, and was disappointed when the river was hidden by buildings and their cab became one small vehicle among many. But the drive had already been eventful; and she had recovered her gaiety.

Once more they entered a station yard. Once more Carl lugged the cases out of the cab and gave the driver money which this time pleased him so much that he waved his whip in farewell.

They were in another station; the sovereign reappeared; the face at the little window split into what appeared to be some urgent cry; and Carl returned in a tremendous hurry.

'Come on, quick!' he shouted. 'The train's just going. Run!'

They ran, to the joggle of cases which had obviously become heavy and difficult to carry. A few people stood or moved in their path, a barrier was reached; the ticket-collector was as urgent as the man at the window had been; a guard holding a green flag looked at his watch and shouted.

'Hurry along there!'

'Hurry. Take your case,' panted Carl. 'Here's your ticket.'

'Hurry along there!' shouted the guard, blowing his whistle. He flung open a carriage door; Constance, now for the first time impeded by her case, ran; and as the man pushed her into the carriage, shoving the case against the backs of her legs, she looked back, only to see Carl beyond the barrier, already turning away as if he were glad to be done with her. The next moment she had lost sight of him altogether; for the train was in motion and her sight was blurred. If she had recently been a delighted child, she was now a child from whom joy had departed. She was alone. There had been no farewell. Tears started to her eyes.

2

She did not allow herself to cry; but sat down rather clumsily in a vacant space, while a strange man picked up the case and thrust it somewhere above her head. He did not look at her as he did this, and his arms were raised in such a way as to hide his face. Nor, when she thanked him, did he return her smile. He retired behind an evening newspaper.

The carriage seemed to be full of evening newspapers; and although she caught sight of several pairs of appreciative eyes peeping over their tops the eyes quickly disappeared, so that papers dominated her vision of the fellow-travellers. All were men; all were very trimly dressed, with starched collars and striped trousers; all had clean white hands which looked as if they never handled spades or brooms or boot brushes. She took them for City men who were returning home after working late at their offices. They exchanged no word with each other. Apart from the train's jolting over points and the roar as it passed over bridges or through short tunnels there was no sound at all, not even a cough. Exemplary men!

Now she could look forward only with dread. Wilmerton lay before her, a cold, musty house, chilly winds, a dying father, and terrifying responsibilities.

She wished Carl had stayed with her for this journey, to support her in all the misery she would find at the end of it. Had she been right in suspecting that he was glad to send her off alone? He had turned away quickly; was it in relief? It might have been no more than shyness . . .

How pale he had grown. Poor lamb, he must be very tired. The cases had been too heavy for him. He wasn't muscular, like Hurd; yet he had deliberately saved her from all physical effort. That was chivalrous; she loved him for it. He was 'a parfait gentil knight'. Wonderful! If only they had been able to kiss goodbye! If only he had whispered—even once—'I love you!' There had been no time. Time was cruel!

Thoughts went back through the day's sensational happenings. That loathsome Hurd! Loathsome! And yet, of course, very exciting! She touched the corner of her mouth, where blood had dried and been removed by her wet handkerchief; and her breast was still sore from Hurd's brutal grasp. Hurd was a fiend. But she had fought him. His cheek, where she struck, would be as sore as her breast. How furiously he had sworn! Like a maniac . . .

Maude had shown herself a true friend. And a prophetess. How did she know what Hurd would say and attempt? That was very peculiar. What, in similar circumstances, would she have done? How had she guessed that Carl would come to the station? She had been surprised to see him carrying his case; so there were some things she did not know. For example, about Carl's love. She had never once teased; she had tartly criticised him—as Carl had criticised her. Was it mutual aversion, or part of some curious sport between them?

Where was Carl now? Where did his friend live? The friend must be a man; he had never mentioned a friend. Could it be a woman? He was as secret as a sealed envelope. Why had he flushed so deeply at Victoria, after speaking to the man at the ticket office? She had never before seen those pale cheeks red, except from grease-paint, when he was her stage lover. He hadn't looked at her as he came back; but there had been extraordinary pride in his bearing. Almost as if he were embarrassed, which with his cool temperament was impossible.

Was he so cool? A strangely amusing notion came into her head. The flush, the pride, the renewed taciturnity were all responsible for it. Had he perhaps—from ignorance!—supposed that Victoria was the only other railway terminus? It was a lovely guess. He had blamed the cabman; but he hadn't spoken sarcastically to him. He had done everything, all along, to impress her with his omniscience. Oh! Oh! He was a fraud! He was a darling!

Much more passed in her mind as the train rumbled through darkness and lighted stations. Waves of knowledge spread,

sometimes passing into remoteness and coming back with
increasing subtlety, increasing force. Things referred to by
Maude as they were undressing, the infatuation of Miss Delmaine,
the cringing of the other men in the company before Hurd's
tyranny, the allusions to Masefield's lack of interest in women,
mysterious suggestions in old plays to corrupt behaviour,
lechery, cuckoldry, and even the hint that darling Ellis had been
seduced by Hurd. Carl was no seducer; he wore a mask of
sophistication, which until now had bamboozled her ...

Suddenly she became convinced that she knew everything
about men. She had received a special revelation, not from God,
but from the eternal wisdom of the ages, vouchsafed only to
women!

'It's clear!' she exclaimed, speaking aloud to the astonishment
of the city pillars who, buried in their newspapers, had been all
the time aware of her and in spirit unfaithful to the wives who
were so familiar to them. 'I know the whole *gamut*, from C
to E!'

It took a little time for surprise to pass. The train stopped
several times as it neared Wilmerton, and when it stopped
passengers left to go to their homes. Each time the carriage door
was opened a salt-laden breeze rushed in, reminding her of
Wilmerton and all that it had so far meant in her life. Wilmerton
had been her birthplace and home, the scene of wild Shakespearean defiances to the rolling breakers and splendid oratory to the
uncontrollable gales, and the beginning of this, her first adventure
with life. It was now a place where she was to endure something
in which splendour had no part.

The Rectory would be shabbier than ever, hushed with the
solemnity of illness, shrunken, it might be, as the result of her
association with the world. How much she had changed since
leaving it! How much she had learned! She began to think of
immediate practical problems. Would she be able to find a cab
to carry herself and her case? Would she have to struggle alone
through the dark streets? Would the waves be high and audible?

And, at the end of the way, would she have courage enough to ring the bell?

Father in bed, gaunt and hollow-eyed, staring at somebody he had forgotten; frowning with distaste or bewilderment or bitter surprise. 'I'm Connie, Father. Your daughter. Your prodigal daughter. The one who went on the stage. The one you paid fifty pounds to be rid of . . .'

No, no, no; she was no prodigal. She was there because Pen had telegraphed, summoning her to the bed of a dying man. Penelope. Penelope. Penelope. The train jogged out Pen's lengthened name. Penelope Rotherham. Listening to it, Constance closed her eyes in weariness. The day had been too long, and too full of violent sensation; her nerves were exhausted. Her heart cried out for love.

'Wilmerton. Wilmerton.' The voice of old Thompson, the porter, broke her dream. She started awake; and as the door opened once more, admitting the familiar Channel wind, and almost the last man in the carriage, seeing that she rose, kindly reached for her case and lifted it to the platform, she recovered perfect self-reliance.

'Can you manage?' asked the man, with the arch courtesy accorded by middle-age to youthful beauty.

'Thank you, yes. Thank you very much.'

She did not remember ever having seen him before; but it was possible that he knew she was Father's daughter, for he raised his hat in farewell. The stormy wind caught her dress and blew the skirt close about her knees. She braced herself under the light of a swaying lamp, growing used to the strangeness and familiarity of it. Instead of rejoicing at a return home she was oppressed by loneliness and dread of the trial ahead.

Yet she was not alone. 'Connie! Connie!' It was the old cry; once detested, but now a cause of exquisite relief. Pen's small figure darted from the shadow; impulsive arms held her tightly; looking down into that eager face, she was suffused with tenderness.

'Oh, dearest! dearest!' She had never before felt or expressed such love for Pen.

'Connie, I'm thankful you're here!' There was a sob in Pen's voice.

'So bad?'

'Almost unbearable. But you *are* here. That's everything.'

That was all for the moment. Thompson, having signalled to the guard, came towards them with a gruff word of greeting, and picked up the case. The train drew away, grinding into the darkness and boisterous wind. The girls, chilled, but with their arms about each other, moved towards the exit. Constance could not help noticing that Pen's light step, as in the past, was shorter than her own, a little patter beside her longer stride. The sound, emphasising her sister's youth, increased her emotion in this reunion.

'You did get my telegram?' she asked.

'Yes. I found the old A.B.C. timetable. I saw what train you'd catch to London, and then tried to calculate what you'd catch at Fenchurch Street. I hoped you'd be here an hour ago.'

'Oh, we stayed to have some tea. I wish we hadn't. You haven't been waiting here, have you?'

'An hour, yes.'

'Oh, dear, dear!' Constance was full of self-reproach. 'In this wind? Poor kid, frozen. You oughtn't to have come.'

They had reached the station yard, where Thompson had put the case into the one remaining cab. He held the cab door, did not expect a tip even from one who had become a fine young lady, and hobbled off; and then, while they, hand in hand, swayed through the dark streets of Wilmerton, they spoke again. Constance said:

'I haven't asked how he is.' There was a silence of suppressed anguish. The hand clasping hers held more tightly. 'Am I too late?'

'That's why I couldn't bear to stay at home.'

'What, alone in the house? What about Mrs Randall?'

'She went a week ago. Worn out, she said.'

'How monstrously cruel!' But something whispered to Constance—it certainly was not Pen's voice—'What did *you* do?' She closed her ears to the whisper. 'You didn't tell me, Pen. I don't know what I could have done . . .'

'You were playing Jessica. That was such a . . . I didn't want . . .'

Their cabhorse had one jingling bell. The sound was in their ears, together with the clop of his hooves and the rattle of the cab; but both were lost in personal feelings.

'How on earth have you managed?'

'People have been very kind. Several of them have helped A nurse has been every day. But just this evening . . .'

'When you wanted somebody most of all!'

'I told them you'd be here. I didn't want them. They were fussing.'

Constance did not misunderstand. The jerking of the hand within her own told her of deep shudders running through that slight body. Her own lips were trembling; her own voice had been unsteady.

The cab stopped. They were at the Rectory gate. They were within the house. Cold and darkness made both shiver; and both instinctively tiptoed, in order not to disturb the dead. Father was terribly present to them now, a lonely prostrate figure more impressive in death than he had been in life.

When they had coaxed the drawing-room fire into flame and Pen had made a warm drink, they sat whispering. Pen, more composed than she had been, and wishing to tell everything she could, gave a coherent account of what had happened.

'It was about three o'clock. I stayed away from school—I've done that a lot, lately . . . I was just sitting. I don't remember what I was thinking about. I thought he was asleep; but he suddenly struggled up on his elbow and shouted; a dreadful shout. It was: "No! No! It was never true! Never!" I ran to help him; and got him to lie down again. He was quite quiet, as if he'd dropped off to sleep. Then he said, just in his ordinary way: "I'm sorry if I frightened you, my darling. I was thinking of something that happened long ago. You wouldn't remember. Is Connie there?" I said: "Not yet, Daddy. She's on her way. She won't be long." He said—it was a sort of mumble: "Good. Very good. You won't be alone. Give her my dear love. Say I . . ." Then he shut his eyes, and lay still. I think he smiled; but I was so upset . . .'

The excited murmur ended in a sob.

Constance too, was crying, touched to the heart by her father's remembrance, penetrated with sympathy for Pen. Because she could not bring herself to show all she felt, she did no more than hold her sister's hand. There was some meaning in that wild cry of negation which as yet she could not fathom. Indeed, she was too tired to understand anything at all but the fact that she was at home, with Pen, in an hour when time had no significance.

Only later did she believe that it could be explained by her mother's story of a vision, an accident, a lifelong struggle with uncertainty. In the end he had resolved that his vision had been delusive. He had proclaimed, as an honest man, what he thought to be the truth. Looking down upon his dead face, from which all suffering had passed, she felt sure that despite what seemed to Pen to be a cry of agony he had died at peace with his conscience.

THE SECOND ACT

# Parallel Lines

# SCENE SEVEN

## *News of Erasmus*

### I

THERE was Pen's key in the door.

She could always tell which of them it was. Carl's key was impatiently rattled in withdrawal, as a relief to whatever nervous strain he might be suffering from that day. The strain expressed resentment of a slight or affront received at the hands of some incredibly boorish agent, or a surge of artistic arrogance, or fear of her own pitiless judgment. Pen, on the other hand, showed no signs of nervous strain. She calmly let herself in, put her key away in silence before closing the door and wiping her shoes on the mat, and listened, like a cat, for the sound of voices. Then she whisked in, sometimes with a cheerful 'Oo-oo,' but generally on dancing tiptoe. Always the ballerina!

'There's a lot for the psychologist in the handling of a key,' meditated Constance, who boldly thrust hers into the lock, and turned it in a single movement. 'It's a guide to character. I hear; I conclude. I should do rather well as a blind person. Acute senses . . .'

The question was whether any dramatist could be persuaded to cast her in the part of an all-hearing, all-comprehending blind woman. It was a splendid dramatic idea; one of her inspirations. The blindness would have to be the result of some illness; not hereditary, and not through disfigurement by injury. Disfigurement was unthinkable. Vanity, of course; but if looks were a part of one's stock-in-trade it would be folly to present them as visibly damaged. Audiences were liable to convert first impressions into prejudices. 'Oh, I saw her in *Blind Woman's Bluff*. She looked horrible! I never want to see her again.' But everybody loved and pitied a beauty sanctified by blindness. 'She was so sweet; so noble . . .' Surely a young dramatist, the sort Carl admired because he was 'serious', had the courage and ingenuity to tackle such a theme? . . .

The year was 1910; the month May. In 1909 a French aviator, Monsieur Blériot, had flown the Channel, and aeroplanes were the latest fad. Taxi-cabs and motor-omnibuses (the latter still occasionally to be seen derelict by the kerbside as a result of mechanical failure) were as common as grey cats at night. Women's fashions were deserting frills and ample skirts in favour of the sheath; while women themselves were rioting for the Vote. Romantic fiction and drama had given place to benign realism or suburban revolt. The world was changing very fast, as Carl said it must do. Victorianism, his *bête noire*, was at an end, like Kipling's bourgeois Imperialism. Carl's favourite phrase was 'Now we can get something *done*.'

John Rotherham had been buried three years earlier beside his wife in Wilmerton churchyard; Constance and Carl had married soon afterwards; and, along with Pen, formed what Pen called a *ménage à trois* in Battersea, near the southern end of the Albert Bridge. Most of John's massive theological books had been bought by a dealer as junk; some hefty mahogany furniture from the Rectory crowded the flat's drawing-room, which then resembled a repository; the winds and high seas of Wilmerton were far away; and Pen, at very nearly eighteen years of age, had developed extraordinarily. No longer a clinger, nor a schoolgirl, she had become a precious miniature beauty who so glowed with spirit that, on seeing her, people involuntarily smiled as they would have done at a radiant baby.

This fact, however much she might suspect Pen of self-exploitation, gave Constance no qualms. She was sustained by the assurance of every mirror that her own beauty had increased. Beauty was almost an inconvenience. The cautionary episode with Hurd was unforgotten—and unconfessed; London was full of predatory males with ambition comparable to his, which was the possession, fleeting or otherwise, of her body. Though flattered by all lecherous glances, she remained unmoved. She was no longer the innocent tyro among Strollers, nor the conceited child who imagined, on the strength of two triumphs, that she understood men from A to Z. She knew one man through and through; the rest were subjects of interested speculation.

'I'm not vain,' she reflected. 'I'm like Yum-Yum, in *The Mikado*; "a child of Nature, and take after my Mother".'

Yes, it was the unreadable Pen who had let herself into the flat. Pen was silently wiping her shoes, smiling like the Mona Lisa, keeping her own counsel, secret as a Chinese diplomat. In another moment she would burst into the room, full of *élan*, full of charm.

'Ah, there you are! Your boudoir!' It was an exquisite voice, small in volume, but crystal in quality. Did she realise that? She must do. And yet, since one didn't hear one's own voice as others did, this continued to be another mystery. Diabolical little demon! 'I hurried home. He's dead.'

'I guessed it. What's going to happen now?' Constance did not need to be told that 'he' was the King, Edward the Seventh, a stout, rolling figure of instinctive majesty whom they had seen with the French President two years ago at the new White City; and that Britain was without a sovereign.

'All the theatres will be closed, for one thing, Madame says.' Even in taking off her gloves Pen showed her fastidious grace. Her fingers were long and exquisite. They fluttered like butterflies. Constance thought: 'Why can't I suggest such delicacy? Perhaps I do?' She learned much from Pen in the matter of gesture; but she believed that Pen, who was so quiet, also learned from her.

'As none of us have jobs, we shan't be affected,' she responded. 'Carl says things can't get any worse in public affairs.'

'Carl's an old Tory!' Pen threw down her hat with the easy swiftness of her entrance to the flat. 'Of course he wouldn't like anybody to say so.'

'I *have* just mentioned it!'

'In a whisper; under your breath,' said Pen. 'Testimony to a genius.'

'I'm tactful. He's easily depressed.'

'And you're the model wife! I must get used to the idea. But whatever you say, or don't say, he doesn't alter. He can't.'

'Are you deriding him, darling?' Constance was quite comfortable. She had been making a new dress, and was sitting with her back to the window, admiring her handiwork as it hung, perched, from the top of the mahogany sideboard. 'Tell me how you like this.' The dress was of pale blue, with a high collar; and she expected to wear it on the morrow, for a tour of selected agents. Pen would certainly pass judgment with candour.

'Very fetching. Can you walk in it?'

'It's only half-hobble. Little mincing steps.'

'Quite Japanese, I suppose. You'll wear your gold brooch?'

'If I can find it.' The tone was so significant that Pen looked sharply at her.

'You don't think he's . . .'

'Of course not. Still, things have a habit of disappearing.'

That was all. Both knew that Carl was suffering from one of his periodic fits of exasperated despair. Both knew that it was being indicated by moroseness, followed by sudden plunges from the room and a slam of the front door.

They were not unsympathetic to Carl. They knew that he must be tired of 'resting' after the failure of an intellectual comedy from which he had hoped to draw sensational fame. The play, aiming at originality, missed fire in the theatre; Carl himself had hardly been noticed by bored critics; and his rejection of a chance to tour in a Number Two company presenting farce had displeased a well-meaning agent. Having said 'West End or nothing. Trial runs in the Provinces, yes; but not without a guarantee of London production', he had suffered the humiliation, before a party of hangers-on, of the agent's contemptuously shouted 'Nothing for you, Stockhouse.' This had made him furious. 'I won't give in,' he snarled at Constance. 'They want to cow me, crush me, eliminate me. They shan't. I won't have it!'

And now the brooch was missing, as other treasured possessions had been missing. He insisted, rightly, that shabbiness and
empty pockets would be fatal to his career.

Constance, more fortunate than Carl, could make a new dress
for herself. Also, she had been luckier than he; but only in very
small parts, sometimes in musical comedy, where she had to say
ridiculous things such as 'What fun!' or the cue-line for a song,
and understudy minor leads who were never ill. She could have
been engaged for tours in these same musical comedies, playing
the understudied part; but Carl would not hear of separation.
'If you went,' he protested, 'I should be alone. I can't look after
Pen. We stick together.'

The truth was, that he was afraid of losing her. On tour, anything might happen; and she was his sheet-anchor. She did not
tell Pen; but she believed that in his scheming mind she was cast
merely as a counter in the intricate game of Stockhouse versus
the Profession. Artful Carl! But was his wife a goose?

Pen received no confidences; but Pen knew everything. She
was one of those devilish characters who judge for themselves
and say nothing. She was both dove and demon, storing every
detail of speech, silence, mood, and significant gesture for
subsequent mimicry. One didn't know that she had read deep—
until it appeared in merciless burlesque. She could not miss
Carl's aversions. If ever she revealed her knowledge, their
*ménage à trois* would be shattered. A terrible day!

Pen's face told no secrets. It could be grave, mocking, poetic,
pensive; but never distorted by emotion. Whatever lay within,
it remained calm. She had matured extraordinarily in the past
three years, growing from a child to a woman. In those three
years she had received tuition, not at the Academy founded a
short time earlier by Beerbohm Tree, but at a private school
recommended by Miss Gosling, of Pickering's. There Madame
Roselli—born Jane Grey—taught the whole art of mime, from
ballet to wordless speech.

Madame Roselli, an ugly, witch-like little figure, with grizzled curls and a hunched back, was a genius. She had great fame, and such power in the theatre that glory might come to her pupils at any moment. She had instantly seen Pen's quality. 'Give me three years,' she told Constance at their first visit, 'and I will make your sister an actress of the highest class. She needs only technique, which I will teach her.' The exacted period was ending—along with Pen's share of their father's small fortune;—and the consequences were to be realised.

Would they bring success? Nothing, with Pen, seemed impossible. Her quickness was astonishing, like the range of her talent. Constance, always afraid of conceit in others, watched her with reluctant admiration. This afternoon, however, Pen was a sister, the one person capable of sharing a humour incomprehensible to Carl and his fellow-apostles of the Serious Drama. This was the rôle in which Constance loved her unreservedly.

'Who's to be dazzled tomorrow?' she asked.

'The lot,' was Constance's reply. 'Blackstone, Clerihew, Peach . . .'

'Very tiring. What would you do if they all offered you leads—as they will do?'

'Those hard-hearts? But they might, of course. What does Madame say about you?'

'She looks in her crystal—"a tall, dark man will bring you riches".'

'How? Will he have a part in his pocket, or his hand on his heart?'

'The hand will be outstretched holding the part, and a contract. So I gather.'

'Hm. You'll be careful, won't you! They tell me tall, dark men are dangerous.'

'All men are dangerous. But you shall come as chaperon. No, that wouldn't do; he'd slip it into *your* hand, instead of mine. I wonder if Carl would approve of that.'

'Yes, it's a problem.' Constance did not refer to a possible transfer of the part. Nor did the all-comprehending Pen suppose her to have done so. Both explored the complexities of Carl's mind; Constance with greater and more pessimistic intimacy, Pen with her own mischievous penetration. Both smiled.

The smile had done no more than appear when a noisy rattling of Carl's key advised them of his unexpected return. He was in haste; not, it struck them, in a temper, but with some private urgency.

'He's got a job,' said Pen.

'Not as late as this,' was her sister's more experienced interpretation.

They heard his hurried step; and the door of the room was thrust open. There had been no time to remove his hat, which he still wore. That was significant. It meant that Carl was in the grip of an obsession. To Constance he was now no longer the enigmatic trouper, but an impatient child who considered his own affairs all-important. Therefore his present air of triumph suggested that Pen, after all, had been right. Leaving the door open, he advanced, smiling his old smile, in which malice gleamed like the internal fires of Vesuvius at midnight.

'Well,' he cried, responding to the unheard plaudits of an audience. 'I've got some news!'

'Pen's just told me.' Constance bit her lip, lest her words should have spoiled a dramatic impersonation. She had been too impulsive.

Carl stopped short, exasperated.

'What? She couldn't know.'

'That the King's dead.'

He brushed aside the explanation.

'Ridiculous! Much more amusing. It's Hurd. Do you understand. Hurd's dead!'

The girls exclaimed; Pen, because she had not met the man, with less vehemence than Constance, who at once vividly saw that face, hideous with lust, close to her own. She shuddered.

'Naturally?' she asked, picturing the hideousness fixed in death. 'In his bed?'

'That's the best part of it, no! He's broken his neck. How right! How appropriate! How exactly what one would have wished!'

The savagery was shocking. It made Carl diabolical.

'It seems to me dreadful. Are you sure?'

'Of course I'm sure. I ran into Moore in Oxford Street. Coming the old actor—bleary and tottery, as you'd expect. "Terriple newce; terriple newce, Stocky, me poy!" His old quavering hand up—like this.' The quavering hand was mimicked; they saw a medieval Pope blessing the multitude. 'I told him not to be a fool, but consider the rat in the arras!'

'Poor Old Moore!' Constance was full of compassion. 'He probably did feel tottery. Don't forget his age.'

'Oho, I don't care about that. Simply a lifelong lickspittle. By God, I'm avenged for all the indignities the Devil put on me.'

'He put fewer on you than on anybody else.'

'He was afraid of me. He knew I knew he was an impostor.'

Constance dreaded to hear once again a catalogue of Hurd's plagiarisms from old mouthing players, and charges of raids on antique costume-boxes. Those, at this moment, would be indecent. Hurd still represented, for her, the true histrion, and, as a man, somebody more exciting than Carl would ever be. But for Hurd, she would not have known the fever of passion. Poor furious, demanding, lustful man! Now he was dead, the roar silenced, the lust exhausted . . .

She roused herself.

'Did Moore give any details?'

'There weren't any. Hurd was found at the bottom of a staircase in some back-street theatre. Missed his footing. Crash!'

They imagined the stumble, the desperate effort to recover, the final contact of a head with stone; and could not speak. Then a terrible thought occurred to Constance, born of memory of that last encounter. She saw a blanched face, uncertain movements of pale hands, heard an agonised voice. Miss Delmaine. Drunk.

Pleading? Following Hurd to a landing? Maddened by some final cruelty? It could happen in a second . . .

'Was he alone?' she breathlessly asked. 'Did somebody *see* him fall?'

Carl was too cruelly exultant to hear the question as it was intended.

'I don't know. Moore saw him before he was taken away. Battered. A bloody mess. Past help. That's all the old fool was able to blubber. Of course he wanted me to join in in the keening. I didn't. I congratulated him on having been in at the death. Oho, that was enough. He tottered off, mopping his eyes with a dirty hanky. Well, that devil's finished. By God, I'm glad!' He moved among the heavy furniture, catching sight of the new dress; but too joyous to remark it.

Constance brooded. All the Strollers would be in the street.

'What about Maude, Masefield . . . Miss Delmaine? What's to happen to them?'

Carl's triumph did not lessen.

'Delmaine's gibbering. On the bottle, I should think. It's the end for her. The others—you'll meet them all in Maiden Lane and Charing Cross Road, trying to pick up crumbs. Moore says they're all here. Whine, whine, whine; "I was with Hurd". That'll do them no good. They'll get fleas in their ears.'

Constance, saddened, remembered that these people had all been kind to her. She again saw them anxiously searching the advertisements in the theatrical papers. They would be doing it now with even greater concern. Poor creatures! They had stayed with Hurd because—apart from Carl and herself—they had not been able to get away. And even Carl, more gifted than any of the others, was trying in vain to pick up crumbs. He would do it one day, because of his talent and his obstinacy. Moore, Devlin, Simon, had less chance. If they starved, who would care?

Miss Delmaine, gibbering in grief, roused no pity in Carl. He had not seen her, as Constance had done, abject before Hurd, and being abused by him as a drunken wanton. He did not grasp the cause of her suffering. Maude had done so; Constance, instructed by Maude, had done so; nobody else. Well, then, the poor creature was at the end of endurance. Had she seen Hurd fall? Had she caused the fall, not deliberately, but by some uncontrollable movement? If so, what must her horror have been? What must be passing now in her tormented mind? Constance saw her standing, aghast, heard her screams . . .

This vision returned again and again. Again. Again, until it was with difficulty that she restrained screams of her own.

Carl, ever sensitive to atmosphere, realised that his vicious delight was unshared. Jealousy of Hurd as an actor revived and, although the man was dead, became hysterical. He frowned, pressing his lips together until they were no more than a dark line in his colourless face. With a savage glance, first at Constance and afterwards at the coolly observant Pen, he turned and darted from the room. They heard the outer door slam behind him.

2

Constance awoke the next morning to find Carl lying with his back to her. And he had crept into bed without awaking her. This indicated that she was unforgiven. A true wife would have shared his rapture at Hurd's death; one with greater finesse would have pretended hypocritically to do so. She was not, then, a true wife; and she was deficient in finesse. On the stage she could assume any part, as Carl did: that was the mummer's craft. In real life neither could sacrifice that superlative ego which is essential to practitioners in the craft.

Carl was childish. He required subordination from his wife. Otherwise, he sulked. She ought to have seen it at once. She had not done so. Fascination with his enigmatic silences, and the longing to be loved, had blinded her. She knew better now.

The silences were evasions, calculated strategies, self-protective retreats into nullity. Three years of experience of his ways had filled her with loving but unsentimental knowledge. She could have given a truly startling performance in the part of Carl Stockhouse.

'My best rôle,' she thought without rancour, eyeing the back of his neck. 'Better than Beatrice, which on the whole is my favourite. Far better than Katharina, with her artful "kneeling for peace" and "putting her hands beneath her husband's boot". Katharina is a jade; Beatrice my dream. I could dance my way through *Much Ado*. But as Carl I should bring the house down and break his heart. I *mustn't.*'

Carl. Everything he had told her about himself, about his mother—the clinger—and his father—the self-engrossed nomad —was significant. Heredity, and his situation between two incompatibles, one of whom grandiloquently deserted the other, while the other, fundamentally stupid, could think of no better retort than possessiveness of an only child. Carl, too, had absconded, in filial imitation of his father. How senseless it all was; and what unhappiness it caused, at the time and afterwards. Was all life like that? If it were, if vanity was the spring of human action, what prospect was there of Utopia? Oho, this was deep stuff! . . .

Carl was set on success in the theatre—to prove that he was a greater man than his father. It was to be success, not in conventional parts, not in classic parts, but in parts apeing contemporary manners and expressing the ideas of equally discontented dramatists. The idea would never be his own, because those he had impressed her with three years ago were all, she had found, borrowed. He saw himself as rising to fame through Shaw, Galsworthy, Barker, and Euripides; but he had been rejected by the new Frohman-Barker Repertory Company.

'They've got their own gang,' he grumbled, bitterly. 'It's a clique, with Shaw messing up the whole thing with rubbish like *Misalliance*. Barker's a weak man; he's only in the business to get his own plays produced. All that palaver about the Censor is to draw attention to himself. And what he's doing is not repertory at all; just opportunist hotch-potch. Sentimental stuff by Barrie; an old costume play of Pinero's, and nothing serious except Galsworthy's *Justice*. No constructive idea. I shan't have anything more to do with it. I wouldn't, even if they offered me a lead, which they're determined not to do. Money, money, money; that's all they care about . . .'

There was much more in the same vein, to which Constance listened with gathering doubt. He was looking for—what? Did he still believe in his star? Nothing had been said for a year of scheme or plan; it seemed as if all the disappointments, souring his temper, had also sapped what she had ardently believed to be unconquerable idealism. Any attempt to encourage him produced only further dissatisfaction. He considered her incurably light-minded—ready to compromise, ready to take any part that was offered in any kind of show, instead of standing by him in the battle for independence.

Constance had no difficulty with interpretation of his attitude to her.

'I'm cast as perpetual second fiddle,' she thought, considering that averted head. She was tempted to tickle his ear by blowing upon it. 'I can play the part; but I can't live it. If the little man weren't deceived by his own egotism, he'd allow for mine!'

He wasn't asleep. He was rigid, knowing that she was awake, and waiting for an apology for imperfect sympathy. 'Of course I understand your feeling, darling. He was a bad man. I was too slow in appreciation. I'm sorry.' Then he would magnanimously forgive, would torment her with hard little experimental, explorative kisses, and proceed to enjoy masculine victory over a grateful slave.

'No,' said Constance.

She did not feel contrite. She did not feel submissive. She needed her own victories. How strange it was; this realisation had grown up within the last few months. It was increasing, to the point of impatience with their way of life. Carl, engrossed in his own grievances, suspected nothing. One day there might be an awakening!

She set her sharp little teeth. Her open eyes roved over a sunlit wall which was papered with thornless rosebuds. The thorns, like a cat's hidden claws, were unquestionably there. Now she would get up. A significant act of revolt!

That day represented a turning-point in Constance's life.

Having awakened to sunshine and not quite charitable meditation, she went on to receive a succession of compliments, an outstanding victory, and, through Pen, a supplementary delight. If, in the evening, very black clouds arose, these clouds were natural in the variable English climate and the life of a born actress, and they did no more than check the radiance of her destiny.

'I was born for affluence,' she decided. 'Affluence and comfort. Not poverty and servitude to curmudgeons.'

What had happened to her childish dreams of love-stricken men entreating her favours? They were still there, stored in spiritual tissue-paper, and ready at any time to leap into reality. She had not changed; she would never change; she was that incomparable being, Constance Rotherham, born not only for affluence and comfort, but for power over men.

The new dress had its share in new hope and triumph. It was exquisite; and while, according to the new fashion, it restricted the movement of her legs, she always took shorter strides when walking with Pen, and did not feel crippled. Furthermore, it received Pen's approval, as was shown by a quick scrutiny and a nod.

The nod was enough to satisfy Constance. No fulsome praise ever issued from Pen's lips, the little scamp! Neither praise nor blame. She could bear pain or joy in complete silence. There were times when Constance felt deadly fear of her; if the head had been shaken the dress would have lost all virtue. Pen was a killer. A racing mind, impenetrable self-confidence, love, scepticism, and ribaldry combined to make her a cause of pride and trepidation. Men would feel this as soon as she embarked on the world. Constance pitied them in not quite sorrowful forecast.

Carl, of course, made no comment. He disregarded the dress, maintaining an indifference much less impressive than Pen's would have been. He drank a cup of coffee, ate none of the breakfast prepared by guilty Constance, and read his morning paper. This, being full of trite material about the late King and the country's social and political disorder, drove him to thought of Hurd and his wife's infamous concern with Hurd's Strollers. Without himself the Strollers had long been doomed. Now they might beg him to go back and lead them. He wouldn't do it. Stockhouse's Strollers; no, he was done with that sort of thing. In any case, Moore hadn't the intelligence to suggest it. The intelligence or, perhaps, the courage.

Hurd's death was not mentioned in a London paper; proof of that rambling hack's unimportance. 'It will be different when I die,' muttered Carl. Hurd was properly ignored. That was gratifying. All the same, Constance seemed not to realise her offence; too busy thinking of her dress. He frowned.

By nine o'clock, still condemned to a student's hours, Pen slipped out of the flat on her way to Madame Roselli's. Half an hour later, as Carl lounged morosely over a novel by Leonard Merrick called *The Actor-Manager*, which he had bought second-hand in Charing Cross Road, Constance prepared to visit Mr Blackstone, the agent, who, by a coincidence, had his office in that very thoroughfare.

'Goodbye, Carl,' she called, from the doorway. 'There's lunch for you in the larder. I'm just off on the grisly round.'

Receiving no answer, she would have felt snubbed if she had been less pleased with her appearance. After hesitation, she darted back, kissed him lightly on the top of his head, and scampered off, laughing affectionately enough at a back stiffened with reproach.

# Parting of the Ways

I

ONCE out of doors she was free. The air was beautifully fresh, and the sky untroubled by cloud. After pausing on the Albert Bridge to watch a tug bringing two barges up the Thames, she walked on as briskly as her skirt would allow. The river had raised her spirits. Though never as thrilling as the sea it offered the beauties of a running tide, a tide which, she reflected, 'taken at the flood, leads on to fortune'. Fortune! Her eyes sparkled. This was a happy augury!

Thoughts of Maude, Moore, and Hurd dimmed the scene; but the sunshine routed them, substituting imaginings of Messrs Blackstone, Clerihew, and their fellow-tyrants with smiles on their faces. Surely they would all be softened by the morning? And the dress? Of course they would. Though none of them was tall and dark, as Pen's crystal-gazer foretold, even a dwarf would appear gigantic if he had a contract in his hand.

'Something tells me,' she thought, 'that this is a day for luck. I wish Carl had come. He only needs one splendid bit of luck. If I have it, we'll go to the theatre tonight!'

Going to the theatre was still their favourite recreation. Carl sent his professional card to theatre managers, asking for free seats; and occasionally tickets would arrive. If there were no tickets, they went to the pit or even the gallery, listening and watching with the attentiveness of cats, and pronouncing verdicts from which there was no appeal.

How the actors would have quailed if they had heard them!

Carl's were always astringent; Constance, more sanguine, was entertained by what he despised, and cheerfully tolerated three hours of serious drama which she found a bore. She was learning, and knew that she was learning, the whole time.

'I don't think Carl learns anything,' she thought, walking northward from the bridge. 'He already knows the *gamut*. *Gamut*; *gamut*; why is that word so familiar? I adore it. *Gamut*, gambit, goblin, grandeur—words beginning with G are always Good. The K sound is good, too, King, crown, conquest, curlywig . . . Come to that, Constance is pretty good. Well, I am, you know!' She laughingly added ruefully: 'Carl used to think so. He doesn't, now. Especially since last night . . .'

Even this thought did not destroy her optimism. She looked into a shop window, where, besides other pleasant objects, she saw her own gratifying reflection. Hat, gloves, and shoes were all smart; her dress was not only beautiful in itself but the cause that beauty was in the wearer. Not the sole cause, she agreed; there was something about the wearer which to an optimist promised excellent acting in every part from that of *ingénue* to that of Mrs Erlynne, in *Lady Windermere's Fan*. Wouldn't the agents agree? They might do so. Why not? Elated, she went upon her way.

The bus was crowded; and everybody in it paid tribute to a most interesting passenger. Young women eyed her enviously from top to toe; older women, with nothing to lose, admired without stint, smiling at the bright face under the monstrous hat; the two or three men could not restrain their glances, which were most flattering. By the time she alighted at Piccadilly Circus she had changed the morning outlook of quite a dozen people, who either forgot their preoccupation with pains and bills or resolved to wear just such frocks as the one they coveted. The conductor, running fingers through coppers in his money-bag to the accompaniment of a whistled music-hall air, gallantly and grinningly helped her to the pavement; her departure evoked a chorus of sighs.

'Very good,' thought Constance, with simple pleasure. 'I was a success.' She had missed nothing of the effect she produced.

Optimism was still with her when she reached the narrow and discouraging staircase which led up to Mr Blackstone's office. The stairs were covered with well-worn oilcloth. They had been trodden with hope, and re-trodden with heroically concealed misery by at least two generations of aspirants, some of whom now enjoyed bright lights outside theatres in Shaftesbury Avenue and elsewhere. And they led to a waiting-room in which Constance knew that she would see again a number of familiar faces. On the walls of this room were flamboyant photographs of the lucky ones, inscribed with enormous signatures, together with posters of theatres and a country scene which was believed to represent Mr Blackstone's birthplace in the Cotswolds but which really represented the home of an actress who had married money. Constance, having learned the truth, disliked this picture; she regarded it as a bad joke of Mr Blackstone's; a taunt to the unsuccessful, and a hint to pretty girls to marry before their hearts broke.

Sure enough, two young women and an older one, heavily painted to minimise her fifty-five years, murmured greetings of false pleasure, and commended the May morning.

'Makes it good to be alive,' said the youngest. 'Hedges looking lahvely.'

'Oh, quate,' added both the others.

Apart from this little flurry of welcome they indulged in no further conversation, because the door of Mr Blackstone's private room opened suddenly to allow a man to depart. The man was very tall, very statuesque; his face was as pale as ivory; and he hastily assumed an abstracted smile for the benefit of the watchers. It was Masefield. He started at sight of Constance, bowed gravely without speaking, and disappeared on his way to the street.

'Edward!' called Constance, wishing to condole and question him about the Strollers. She rose to her feet, and took a couple of short steps; but was too late to catch him before the door shut with venom. It was a moment of painful chagrin.

The other women exchanged glances. They saw only that he had been unsuccessful with Mr Blackstone, and had no clue to the rejected encounter.

'"Abandon hope all ye who enter here,"' said the youngest. 'Makes me feel I want to get back to Mother.'

'I haven't got one,' replied her companion. 'She died when I was three.'

The older woman said nothing; she was past lightness of remark, and hoped for nothing better than the part of somebody's mother, crabbed with age, on tour.

Such rueful humour reminded Constance of Maude, who would stoically have relished it. Already moved by the sight of Masefield and his evident unwillingness to treat her as an old comrade, she lost heart. Masefield was a poor stick; but he belonged to days when she was sentimental, and she had been much attracted by his beauty. And Maude? Poor old Maude! Where was she now, and what would she do? 'I really must write to her. I've never answered her last. It's too bad of me. Too bad.' She resolved to write as soon as she got home, and perhaps would have done so if other happenings had not driven the resolve from her mind.

The first of the happenings came now.

'Oh, Constance!' exclaimed a voice. It was that of Mr Blackstone himself; and Mr Blackstone, so far from being a tall, dark stranger, was a tiny, plump man whose old fairness had given place to puffy red cheeks and hair, eyebrows, and moustache of a greeny-yellow colour. So insignificant was his appearance that Constance had to recognise him afresh every time she saw him.

Mr Blackstone always wore a cut-away morning coat, to show that he was a gentleman. This was a trifling pretence, which only people like Carl ridiculed; for the agent was a hard and shrewd man, without sentiment, who knew every detail of the theatrical world, every scandal attached to leading actresses, every profit or loss being made in all the London theatres. He called all his professional friends by their Christian names (which he never forgot or misplaced); and was regarded by clients as the most reliable of a disheartening tribe.

Carl said his name had never been Blackstone; but he answered to no other, and Constance thought Carl was unjust. The injustice was based on common antipathy. Mr Blackstone, always kind and regretful to herself, was irascible with Carl, and Carl was at his most resentful in consequence. What passed in Mr Blackstone's mind concerning herself she was not learned enough to read; for his mind was as impenetrable as the Minoan script.

'Oh, Constance!' said he, briskly, 'The very person I want to see!'

This address was so exceptional that everybody in the room, Constance included, felt sharpened interest. The older woman, like an unwanted dog in a home for strays, which sees one of its companions adopted by some new owner, stared yearningly at Mr Blackstone. The eyes of the younger ones darkened with jealousy. This was a rival, favoured because she was a blonde. They hated her.

'Just a minute, ladies,' said Mr Blackstone, to the gazers. 'Come in, will you?'

Constance followed into his office, where a woman secretary sat at a desk efficiently reading shorthand notes and rattling away at a typewriter. As soon as the door was closed, Mr Blackstone's manner changed to one of urgency. 'Now look here, Constance, I've been trying to get hold of you; but of course you're not on the telephone, and neither Tom Moore nor Ted Masefield—you saw Masefield just now; I couldn't do anything for him—knew your address. It's very difficult, you know; you ought to be on the telephone. Well, after this you may be able to afford the resources of civilisation, ha-ha. What you must do at this moment is to cut round to the Regent in Frith Street. Cupples is using it as an office for work and rehearsals. Soames Cupples; ever heard the name?' He laughed again in asking this jocose question.

'He's my dream hero, Mr Blackstone.'

'Of course he is. More tangibly, he's got a bank balance.

Insist on seeing him. He's not easy to see; and they'll try to put
you off. Tell him you're the girl I spoke to him about. You're
just the type he wants. He'll ask you to say a short piece; test
your voice. By the way, can you sing?'

'I'm not operatic,' replied Constance. 'I know my notes, and
I sing in tune.'

'That's enough. Few can do it. He thought of Barbara Tuke;
she's a little old, and although she's clever she's got no ear. I
think he'll jump at you—looks, voice, carriage. Queer chap,
Soames; a bit slow, by my standards; but able, able, and his
backers are sound. Claude Marrington, Sealby, somebody else;
forget . . . Cut off, now. If it's all right, come and tell me, so
that I can draw the contract. I may say it's a matter of ten pounds
a week; a nice little comedy with one or two songs and a bit of
drama. They call it *Clothes and the Woman*—a sort of skit on
Shaw's *Arms and the Man*. Quite smart. Give you a chance to
show your paces—and your figure, ha-ha;—and give me something solid to work on for the future. Now I must see those
other girls. Nothing for them; but I'm kind-hearted. Good luck!'

He shook hands; something he had never done before. He
smiled, showing large irregular teeth. He pushed her elbow, to
emphasise the need for haste. Brimming with hope, Constance
sparkled upon the waiting trio, who had been joined by a
stranger, and ran down the stairs into Charing Cross Road.

Her journey was not a long one, and she therefore had no
time for more than hasty speculation; but amid the jumble of
feelings aroused by Mr Blackstone's optimism she was conscious
of quick gratitude for what had obviously been a generous
recommendation, and she found a single great curiosity. What
had he said about her to Cupples? Apparently they had not discussed her ability to sing; it was her looks that mattered. The
importance of the new dress was manifest. If the dress triumphed,
her labour with needle and thread would be vindicated. So would
her eye for style and the steadiness of her hand in cutting out
flimsy material.

'Ten pounds a week! Good heavens, they would be rich! It was forty pounds a month—well, more than that. Thirteen weeks, if the play ran so long, would be a hundred and thirty pounds; and twenty-six weeks . . .' Stop! Stop! She mustn't speculate so crazily! . . . Carl would be able to have a new suit, which would be a marvellous asset. It might produce an engagement, and probably an unobtrusive restitution of missing trinkets. She didn't like that trait in him. It was worse than secretiveness. But he'd had a very hard time, poor boy, and of course he didn't want to confess that he was broke. Now he'd be whipped out of his bitterness into the drollery of their early acquaintance. What fun they would have!

And she? 'A chance to show your paces!' Wonderful!

Ha! The usual dingy little doorway that was thought good enough for professionals; a strong smell of damp, dust, and tobacco-smoke; a dimly-lighted sentry box; a baleful eye. The eye, set in a face the colour of teak, seemed to be the only one the doorkeeper possessed, for the other was closed; but it held a lifetime's hostility to womankind. A drunken mother, gadding sisters, a flighty wife. Perhaps no mother, no sisters, and no wife at all . . .

A surprisingly high-pitched chant reached her ears.

'Mr Cupples can't see nobody today. He's busy.'

'He's going to be busy seeing me,' declared Constance, with spirit. She was upheld by the knowledge of Mr Blackstone's warranty. 'It's what he's here for.'

'Hm. They all say that.'

'I'm not "they". I'm "me". And what I tell you is true.'

'Is it?' The man was suspicious of her gaiety. 'Got an appointment?'

'He's waiting for me. I'm Miss Rotherham.'

A misogynic silence lasted for sixty seconds, while the eye accused. Very reluctantly, and with a cry of 'Wait there!' the creature pushed like a modern Caliban from his box and hobbled along a dismal passage. A true gaoler! Old Wilfred Shadbolt! Constance, for all her boldness, clenched her gloved fists as she

waited for his return, feeling the kid constricting her knuckles.
What a long time he was away! Probably begging permission
to cast an interloper into his deepest dungeon . . .

She had an opportunity to peep into the box, where she saw
an old greenish bowler hat, a battered oblong tin used for storing
her enemy's shag, and an open book. She could not read the
book's headline, which was in small print on poor and dis-
coloured paper; so she was left with the problem of a one-eyed
man's ability to decipher anything so ill-printed.

'I suppose troglodytes—oh, no, it was Cyclops, wasn't it?—
can read as well with one eye as two. Don't they call it com-
pensation, or something? All the same, it's an evil eye. It bodes
no good.'

She sought to recover confidence by thinking of Mr Blackstone's new cordiality and the glorious multiples of ten pounds a
week. In a year, that would amount to . . . Her hands unclenched.
She used her fingers to calculate. Ten times fifty-two . . .

'Mr Blackstone's commission would make a big hole. Fifty-
two pounds! Carl would be sure to grudge that!'

At last the sounds of a hobbling tread promised the troglodyte's reappearance. His eye glared. She thought it had reddened, like the eye of a rhinoceros, with a sort of charging rage.

'All right.' The man was as rude as ever; he had been defeated
in his effort to secure her dismissal. 'Along the passage there.
Up the stairs. You'll see the door.'

Constance drew a deep breath. She and Carl had several times,
in the last three years, watched Soames Cupples from seats in
the pit; and even Carl admitted some quality in the large, impassive, hoarse-voiced man. His comment had been: 'The play's
tripe; he's prostituting himself; but he acts everybody else off
the stage, as I do.'

Such praise was munificent. Coming from one who rarely
commended, it was as if one should say the Elgin Marbles had
their points. Being a woman, and more naturally sanguine,
Constance formed a higher estimate. She thought the play full
of wit, and Cupples, although he never exerted his full powers,

and took little interest in the Serious Drama, the best actor she had ever seen. Much better than Hurd. Oh, *much* better. For the first time she appreciated Carl's denunciation of Erasmus as an antediluvian ranter. It was true; Erasmus was florid, quite obviously the actor, yet less actor than orator. He aimed at the sonorous, the superlatively histrionic, the over-elaborate. He was old-fashioned.

Cupples, on the contrary, was natural. He used no exaggerated pauses or gestures. He never raised his voice in declamation. The smallest turn of his head was enough to reveal thought, discomfiture, wicked glee in the discomfiture of others. He could be droll and serious in a couple of sentences, imposing silence on his audience by means of silent magnetism. That was marvellous. That was the perfection of style. She grasped its implications, and resolved to practise ever after a similarly effective restraint. To Carl she revealed nothing of her determination.

And now she was to see Cupples, not from the pit, but face to face. The prospect called for all her courage. She must not strike him as a tyro, bent on impressing; must not be too cool, nor too self-reliant. 'In fact I must dissemble . . . *act*! . . .'

The stairs, which were steep and winding, did not increase her assurance. Nor had she any chance to recover her breath on the landing; for the door of a large room stood wide open, and she could see Cupples at a desk, looking towards her. He would watch, to assure himself of her aplomb in entry. He would watch, to see how she sat down . . . Walking forward, therefore, she braced herself against the intimidating shout which Hurd would have used.

It did not come. The room, a bigger one than any she had seen in small provincial theatres, was fit for rehearsals and light enough to disclose at one glance every spot and splinter in the uncarpeted floor. A moving spider would have been visible; and there was no spider. There was only the one big man who had mastered his profession; and who was as much unlike Hurd as Carl was unlike the troglodyte.

Her reception, also, was different from the first encounter with Hurd. Cupples, a dominating figure, tall, burly, and light on his feet, and capable, she was sure, of superb dignity in tragedy, if he should ever play in tragedy, came across the room to greet her, shook her hand firmly, indicated a chair, and, when she was seated, continued standing. His smile and grave courtesy dismissed every fear.

He was without restlessness; but looked quickly at her in a way to cause no embarrassment, and, showing no vaunt of power, spoke in a low tone. She had heard him speak just as quietly and as audibly on the stage. On the stage, however, he was sustaining a part. If he now played a part, as was probable, it was one appropriate to their present situation, to which she must carefully address herself. She thanked God that three years of marriage to Carl had given her this perceptiveness.

The perceptiveness told her that he was being Soames Cupples, a man of fifty, who, knowing his own mind, and already satisfied as to certain matters concerning herself, sought to test her ability for comparable directness. He did not forget that she was very young; but he was unobtrusively exacting. Could she satisfy his exactingness? Was he as direct as he seemed? Was he as confident of her as his manner implied?

Constance could not tell. She could only rely upon her own cleverness in the art of hiding personal emotion. She believed him to be sincere; therefore she must be sincere in turn. She was to find his character much more tortuous than this first encounter suggested; but in obedience to her instinct she plunged into candour.

'Mr Blackstone thought you might be able to give me a part,' she said.

'Mr Blackstone,' he replied, 'told me you were the type I was looking for. I can see he was right. He also said you were willing to take advice.'

'To do as I'm told,' corrected Constance, smiling. 'I am.'

Cupples also smiled.

'Shall we say, as he did, that you're intelligent? I'm sure you are. I understand you were with Erasmus Hurd. Did you play anything but Shakespeare?'

'Not with Mr Hurd. I've played some small parts in London since leaving him three years ago. Very small.'

'Hm. You have a beautiful voice. Can you sing a song?'

'Mr Blackstone asked me that. If it's not an operatic *aria*.'

'No. Quite a simple song. You sit on a table while other people do the work you should be doing; and entertain them—charm them—with what the author calls a ditty. The point, there, is that you're an accomplished charmer who knows how to get her own way and escape drudgery. Is that a rôle you fancy?'

Constance laughed: and she saw that her laughter pleased him.

'It's a rôle I should *like* to play,' she said. 'I've had no chance, so far.'

'I'm sure you'll play it very well with practise,' replied Cupples, drily. 'Now I'll get you to walk about a little, speak a few lines—not too Shakespearean—and sing a few bars of some familiar song, to show you have the necessary light touch.'

'Now?' Constance rose. 'This skirt's not ideal for walking. I hadn't really thought I should have to show my paces.'

'All the better. Yes, walk naturally to the other end of the room; turn; walk back. Excellent. Your carriage is admirable for this part. Now repeat something you've learned; not too ambitious. Don't "act"; repeat. Yes, Elizabeth Bennet's rejection of Darcy will do perfectly. I wonder why you thought of that?'

'It amuses me. I learnt several of her speeches, for fun and practice.'

She became Elizabeth, speaking with animation, while he, not in the least like Fitzwilliam Darcy, watched and listened with his head on one side. When, having dismissed Darcy, she looked at him inquiringly, he nodded.

'That's just what I wanted. Thank you. Finally the song. Any Cockney?' He laughed when she suggested Marie Lloyd's *Rum-tiddly-um-tum-tay*; and laughed again when, with admirable mimicry of that great artist, she had given him one verse and chorus.

'Splendid. Perfect. Well, I think that's everything. I should like you to come again tomorrow, at ten o'clock. I'm then reading the whole play to the cast; and you will be given your part. You'll find the others a pleasant lot. Marie Biggs, Frances Lowe, Jane Parker, and of course Jack Everard, who plays your lover. You dismiss him in the first act rather tersely, more tersely than Elizabeth would have done; but relent for the final curtain. You'll find Jack a very pleasant fellow. Two or three others. We shall try out in Brighton in July; and open in Town, I think at the Renaissance, at the beginning of September. I hope we shall run through Christmas. Thank you very much, Miss Rotherham.' He held out his hand.

'Am I really engaged, Mr Cupples?' Constance could hardly believe the glorious fact.

'Engaged with confidence. I think you'll find the part congenial, and make it extremely attractive. *Au revoir.*'

Laughing, but with her eyes full of tears, Constance ran down the staircase. She paused by the doorkeeper's box, to find him poring over the ugly little book, holding it near to his single eye.

'Goodbye, doorkeeper,' she said. 'You'll see me again. Often. So make a note of the face!'

In spite of this gay rebuke, however, she was still so much shaken by her triumph that she was forced to seek a tea-shop, order a cup of coffee, and sit for a quarter of an hour, until the first incredulous joy had passed. Only then could she return with any sedateness to Mr Blackstone. Her head was full of two stupendous excitements. The first was Soames Cupples, whom she saw as a prince among actors and a king among men; and the second was a new vision of the world as a gargantuan oyster.

'"The point is,"' she quoted Cupples as saying, '"that you're an accomplished charmer who knows how to get her own way." Thank you, Mr Cupples, I'll remember that. And I shall make the part "extremely attractive". Ha-ha!'

## 2

The flat was unoccupied when Constance reached home. As the lunch she had prepared for Carl had not been touched she felt herself entitled to eat it, and did so. Seated at one end of the table, she looked around the room and resolved that when Carl's new suit had been paid for she would change the great sideboard and fat-legged chairs for furniture better suited to a small room. Sheraton or Hepplewhite would be lovely; reproductions, of course. Some modern pictures, new china, even a maid. Well, not here; but in a larger place, where they could entertain . . .

They mustn't be too bold; the play might not run. Oh, yes it would. Mr Blackstone had assured her that it would last into the new year, seven or eight months ahead. Seven or eight months: how wonderful! The vista was intoxicating.

'It will show Master Carl that I'm a real actress, who can get real parts. I mean, being engaged by Cupples is like winning the Victoria Cross. Mr Blackstone says Cupples never has a failure; and with dear old Marie Briggs in the lead it might go on and on. I wonder if she'll like me. She's supposed to be very kind if she does, and frightful if she doesn't. She'll be my friend, and ask me to her parties . . .

Another thought came: Carl might grumble because she was to appear in light comedy. He would accuse her of betraying the Serious Drama. He would sneer about taking the cash and letting the credit go. Would he refuse to buy new clothes with the wages of sin? She would have to be very delicate indeed.

'Hm. Hm! I don't think he'll refuse. Circumstances alter principles. I'll explain that taking a present from me, his wife, isn't the same thing as being bribed by a corrupt manager . . .'

She would go with him to the tailor, and make sure that he wasn't cheated by an unprincipled man with a long tape-measure dangling from his neck and a great lump of chalk in his fingers. Good heavens! Good heavens! That would never do!

If he thought she was being proprietorial he would fling the money in her face. 'You haven't bought me, you know! This suit is to be mine!' 'Yes, yes, of course, darling. I only thought . . .' 'Then don't think!'

How touchy men were! They stood on punctilio. That was a beautiful word; she was not very clear as to its meaning. But it meant, roughly, that as long as she kept the gift a secret between themselves his pride would not be upset. Pen, without a word being spoken, would know all about it, but would never blab, even in a quarrel. That made her safe and dangerous. Pen could have a new tailormade costume. New dresses . . . This dress must take some of the credit. It was a lucky dress. She would always keep it; would feast her eyes on it when she was dying. 'In that dress,' she would mumble to her nurse, 'I conquered the great Cupples!'

There was a further secret satisfaction. Pen might fulfil that woman's prediction, and be in the West End by the time she was thirty; but if she arrived there she would find her sister, Constance Rotherham, already established. Cupples had spoken! 'You'll make it *extremely attractive*.' If she was attractive in one part, she would be similarly attractive in others. Cupples had been delighted with her imitation of Marie Lloyd. Cupples had twice shaken her hand. Cupples was the best judge in the world. Carl admitted that as an actor he was good. Mr Blackstone said he had good backers. What if he should want her to remain in his company?

'Oh,' Mr Blackstone had said: 'We'll have all the managers after you.'

'Careful! Careful!' exclaimed Constance. 'One swallow doesn't bring the cows home!'

Oysters, swallows, cows, contracts, new suits, new furniture, glory: her visions were advancing in delirium. She could not sit still, for the dazzle of a wild dream. This Cinderella ball-dress must be taken off. She must put on an old frock, wash up her lunch plates and Carl's breakfast cup and saucer. Then sweep, and dust, and tidy until the place looked fit for a theatrical star to live in. Domestic work was needed to quieten spirits. Otherwise she would ignominiously break down and weep.

Domestic work was still in progress when her ear caught a faint sound at the front door, of a key being used with something less than Pen's normal precision. Pen was excited. How extraordinary! Constance, her head swathed in a scarf, and a dustpan in her hand—the perfect drudge!—paused, to see Pen swirl along the narrow passage as if she had no need to put foot to the ground.

'And so what?' she demanded. Her first thought was that Pen was in distress; but distress had no part in the eager arrival. Pen was a child again, needing Constance. 'And so what?'

Pen caught her arm. The quiet eyes were radiant. Flushed cheeks produced exquisite animation.

'So everything what!' she exclaimed; after which, recovering, she was her demure self. 'I think you might try to guess, Connie.'

As Constance was anxious to communicate her own news, she could not feed Pen's vanity by a series of preposterous guesses. She said at once:

'Madame Roselli?'

Pen replied: 'Better than that, darling.'

'The tall dark man?'

'With contract. At least, with offer.'

'Good gracious! The heavens will fall! We only want Carl to gallop in, saying he's leading in a new Galsworthy . . .'

'Does that mean you, too?' Pen's gaiety was hardly dimmed.

'It does. Ten pounds a week. What's yours?'

'A tour in a new children's play. I'm Queen of the Fairies.'

'You always were. How much?'

'Ah, that's where I'm not so good. It's a tour, you see; and I shan't get much more than pocket-money after expenses are paid. But if you have ten pounds we shall be rich.'

'We shall be rich.'

'In London?'

'Soames Cupples.'

'Phew! How will Carl like that?'

'I've been wondering. Tell me all about yours. No, you first, because you're the youngest. Admire my restraint. It's very noble. Mine's a Saga of Blackstone, Cupples, and the One-eyed Doorkeeper.'

'You have no nobility. You merely want to have the last word.'

'That's true. But yours, in a way, is more wonderful; so there's a certain justice. Who is the tall dark man?'

Pen smiled mysteriously. She rarely laughed.

'His name is Mortimer. He's not tall, and he's not dark; sort of nondescript. A little bald, and snub-nosed. But he's real, and he's got this fairy play. If it's a success on tour, he'll bring it to London for Christmas.'

'Blackstone says *we* shall be playing through Christmas.'

'You and Cupples?' It was mischievous.

'One or two others. Marie Biggs, for instance.'

'Oh, Connie! That quite disconcerts me. Mine are only children. Almost all of them will have to get a magistrate's permission every week. Madame says magistrates are a whimsical lot, who may refuse any child leave to appear. That would be fatal. But it's a six weeks' tour, mostly number one towns.'

'Our try-out is at Brighton.'

'But you're not a Fairy Queen.'

'I sing a song. And Cupples says I shall be "very attractive". I'm not sure that he didn't say I *am* very attractive.'

'You devil! Of course you will be. But you won't have wings.'

'Mine are the real thing.'

'And what about Marie Biggs? Have you met her?'

'Tomorrow. I don't know much about the play yet. Oh, yes, I have a lover. Jack Everard. As you know, he's charming.'

'Connie! This is a dream!'

'Two dreams, darling; yours and mine.'

'Yes, two dreams. Yes, two dreams.' Pen grew quiet. She was considering many implications. Constance, watching the little face, which was now serious, feared that this might be the

end of artlessness between them. Secrets were bound to develop
the most intricate strands. Hitherto they had made their common
boasts in comfort, each having little to boast about that the other
could envy. Now they were to be rivals. Remembering the
school play, she knew that she did not want to be surpassed by
Pen, in art or career.

For perhaps half-an-hour they entered into more elaborate
detail, repeating the various speeches made in their momentous
encounters; and Constance heard how the stranger who was
neither tall nor dark, but snub-nosed and a little bald, had sat at
a table in Madame Roselli's studio while Pen obeyed her teacher's
instructions. Another pupil was also made to speak various lines
and give an exhibition of dancing; while several children, all of
them beginners, watched with interest from a form placed
against the wall. The stranger had then conferred with Madame
Roselli before speaking cordially to Pen herself. He had made a
definite promise; and Madame, winking in her witch-like way,
had expressed satisfaction. Everything was settled.

In return, Constance told how she had seen Masefield, exchanged hostilities with the one-eyed Cerberus, and been complimented by Cupples. She had just finished the story when
Carl's key rattled and he came dejectedly into the room.
Constance saw from his averted glance that he wished the overnight episode to be forgotten, and in one deadly flash of intuition
that he was afraid of her. The effect, although love protested at
it, was instantaneous and permanent. Nevertheless, she responded to his wish by saying, gaily:

'This isn't a conspiracy; we're celebrating.'

He stared, lifting his head in a movement learned, she thought,
from Hurd. It was entirely theatrical. The satirical smile with
which he disguised feeling showed him to be on guard. She
hastily told the good news, her own first, and very briefly, Pen's
with greater humour, as something they should enjoy as a child's
prize-winning effort. She did not know whether Pen would
approve; she obeyed instinct. It then struck her for the first time

that Carl could be slow in assimilating information, for he looked puzzled. Then his face lighted up.

'Why, this is glorious!' he cried, in the tone of Cassio exclaiming ''Fore God, this is a more exquisite song than the other!' 'I don't wonder you're celebrating. We must all celebrate! Where's the champagne?'

'We must buy a bottle.' Constance pretended to share his assumed gaiety.

Pen said: 'Have we any money?'

'Well, no; only three and fourpence. But we still have that half bottle of claret.'

'Claret!' cried Carl, brushing poverty aside. 'This calls not for claret, but for Cliquot!' A stranger would have imagined that he had sovereigns in his pocket, which the others knew to be empty.

Constance was downcast.

'I ought to have asked Blackstone for a sub. I'm sure he'd have understood.'

'But you didn't think of it,' said Pen, without moving. Her tone was derisive. Very slowly indeed, she added: 'As a matter of fact I've got ten shillings—hidden away from possible marauders.'

Carl's start was, this time, not ostentatious. It confessed suspicion of a charge against himself. That was very bad indeed; so bad that Constance hurriedly urged Pen to produce the money.

'I'll pay you back out of my first wages,' she promised. 'And Carl shall get the Cliquot. You don't mind, do you, darlings? And while you're gone, as the larder's rather low, I'll prepare some Welsh Rarebit. It's the best I can do at short notice. I've been too excited . . .'

She did not want Carl disturbed; and her proposal that he should handle and spend the money was meant to soothe. This evening must be without flaw. Sure enough, when Pen's secreted half-sovereign was placed in his hand he gripped it as a starving man would have done, at the same time gleaming with the satisfaction of a miser. Constance pictured him as Caspar, in

*Les Cloches de Corneville*, running gold through his hands and over his head.

'I'll go at once!' Carl raised his arm with a theatrical flourish, summoning troops to the assault.

'You'll bring the bottle back, won't you!' Pen's tone, but not her meaning, was innocent.

He paused, with a haughty glance.

'Of course,' he exclaimed. 'When did I ever . . .'

'Go along. Go along.' Constance turned him to the door.

When they heard the subsequent forceful crash, the sisters looked at each other with comprehension. They did not speak. Neither reproof nor defiance passed between them. But Constance knew, as if the words had been uttered, that Pen's reflection was: 'I bet he'll get it on tick, and pocket the ten bob!' Or had this thought been her own? If so, it was dastardly. She was seized with one of her fits of melancholy.

## 3

All melancholy was dismissed when the cork popped and the golden wine sparkled. To the girls, who had never before tasted champagne, the first encounter was half-disappointing and half-delicious; but the wine made their meagre feast taste wonderful. As for Carl, who bore himself as the third in a galaxy of victors, he refilled his own glass and gulped the drink with enthusiasm. He asked keen questions about Pen's fairy play, and praised Mortimer as a man of taste.

'He's good. Knows all about the German theatre. Probably studied all the folk-lore!

Constance felt bound to celebrate her own patron.

'I shall drink to Cupples!' she cried, jovially. 'He's the man for me!'

'Hm. Cupples isn't an artist,' grumbled Carl.

'Oh, darling! I thought you admired him!'

'No, no, no!'

'Didn't you say he acted everybody else off the stage?'

Carl grew restive. The champagne had produced an instant effect.

'What I said was that he knew all the tricks. So he does know them. He's not really good.'

Should she protest? If she remained silent, would Carl find her obstinate?

'I can't hear a word against him, today, whatever I may think of him later. He's given me a job. And he was very complimentary.'

'All manner, as you'll find. He knew he was dressing the stage.'

'Even that is good, isn't it? It seems to me miraculous. Don't forget I'm playing with Marie Biggs!'

'Hoh! She's just an old bundle. The same in every part.'

'I've always looked on her as the ideal low-comedienne. Don't you admire her?'

'Not a scrap. No subtlety. That's my complaint about the commercial theatre. It's all show. No brains; no guts! No; you've fallen low, Connie. Taken the first thing that offers.'

'Ten pounds a week, Carl.' It was Pen who spoke. 'It will be rather useful, won't it?'

He drew his breath sharply, and rocked from side to side.

'Money. Money. The curse of the theatre.'

'But lovely to handle. Just think. Twenty half-sovereigns every Friday!'

Reference to that secreted coin irritated Carl. Was it still nestling in his waistcoat pocket? They almost expected him to fling it on the table in sudden temper. He did not do so. He pressed his lips together, again rocking. A moment later his face cleared. With a sudden gesture he turned the champagne bottle upside down, pouring final drops into his own glass and draining them upon an insatiable tongue. Having done this, he looked covetously at the small quantities still visible in the other glasses.

'This does me good!' he ejaculated. 'I wish we had another bottle! I suppose you haven't any more money, Pen—hidden from marauders?'

'Have the rest of mine, Carl,' suggested Constance. She handed it to him.

The gift was accepted with a royal gesture; while Pen drained her own glass.

'You should have left a kiss within the cup, Connie,' she remarked, derisively.

His darkling glance of resentment caused both girls to laugh; and Carl joined in the laughter, to show that he was equally merry.

He was long in coming to bed, sitting at the table and smoking many cigarettes. Constance, waiting for him, and expectant of his arrival in good humour, pondered the exchange of speeches. She was now used to his depreciation of other actors, which was due to the impulses of jealousy, and not to any settled conviction. Therefore she did not take them seriously. She believed that he was too honest to maintain lasting contempt for anybody. If, by any means, she could induce Cupples to give him a part, Cupples would become the greatest actor in London.

Appreciation: that was what every artist needed. Needing it as ardently herself, she had been happy all day. She was still happy. She was not troubled by Carl's attitudes; but she felt they were unworthy of his talent. She was still sure of that talent, sure of its recognition in time. It was the interval, which had lasted too long, that set her thoughts roving into dread of deeper discontent, if her engagement with Cupples went on, as she hoped, into the future.

There stole into her thought an imagining of their inevitable break. He still did not come to her side; and gradually the wish for his love-making in this hour of delight subsided. She said to herself: 'Oh, well, if he's going to be silly . . .' Her melancholy returned, with, at its base, an impulse of cruelty. She was necessary to him: one day he might find her unreachable . . .

After a little indulgence in this hardness she put it away; and within seconds was fast asleep.

Perhaps two hours later she was awakened by Carl's restless tossing. It was quite convulsive, and was accompanied by deep sighs. She did not move; but listened. There were muttered words, like the mumblings of a dreamer. Then further tossings. At last he seemed to fall into more normal stillness, and she believed that he slept. Her own wakefulness continued, with anxieties about Miss Delmaine and the other Strollers, abrupt jubilation about her new ideal, Cupples, ridicule of the one-eyed doorkeeper, and Carl again. No love for Carl; but a mingling of impatience and pity. His tossing was resumed. She heard him groan; and all unkindness departed.

'Aren't you well, Carl?' she whispered. When there was no answer she put an arm about him, as she might have done to a troubled child. She felt him shudder and move to evade the arm. 'Carl! I know you aren't well. Are you unhappy? Is it . . .'

'I wish you'd leave me alone,' came in a strangled voice.

She withdrew her arm.

'Is it because you're worried about my taking this job?'

No answer. She repeated the question, and heard a grunt, followed by the words:

'Certainly not.'

She did not believe him; but she could not bring herself to say: 'I'm very sorry that you shouldn't have had just such luck as mine.' It would have introduced—although she knew it to be true—the very comparison that instinct told her to avoid. For the same reason she could not attempt any encouragement, any assurance that his turn would come tomorrow, or next week, or the week after. Nor could she urge him to be more conciliatory to Blackstone: that would evoke a tirade against all agents, and all compromise with principle, which she would find boring and unanswerable. What would it be wisest to do? When in doubt, say nothing. Think. Oh, but thought would call in question all the happiness of their early months together. She must not think.

Without warning, there began quite another tirade, which was an arraignment of herself. He had half-turned, careful not to touch her, and was speaking in a hoarse tone, as if tone and throat were dry as cinders. A horrible voice.

'You and your bloody sister. Artful, peeping little bitch; butter wouldn't melt in her mouth. Never any understanding of me or the necessities of civilisation. Common. Thoroughly common and mean. Thinking of yourselves, your absurd japes and conspiracies. Do you think I haven't seen it all? Month after month. Month after month. Using me as a convenience. The true parasites' contempt for originality. Thinking of yourselves as people on the highroad to money. Throwing me aside into the gutter. That's quite wrong, as you'll discover. Quite wrong. The mistake I made was in thinking the smugness of a seaside rectory could be eradicated. You'd be nothing but for me. Still sucking up to Hurd, blast him! Left on the road now, with Moore and his kidney. Knowing no better. Well, you know no better. You think prostitutes like Biggs and Cupples are the cream. That's because you're a natural prostitute yourself. Covetous egotism. No standards. Invincible ignorance. Invincible selfishness. The pair of you. Inferior to the core . . .'

The speech ended in a sob. He turned away again, humping his shoulders, covering his head with his arms, perhaps believing that by doing this he could deafen himself against hysterical self-justification.

Constance, hitherto enthralled by the sense of good fortune, had listened in amazement. She learned for the first time some of Carl's harsh beliefs about herself. They were absurd; but he gave them credit. They were not, clearly, immediate reactions to her luck; they had formed and developed during the past three years, growing like cancers in his brain, and now revealing themselves as malignant tumours.

Unable to account for the faults she was accused of, she lay cold and aghast. Evidently the silence affected him still more strongly than protest would have done. She heard him leave the bed, heard cracks and rustlings which suggested that he was dressing, and at last heard his tread across the room.

'Carl! Where are you going?'

'Out!'

The door was pulled open and left open. The outer door of the flat was slammed. Hearing the crash and its echo Constance was at first appalled. Every dream of domestic happiness, present and to come, was blasted. She lay with rapidly-beating heart, lips trembling, eyes burning, lost in the charges brought in that hoarse voice of hatred. She was deeply, dumbly unhappy.

Minutes passed. The silence was broken by her heart-beat, perhaps by sniffs that escaped an agony of sobbing. But before the sobs could come Uncle Terence's ghost—it must have been Uncle Terence's ghost, since nothing else could have suggested them—whispered into that paralysis of thought some diabolical and derisive words:

'Nora. *The Doll's House.* He's plagiarising the symbolic slam! But he'll be back in the morning for a good breakfast. Poor boy! *To think that I once loved him!*'

# 4

It was eight o'clock on a September evening. A new king was on the throne; but he had not yet been crowned. London was itself again. Outside the new Renaissance Theatre near Charing Cross lights glittered: SOAMES CUPPLES MARIE BIGGS, with no mention of the play's title, and of course no reference to the play's author, Thomas Waring. The management knew its business.

Car and carriage doors slammed; the *foyer* brimmed with a jostling crowd of men in tail-coats and women who looked like fashion-plates; and the noise of their greetings and high-pitched chatter (for as this was a very fashionable first night most of them knew each other) would have deceived an octogenarian into the belief that his hearing was restored.

Within the auditorium programme-ladies ushered patrons to their seats among a great thudding of new tip-up seats; and the visitors stood in appraisal of the theatre's decorations. Aloft, where seats did not tip up, and where, after a long wait in the street, gallery-ites craned to watch the aristocrats below, eager hands were ready to clap every entering celebrity.

Scattered among respectable stall-holders, and unapplauded by the multitude, sat a number of outcasts who sharpened their witticisms for the next morning's press criticisms. The power of these anonymous persons, well understood by the actors, lay in what they would say about the entertainment. If this was adverse, thousands of readers would stay away from the theatre. If cordial it would speed bookings and contribute to the play's success. Everybody behind the curtain assumed indifference to the press; everybody felt secret fear of bad notices.

To Constance, making her first conspicuous appearance in London, the outcome of this night seemed all-important. She was painfully nervous; and would have been panic-stricken if Soames had been less confident. Unlike Hurd, he was imperturbable. He had rehearsed the cast so thoroughly that each member was word-perfect, and knew to a hair's breadth what movements to make at every point in the evening. Marie Biggs, so experienced that she commanded the stage whenever she appeared on it, was the only one to confess her terrors with laughter. The others visibly shook as the hour of ordeal approached; but Marie was able to press Constance's hand, whisper encouragement, and make one of her plump, chuckling jokes.

'If every one of those bow-windowed printers' devils collapsed in his seat during the show, and was swept up with the shoes and gloves, I shouldn't turn a hair,' she said. 'Well, I know it's a wig; but I always wear a wig. It's to hide my own hair. That turned white long ago, and though I dye it I'm always mottled. How's yours, darling?'

'Natural colour; but standing on end,' confessed Constance.

'It looks beautiful, child. So do you. Beautiful. That pink frock suits you. I'll tell you my motto. It's "Never worry!"'

'I'm past worrying. My teeth are chattering.'

'Never mind that, as long as you don't bite your tongue. You're lucky to be on when the curtain goes up. The set's so *chic* that they'll applaud it; and you'll be off to a flying start. Nothing better than a flying start. You'll see.'

Constance did not believe Marie, whom she had learned to love in the last four weeks. Nor did she think Marie immune from the artist's nerves. Nobody, not even Soames, who had been pacing up and down for the last twenty minutes, was immune. The one comfort, indeed, was that these seasoned professionals were as excited as she was. All joined in Marie's execration of dramatic critics; and all hoped for impossibly enthusiastic notices on the following day.

Constance alone had no hope. She thought: 'I shall be a flop. I shall dry up. I shall spoil the scene with Marie. Soames will scowl.'

Soames would scowl. She had never yet received anything but grave courtesy from him, with a nod of approval, and the priceless words of praise—'Very good.' Nevertheless she felt sure he would scowl tonight, the all-important night. She heard with dismay the calls for beginners, and saw the mechanical smiles of her fellows as fixed stares of hatred. They must dislike her; they must know she was going to betray them all by incompetence . . .

Only the little scuffling that accompanied the dressing of the stage, and the perfect skip with which she perched on her table, produced any confidence. Harry Jones, the hatchet-faced stage manager, took his final survey. He rebuked one girl for over-archness; told them that in the crowded house at least two Cabinet Ministers were there to improve their minds and policies; told them, also, that they must put a special kick into their performance because his pessimistic wife would blame him for anything that went wrong; and left them giggling.

They heard, far away, the orchestra's lively crescendo, some scattered applause, silence as the auditorium lights faded, the few slithering bars of a musical prelude, and—

Now!

Up went the curtain. Applause for the set followed, as Marie had promised. It was very beautiful; for it represented the show-room of a Court dressmaker, and was draped with silks and velvets the blending colours of which were reflected in so many long mirrors that the miracle of Aladdin's cave was recalled. Hence the encouraging welcome from every woman in the audience, who imagined herself in Paris with a bottomless purse.

Besides Constance as the star model whose charm dominated even her rivals, there were half-a-dozen attractive young women whose business was in contrast to the comfortable ease of their leader. The young women were not a chorus; they came and went in great activity while Constance sang about her expectation of marriage into the nobility. The song proved that she knew her value in the realms of coronets and country houses; and its tone was cynical. Being sung, however, with Cockney mockery, it prepared the way for the author's laughing mixture of satire and social criticism. It struck, in fact, the keynote of a play containing a little seriousness but more ridicule of current fashions in clothes, thought, and politics.

The appearance of Marie Biggs produced extraordinary enthusiasm. It did not cause Constance to leave her table, because she was supposed to have the confidence of a spoiled darling; but it did give her the opportunity, as an actress, of observing Marie's technique in seizing control of an audience and reducing it to absorbed silence. Ellis Rooke had been very good, but in parts known to the audience as classic, where famous speeches ensured attention; Marie had no such advantage.

She was creating a character with words of only normal meaning, giving them quality by her own art. She had no physical help. At first sight she aroused merriment, affectionate

indeed, but of a kind which could have tempted a lesser actress
to caricature. Marie was not tempted. Having good lines to speak,
she delivered them superlatively. Any author would rejoice at
finding his meanings raised to perfection.

Was the author in this case present? Constance had not seen
him at rehearsals, and his name, Thomas Waring, was unknown
to her. She had been told that he was in America, very ill, believed to be dying. Then she heard he was better; but forced to
remain in a clinic in Switzerland; that he was coming to London;
that he was visiting his mother in Llangollen or Shoeburyness
or Lancaster; and that he would definitely not attend the first
night. He was shy, impudent, contemptuous of the public. In
any case, she learned, playwrights did not matter. They were
subordinate figures in the theatre, as was shown by the fact that
while Soames and Marie had their names in lights Thomas
Waring's name appeared in small type in the programme.

She herself had no lights. The audience, laughing at her song,
would have encored it if this had been allowed. After Marie's
first appearance no attention was paid to the singer; and Constance, full of admiration for a principal, withdrew into the
general picture until it was her turn again to exercise juvenile
charm. In this she obeyed Marie's comprehensive injunction:
'Always be unselfish on the stage, child, whatever you may be
at home. I've known murder committed from conceit. It makes
for bad feeling. I'll see you get your chances.'

At this time Marie and Soames could do no wrong. Therefore,
as an actress, whatever the envious might say in later years,
Constance accepted subordination. She was in this play, as in
all plays, scrupulously unselfish.

Not a slip marred the performance. Rehearsal had been
thorough. Soames was a rock; Marie a treasure. Even Jack
Everard, who was apt to play the fool behind the scenes, managed to be simultaneously a light-hearted tease and a devout
lover when he and Constance had their several brushes. He
helped her so much that they could hear the inspiriting murmur

of a delighted audience throughout. Some of the exchanged banter reminded Constance of her favourite sharpnesses between Beatrice and Benedick; but they were lighter, and were conducted in Cockney accents, of which London-born Jack was a master. She determined that when, years hence, she crowned her career by re-creating Beatrice, the Benedick should be bigger than Jack. Nevertheless she found no fault with her partner. She was in such high spirits tonight that she found no fault with anybody. Her proud thought was 'They like me!'

As the curtain fell on the play's happy ending there was cheering as well as stormy hand-clapping. As it rose again the entire cast bowed very low, as Constance had always wanted to do on such an occasion, Soames and Marie in the centre and the others modestly deployed on each side of them. The curtain fell, and the minor persons scampered, grinning, to the wings. It rose on Soames, Marie, Jack, and Constance, bowing gravely as before. Then, as Jack and Constance would have withdrawn, Soames peremptorily called them back.

'Stay!' he shouted. 'They'll want you.'

He was right; and this time, with faithful instinct and one of those gestures of kindness which made her so popular, Marie drew Constance to her side, seized her by the hand in affectionate pride, and kissed her. The effect on the audience was magnificent; on Constance it was so great that she saw the auditorium and the standing crowd in a mist. Cheers came from the wings. This was glory indeed!

'Lovely!' said Marie, in her ear.

'Very good,' Soames agreed.

'I think somebody ought to kiss me, too,' whispered Jack, who, as an Adonis, was used to caresses from the fair. 'Soames has missed the chance of a chaste salute.'

'Never mind Soames. I'll kiss you.' Constance kissed him, being caught in the act by an unexpected rise in the curtain, to an accompaniment of further cheers and laughter.

Then arose shouts which she had never heard before: 'Author! Author!'

'Not here,' whispered Jack. 'A pusillanimous fellow, they tell me. Afraid the whole lot would want to kiss him.'

'Is he like that?' asked Constance.

'Shy. Something we don't understand.'

Soames stepped alone to the footlights; and the cries ceased.

'Ladies and gentlemen,' said he. 'I'm sorry that the author is not in the theatre. He was to have been here; but he's coming home from Spain, and he's been delayed by fog in the Channel. I shall tell him of your great kindness. Meanwhile, on his behalf, and on behalf of us all, I thank you. Good night, ladies and gentlemen; you have made this a very memorable evening.'

Bowing again, but this time with dignity rather than humble gratitude, he suffered the curtain to fall for the last time as he stepped back. The orchestra scratched out some bars of an anthem to the as yet uncrowned King George the Fifth. The footlights were switched off. The play had ended.

5

Not so the evening's excitement. A celebrational party was to follow; and the cleared stage was invaded by celebrants. They poured from stalls and boxes into the wings, bringing incredible tumult. Already discomposed by so many thrills, Constance could only smile and say 'Thank you' to all who surrounded Marie and herself, exclaiming, forcing handshakes or kisses, and shouting until she felt dizzy.

The play, she heard, was a work of genius; her own performance had been more wonderful than anything ever seen before.

'Wonderful! Wonderful!' was the cry. 'You were marvellous!'

'Always the same, darling,' Marie muttered ventriloqually. 'Not a word of truth in it. They get wild at first nights; and then go away and pull us to pieces. I'm clutching your arm to save my poor old legs from breakage, as well as protect you from abduction. Mercy, what a row! Like wild beasts! Keep hold of me: and keep steady!'

Waiters from a restaurant nearby, who had lurked behind the scenes during the last act, and who now struggled through the crush, miraculously bore champagne and little oddments of food among the crowd without spilling or dropping either. Some of the guests, bawling, and brandishing little forks and skewers in their left hands while raising the bubbling glasses with their right, quaffed recklessly, toasting everybody and keeping close to the waiters for more refreshment. Some of them dropped their glasses and trod the fragments under foot, laughing at the mishaps and feeling that their souls had been liberated.

'That's because it's free, you know, darling,' confided Marie, without perceptibly moving her lips. 'In the morning they'll have forgotten all about us. I hope so, anyway.'

'Oh, Marie, dear!' screamed a diamond-bedecked stout woman with gleaming shoulders and as palpable a wig as Marie's own. 'You were ab-so-lutely priceless! And Miss Rotherham, too: what a picture!' Once-blue eyes examined Constance's face with a hardness out of keeping with the gushing tone. 'I loved every minute of it!'

'The sets were divine!' cried another woman. 'Rachovitch is such a genius!'

'Excuse me, Miss Rotherham,' said a deep voice. 'I can't resist the temptation to tell you how much I admired your perform- ance.'

The speaker was a middle-aged man who apparently belonged to the screaming stout woman, but who spoke with none of her galvanised exaggeration. He was tall, heavily built, and imposing. His face was unlined and very pink; he had a rather bald head, and an expression of dignified affability which suggested wealth and breeding. Constance knew that he was Soames Cupples's financial backer, Sir Claude Marrington, and she was naturally elated by his notice. He was the finest fine gentleman she had ever met. The stout bejewelled woman who had screamed at her must be Lady Marrington, a popular figure with gossip writers as a giver of parties. They were very rich indeed, and they lived in magnificence. That would be something to tell the family!

No mob would ever alarm Sir Claude; no angry King, emperor, or president dare to offer him an affront. Good though Soames's manner was, it was that, ultimately, of a simple-minded servant of the public, a man committed to the playing of many parts, and studied even in seeming repose. Sir Claude had one part only: that of a suave commander of wealth and circumstance. He made her think of that other, long ago at Wilmerton, who had indulgently heard his woman friend's prophecy that Pen would be in the West End within twenty years.

The memory was startling. It stabbed her heart.

'They didn't think I should ever get here,' she exclaimed to herself. 'But I've done it. I've done it. And I'm a raging success, too!'

The boast, she felt, as the social élite stared and smiled and dropped their little words of flattery, was justifiable. Handsome young men, gay young women, all sought to know her. She was the centre of observation. She was a new star in the firmament who would be asked to grand houses and driven, not in the hansom-cabs of her childish ambition with their clopping of horses' hooves, but in silent limousines. The vision was intoxicating.

All the same, the ambassador's manner, by recalling a day in Wilmerton, had reminded her of Pen. Pen had been in front all the evening. Pen had promised to come straight round as soon as the curtain dropped. 'Where *is* the child? What's happened to her? Little monkey!'

Released by Marie, but still dominated by the excitement of success, she looked in all directions for Pen, thinking to introduce her to these fashionable people and gain credit for them both.

'I'm hunting for my young sister,' she explained to the ambassador.

'She must be young indeed,' was his gallant reply.

'Ah, there she is! That dark girl in green. She's all right. Apparently she's met a friend.'

Pen, sipping champagne in her own fastidious way, and looking, thought Constance, 'as wicked as I know she is; but as if butter wouldn't melt in her mouth,' was not a fairy queen tonight; she was a woodland elf. She was listening to a young man who resembled an ambassador less than an all-night traveller who had come straight from his cramped seat on a long-distance train. He wore a rumpled tweed suit, whereas the ambassador was immaculate in tails; and was so slight, with sleepy eyes under heavy lids, and fair hair pushed back from his forehead, that he had the aspect of a tousled schoolboy. Though obviously intelligent, he was out of place in the polished company. A rough diamond; an unceremonious interloper; for some unexplained reason an embarrassment to her. Spoiled by so much surrounding gentility, Constance became a snob.

'Hm,' she thought, observing an ingenuous smile on the young man's face. 'No manners. Provincial. And he grins like the Cheshire Cat. How can Pen tolerate him? I couldn't. I certainly couldn't. And why—that's what really bothers me— is his face disagreeably familiar?'

This would have become a problem if she had not been beset by several other young men who wanted to declare themselves her admirers. These others were as smart as daisies. She lost sight of Pen, found her again after an interval, and realised that the stranger's grin was a particularly *naif* smile. Also that he was amusing Pen very much by some chatter which, from the constant gleams from under the heavy lids, seemed to be about various members of the crowd. What was he saying? She felt intense, unwilling curiosity. He was plainly one of those disconcerting young men who are primed with ridicule. Horrid! And where on earth had she seen him before?

'Ah!' cried Marie, suddenly. She had followed Constance's glance. 'There's the boy who's responsible for it all!'

'Oh, who?' screamed Lady Marrington, producing a lorgnette,

and staring. 'Do you mean the author? I don't know him. I must.'

'Who does know him? A very shy bird. But he's evidently happy with that enchanting little sprite in green. A mere child. Come along, Rachel. I'll introduce you.'

There was a general movement, led by Marie, towards Thomas Waring and his sprite. Both disappeared from Constance's view.

Tempted to follow, she was prevented by a whisper from behind. It came from Pen, who had taken advantage of the screaming descent upon her companion to slip away from him.

'Sh! I'm here, Connie. I've been trying to get to you; but I was waylaid by that drowsy-looking youth. He almost knocked me down, blushed, and began a stammering yarn about some wild journey across Europe. Something about "an earth to cleave, a sea to part". I couldn't make much of it, owing to this frightful racket; but he's a pet, and makes jokes every minute.'

'No wonder. Marie says he wrote the play. Did he tell you that?'

'Not a word. I didn't know who he was. How attractively modest of him!'

'Have you ever met him before?'

'No. I told him you were my sister. He was speechless. It's his stammer. Then I found that owing to his fantastic journey he'd arrived late, and missed your song. I said he must come again, to hear it. He said he'd come ev-ev-every n-night for a w-w-week.'

'Fancy! No longer?'

'Ah, that I can't be sure. But I did tell him he'd missed something good, and that the author had given you the part of a lifetime. I now understand why he laughed.'

'You made friends rather quickly.' Constance became the prudish elder sister.

'I do.' Conscious charm made Pen complacently enigmatic.

'Don't smirk! Of course, an occasion like this is the same as a masked ball. Everybody speaks to everybody. Dozens have done that to me. I suppose it's the atmosphere.'

'Which is a mixture of draughts, grease-paint, and fumes.'

'Did you think I was all right?'

Pen laughed at the anxious question.

'Modesty's the fashion! You *know* you were very good.'

'I hoped I was; but one's so easily dashed.'

'I'm not.'

'You never were. I am. Marie's already dashed me, by saying the rumpus means nothing. Thoroughly insincere. They'll go home, spitting venom. So if you'd been malicious . . .'

'Which I never am.'

'I expect you call it something else. Oh, I don't know. I've been so lost in the part that I'm thinking of adopting it as a model.'

'I saw that. I thought: "She'll never be the same again!" and wondered if Carl could stand it. By the way, I met Carl just now, skulking in a corner, trying to escape without being seen. He told me not to say he'd been here.'

Constance felt her last pang on Carl's account. She was grim.

'Idiotic! I offered to get him a ticket; but he said no, he was busy tonight.'

'Poor boy. The stiff upper lip. His only resource.'

'Against what?'

'Your diabolically hard heart.'

'Ridiculous!'

The hurried exchange was interrupted.

It was interrupted by Marie, who had stumped back on her short legs and painful feet, bringing Thomas Waring to meet Constance. He was grinning, in what she considered a decidedly sheepish way. But she noticed that although he shook her hand, laughing and stammering his thanks with boyish gratitude, he immediately afterwards glanced from under his heavy lids at Pen. Did he wish that she, too, had sung a song in his play? It was obvious that she fascinated him.

'My sister says she's already told you what a wonderful part you've given me,' said Constance boldly.

'Y-y-you transformed it!' Waring spoke slowly, not with a drawl, but as if words came to his lips with difficulty. He looked straight into her eyes, immediately afterwards concentrating upon her dropped hand. 'I . . . I . . . must write you another.'

'Not too soon!' commanded Marie, with a warning shake of his arm. 'We want to keep her in this play for a long run. Remember it's our bread and butter. Only dramatists live on air.'

'On th-their royalties.' How slowly he spoke! 'So the m-more plays they write . . .'

'The sooner they kill the golden goose!'

'Yes, that's true.' For one who was half-asleep he was perceptive enough. 'I must bide my time. But I'm getting ideas every minute.' He again glanced sideways at Pen. Constance thought his next play would be about a sprite. It was impossible to warn the laughing boy against such an undertaking. She was sure she had seen him before. He hadn't laughed then . . .

'Oh, well, I don't know how you think it all up,' exclaimed Marie. 'I suppose you'd say I'm an old fool.'

'You're a genius!' cried Constance. 'As you've shown tonight.'

'Thank you, darling. Mr Waring doesn't tell me that.'

'But I wrote the play for you, Miss Biggs!' protested Waring, from dreamland. 'Don't you remember?'

'You wrote it for yourself, darling; and we all love you for it. Even the critics; though they won't say so tomorrow morning. They never do.'

'We're all heavily burdened, Marie, dear.'

Constance saw his eyes gleam again under the heavy lids; and knew that he was not as modest as Pen had declared. He was rather conceited, in fact, like Pen herself; but he hid conceit under his lethargic manner. Did Pen see that now? Where was Pen? She was close at hand, calmly observing and memorising the boy's idiosyncrasies, estimating his talent and his damnable secret satisfaction with that talent. All authors were conceited.

'I'm not hard-hearted!' The thought flashed across her mind.

'Pen's a demon. We've all had a great success—including himself; —yet he's thinking only of her. He's infatuated!'

They were separated as the guests began to depart, this time by the big, quiet Soames, who had but to move in a crowd to scatter it from his path.

'Like a mounted policeman!' thought Constance. 'And I love mounted policemen. They dwarf the rest of mankind, including the clever Master Waring!' The deep voice gave her equal delight.

'Well, you've done well tonight, my boy. We shall run through Christmas, and probably into March.'

'Like a panto.' Marie was brisk. 'I've always wanted to be in panto.'

'No field for you, Marie. And we can't spare you. Nor Constance. Both were superlative tonight, and this chap's lucky to have you in his grand play. All lucky, in fact. Now, Tom, I'm sorry to interrupt. I like to see such a happy group. But can you spare a few minutes? The Home Secretary is just going; and he wants a private word with you. He says you've given him some ideas.'

'I'm . . . full of them,' declared Waring.

'I know. He has that impression, too.'

'We-well.' There was a grave assumption of self-importance. 'I can spare him a few.' When they laughed, applauding his concealment of pride, he straightened his back, turned with three bows to Marie, Constance, and Pen, and said: 'I must go now. I have urgent b-business with an Officer of State. Good-bye.'

'Come, Tom. We mustn't make him wait for those ideas.'

The phrase 'I must go', and Soames's 'Tom' startled Constance. Put together, they gave her the clue she had sought in vain. She knew where she and Thomas Waring had met before. She watched his erect departure with something of the emotion she had felt more than seven years earlier, when as a boy he deserted her upon the Downs behind Wilmerton.

## 6

When the shouting died, they were sent home to Battersea in Soames's luxurious new car, into the cushioned seats of which they sank with rapture. They passed through the deserted streets like skaters in a dream. Opulence was here at last; and it was good. The car was so well sprung that it made no noise, gliding over the asphalt as it might have done over a frozen lake. They saw shops with drawn blinds, a few late pedestrians, a rare police-man; nothing else.

'Magic carpet!' breathed Pen. 'Oh, Connie; this is the life for me!'

'And me. I wish it would go on for ever.'

'It may, you know.'

'That would be bad for us. Ruin our principles.'

'I don't care overly about principles. Daddy had too many of them. They worried him to death. Principles and scruples. They made him thoroughly wretched. I decided as I heard him rambling that I'd never be like that. So I shan't.'

Constance thought of somebody else who had been neither wretched nor self-tormented. She said:

'I wonder what Uncle Terence thought of him.'

'Uncle Terence was probably the same. A mass of conscience. They were both Victorians.'

'Yet he seems to have died happy; unlike Father.'

'We weren't there. I mean, we didn't see him die—meeting his Maker. It was their nightmare.'

'That wasn't what he said to Mother.'

'What he said to Mummy might just have been bluster. He saw she was getting hysterical with respectability, and did a bit of acting. Like us. She'd be taken in.'

Constance was too much astounded by this new light on an old character and revelation of a sister's mind to make any further comment. She concluded that as a result of exhilaration after the show, the champagne, and the glittering company, Pen was deliberately talking nonsense.

They saw the river within ten minutes of leaving the theatre. It was flowing darkly under the bridge, without reflecting lights along its banks; and, quite suddenly, they had reached their journey's end. Sighing for lost Paradise, but a little comforted by the chauffeur's smiling salute, they bade goodnight to the car. They could still imagine themselves as princesses adored by a loyal subject; and the lovely breeze of early morning under a cloudless sky was like nectar.

Only after opening the locked street door were they aware of chill. The place smelled dank, as if sunshine never touched it; and their hearts grew less light. Constance, in particular, was oppressed by the realisation that she was now to meet Carl.

'I don't want this,' she whispered to Pen. 'It's anticlimax.'

'I know. I understand. But you'll be back on the stage on Monday night; and that boy will hear the song—so shall I.' Pen linked arms for the climb through intimidating darkness to their flat. 'And it will happen again, night after night, until it's stale and you go on to something else. Lovely! I wish it was me.'

'I think you ought to say "I",' objected Constance, becoming a grammatical purist.

'That's your swollen ego.'

'Oh, I haven't a swollen ego.'

'You have. It will grow and grow. You'll be insufferable.'

A striking clock checked Constance's protest—one, two, three . . .

'Heavens! We've never been as late as this before. I expect he's gone to bed.'

She thus betrayed, and knew that she had betrayed, the cause of hidden depression.

'We'll rout him out,' whispered Pen.

'He won't come. He'll pretend he's been in bed all the evening.'

Hushed, and made uncomfortable by the thought that while they had been lost in festivity one person had missed all the fun, they reached the third-floor landing. Pen produced her door key and turned the lock without a sound. They crept into the flat, which was in darkness and reproachful silence.

'What did I tell you?' whispered Constance, as they entered

the sitting-room and blinked in its swift illumination. 'Has he left any note?'

'Not a sign.'

Guilt was heavy upon them.

'I'll just make some coffee. We'll put on our dressing-gowns, and relax. Are you tired?'

'As bright as day. Aren't you?'

'I shouldn't call it "day". A sort of coruscation, fireworks, illuminated jewels. Something from the Arabian Nights.'

'I shall dream of that boy giving Winston a few ideas. I wonder if he'll dream of me?'

'I shouldn't be surprised,' said Constance, drily. 'He's an original character, and quite silly.'

She went, still cloaked, into the kitchen, where she filled a kettle for their prospective brew.

This done, she slipped into the bedroom which she continued chastely to share with Carl. The room was black; and at first, hesitating to waken him, she made do with the dim beam coming from the kitchen. When, however, she saw no long mound in the bed, she switched on the light and saw that nobody was there.

'Well!' She drew a quick breath. Was Carl, exasperated by what he had seen and heard in the theatre, so displeased that he still wandered in the streets? Grudging her success; hating the play; disliking her as of late he had seemed to do; punishing her for enforced absences from home and concerns with matters in which he had no share? Difficult boy! But he would soon return, as he had done before. She would set a third cup on the tray. They would all sit for half-an-hour. Hark! Was that the rattle of his key?

It was not. Silence was complete. A slow dread encompassed her. She spoke aloud.

'He's not really petty. Just temperamental. I'm temperamental myself. Pen says I shall be more so. Pen says I've got a diabolically hard heart. What about herself? Does Carl think I'm hard? I wish he'd come. He's ridiculous!'

She took off her dress as she spoke, and examined her face in the mirror. A little tired; but that was to be expected, after a long and over-exciting day. Hair, skin, mouth, all satisfactory. And she'd been good. Not a line fluffed; every movement as re-hearsed; very nervous at first but not after the roar greeting her song. Had Carl heard that? Soames had been pleased; Marie lovely and kind; Jack Everard quite splendid, and very unselfish indeed; the others full of admiration. As for Master Tom Waring, he'd said she transformed the part he had written. Blarney; but it might be true. He'd improved. She had been depressed for a few seconds after recognition, by re-living the unhappiness of that afternoon meeting with him, Blanche, and the Frenchman; but that was past . . .

Yes; but where was Carl? He'd been present, after all. He couldn't keep away. Now he was thinking things over. He would soon be here, and his crossness with her dissipated; and they would be lovers again. In obedience to sudden impulse, she raised the nearer pillow and felt for his pyjamas. They were not there.

What did that mean? She looked around the room. One drawer in the chest, where he kept his clean shirts and collars, was not quite closed. She pulled it open. The drawer was empty. The two shirts she had given him a month ago were gone, together with the old mended ones. She darted across to the big wardrobe. Only clothing belonging to herself hung there; even his new suit, bought in spite of proud refusals, was missing.

She remembered their arguments. 'You *must* look smart. It's the sort of thing agents notice!' 'I know. I know. But I don't want . . .' 'Please, Carl!' In the end he had agreed; and when the suit came home she had warmly praised its colour and fit, turning him round with critical firmness. 'Very nice. Excellent. Princely!' Had she spoken too much like a mother? Been thought patron-ising? She had been careful not to mention agents, in case Carl imagined her to be reproaching a lack of success. Without thanking her for praise or suit, he had worn it forthwith. There had been no tangible result.

What else? She was confused between anxiety and suspicion;

and on finding her last trinkets undisturbed was ashamed of her doubt. But his handkerchiefs and ties, and his second pair of shoes, were not there. Nor was the big suitcase he had carried on that wintry day three years ago when they fled the Strollers.

'Well!' exclaimed Constance. 'A clean sweep!'

She was disconcerted, pondering what seemed to have been a hurried and unceremonious packing; and amid the confusion of feeling was startled to hear a cautious voice from beyond the doorway.

'Is he asleep?'

She answered mechanically, in the same low tone.

'Very extraordinary. He's not here at all. Come in.'

Arm in arm, they surveyed the room.

'The open drawer is my doing. It was shut. Look! Clothes, shirts, suitcase—all taken. Even his new suit.'

'How defiant!'

'Well, it was his!'

'I know. But . . .' Pen's thoughtfulness seemed to bring Carl's nature, and especially her secret estimate of his character, into cruel focus. 'I should have thought his pride . . . He must have dashed back here after I met him.'

This suggested a headlong journey, a frenzied rifling of drawers and wardrobe, and a furtive flight. Constance shook her head. Such, she knew, was not Carl's nature; and there had been no sign of haste.

'More likely during the show,' she said.

'It couldn't have been. He was there for the curtain. He'd heard the song. I asked him.'

'What did he say about it?' In the midst of speculation, Constance wished for his praise.

'Just mumbled something.' Pen dashed her hopes. 'I was in a flurry. No, I wasn't; I was just happy. I asked if he was coming behind with me; and—you know how he is—he gave that sour smile, shook his head, and vanished like a genie. Probably got a cab at once.'

Constance searched in memory for any hint that Carl might have given. There was none. Her head, already over-taxed by excitement, began to ache. In spite of the dawn's warmth, she shivered.

'What about money?' asked Pen.

'There wasn't any. Do you feel I'm to blame?'

'Only in a general sense. You didn't flatter him enough.'

'I didn't flatter, because he always brushes aside any praise. The only judgment he values is his own. Besides, I was being careful not to commiserate. You know, in case he thought I was despising his principles. I agree that principles are a handicap. I don't think I shall let them bother me in future. Well, we'd better have our coffee now. There's nothing we can do. I can't cry. I don't even want to. I feel worn out.'

They returned to the sitting-room, among the massive furniture, and sat drinking the coffee.

'I suppose tonight's enthusiasm was the last straw,' ruminated Pen, after a long silence. 'He couldn't stand it.'

'Deeper than that.' Constance had many incidents of the past to assemble. 'It wasn't envy, if that's what you're thinking.'

'Wasn't it? I've never known anybody so envious. Remember his disparagements.'

'They were the results of his principles. Oh, dear, how I hate that word! Carl's used it too often. But you like him, don't you?'

'Mmm.' It was a doubtful drawl. 'I've come to the conclusion that I like very few people.'

'Don't you like me?'

Pen was all mischief.

'Sometimes. I think Carl's pathetic. Always trying to impress you; and you showing that you weren't at all impressed.'

'I was.'

'At first, perhaps. Of course you know he's terribly in love with you.'

Constance was aghast.

'Pen! I don't think he ever said, in so many words, that he was even interested in me.'

'He's a curmudgeon. Afraid to show anything, in case his vanity's wounded. You know how you laugh at sentiment.'

Again Constance was stricken; this time with fear of Pen's insight.

'How on earth do you know all this?' she demanded.

'It just comes." Pen was innocently complacent. 'And I'm right about Carl. I've watched him. That's why he'll never do anything on the stage.'

'But he's done splendid things on the stage.'

'You thought they were splendid, because you were in love with him.'

Alarmed lest the same capacity for destructive judgment should be turned upon herself, Constance attempted no further argument. Instead, she sighed, and looked back yearningly to the happier experience of an hour ago, when everything was brilliant. All the people in the theatre would now be in their own homes, laughing at a happy evening. The critics would be in their newspaper offices, scribbling opinions. Only she and Pen were confronted by an empty flat and, in her case, heart-searching about the absentee. She said:

'What a typical end to what I thought was triumph! The triumph's evaporated. I shall feel lonely and guilty all night. Look! The light bulb's gone yellow. I can see dawn peering through the window like a table-knife. We must go to bed. I shan't sleep a wink.'

Pen rose at once from her chair.

'You'll be asleep in five minutes,' she amended. 'And to-morrow morning you'll wake up late, singing. But I bet— wherever he is—Carl won't sleep. He'll be giving a performance; swearing at you; at all women, working himself up into a mixture of Othello and Timon of Athens, poor little devil!'

'Hideous!' shuddered Constance. She added, with agitation: 'And it's my fault. All my fault. I've broken his heart!'

'Don't you start!' Pen was stern. 'What you're really feeling is "He was boring me to death. Thank heaven I'm free of his scowls and grumbles! Now I need think only of myself!"'

'Horrible child!' cried Constance, in terror lest the prognostic should be true.

THE THIRD ACT

# Triumph

# The Lights are Dimmed

I

THERE were no lights outside the theatre, because all the celebrated lights of London had been dimmed by Government order. They were not wholly extinguished, as they were to be in another year and in another quarter of a century; but the town had resumed the darkness of the eighteenth century, when Boswell engaged in furtive adventures among the shadows. Faces could still be half-identified in passing; prostitutes were able to withdraw into doorways without losing their identity; cars and omnibuses still functioned. The cry 'Business as Usual', a call to steady nerves at the outbreak of war, had given place to another and more ambiguous exhortation, 'Keep the Home Fires Burning'.

These fires burned miserably for wives, widows, and the elderly, who anxiously listened for warning maroons and thudding anti-aircraft guns; but night clubs were packed, and in theatres, once the darkened foyers had been passed, it was possible to see glittering shows for the distraction of weary and sex-eager troops on leave and the encouragement of laughter and emotion among civilians. That blessed word 'escapism', although invented, was not yet a reproach. Nor did many condemn the mixtures of colour, dancing and farce offering relief from mud, lice, tedium, and fear. A sort of freedom prevailed. 'Drink, dance, and be merry; for tomorrow the young men will die.' Millions were already dead.

Constance Rotherham, twenty-eight, quite grown-up, and too

much occupied with work and lovers for profound thought, no longer interested herself in Carl's lectures on the higher drama and the playing of an ideal Beatrice. Her success in Tom Waring's play had been exceeded by other successes; and she was now called flatteringly the youngest and brightest theatrical star of all. Some vulgar newspapers referred to her, for purposes of quotation, as 'Britain's Wartime Sweetheart', a description which formerly would have offended her taste, but did so no longer. She was surrounded, off the stage, by just such a crowd of warriors and suitors as she had imagined in childhood.

'I'm "doing my bit",' she quoted, reassuringly, in moments of doubt. 'And the audiences love me. That's enough for the time being. "*Après la guerre*" they shall see!'

At present she was appearing in a play called *Hearts and Home*, the work of a middle-aged cynic who fed popular taste with themes of adultery, spiced with double meanings and general mockery. Constance knew the play to be rubbish, and despised the middle-aged author as a decadent baldhead; but she gave her charm and energy to every performance because it was her nature to do so, and had strength enough to carry her vivacity into ever-increasing social life. She could have wished, on her own account, that the War would never end. If she had been told that her condition was that of hysteria she would have been deeply resentful.

In *Hearts and Home* she played the part of a young woman of unscrupulous daring, who conducted three love affairs at once, and at the close brought a deceived husband to his knees. The husband was Claude Redfern, an experienced actor of the second class who knew that his place in the comedy was entirely subordinate to that of the *prima donna*. He was not personally attractive to Constance, who found him unsympathetic; and in fact, as instinct told her, he detested his stage wife. Behind a secretive hand he told his friends that she was a prize bitch who sacrificed everybody else to an insatiable vanity; but before an audience, as was required, he turned in chameleon fashion from the debonair to the suspicious, from suspicion to fury, and from rage to shame, so that he made an excellent foil. Crowds rejoiced to see a man humiliated by a mistress of resource.

In a smaller, but still important, part, that of the heroine's ridiculously fond mother, Marie Biggs repeated the performance she had given for the past ten years. The War had aged her. A much-loved only son had been killed in action; a less-loved husband was in a mental home. She was a lonely old woman. Her short legs, under the ample skirts which she wore to conceal them, were sadly bowed; nothing could hide her sagging dewlaps; without make-up she looked like a melancholy toad. On the stage she was forced to play for laughs by ever more extravagant bustle and grimace. Her genius for comedy, once unquestioned, had decayed.

Watching Marie one night, Constance was struck by incongruity.

'How extraordinary,' she thought, 'that six years ago—was it six? I forget—I was out of my wits with joy at the prospect of meeting, and playing with, Marie. And then my pride when, before that raging audience, she kissed me. I thought it was the most wonderful thing in the world. Now—what a change!'

She saw nothing, in the future, for herself, but increasing triumph. She sometimes imagined fields in which she could prove the versatility of, not genius perhaps, but great talent. Comedy, obviously, offered the widest range; but she also hankered for experience in drama, and the creation of 'strong' parts such as those of an innocent woman standing trial for murder, a woman sacrificing herself heroically for the man she loved, or a woman who, after defying a tyrant and sending him to perdition, was left, as the curtain fell, on her knees, sobbing in agony for love of him. In every case beloved by audiences for qualities of character, and courage. The plays must not be too heart-rending, in case the audiences should come to associate her with pain, which could bring an end to prosperity.

Why didn't somebody write her a play of this order? She felt more confident each night of being able to dominate the stage, as all great actresses have done, to take liberties with the author's text, to indulge in mischievous little parodies of other actresses. She was already regarded as the embodiment of vivacity. She had—what was it that Chaliapin sang in *Boris*? 'I have attained to power!' What a grand phrase! What an intoxicating assurance! It was here! Hurray!

Yes, poor old Marie: a splendid generous old warhorse! One must always be kind to her, out of gratitude for the past, and, less admiringly, in testimony to the present. Marie's voice was failing: by the end of the show it was hoarse, and in conversation afterwards a whisper. One day it would go altogether. She no longer commanded the certainty of attack which had made her such a marvel. Sometimes her expressive hands jerked, and her mouth, sagging, could not effectively pronounce the words. Playing opposite to her, and noting the troubled eyes, one could tell that she knew her defects, and accepted them with the stoic fatalism of age.

One must be kind, and, as an actress, demonstrate the kindness. Therefore at the final curtain, when many in the auditorium stood to cheer a dazzling young favourite, Constance always put an arm round Marie's shoulders, drew her forward, and kissed her with radiant modesty. She could almost hear the audience exclaim 'Charming!' and Marie, amid the ready tears of the profession, always acknowledged the embrace by whispering: 'Thank you, darling; you were better than ever tonight Better than ever. Always! Always!'

Dear Marie! Dear vulgar great-hearted old woman! It did one good to experience such gratitude. When the play was being cast, Constance had put in a word for her. She believed the word had been decisive. Afterwards, before the first rehearsal, they met in the street; Marie in terribly ostentatious furs, her face highly rouged and her yellow wig frizzed.

'I'm to be your mother, darling!' she shouted, from twenty yards away.

Constance, the rector's daughter, had been taught never to

shout in the street. She hastened to Marie's side, and was embraced.

'Of course you are! The best in the world! You shall always be my mother!'

Marie, greatly moved, dabbed her eyes with a vulgar spotted handkerchief, memento of an old success. Her poor old gaping lips, smothered in what looked like red-currant jelly, trembled.

'There. I'm better! Have I blacked my cheeks?' she demanded. 'This stuff runs abominably!' On being reassured, she continued: 'Your grandmother, more like it.'

'Nonsense!' Too quick. Too quick. One should have laughed; taken time.

Marie, apparently, had not noticed the excessive promptitude. She had a candour peculiar to herself, and innocently attributed the same candour to others, who sniggered secretly and felt superior to her.

'I was sixty-seven yesterday. Nobody took a scrap of notice.'

'Oh, Marie! I didn't know. I'm ashamed.'

'That's all right, dear. I didn't want anybody to know. I'm "one of the ruins that Cromwell knocked abart a bit".'

'You're young in heart. As young . . .'

'No, dear. I'm old. No illusions left. But I've had a good run; and thank God I can count my blessings. You're one of them.'

'We're both alive, at any rate.' Constance, thinking of kindness, and their escape from bombs, remembered too late that only a few months earlier Marie's son had been blown to pieces on the battlefield. She reproached herself for a second *gaffe*. Marie remained unconscious of either. She said:

'Only just alive, in my case. I shall have been on the stage fifty years next May. I never had your beauty—or your voice. What I had was piquancy. I was saucy. They loved it. Eh, dear; fifty years ago, and, like you, full of ambition. Well, it's gone. I never expected to play Lady Macbeth. An *ingénue* in Barrie or Pinero—my favourites. Now, by the time this cruel war is over, darling, they'll be tired of tinsel and waddling old dames like me.

You'll go on; but I shall be scrapped and forgotten. It's the mummer's fate.'

'Don't frighten me, Marie! I don't want to be forgotten!'

'You've got another forty years; a lifetime. But I . . . What does the Bard say about "unregarded age"? This year, no birthday cards; next year, perhaps, no birthday. I shall struggle on as long as they let me; but one day—pop!—I shall be gone.'

'No, no. I shall catch you before you fall.'

'Oh, I shan't fall, darling. Make no mistake. I shall be pushed.'

Constance never forgot the briskly-spoken words. They returned to her in all fits of melancholy, a knell to bright hopes of an idolised age. 'Scrapped and forgotten. It's the mummer's fate.'

The mummer's fate! Was not memory the most treacherous of illusions? She herself had lost sight of everybody she had known before the outbreak of War. The Strollers were dispersed. Old Moore was dead. Miss Delmaine, certified as a person not responsible for her action in causing Hurd to break his neck, was under restraint. Masefield was with the Army in India. Carl, she had been told, was at sea in a minesweeper after a spell of intellectual so-called conscientious objection to military service. Poor tortured boy, still her first love, but long ago supplanted by Soames! The rest had disappeared. Even Maude Marsh was silent.

'Dear Maude. Not a good actess. She knew it. What she said about chambermaids was true. If I can find her address, I must drop her a line. She'd enjoy this play. It would suit her homespun mind. We could compare fates . . . Heavens! What a long time ago it seems!'

The letter was never written. In the theatre one continually makes new friends, enters new circles, glimpses finer social prospects. Maude, married at thirty to a Bradford cloth manufacturer, had written a few congratulatory messages, insinuating requests for free seats; but, after one or two hurried backstage meetings when the favours were granted, relapsed into good-natured neglect. The War made further communication difficult; and now, with three young children, and her hands full of local work, she cared nothing for the metropolitan stage. For Constance it might be said that Maude had served her turn.

'She can't say I've dropped her. There's nothing snobbish about me. It's just—well, she's made her marriage-bed; and wants nothing else. A warm-blooded nonentity who opened my eyes a lot. Good luck to her! She was a help over Hurd—I've a kindness for Hurd, though, the little monster!—and she certainly yanked Uncle Terence out of what these new-fangled psychologists or psychopaths—whatever they call themselves— would call my sub-conscious. Uncle Terence has been my guardian angel ever since, bless him! Poor Mother! Poor Father! I wonder what they'd think of me now!'

These amusing whimsies occupied her secondary attention while she was making-up for the third act of *Hearts and Home* in the sumptuous star's dressing-room of the Goldsmith Theatre. The room was exquisitely painted and mirrored and flower-strewn; altogether unlike those kennels into which the Strollers had been crammed a lifetime ago. She could, and did, entertain in it, knowing well that she could bear the closest scrutiny of her admirers, and finding this adoration a delightful stimulus. All, tonight, were back in their seats; in three minutes the curtain would be up; her only companion was Jenkins, the bony grey-haired dresser, so efficient that one forgot she was human.

Maroons were sounding for the first time that night. At any moment one of those wretched Zeppelins might drop its load on the theatre, and put an end to all plans for the future. Nobody heeded them. The orchestra was playing its lively *entr'acte*; the stalls were full of middle-aged men, soldiers, and smartly-dressed women; danger added spice to every risky joke. Somewhere in London people were being killed; they were being killed all over the globe. If one thought of the slaughter one would not be able to play at all; so forget the horrors, and 'on with the motley'!

Constance was meeting her pet cavalier when the show was over, and they would go on to a high-class subterranean nightclub and perhaps back to her flat in Chelsea. Thank God Sybil, her maid, well used to the constant attendance there of Soames, and always well-paid and well-tipped, didn't lift an eyebrow at early morning arrivals, and, however long the visitors stayed, remained cynically sphinxlike in face of all odd happenings. Thank God, also, in the present state of an inevitably brief *affaire*, Soames was up in Edinburgh, too old for active service, but superb in a red-tabbed uniform, and as content with her as he had always been, the darling!

As for Pen, she was overseas, fighting the War in her own way, and probably making mincemeat of the troops who guarded those mysterious regions, the outposts of Empire. She had seen little violence, and in frequent letters made light of discomforts. But, apart from parades, dances, concerts, and the rest, what was she really doing?

'Up to no good, I'll be bound,' decided Constance, laughing, as she rose from her dressing-table in answer to the theatre bell, and winking boldly at Jenkins. 'Like me.'

2

The crowd at Hockley's was large, and much as usual. Tables were full, and seemed to remain so despite occasional dartings on the part of suppers to augment the clumsy jostle on a very small dance-floor. Constance, who refused to rock breast to breast and suffer bruises and bumps from uncouth strangers, remained secure, the back of her chair against a wall, while she watched the scene. She knew that her host, Rory Alison, was regarding her with a sort of well-bred soldierly ravenousness; but at the moment of entering the club she had been stricken with one of her fits of melancholy, and the delights of love were very remote.

As a rule, these fits passed quickly. She attributed them always to some uncalculable inheritance from her father. But tonight she could not escape, in spite of the usually stimulating clatter, raised champagne glasses, and only half-intentional contact of her own fingers with Rory's. She looked beyond him at animated crowds of precocious girls with subalterns or other sleek juniors, older women clutching at evanescent youth, baldheads lavishing wine and attention on their too-early-sophisticated partners for the night's entertainment, and middle-aged couples resolutely forgetting business and the War for a couple of hours. Hockley's band was working hard; its South American leader, whose dark face suggested good feeding and an acquaintance with all evil, saw everybody present as a puppet engaged in the dance of sex.

Melancholy made her pensive. How inexplicable it was that one instantly summed-up a gathering, assessing at a glance all types, characters, social classes, little betraying gestures, the old, old, old, flirtatious touches of hands and peeps through feminine eyelashes, the assumptions of possessive masculinity, the disguised calculations behind pretty faces, the anxieties of women whose youthful confidence was impaired. These unerring impressions were wonderful material for an actress. Normally she would have accepted them without further thought, and turned zestfully to her handsome cavalier.

Damn this sudden depression! It had come suddenly in the midst of their journey through the darkened streets, when she had held Rory's arm and pressed it to her side. He, and the thought of the time she would spend in his arms, had filled her thoughts. She had been brimming with merriment, almost dancing with pleasure. And then—'pop', as Marie would say—a black cloud had descended. Heavy silence was in the air, prelude, it might be, to some as yet undelivered or returning attack. Through a movement in her nerves, or a mysterious thinning of the blood, she had lost delight. She shuddered.

Rory was as fascinating as ever; very striking with his black hair, steady eyes, and, below the small black moustache, those firm lips which were to carry her to ecstasy. His face was thin, almost fleshless, with high cheekbones and small ears; all satisfying to the eye and gratifying to the taste as signs of breeding. And his carriage was that of an athlete. None of her previous lovers, from Carl to Soames, and from Soames to the chance men of wartime—all now forgotten—had been his physical equal. And yet . . . and yet . . . in the midst of anticipation this terrible melancholy had descended. The sense of impending calamity was terrible.

She tried to escape from it by smiling at the noisy crowd, by thinking of past happiness; but in vain. Could it be that danger threatened? To herself, to Rory, to Pen? Where was Pen? Though her situation had been no more than hinted at in letters it seemed to lie in some distant land: she could hardly have been brought home on leave from far away. Besides which, she gave no indication of fighting. She must be safe, thank God!

Could the danger be to Soames? He had written of no alarms. He would never do so. He was the calm, protective man of middle age who refrained from all betrayals. They would have displeased him, and interfered with that remarkable self-portrait in which he was shown as impervious to shock or disaster. It might be Soames, approaching her through her conscience . . . Absurd! She had no conscience!

Was there, then, danger here? A bomb on such an assembly would be carnage. All the laughter and talk and movement would be revealed as hysterical folly . . .

She saw Rory's concern for her mood.

'You're *distraite*,' said he. 'Are you bored? Do these people irritate you? Or have I said something amiss?'

This was exactly the impression she did not wish to make on him. She laughed with effort.

'No, no, no. To tell you the truth, you haven't said anything at all, lately. Or, because of the noise, I haven't heard it. Nor am I bored. I'm never bored. Never. Especially now.' She sought hastily for justification of inattentiveness; and snatched, as she had done on other occasions, at Pen. 'I was speculating about my sister. You don't know her . . .'

'I should like to know her . . .'

'Perhaps you will, one day. I was thinking how much this scene would amuse her.'

Rory, eager to learn all that concerned herself, showed further interest in Pen.

'Your sister likes crowds? You were imagining her here? Do tell me about her.'

Constance finessed.

'Oh, a mischievous little thing. She'd see all these people with merciless understanding.'

'Your own, I'm sure, is very merciful. You look at their faces, read their characters—if they have any, which seems unlikely—and judge them with your own kindness.'

Constance looked again at the faces near her.

'Yes, I like your reservation. They look fairly silly.'

A burst of laughter from half-a-dozen youngsters at a neighbouring table greeted the performance of one of them who, meaning to be funny, had tried to balance a glass of wine on his forehead with sorry results to himself and the girl next to him.

'Silly enough there,' agreed Rory. 'Not so abject elsewhere, would you say?'

'All sorts.' Constance was disdainful. 'I wonder why you think I'm kind. I'm not. We won't discuss that. I do notice faces; but quite superficially. The theatrical temperament that spots and stores types.'

'Ah, this is interesting.' Rory's animation increased. She saw him watching her with delight, smiling, but with devoted eyes; and the sight was exhilarating. How intensely she wished to prolong that interest! 'Your sister, I think you said, is not an actress?'

Constance was caught and amused by this pertinacity and his obvious inability to grasp Pen's nature from a few hints. Gloom lifted. She would have liked to tantalise him, as Pen would have done—to give, in fact, an impersonation of Pen. That was impossible. She remembered the vivid, mocking, irresponsible child who had made Blanche's affectations ludicrous, the critic who had revealed Carl's incapacities, and the sister who might at any time produce a scathing exposure of her own faults. Terrifying Pen! A creature of unfathomable mind. And Rory here, through love of herself, blundering into complete misconception of the two Rotherhams. He was a simpleton!

There was a further roar of laughter from the youthful gathering close at hand. It was not unpleasant: and she thought Pen, being nearer to the age of these other children, would have been tolerant. She would have contemplated them from behind her mask of innocence.

'My sister is never anything but an actress. Her mind's as quick as a dissolving view. But that's a bad simile, because it suggests softness; and she's never soft. Rather hard, I suspect, under the dove-like air. A latent cruelty. She could hurt very much.'

'But doesn't?' Rory seemed loath to believe any ill of Pen. 'In that case, she's as merciful as yourself.'

'I can't be sure. Only that the capacity's there. I can't "place" her any longer.'

'But you could once? What is she doing now?'

'I used to "place" her as my younger sister. A child. Then I found a stranger who was also myself—more than myself. Then . . . I don't know. I don't even know where she is at this moment; nor what's she doing. Her letters are quite cryptic. She may be cooking, or nursing, or playing in Lena Ashwell's theatrical party for the troops, or just—somewhere—holding soldierly hands and shedding charm.'

'Very sisterly!' muttered Rory, whether of herself or of Pen she could not tell. 'Is the charm deliberate?'

'What do you think? She's a pretty girl, with a natural grace, like a thrush running. Of course it's deliberate.'

'Like yours?' He was smiling broadly.

Archness for archness: Constance said, demurely:

'You can hardly expect me to make that comparison—especially to you.'

'You could do it without fear.'

' "He jests at scars who never felt a wound"! She makes me feel slow.'

Rory considered, or pretended to consider. He was very artful.

'You're not that, as you well know. Has she your candour?'

'Oh, heaven! She's inconveniently candid. No, I know what you mean. I'm not at all candid, in your sense. And she has a thousand arts, all hidden. Somebody once, just seeing her at a distance, called her a "sprite". It was rather good at the time; she looked lovely, and very pleased with herself, as she always is. But fundamentally she's a *gamine*. I had a great shock when I first realised that. I still remember the shock—I was thinking of it a minute ago. So I'm distrustful of her candour. You understand?'

'Do you mean you think she knows too much about you?'

'Pretty well everything. As a child she was very dependent upon me; rather a bore. She was timid; I was the protective elder sister—a part I hated. I was almost—not quite—made to hold her hand when we went to school. That lasted for years, as long as my mother was well. After Mother died, I couldn't stand it. I felt I was being stifled. So . . .' Constance knew that her behaviour at that time might, to a soldier, seem like desertion: she became hurried and defensive—'So I left home; joined the profession; and here I am! My sister stayed behind. My father idolised her.'

Again his attention became acute. Or was he listening to something he could hear above the band and the chorus of voices? The band was playing *fortissimo*.

'Your father: what was he like?'

What could she say? Not, certainly, that her father had been insane. Nobody would betray such a fact, even if it were true. But had he been insane? Where did obsessive melancholy pass into madness? In pausing to reply, Constance also listened. Were there not, behind the music, thuds louder than those produced by the big drum; thuds of anti-aircraft guns? She glanced at Rory, whose face expressed nothing but anticipation of her reply. She must have been mistaken.

'My father? Well he was very tall, thin, quiet; rather moody. And he thought me a noisy, rebellious creature. I've never forgiven him for that; chiefly because I wasn't noisy. I felt it was an injustice.'

'Perhaps he was shy of you? That could be possible.'

'I don't think so. I think he really disliked me, and was glad when I left home. In fact, although I didn't know it at the time, he paid some sort of premium to the company I joined. A sort of bribe! Then he fell ill. While I was touring all over England—I now shiver when I think of the discomforts—my sister watched him die. It made her grow up suddenly. I went back, to find him dead.'

'Another shock.'

'Another shock; and I had nobody to advise me.' She made no reference to Carl. She had forgotten Carl. Almost forgotten him. And Rory had never heard of him. Why say that Carl had helped her? Rory, following the story she told, here prompted.

'And responsibility for your sister?'

This reminder was for some reason so unwelcome to Constance that she exclaimed:

'I hate referring to her as my sister. Let's call her by name— Pen. I doubt if I've ever worried about responsibility. She's quite a decided character. I couldn't influence her.'

'That seems incredible. She may not wish you to think you do?'

'I suppose she wouldn't want to give me that satisfaction. But in any case there are times when she's incomprehensible to me. Absolutely incomprehensible.'

He smiled, and spoke very low, with an air of wisdom.

'You probably understand her as nobody but a man she loves will ever do.'

This was a further shock, suggesting unsuspected sentimentality in him. Constance could not imagine Pen in love. Pen was like a fairy without a heart. Chill came again, increased by a curious diminution of chatter around them, as if everybody were listening in spite of the general gaiety. A few faces had whitened. She could not refrain from saying to Rory:

'Do you hear what I think I hear?'

'I hear nothing but your voice. It's very beautiful; and what you tell me is absorbing. Talk on!'

He stretched his hand, warm and dry, across the table, and took hers. The heavy thuds died away; after a few minutes the crowd chattered as before.

'Don't let's talk any more about Pen,' Constance said, abruptly. 'Let's talk about you.'

'About me? Oh, but that's a terrible come-down!'

She saw the gleam of Rory's teeth. His was a confident smile, not of sexual assurance regarding herself, but of inner serenity to which she had no key. Sadness, born of a suspicion that he did not trust her, or that, after all, she was no more to him than any other pretty fool, returned almost overwhelmingly.

'Nevertheless,' she persisted; 'as I've been, so far, very garrulous . . .'

He must have perceived tears in her eyes; for his manner changed.

'What shall I tell you?'

Constance could not reply with equal directness: 'Tell me that you love me. What else matters?' She was forced into insincerity.

'Almost anything. When your leave is up, for example.'

'It's the shortest story in the world. Tomorrow morning. At the crack of dawn.'

'So soon? Then I must be very kind to you tonight.'

'You've been nothing less, as always.'

'Why didn't you tell me before?'

'I didn't want to lessen my own happiness. Dare I say, yours, too?'

'You may indeed. Oh, dear, so soon! And I've been talking stupidly for the past hour. Being what you called "*distraite*". Too bad! Why does everything sound so much more flattering in French? In English the word "glum" would have been ample.'

'But "glum" is both ugly and inapplicable. The last word I could apply to you, the epitome of gaiety.'

'It was about you that we were to speak, remember.'

'I hoped you would have forgotten that. Evidently I have no conversation *finesse*. Another French word, you see: one picks them up, as one does so many other things, in France.'

'Yourself!'

'Yes, yes. I'm a professional soldier. You say you know that. Otherwise, what? Not interesting, I'm afraid. I take great pride in my men. I trust them. I feel responsible for them. As you see, not romantic, and therefore, to a woman, not interesting.'

'You think we care only for romance?'

'I think, for you, it colours the whole of life. For you, a rainbow; for me, khaki, mud, trenches, duty. No romance there.'

No romance, except that he transfigured all ugliness, all suffering, by stoic endurance. He was returning to his task within hours, resuming pride in his men and loyalty to them. Within twenty-four hours he might be dead or maimed for ever. Experiencing horror, she protested.

'The very core of romance. Our vision of you tells us that.'

'And our vision of you keeps us going. Remarkable contrast! I can't tell you what it will mean to me henceforward. This evening in particular.'

'When I've been glum, garrulous, and stupid. I hope you'll have a more agreeable memory of me than that.'

They looked directly at each other, eye to eye. Both smiled.

## 3

Coming, as they did, from noise and brilliance, they were struck by the chill silence of a deserted side street. Rainy wind made Constance shiver and take Rory's arm, which she pressed to her side. In doing this, she heard again the heavy thudding of anti-aircraft fire, not near, although its echo was enough to hold threat. No starry lights were visible in the sky, darkened as it was by scudding clouds; but when she looked back over her shoulder she saw one such light, from a bursting shell, while beams roved across the clouds, probing for the unseen enemy. Underfoot the pavement was treacherous with moisture. If she had been alone, she would have been afraid. With Rory she had no fear.

'I see in the dark,' he assured her. 'We go down here, turn right, walk a little way, and then . . .'

'I sent my car home as we left the theatre.'

'But I also have a car. A borrowed car: mine for the night. What's more, I remember where it's parked. Once aboard the lugger; and half your troubles will be over.'

'Half? I have no troubles. Meanwhile the gunfire gets nearer.'

'That's as may be. Would you rather shelter? It's a mile away.'

'I stay with you; and you with me.'

They trudged on. Somewhere under her excitement stirred consciousness that wet from the pavement began to penetrate the soles of her shoes. Who cared? Not she! They were together. Danger, if there were danger, was to be shared. Present discomfort would yield to the warmth to follow. How exquisite to feel his strength, and the benison of his courage! This was life indeed! The men under his command must always be strengthened, as she was, by his presence. Their strength would all too soon be renewed, while hers—.

'Oh, gosh; I can't bear to think of it!' she told herself, pressing the arm closer. Her pace increased. Soon she was running at his side as his long stride carried them forward. Magnificent Rory! While her ears strained to catch louder gunfire she exulted in prospective deliverance. They would be alone together in his car. They would very soon be at home by a warm fire, with Sybil discreetly in the background. Blinds all over the house would be drawn. Even before they reached home the 'all clear' would quieten anxiety; and, after that, she would atone for all her dullness in the club. Melancholy had passed; excitement, heightened by anticipation of delight, alone remained.

' "What cares these roarers for the name of King?" ' she exclaimed.

'I didn't hear you.' Rory bent his head.

His cheek was so near her lips that she kissed it with entirely returned gaiety.

'I addressed the elements!'

He stopped. Despite the rain and the wind, they kissed very sweetly; and afterwards, at the run, reached his borrowed car and were inside it.

Sidelights were enough to guide their progress through pitchy night; and Rory drove with confidence. He needed occasional advice as to turnings, and two or three times they were forced to pause as another palely lighted vehicle strayed across the street; but his boast that he could see in the dark was justified. Constance had no fear, even when, at one point, some unidentifiable fragments from the air bounced from the road surface. This was the only moment of danger.

'Poor devils farther east must be getting it,' Rory murmured, as if to himself. To her, he said: 'Not much further now. I think the affair's over, in any case.'

'Over. Over.' The word echoed in her head. In three hours, at most, probably less, their night would be over. He would be on his way to Victoria—good heavens, how learned she was in railway stations; her first brief visit to Victoria had been made through Carl's absurd ignorance!—and she would be alone. More alone than she had ever been; calculating the progress of his train, imagining the journey to France, across France, to mud and boredom and the questionable romance of suffering endured! She shivered again, again, again, not solely from fear, knowing that however great her emotion upon arrival she would present to him the image, carefully designed, of assured calm. What fraud, when her heart throbbed and ached, she would then commit!

'Hullo!' muttered Rory, as the car, rounding a corner, entered the street in which her home lay. 'You see that?'

She saw what he, trained to guard against every surprise, had

seen an instant earlier. At once all her premonitions of disaster
rushed back, reawakening earlier dread. Something—it could
be nothing but evil—must have happened. Another car stood in
front of the house, without lights, and accordingly full of
potential menace. It was a very big black car.

'Service, I think,' said Rory. 'Is it familiar to you?'

What thoughts had arisen in his mind? Were they suspicious
of herself? Had his tone become suddenly harsh? She was frozen.

'Quite unknown,' she answered, succeeding very well in
an assumption of confidence. 'Could it be for you? Extended
leave?'

'No.' He was brief, decided; there was a barrier between them.

'It may be next door,' she said. 'Some mistake.'

'Possibly.' He brought his own car to a stop behind the
stranger, while Constance, now used to the darkness, opened the
door at her side. She did not wait for him to join her; but ran
forward, peering into the empty car without identifying it, and
so under the house portico, puzzled, apprehensive of ill-news and
Rory's ill-opinion, and unprepared for any further speech. She
had drawn out her key to the front door by the time he joined
her.

'I'm as baffled as you,' she told him, in a low voice. 'I receive
no visitors at this hour—or any other.'

He did not reply. She sensed wariness. Good heavens! Did
he suppose her capable of some treachery to him? A shadow of
indignation crossed her mind, to be lost immediately in confusion of thought. The door was unlocked. He did not touch
her as they entered, seeming to hold himself aloof. From
suspicion? From surging consciousness of intrigue? It was
impossible to guess. They stood, speechless and breathless, in a
hall which was as black as a vault.

No light showed from any of the rooms; but, since she knew
that the lintel above the door was obscured, Constance reached
for the light switch, thereby flooding the hall in an amber glow.
She then moved quickly forward, opening the door on her left,

and looking back at Rory so that he should follow.

'Here we are,' she said gaily. 'Safe and sound. And there's a splendid fire. Come in; warm yourself; and I'll make enquiries of my maid about that car of mystery.'

Rory, holding himself very erect, advanced into the room, which, as she had known it would do, heightened the beauty of her clear skin, her dress, her cloak. The cloak was a little damp, but its blue was not seriously affected by rain; while the paler blue dress beneath it shone like a cloudless sky under the golden light. As she cast aside the cloak she expected to see him smile at the renewed sight of exquisite shoulders.

'I really am looking my best tonight,' she thought complacently; for of course she knew where every mirror in the house hung, and where every reflection might be observed. 'Does he feel complimented?'

Rory did not smile. His dark face had become immobile, only the eyes were intent as if he still listened to distant guns, as if he heard stealthy footsteps. There were no guns; there could be no footsteps but Sybil's. But as Constance stood, ready for an embrace which should precede her inquiries about that sinister car, she saw his glance pass beyond her, to the door which she had left open. The glance became dark, fixed, aquiline.

Following its direction, Constance felt her heart jump. Her own movements, for one moment, stiffened as his had done. She experienced panic; for Soames, big, kind, red-tabbed, and unmistakably commanding, stood in the doorway; not grimly, with an aspect of jealousy, or proprietorship, but as one tranquilly confident of his power. Having paused with the actor's instinct for effect, he advanced courteously, his hand ready, she could tell, for the clasp he would offer to an unknown but welcome visitor.

It was obvious that he was at home. Rory, whatever other thoughts he had, must at once have recognised this, noticed the red tabs—his own rank was that of a major in a combatant regiment—and the fine carriage of that noble figure. He did not salute, but he stood to attention.

Panic was suppressed, to be replaced by what some would have called effrontery. There must be no quarrel. She must simultaneously cajole two men of character. Though all that she had planned or dreamed was in ruins, she had played that night on the stage a wanton who impudently deceived lovers; and experience inthe part supplied her with resource. There were two differences; one that her heart was now involved, so that it was hard to keep from sobbing, the other was that in cynical comedy rivals can always be kept apart by the dramatist's skill, whereas here they were face to face. She looked from one to the other so swiftly that neither knew she had done so.

There was no hestitation. She was an artist.

'Hullo, Soames! How splendid! Rory, you must meet Soames Cupples: you've seen him many times on the stage, I'm sure. Soames, this is Major Alison, home on leave—until tomorrow—from France. We've been to Hockley's, and were held up by the raid.'

Nobody could have guessed from Soames's manner that he judged either herself or Rory. He was apparently the phlegmatic man whom he had so often represented in pre-war comedy; and his bow and handshake were masterly. She could detect no reserve. By contrast, Rory, the soldier, who bore the horrors of the trenches without fear, was a less successful actor. Standing almost at his elbow, with her head raised, Constance was aware of faint perspiration under his brows, and amid her own concealed agony she had pity for one unversed in disguise. Such was her temperament, however, that she took pride in desperately- achieved composure and even felt amusement at his ceremoniousness. It reminded her of a stiff-legged cat passing another from which it expects attack. Nevertheless he recovered with splendour, gripped Soames's hand, looked directly into his rival's eyes, and —it showed, not duplicity, but heroism—smiled with the charm she knew.

'Yes, indeed, sir; I've seen you with admiration—in less hazardous days. But you've embraced a new profession.'

'Which doesn't suit me as well as the old.' How familiar and full of dignity the deep voice sounded! 'I'm only a civilian dressed up; but I judge you to be a regular.'

She was out of their sight during this exchange. They measured each other simply as men. By the use of the word 'sir', Rory emphasised Soames's age; Soames, by deprecating the reference to his new profession, expressed regret for that age and a brave man's respect for another's valiance. Rory, taken by surprise in a strange house, was at a disadvantage; Soames, who never showed surprise, and whose understanding of human nature had long moved her to marvel, had greatness enough to embrace the unexpected guest as if his presence were the most natural thing in the world. She had never admired any man as much.

One other thing she noticed was that Soames did not behave as the master of the house. He looked aside at her, gravely smiling, his broad brow and wide mouth combining with the rather swollen flesh about his eyes to indicate his profoundly thoughtful kindness. She was torn between love for him and passionate longing for the equal passion which she believed Rory to feel for her.

She dared not sigh, she could not weep; the moment demanded that she should bear herself to the one as above suspicion, and to the other, not as a disconcerted mistress, not as a two-faced harlot, but as a charmer whose kindness he had perhaps misconstrued. Was that what her actions must suggest? Should she declare openly that she could not forsake him? Soames would understand that; he would remain considerate to the last. But, since much else was involved in their relationship, she must not be mad. Could one, for one night's spoiled ecstasy, sacrifice his respect for her? What of Rory's respect? Was not that already forfeited? How curiously his manner to her had changed at the first sight of Soames's car! This was the unhappiest reflection of all.

And yet was she not an actress? An actress of quality and finesse? Since that was her trade she must now act as she had never done before.

'Soames,' she cried, with a return of gaiety; 'Rory and I were drinking champagne at Hockley's: we must all have wine together. I'll get Sybil to bring it. You two talk together while I see the girl. Sit down, both of you. Two brother officers!'

She saw them sit, Rory with an air of embarrassment, Soames as he might have done in any situation, whether at rehearsal or stage tea-party; and hastened from the room.

'Sybil! Sybil!' she called, in a low voice.

There was a rustle from the kitchen doorway. She whispered her request, heard the hushed response, and ran into her bedroom, where for the first time she could allow herself to groan in despair and, shuddering convulsively, press both hands against her mouth to check the sobs which struggled for release.

Those minutes of bitter pain were followed by a determined recovery of self-control. Between clenched teeth she muttered: 'That's enough. Stop!' This was emergency; not a time for collapse. 'Quickly! Quickly!' She went to her dressing-table, mechanically noted the stricken pallor which could be and was dealt with by rouge and powder, stood back, again approached her face to the mirror, listened, and waited. Sybil was on her way back to the kitchen after taking wine to the two men. Therefore she must steady her nerves and return to whatever fresh trial the hour might bring.

Sure at last that she looked as confident as ever, she swept out into the hall and to the sitting-room door, hearing as she opened it the final words of an interchange which again quickened her pulse. Soames's deep voice, always so penetrating that even now, when it was pitched low, every word was audible, delivered a thrust to her heart.

'As you can understand, the news had to be broken to her at once. That's why I'm here. I caught the morning express.'

What news? Express? Had to be broken? Pen? It must be bad news. She could bear no bad news tonight. Yes, but if she broke down after all, her hysteria would seem natural enough. Her thoughts flew to every possibility. Not Pen. She would have heard any news before Soames. It would have come directly to her . . .

A clue to the puzzle was supplied by Rory's muffled reply.

'But if she hasn't seen him for so long . . .'

'That I can't estimate . . .'

Soames, realising that she was there, stopped speaking.

Both men were leaning forward in their chairs to exchange these confidences. They were very grave. Neither showed consciousness of any rivalry. Concealment of such an emotion would be child's play to Soames, whose mastery of his art was complete; but Rory? Normal clairvoyance was defeated. She was at a loss; her misery penetrated by curiosity.

As she closed the door behind her, they rose.

'We waited for you,' cried Soames, turning at once to the tray which Sybil—diplomatically, or at a sign from him which Constance, familiar with every gesture, could imagine—had set on a side-table near the curtained window. So laid, it obviously implied that Soames was as much a visitor as the stranger. 'May I?'

'Please!'

She searched for the meaning of those overheard words. 'Him': therefore Pen was safe. Tragic mischance to her would alone be irreparable calamity. But 'Him'? Men of all sorts were known to Soames and herself; none, not even the wayward Tom Waring, who was in 'intelligence', could have caused him to make a sudden journey from Scotland. The journey was inexplicable. Had his reference to it been no more than an excuse for his nocturnal visit, offered to defend her good name with a high-spirited lover? That would be too ridiculously quixotic—even for Soames, whose notions of chivalry were Victorian . . .

Soames had moved to the side-table, so that his back was towards her. A movement of his strong wrist produced the subdued explosion she listened for. Rory, his face averted, brought forward another chair. He had flushed darkly, she supposed at the news communicated by Soames; but he was as courteous as ever. Was this the wonderful British upper lip? Was it the protective of the male in every species? Testimony to her own continuing value in his eyes? 'Him.' 'Him.' That must be an invention. What else had they said in her absence?

Amid these perplexities rose marvel that Soames's calmly sober presence was relieving her agony of disappointment. Rory, who must be accusing her of duplicity—'But my God! My God! I never meant it!'—had every charm of looks and manner; yet now, when everything demanded the most comprehensive finesse, he left her without aid. He was stupefied because, being infatuated, he had supposed her immaculate. Soames, on the contrary, was a rock. Too wise to be deluded for a moment, he was supporting her; and he had already imposed his personality on the situation. There would be no row, no reproach. Although he must know what she had intended, he was unruffled. She watched him from under heavy lids.

'There!' said he, bringing two glasses, of which the contents brimmed and bubbled, and embracing Rory and herself in one benign smile. She saw that his hair was greyer, almost white, and his ironic mouth broader than ever.

Rory was no longer flushed. He took his glass and waited. It was Soames who first raised his own. Not by the smallest change of expression did he betray his thoughts. And as Constance drank she felt her heart ready to burst.

'Soames, I couldn't help hearing something you said to Rory as I came into the room. Is there some bad news for me?'

Suddenly, as she put her question, she knew that they had spoken of Carl. He must be dead. Oh, but so many were dead. So many were dead. And to her he had long been a forgotten sorrow. She could hardly recall his face. Her emotion concerning this news was one of surprise only. Ought she to simulate more? When her present task was to pretend to be calm?

'Bad? Good? Important, I think,' answered Soames, gravely.

'It's Carl, isn't it?'

'Yes, Carl. His little boat was sunk with all hands, yesterday, in the Channel. I saw the official report. I was afraid you might hear it in some clumsy way.'

'That was good of you, Soames. Thank you.'

She drank no more. Obviously she must show some feeling, or they—Rory—would think her heartless; but she was numb with excess of feeling. This was the very pretext she needed for a 'scene'. Even if Rory, fine chivalrous Rory, assumed that hysteria would be proper in a bereaved wife, Soames would detect insincerity and despise her. His respect was already in jeopardy; she could risk no more. As for Rory, he was lost. No man of his temper and training would make love that night to a woman whose husband was just dead.

He must go, unsatisfied. She must dismiss him quickly, in front of Soames, with as little discredit as possible. That, however horrible, was certain. Her impulse to scream must be repressed. 'Oh God! Why have I this . . . this . . . this to bear?' She had once loved Carl. He had been her first lover; and memory of his white face, the trembling lips with which he delivered noble lines or angry speeches to herself, the occasional dark glances which Pen said were the despair of love, flashed before her, piercing numbness. He was dead. The speech he had quoted to her as the Devil's, 'Thank God I am done with him!' whispered in her ears.

Re-possessed at last of the power to speak, she handed her glass, not to Soames, but to Rory, who had not once raised his eyes to her face.

'Long ago. I was very young,' she said. And, to Soames: 'You have no details?'

'None. Simply the fact. "All hands." I recognised his name.'

'Yes. That was very kind.'

'Or officious?'

'Soames!' But she understood that he was really defending her from Rory's possible supposition that she had schemed a humiliation for him. 'Only kind. As always.' Finding that more was expected of her, she began to speak almost inaudibly. 'I knew he was at sea. I think Pen told me. I suppose he wrote to her, meaning that she should tell me. They corresponded—part of her nature . . . It's a shock, naturally. I can hardly grasp it. He was a nice boy. Difficult. Full of ideas; but inarticulate. I'm very sorry. I expect I shall feel it more tomorrow. Yes, tomorrow. Not tonight.'

Her eyes filled with tears. She was seized by one of her fits of shivering; and heard both men exclaim in trouble.

'It's all right. I shall be better in a minute. Rory, dear; you'll excuse me. I hope you'll forgive me . . . forgive me . . . I know you have to go back in the morning. Morning; why, it must be nearly four o'clock already. I wish so much it could have been otherwise.'

They were all standing; and the wineglasses had been set down. Constance realised afterwards that Rory's firmly closed lips had been white; but, being blind now, she took his hand in both her own, clasped it as if she could not bear to let it go, and then, with a gesture free from art, raised her arms to his shoulders and kissed his cheek.

'Not goodbye,' she whispered. 'Never goodbye.'

She did not look at Soames; the parting was between herself and Rory, as Soames would understand. Soames could and would understand everything. Otherwise, whatever the consequences, she had only to leave him. Women did not pay debts of gratitude.

Rory gave her one direct glance, bowed, went to the door, looked back, and was gone, she believed for ever. She heard two voices outside the house, the sound of starter and engine, at first a roar in the silent street, and then fainter until it died altogether. When silence became absolute she was so unhappy that her sobs could no longer be wholly checked.

## 4

Soames did not immediately return; and by the time he was with her again Constance sobbed no longer. In imagination she was following Rory through the streets, which by now were probably lighter with the first chill of the coming day. He would go—where? home? to some hotel?—and in time would join those other hundreds of men who were doomed to the foulness of muddy roads and trenches. To reach that foulness he would cross the sea within a mile or five miles, it might be, of Carl's grave. The smell of the sea at Wilmerton was in her nostrils, and the sound of bitter grey breakers in her ears. Carl, Rory . . . She shivered again.

Nevertheless she was standing by the fire, looking down at its flames and glow, when the door was again closed and she knew that Soames was there. He came, as was natural to him, to the middle of the room with that singular small-footed grace which she had remarked on first seeing him act. It was not necessary for him to look at her; he had the gift of absorbing all details while seeming to remain unaware of them.

Pausing, therefore, he remarked thoughtfully:

'I liked that boy.'

'Yes, he's very nice.' Constance did not recognise her own voice.

Soames took up his deserted glass, sat down again, and brought her own.

'Better finish this,' he told her. 'I'm sorry to have been heavy-handed. I should have been more adroit if we'd been alone.' He sipped.

'It would have been all right if I hadn't heard what I did, and asked you. But I wasn't really upset. I ought to have been. I was confused; but apart from the horrible death . . . Well, you know how I felt about Carl; and yet I begin to reproach myself.'

'Don't reproach yourself, Connie. There's never any reward for that; only a useless searching of the mind.'

'I keep thinking of what Pen said about him. I mean, that he was fond of me.'

'Who isn't?'

'I'm not, myself, at this moment.'

'That will pass, too! He was smiling with the greatest kindness. 'You weren't born to take a black view of yourself for long.'

'You mean I'm shallow?' She had not drunk again from the glass; but stared at the slackening bubbles, finding them symbolic of her state, perhaps of her nature. The desperate longing for Rory had subsided; she could only think of him in the grim dawn of a troop-train departure, missing her face from among those who bade farewell to loved ones.

'On the contrary, rich in quality.'

'You say that—now?' She referred to his discovery of her in Rory's company.

'Always. One quality is resilience. Look at the wine. I move the glass; and life returns to it. You'll go on the stage tomorrow as if nothing had happened.'

'I should be a bad actress if I didn't.'

'My fear was that you would hear about Carl just as you were going on. That's why I came. One reason why I came. Another was that I miss you very much.'

She put the glass to her lips, fearing to be seized, in spite of the fire's warmth, by another fit of shivering.

'I don't think I want any more wine. I drank it at supper because I was trying to be gay; but it's turned sour.'

'I quite agree. The moment for it is past.' He took the glass from her and set down his own, returning to her side, and standing with his back to the fire. 'Also, I must go. I have to be back in Edinburgh tonight.'

Thank God! She had been afraid he might stay, which would have represented outrage. Once again, wonderful Soames!

'Is there anything Sybil or I can get you before you go?'

'Nothing, thank you.'

They were talking quite simply, from long, on her part,

passionless intimacy. He was her father, brother, true husband; she loved him; but she had desired Rory more than any other man, and Rory was gone, she believed, for ever. If she spoke of him now she would break down; and Soames knew this. He did not touch her.

'Will you be away long, this time?'

'I can't say. I shall come as soon as I can. You'd like me to do that?'

This question so touched her heart that she turned to him for comfort, her hands against his breast, her forehead pressed to his shoulder, feeling the strong arms rise as a mother's might have done to support a child taking its first steps. He did not kiss her hair; and neither spoke.

As he prepared to leave, Soames moved about the house, collecting what he wanted to take with him; and Constance, having changed her dress and drawn aside the heavy curtains, looked down upon the big car which stood in the street below. The street, otherwise empty, was leaden in the semi-darkness, causing her to think of Rory once more. She imagined the long train moving away, khaki-sleeved arms stretched from every window, handkerchiefs fluttering from obscure figures on the platform, and, for those who remained behind, deep and continuing loneliness until they received such laconic messages as 'missing', 'killed in action', or 'sunk with all hands'. Poor creatures!

Excitement had subsided; sadness alone remained. She heard Soames come back into the room. He had bathed and shaved; and while always heavy pouches below his eyes, and long lines from the base of his nose, emphasised the loss of youth, nobody but herself would have supposed him ever troubled by illness or dark thoughts. He was now approaching sixty, a bulky man with no coarse fat on his bones, whose step and bearing indicated vigorous health. He was not old; he was wise and mature, with an extraordinary sense of rôle but in daily life few of an actor's mannerisms. She knew he took care of his person; what was largely hidden from her was the intense effort of will by which he maintained his buoyant carriage. Did he falter, as she did, when unobserved?

Today there was no faltering. He looked about the room, seeing it as the appropriate setting for a beautiful young woman, memorising it and her for warm recollection, and—she guessed —framing the terms in which he would bid her goodbye. Because he was an artist, those terms would not be drawn from stock; he would never echo ancient parts; but of course tone and phrase must satisfy his fastidious ear. He had been an actor for nearly as long as Marie Biggs had been an actress, and in the centre of the stage, mingling showmanship with sincerity, for nearly half that time.

'I'm just going,' he said, briskly. 'Don't come out; it's a draughty morning, with a few spots of rain. Probably a blizzard by the time I get to Auld Reekie. I'll let you know of my arrival; and I'll give you good notice of my next descent.'

Constance looked sharply, alert for distaste arising from last night's unforeseen trio; but she could not penetrate his air of kindness.

'I wish you might be coming for good,' was her reply.

'Amen to that. Well, it may be so. They say "When bane is highest, boot is nighest"; and I'm a great believer in fibre, as you know.'

'In me, for example.' She was dry, fretful.

'In you, always.' His head was lowered in thought. 'Connie, there's something more I want to say to you before I go. I'm not sure it's the opportune moment. One's never sure. But there it is; words have to be spoken . . .'

Her consternation was so poignant that she could hardly respond.

'Say them! Say them!' she entreated.

'We mustn't be too solemn. What is in my mind—after yesterday's news—is that you might now consider a quiet marriage. It would have certain advantages for you . . .'

The relief, when she had expected something so different,

produced such a flood of affection for him that Constance almost laughed aloud.

'One of them being the making an honest woman of me?' she demanded—overwhelmed with shame for the ribaldry as soon as she had uttered it. 'Forgive me, Soames. I oughtn't to have said that. It was my tongue; not my heart.'

He smiled.

'Your tongue. Very unruly. I know it well. Mine is too ruly. I'm eloquent only with other men's words. That must often check you. One of the misfortunes of . . . '

To prevent his use of the word 'age' she interrupted.

'Are there any advantages for you?'

'I can think of a number.'

'Your unselfishness reproaches me!'

'It's meant to impress, not embarrass you. Take the notion into your thoughts. I must go this moment. Goodbye, my dearest.'

They kissed, not mouth to mouth, but very sedately, like respectable married folk. Constance clung impulsively to him, many eager, loving words unspoken, and felt him withdraw. She was completely alone.

'My God!' she thought. 'It's my fate. "I must go now. Goodbye"!'

She wept at last, in a state of bewildered misery.

5

Armistice Night, 1918. From an early hour London, and presumably every other city in Great Britain, had been a pandemonium of cheering mobs; and as evening fell upon still-darkened streets the crowds continued to mass, freely mingling, making casual acquaintances, drinking more than they could hold, and proving to philosophic observers that British phlegm was a thing of the past.

All was in uproar. Not yet had the revolutionary spirit, which was later to disconcert orderly folk, been developed. Nobody, apart from a few puritans, grudged the people who had cast off an immense load of weariness and suppression some relief to their feelings. Clubs and pubs were open everywhere, lights were shown in many windows which had been darkened for over four years, and morals had never before, since Queen Victoria came to the throne, been loosened to the same extent. Young and old held carnival.

Constance Rotherham—Stockhouse—Cupples was appearing in a new play, *Triumphant Eve*, in which her part was that of a young woman who ruled everybody, from two parents (made ridiculous according to the fashion set by Bernard Shaw) to half-a-dozen suitors. She had learned in the morning that all theatres were to function, and as reports reached her of the tumultuous assemblies in the West End she left home early and was at the Majestic by five o'clock in the afternoon. Having had misadventures *en route* she knew that as large an audience as the theatre could hold was likely to assemble. Battered fellow-actors drifted one by one into her presence, all laughing but dishevelled; as many as possible of them were entertained in her big dressing-room to tea, sandwiches, cakes, and savouries. If two of the suitors were less sober than they should have been, that was unfortunate; but these errant fellows were quietly sobered with cold water, and even if their gestures remained less than precise they retained a tolerable acquaintance with their parts and were unlikely to gag insufferably.

'Oh, Golly!' moaned Marie Biggs, cast once more as mother to the leading lady. 'I hope they won't be rowdy. If they start it will be worse than Boat Race Night!'

'You don't have an Armistice every day, Marie,' warned old Jack Lomax, her stage husband. He rubbed his red cheeks with both hands, and pushed up his ginger hair until it looked like a well-worn sponge. Having reached the theatre considerably flushed and very talkative, he had been reduced to the merest joviality by a wash and a quart of tea. The tea was now making him fidget.

'Pray God what they say is true, that it's been a War to end War,' said Marie. 'They ought all to be on their knees. Instead of which, somebody shouted "It's old Marie! Let's give her a lift!" And they tried to carry me to the theatre. I was afraid they'd drop me under a bus, waving flags and dancing like that!'

'It's begun to rain,' added a late-comer. 'That will damp their spirits.'

'It'll send them indoors till closing time,' retorted another. 'Then the ambulances will be busy. "Bring out your dead! Bring out your dead".'

Marie, thinking of her dead son, blanched under the rouge.

'Oh, well,' she panted; 'let them have their fun, poor things. Connie will look after me. She always does, bless her.'

'I will. I will.' Constance, who had escaped the crowds by slipping through side streets in a cloak and biretta which made her look like a priest, basked in this tribute to her kindness. She had time to think 'I'm kind. I'm kind. Few are as kind as I am!' And she was happy with the general happiness. Only the fear that she would have a boisterous audience made her tremble. She said as much to the stage manager, Jackson.

'That's all right, Miss Rotherham,' he reassured her. 'They'll be waiting for you at the stage-door. You'll go down the circle stairs; and I've arranged for a couple of powerful lads to run you round to your car. Don't worry. Worry never did anybody any good. We shall have a full house, and you'll give a great show. I wish Mr. Cupples was here, though. He'd awe them.'

As she had half hoped, half feared, the theatre was full of merry-makers. They cheered the small band, they cheered the two or three celebrities who were spotted on entry to the stalls, they clapped when the curtain rose, and at her own first appearance the shouting was rapturous.

'Nearly blew me off my feet,' Marie told her. 'They gave you longer than they did me. Well, it's natural; though they all think of me as their own mother, the darlings. Are you going to smuggle me out with you, dear? I'm so afraid I may wake up in a strange bed. Me!'

'We mustn't let that happen to you, dearie!' laughed Constance.

'Oh, they'll be waiting for *you*, dear. We want a lot of police here. Only they'll be busy elsewhere, I'm afraid. I'm sorry it's so wet for them. Of course, it would happen, in England. That's why we've lasted down the centuries.'

The play continued to arouse bellows of laughter; and in the gallery there was a blowing of whistles, some waving of flags, and a fight.

'Indecorous populace!' Marie said. 'If they fall into the pit there'll be a riot, like there used to be in the eighteenth century.'

'Don't pretend you were there then, Marie.'

'No, I wasn't. But I've heard about them.'

These remarks were exchanged in the wings, or in pauses when action on the stage allowed of passing whispers. They helped, as Marie meant that they should do, to reduce the tension caused by what they could see to be restless sections in what was otherwise an audience bent upon enjoying the play. Fortunately good humour quieted the noisy ones, the boxers were persuaded to shake hands, and the third act, in which Constance reduced all members of her stage family to dog-like obedience, was followed with enthusiasm and without interruption. It was at the final curtain that the shouting was resumed; and then it was universal. Everybody in the house stood clapping and cheering.

'More like an opera than a play!' cried Marie, at the third call. She had received her usual kiss, and could expect no more. Instead, she blew kisses to the multitude. At last her legs could bear her no longer. 'I can't go on again. It's you they want, dear. Take this one alone.'

For the first time in her life Constance took a solitary curtain.

The noise was deafening. Even when the curtain had been lowered for the tenth time, even when the band had played 'God Save the King', she could hear din from the auditorium. She stood trembling on the stage; and as she stumbled off, with hardly the power to walk, exhausted Marie was roused to a final effort of adoration. Arms raised in plump acclaim, while the rest of the cast clapped their hands and gave a laughing cheer of their own, she exclaimed:

'You're their lollipop! They'd like to eat you! Listen to them! "Constance! Constance!" Darling, you're the most popular actress in England!'

The words were spoken with Marie's characteristically exaggerated emphasis. They were accompanied by a shower of tears. They ran like fire in Constance's head. She thought:

'I'm the most popular actress in England! They love me!'

Thrusting Marie aside, she ran unsteadily to the dressing-room, where a small number of exuberant cronies had already gathered. These cronies echoed Marie's pronouncement in their own fervent worship of success. They had brought flowers; someone had managed to secure champagne and glasses, which they brought into action. Pop! Pop! the corks as they were drawn made noises like the firing of air-pistols.

'The most popular actress in England!' 'You've won the War!' 'You're the Queen of Hearts!' Never was such flattery, such general joy; and in the Majestic it centred upon one who, drunk with excitement, greedily drained her glass and listened to the storming compliments. She was afterwards to laugh, weep with shame, and dismiss the *furore* as altogether spurious; but nothing could make her forget the gratification she then felt. She was idolised. She had attained to power. Her splendour was unquestionable. She was the best-loved actress in England.

In this hour what Pen was to call 'Constance's megalomania' was born. It affected all her actions henceforward.

## SCENE TEN

# *Soames*

### I

THE early months of peace brought Constance a dizzying rise in social importance. Having begun as a nobody, she was still a nobody when little Blackstone's keen eye led him to recommend her to Soames. Successes gained then and since had ensured amused patronage from hostesses who loved to spice their parties with rising talents; and the shrewd Blackstone handled the monetary and other affairs of his pet discovery with great effect. Through his efforts and the chances of wartime she had long forgotten what it was like to watch her shillings and pence.

At one time, through Pen, who mysteriously kept in touch with him, she had asked if Carl would accept a share of the new prosperity. Pen reported a refusal. 'He simply says "No", she wrote. 'I was very delicate. Told him you were keeping *me* flush, as was sisterly, and wanted to be sure the rest of the family wasn't in need. The answer was a postcard, ignoring my chat, and just the one word—*tout curt* as one might say. So that's that. I shouldn't worry any more.'

Rebuffed, Constance stored the offer and its rejection in memory.

'He can't accuse me of *anything*,' she told herself. 'I've really behaved very well to him, the obstinate character. It's nothing but male egotism; "won't take money from a woman". Very well; I shall buy myself a fur coat.'

She bought herself a charming nutria coat; and a kind world

supposed it to be the price paid for her favours by Soames or some other. Sparkling friends stroked the coat with envy, expecting her to appear in a rash of jewels. When it was seen that she did not wear jewellery they were baffled. It was not long before her association with the widowed and childless Soames was canvassed, her husbandless state being widely remarked. Fortunately at that time Pen was still living with her.

The War made a difference. Flowers and presents were showered upon her by many admirers; Pen disappeared into some auxiliary service; and most people were too much occupied with their own concerns to be over-censorious about a popular favourite. It was known that she and Soames were living together; and until Soames also was accepted for a non-combatant job she was safe from condemnation as a wanton.

With the peace, however, and as the recognised wife of Soames, her position became one of importance. Not only did she share to the full his exchange of friendship with the rich and celebrated, but she became automatically the leading lady in his productions. Authors and literary agents with plays to sell made much of her; fellow actresses and actors paid her new respect because they thought she could influence Soames in the matter of casting. She was besieged with flatteries from morning to night; and in the theatre received applause only slightly less than that given to Soames himself.

Audiences were not the unquestioning enthusiasts of wartime. They were composed of men and women who needed to be tenderly diverted from the post-war drift into pessimism. Since the male lead was played by one of the most distinguished actors in England, they expected Soames, whatever the charms and fancies of his leading lady, to portray a figure of sagacity, nobility, and resolution. He was not to be a farcical cuckold. Adultery might be, as it always is, the secret preoccupation of the respectable, but it must be adultery resisted or exposed upon a high moral plane. Wartime promiscuity was finished. Statesmen were negotiating peace; in the north rumbling anger was heard from returning soldiers who found that, after all,

England was not yet a country fit for heroes to live in; and the general tone was serious, with a call for restraint in humour.

There were times when Constance chafed against this restraint. She missed the guffaws following some impudence of her own. She even, at times, greatly as she admired his skill as an artist, found Soames's integrity as a man less tantalising than she could have wished.

'A good man,' she told herself, 'has the qualities of rock. Very stable; but inelastic. Dear Soames!'

When she demurely remarked something of this to one of her nearer, but still obsequious, women friends, Linda Sweet, who had almost no hope of getting one of her plays produced, Linda tittered.

'Soames has a wonderful range of understanding. He's a very great man indeed—as we both know.'

The sally, with its implication of 'too well', invited confidence leading to intimate ridicule of virtuous dullness, always a favourite gibe of the smart. Linda's eyes were bold and roguish as she spoke, and her cheeks were plump with a toothy grin. Constance was at once on guard. However amusing Linda's malice might be in other directions, she was untrustworthy.

'I wasn't really thinking of Soames,' she replied. 'More of people like Jacky Marshall, who's a prude. In Soames's case the range of interest is quite wonderful.'

'Wonderful indeed!' declared Linda, still arch, and rejecting Jacky Marshall as a red-herring. 'And so inspiring for you!'

'At every performance,' insisted Constance.

'Always the same.' The teasing continued.

'Always sustaining,' said Constance.

'In fact a rock!'

'A great actor. A great man. A great example.'

'Delicious to hear you say so!'

That was all. Smiles were exchanged. Linda did not feel rebuffed. She had roused her friend to defence; and another's defensiveness, to minds such as Linda's, is a great gratification.

Constance afterwards took credit to herself for having been so firm. Nevertheless she dwelt upon Linda's hints. They showed what was being said by some of those—the malicious, the over-sophisticated, or the merely conceited—who enjoyed Soames's hospitality, but did not over-reach him or his financial backers. The backers, Marrington and Sealby, drove hard bargains, and interfered in ways highly annoying to an artist; but in spite of his love of the theatre and its fabricated material, Soames was not lacking in common sense.

The more she knew of his business affairs, the more Constance marvelled at the handicaps under which he worked. He was not a rich man. He was dependent on box office popularity. With no inclination towards what Carl had rather pompously called the Serious Drama, he considered himself a servant of the public, not its tutor. His preference was for comedy. He thought *The School for Scandal* and *The Importance of Being Earnest* the best of all plays; and he did not object to an old situation if the suspense was agreeably resolved. This was the reason why he and Constance were now appearing at the Royal in *Treble Harness*, in which some waywardness in a young wife, threatening at the end of Act Two the ruin of a marriage, was ended by discovery that the potential co-respondent was not only a stealer of women's hearts but a professional burglar. Soames's prosaic but ultimately ironic rôle was that of the patient husband who was also a barrister successfully retained for the defence.

The play, by one Bentham, the author of a dozen similar comedies, had obviously been written for the display of Soames's gravity and resource. The young wife's part could have been taken by any one of a dozen personable young women. These facts, united to those of a lukewarm Press and some faltering in public support, coloured Linda's hint that a more than middle-aged Soames was smothering his wife's livelier talent. The hint was characteristically mischief-making; but an actress bent on success has many opportunities for pondering hints, and it rankled.

Constance knew that she must beware of revealing her concern. Hence the exaggerated proclamation of loyalty. At the same time another phrase occurred to her mind. It was used by a second young woman, Celia Boniface, a hard-up actress to whom, remembering old days when she and Carl were living on the remains of John Rotherham's small estate, she had given twenty pounds.

'You're awfully generous!' said the half-starved and skeleton-thin Celia, who had unreasonably hoped for fifty, and was resolved to spend all the money at once on clothes. 'This will at least keep the wolf from the door, darling. I think you're the most marvellously generous person I ever met!'

No reply was possible; but ever afterwards, as a consequence of two idle conversations, Constance thought of herself as superior to other women in generosity, and as one who suffered the injustice of playing second fiddle to a stronger but emotionally sluggish personality. She still felt great admiration for Soames; but she coquetted with the notion that she ought to star in a play in which he had no part.

'I do wish Tom Waring would write something specially for me!' she exclaimed to herself. 'He gave me my first success. He could do it to perfection. And then! I wonder if Pen's seeing him. I wonder what she'd think of Linda. Of everything. She's an oyster-like minx, bless her!'

Pen had returned to London within a month of the Armistice, wearing a very trim tweed suit, and looking brown from exposure to an eastern sun. She had always tanned beautifully. At their first meeting, Constance was disappointed, thinking that Pen had lost some of the child-like magic of former days. She was too-evidently self-assured, she was coarser, she was less artless in movements of head and body, as if the experience of four years—she was now twenty-five—had taken delicacy, as well as bloom, from her appearance.

At a third or fourth meeting, within ten days, disappointment was adjusted to a new vision; so that the old mixture of admiration, fear, and resentment was alive. Constance was aware of the same magnetic quality, arising from physical grace and quickness of spirit; and was again baffled by inability to penetrate a mind more subtle than her own. Was it more subtle, or only less generous? Pen made her feel slow-witted; never an agreeable sensation, and one provoking defensiveness.

'If she thinks I'm stupid, she's mistaken. Naturally I'm influenced by the sort of part I'm playing. I always have been. It doesn't mean that I'm just an echo, or limited in any way. Far from it. I see deeper than she does. Do I? What's behind that extraordinary air of listening to the spheres? I can't hear them.'

Another question turned on Pen's unexpressed opinion of Soames. Did she find him dull, old-fashioned, a stick-in-the-mud? Of old she had shared their common admiration of his superlative art: had she lost it? Did she immediately see that, as Constance had discovered, he needed much drink in order to stimulate those masterly performances? He was never intoxicated. He was not killing himself. As yet there was no sign of illness or decay. But could Pen read in the pouched eyes something more than a gradual progress towards age?

She behaved towards Soames with easy familiarity, as if she had known him all her life. She was neither timid nor impudent nor ingratiating; and yet something in her manner suggested that she knew every secret that he hid from his wife. There could be no doubt that she was as full of understanding as of craft. And, dammit, Soames responded with comparable openness and enigmatic reserve, like a man who at one glance had read a character, respected it, disliked it—or at least remained unmoved by it—and accepted Pen as he would have done his own sister. Asked whether he found her interesting, he replied: 'She's adorable, of course; a heart-breaker.'

This verdict recurred to Constance's mind one afternoon when she and Pen were sitting together after tea in the Chelsea drawing-room where Rory, now forgotten, had first heard of Carl's existence and death. The room had been newly painted and papered in cream and gold, with fine light blue velvet

curtains and elegantly-upholstered chairs. It was as far away as
possible from the Rectory or that flat in Battersea in which the
Rectory furniture looked elephantine.

Evening was at hand; the sisters were in the comfortable glow
of a coal fire. Constance, seated in her own chair, could see Pen's
face, half-lighted and half-shadowed as the flames rose and sank,
and the slim body curled on the hearthrug like a child.

Lovely girl! Lovely! And in this atmosphere of peace more
dear than ever. It was hard to imagine her in wartime, suffering
the hardships of unpleasant surroundings, certainly on occasion
of physical danger. Was she really as adorable as Soames thought,
and as she now seemed? Constance had once, in anger, struck
her for a devilish impersonation; many times since, exasperation
would have produced a similar blow, if blows had been part of
the Rotherham pattern; but now curiosity was joined with
love.

What passed in Pen's mind? Thoughts of lovers? Was she
still a virgin? What had she been doing throughout the War?

This last question, at least, could be put. It was put, in a carefully careless way which disguised intense curiosity.

'Oh, I've been all over the place,' answered Pen. 'Camps in
England; quite a long time in India; Egypt . . . I've done all sorts
of things; and learned a lot about human nature.'

'Been a good girl, I hope?'

'I took you for my model, dear Connie!'

'You couldn't have done better. And what are you going
to do now?'

'Rep, for a time. I think I shall like it. I played all sorts of parts
in the shows we got up; and did rather well in them.'

'I'm not surprised. Skits, I suppose.'

'No, not always. I played your part in Tom's *Clothes and
the Woman*.'

A spasm of jealousy shot through Constance. Her tone was
quite disagreeable.

' "Tom"? Do you know him as well as that?'

'It was all very informal.' Pen was calm. It afterwards occurred to Constance that the reply could have been evasive. At present her thoughts were otherwise occupied.

'Was that one of your successes?'

'It's a very amusing play. The sort that men like.'

'What, because it ridicules women?'

'Connie! It's a sort of school for charm!'

Constance laughed, not at all unpleasantly.

'I wish I'd seen you. Did you burlesque me?'

'I played it absolutely straight. Some of your business, of course. They knew I was your sister.'

'Yes, they'd know that. They'd seen photographs, I suppose.'

'They were seeing them all the time. The impression was that *you* were doing rather well, too.'

'I've had my days,' admitted Constance, rather smugly. 'In the real theatre.'

'And with Soames? That was a tremendous event.'

'What, marrying him? We kept it very quiet.'

'Still, it was news. He's got a tremendous reputation everywhere. Rather overwhelming. Do you think it could prove—in some way—a disadvantage to you?'

'What, in making me groovy? Is that what you've been told?' Constance was alert with suspicion.

'Yes. One or two of your friends.'

'Any in particular? Linda? Celia Boniface? "Poor old Connie"?'

'Far from that. All singing paeans. But I sometimes fear that with actresses loyalty is a form of spitefulness.'

'Don't I know! Some of them are real cats.'

'And though you're very good indeed—very good—in this new play, the part's fairly silly.'

It was the same story, differently expressed! And the story was true! Part silly; therefore one's self discredited. Hitherto the women she had played, however unscrupulous, had been triumphant; this one, a wanton, cried in ignominy. She had seen that all along. Constance brooded. Then she said abruptly:

'I wish Tom Waring would write another play for me. He

said he would, you know. Before the War. Soames is quite unselfish. He wouldn't mind standing back. Have you been seeing Tom?'

Pen's face was unreadable.

'He's been about. Something to do with his Army job. His stammer's better, by the way. It was always an affectation.'

'A silly one. Was he there when you played *Clothes and the Woman?*'

'Yes. Connie, I must go. It's practically dark; and I have to see Digby Furness. He wants me to play one of Chekhov's "three sisters".' She rose to her feet with the grace of a ballerina.

Constance exclaimed: 'Did he write about sisters? I thought it was only dismal stuff about an orchard. Oh, he's good, is he? Intellectual! Carl would have been pleased.'

The response was a quick look.

'You still think of Carl?'

'One doesn't altogether forget one's husbands, I find.'

'But you don't regret him?'

'I expect I shall feel terrible remorse when I'm sixty.'

'Pretty far ahead,' commented Pen, drily. 'Still, he's remembered. Look here, I'm going. I'll let you know what Digby decides. He's taking the company here and there, hoping to settle in or near the West End in a couple of months. I suppose *Triple Harness* will run so long?'

'I don't know. Soames says it's picking up. But if you see Tom you might sound him about a play for me. Soames would produce, of course, if I liked it.'

Pen's grimace was delightful. She paused in consideration, eyes downcast and lips pressed together, reminding Constance of her performance as Robin Goodfellow long ago at Pickering's. What was the word? Genius? In one's sister? How absurd! Then, waving her hand in farewell, she was gone, leaving doubt behind her.

'I feel as if I'd been caught on the wrong foot,' reflected Constance.

If Pen was seeing Digby Furness, she obviously was not going straight to his office or hotel. Otherwise she would have spent a short time in prinking, so as to impress him. Furness was a pretentious creature, with pots of money; the sort who could have given Carl a start if he had cared to do so. Probably Carl had argued with him. Why do Chekhov? How many sisters had he written about? Why had Pen asked that question about Carl? It hadn't been malicious. Carl had kept in touch with Pen, sending no message at any time to the wife he had deserted. Whose fault was that? A ridiculous question!'

Where was Pen staying? Had she been evasive over Tom Waring? 'He's been about' might mean anything; certainly more than a single encounter. He had watched Pen in *Clothes and the Woman*. What did he think she made of the part—'my part'? Not a word said as to that . . .

'All very peculiar!' observed Constance, to the empty drawing-room. 'Why hasn't Tom Waring been to see me? After all, I created the part, and made his reputation. My name's outside the theatre tonight in letters as big as Soames's. Compared with me, Pen's a beginner. She's jolly pleased with herself. This sisters play won't run if it's anything like the one about the old man boxed in a deserted house. Too morbid. She won't make a name out of Rep. Or will she? Funny that I should be so uneasy . . .'

The room had grown dark. No flame rose from a sunken fire. Driven by restlessness she jumped up to switch on some vivid illumination.

## 2

That night, after the second act, Tom came round to Soames's dressing-room, and was brought to see Constance. Already dressed for the stage, and resting in a chair with a book of verse in her hands, she looked dreamily up, as she might have done for a photographer; and this seemed to amuse the newcomer. He smiled broadly, glancing quickly at the book and a big portrait of Soames which hung on the opposite wall. Since there was ribaldry in his expression, she hardened defensively. Evidently he thought her pretentious. She supposed all actresses, to him, were pretentious. Most of them were.

She at once recognised Tom. His wavy fair hair had been cropped, the small lines about the corners of his laughing eyes were etched deeper by observation and merriment under a hot sun; but he was unquestionably the stammering author of *Clothes and the Woman*, if not the constrained junior of that unfortunate Wilmerton humiliation. Linking his brown skin with Pen's comparable tan, she thought: 'Pen told him to come. After what I said. She's seen him this evening. She knows him better than she admitted, little minx! However, that's as may be. I shan't mention her.'

Beside Soames, Tom appeared slight. Compared with Soames's aspect of ripe tolerance, his mischievously quick glance suggested a flibbertigibbet, unreliable in act or word, looking everywhere for private vanities, and ready to sacrifice anybody and anything to a joke. Another wicked little wretch! Nevertheless he had charm. In addition to the smile which was almost broad enough to be called a grin, there was a slight, confident cock of the head, and something attractive in the movement of the shoulders and arms leading to brown well-shaped hands. The hands, in particular, caught her eye as indications of temperament. They were beautiful; very small, quick, and long-fingered.

'He's improved,' thought Constance. 'What the War's done! First Pen, and now this happy boy. It's aged poor Soames!' The comparison of one man with the other was instinctive and, for reasons known only to herself, saddening. Thought of Soames's loss of radiance was becoming obsessive.

'I've been admiring you from the b-back of the Circle,' announced Tom. So the stammer was being used again, to ingratiate himself, or perhaps from nervousness.

'Recalling your first triumph?' she asked, meaning to introduce at once the subject chiefly in her mind. She included Soames in the reference.

'D-delighting in the thought of seeing you both together,' was Tom's reply. Was it insincere? Before she could do more than feel the suspicion he continued: 'S-sweeping the years away, as if they'd n-never been.' He turned gracefully, and with respect, to Soames. 'I go further back—to our first meeting, and your kindness to a b-beginner.'

A beginner! Constance took a quick breath. He must have felt as she did on that fateful morning; the troglodyte; the climbed stairs; the first sight of a superlatively kind man who set her instantly at ease. Soames! Dear Soames! No awe of him remained; her thankful gratitude was gone; its place had been taken, first by admiration of his sureness as a director, then by triumph at her power over him, and now by almost maternal attachment. But Tom gave no sign that he noted, as she had done in the comparison with himself, Soames's increased girth and diminished vigour. Therefore she must show only gaiety.

'We're a magnificent trio!' she cried. 'What a good night that was!'

'Yes,' ejaculated Soames. 'I remember it.' He was thoughtful.

'Y-you must remember many such. But to us ... to Constance and myself ...'

Too dangerous! Too dangerous! He would make Soames feel an old man!

'I've had a few since then,' Constance exclaimed. 'While you were away, Tom. You wouldn't know about them. And of course you were honoured that night by an almost regal summons. I wasn't. Not a word. No summons; no message. That was because I had no ideas. Your ideas had made an impression. I never heard if they found favour. Did they?'

'They w-were brushed aside. They w-weren't as good as his own. And ... and there were too many of them!'

'Nonsense! There can never be too many ideas. I hope you've come back full of hundreds more—for splendid plays!'

Laughing, he pretended to have lost the use of his pen. How his eyes closed when he laughed! They were quite heavy-lidded. But through the slits the eyes themselves glowed with life. She had never seen any brighter. What colour were they? Was it an agate grey? She must discover!

'I w-wasn't one of the l-literary boys,' he exclaimed. 'Thumbing out the dactyls, hunting up onomatops, cursing the generals in rhyme! I was j-just a soldier—a s-sergeant until they found me out. Th-then I was made a dogsbody.'

'What did they find out? I'm sure you did everything well.' She deliberately fixed him with her own eyes of ardent blue to force the discovery she needed. Yes, agate! No, blue! Impossible to decide! 'Now you're demobbed, you'll be able to say what a soldier knows but can't say.'

'It's a restricted language. Fortunately, I had my own. I gave eloquent lectures.'

'Really? I can't imagine it. But you will come back to plays, won't you?'

Tom shrugged.

'I've lost my innocence, and grown stodgy,' he said.

'Not too stodgy, from the way you say that. In any case, you can put your stodginess, as you call it, into plays. What we loved about *Clothes and the Woman* was the wisdom under its wit. After four years of wonderful experience, your mind must be re-stored.'

'My mind'—he pretended to sigh—'Oh, dear me; a vacuum.'

Soames, having listened abstractedly to the exchange, said in his deepest voice:

'If there is anything we can do to help you, I hope you'll give us that privilege.'

Constance, provoked by his gravity, and Tom's silent mockery of it, protested with a little temper.

'All I'm asking is that you should write us something equal to *Clothes and the Woman*.'

'Just like that, eh? Five minutes; and it's done,' was the unexpected crisp reply. There was no stammer and no mischief;

but a serious directness. 'The social atmosphere's changed. I haven't caught up yet. Women have changed ...'

'They haven't changed since the Garden of Eden. They've only got more dressy. There you are; a ready-made theme!'

'Too reach-me-down. The fig leaf is out of date; and, unlike our gallant soldiers, Adam was a cad!'

'Say so! *Adam and Eve*. Your new play!'

'My new play!' It was the comment of one who had conceived a nonsensical but attractive idea.

'You're a young man,' added Soames, as one waking from reverie. 'Not desiccated, as I am.'

'You're not desiccated, Soames.' Constance was more alarmed than impatient. 'And Tom mustn't give you a dessicated part. Just the old Adam; mature, wise.' Her imagination had been caught by the idea for a play; but she was deeply troubled by Soames's hint of superannuation. Bookings were probably worse than she had guessed, and the outlook was therefore darker. He was seeing himself—Marie Biggs had prophetically done the same thing—as finished; perhaps considering ghastly 'farewell' tours in England, South Africa, Australia. Then 'a little folding of the hands in sleep'. Oh, God! That would be intolerable! It was Hell to be dependent on popular whim! 'All we need is a vital play—from Tom. It's his duty, in gratitude; and for his own good!'

Soames remained impassive. He turned to Tom.

'Do you feel this play of ours is old-fashioned? I've been told it is.'

'An-an-antediluvian.' The stammer—for effect—was back. Silly boy!

'Hm. Fresh eyes. And judgment already at work. That shows the artist in you is active. Splendid! You'll go home full of ideas, determined to show the fogies how to write a model play.'

'For us,' interpolated Constance. 'You'll bring it in next week —or the week after; and we shall extol you ...'

Soames continued to address Tom.

'Not as soon as that, I hope. Take your time. You'll stay to the end of this one, I hope. As Constance's favourite poet says, "the best is yet to be". The *dénouement* always takes the audience by surprise. It's very effective.'

Constance's heart sank. She saw the movement of Tom's disrespectful eyes towards her book, and heard his too-bland reply to uncharacteristic fatuity. She wanted to cry out: 'He's not like that, Tom! Not at all like that!' But it was too late. Tom said:

'Yes, I've heard about the *dénouement*—from Pen!'

Pen! Not sentimentally, though. The minx must have sneered at the *dénouement*. Quite right; but abominably supercilious of her. The result of Chekhov to the head! She'd fallen into the new intellectual priggery! Was Tom involved with Digby Furness? They would lose him. And he—less important to herself, but still lamentable—would lose his way in the snob labyrinth.

'You won't get too Parnassian, will you, Tom!' she entreated, as if her flying thoughts had really been spoken. Did he appreciate what she meant? He smiled. Not a villain; but when one was in earnest, another person's smile could be devastating.

'No,' answered Tom, smiling at her. 'Feet on the ground. Feet on the ground. Th-that's me!'

'Where's your head, though?'

'Shoulder high.' He compared their almost identical heights, his smile deepening.

If he looked like that at Pen he would be irresistible. She hoped he didn't. How sharp all jealousy became! Of course he was much too charming ever to be a prig. But did the smile hide a sneer at herself?

'I'm terribly keen on this!' she exclaimed. 'For your sake, as well as ours.'

'Y-you have a heart of gold,' answered Tom. 'Pen has always said so.'

'How kind of her! But how horribly condescending!'

A bell, warning them that the stage waited, rang as she received this curious intimation; and in the hurry of the moment she had no time to reflect upon it. She could only repeat: 'Remember: Adam and Eve;' and add ' "male and female created He them",' before Soames, always punctual, strode to the door. They did not see Tom again that night.

After the show, Soames and Constance went home together. She took his arm as they sat side by side in the car; but both were very tired and they did not speak. After she had changed her dress she returned to the drawing-room to find him pouring neat whisky into a tumbler. His hand shook; and she was shocked at both sights. The swallowing of this draught, however, seemed to produce revived energy, which showed in a deep breath of satisfaction.

'Better now,' he exclaimed, setting down the tumbler. 'I find the strain of two performances in a day severe.'

'Could we cut out the matinée?'

'No. I must carry on.'

'But if . . . this . . .' She indicated the glass. 'Is it the only way?'

'For me, yes. It's quite all right, you know, darling.'

'I only worry about the consequences. What about a doctor?'

'Look! I despise the breed. One day I'll tell you what they did to my mother.' He held up the hand, which had grown miraculously steady.

She would not protest. The result of a warning from herself could be, not sullenness, which was foreign to his nature, but a return to exhaustion. She must get a doctor to catch him unawares. Which one?

'Yes, wonderful. It isn't only overwork, is it?'

'No.' He drank no more; but sank heavily into a chair. 'There comes a time—every artist knows it—when either the capacity to work or the welcome given to that work diminishes. I was out of the theatre for nearly four years.'

'Because you thought it your duty—your patriotic duty—to do something else.'

'Not quite as simple as that, Connie. Vanity does its work.

All old men were shamed by the loss of young lives. I wanted to show I wasn't old.'

'You're still not old.'

'No, I'm not old.' He became thoughtful. 'No, not old. Young Tom hit the nail on the head when he said, a couple of hours ago, that the world had changed. He thinks this play isn't good enough, you know.'

'It's not. I've felt it all along. That's because I don't like my own part.'

'Five or six years ago you'd have liked it; and I could have carried the play.'

'You mean, I can't?'

'You're playing better than ever. I think I am—up to a point. But I have to work harder; and the dear perceptive audiences—never under-rate them, darling; like British juries, they're always right for the wrong reasons—feel it by instinct. They detect the strain. Also, they've lived a century in four years; and Garrick himself, Siddons herself, couldn't break into a new era. Audiences don't know exactly what they want; they know they need change.'

'All the more reason for getting young Tom, as you call him, back to work.'

Soames looked up at her—she was standing before the fire in dishabille—with a slow smile of affection.

'Yes, you pressed him rather hard,' he muttered.

'Too hard, do you think?'

'I wondered. He's like a racehorse—or a genius. Very sensitive; not, I think, to be driven. I may be wrong. You evidently felt he should be reminded of his duty.'

Constance warmed in rebellion; but she stifled a retort.

'You know more about psychology than I do,' she said, after a while. 'I thought he rose a little to *Adam and Eve*. Do you think I should let him go? What if this play has to close down?'

'More whisky,' was Soames's comment.

'No more! No more!' Misunderstanding the speech, she raised a protesting hand.

'I meant that I should have to work still harder.'

'Or I?'

He must have realised that in her ears he had sounded egotistical; for without alteration of tone he said:

'An old pro always exaggerates his own importance. An occupational disease. In a sense, that's been forced on me by Marrington and Sealby. It's their money. They've invested it in me, as, during the War, Sparkes did in you. You want to go back to Sparkes?'

'I want to stay with you,' said Constance.' Whatever happens. I don't care for Sparkes. I actively dislike Sealby. I think he's a mean little exploiter. Marrington is at least a gentleman.'

'Largely veneer, I think. Very genial in sunshine; under cloud the smile is briefer.'

'He's made a lot of money out of you, Soames.'

'Businessmen have bad memories, child.'

Child! The word made her shudder. It held unbearable implications.

'And no imagination, either,' she cried, roughly. 'They don't grasp the reason women demanded the vote. It was simply a refusal to be treated as children or incompetents any longer. After all, they worked like demons during the War.'

Soames made no reply. Then, as if symbolically, he refilled his glass, while Constance watched, her breath coming fast and her sudden anger fading into something near to despair. She had no power over him, no talent, no place in the world. Without some effort on her part they would both sink.

'I shall talk to Tom again,' she said. 'I won't press him. I'll be a paragon of tact. But I'll make him write us a play for the new era!'

'Amen,' replied Soames, draining his glass. 'And now, darling, we must get to bed.'

## 3

That talk had consequences which were not immediately to be seen. Constance pondered them whenever she was awake, even in the midst of difficulties arising from the quarrels between otherwise unimportant people at home and in the theatre. First her cook threw a rolling-pin at Sybil, who gave notice and had to be coaxed back into good humour. Then two Irish stage hands had a fight over the authorship of the New Testament, which delayed the rise of the curtain for ten minutes, made the audience restive, and gave her a *migraine* lasting through the following day. And finally, while still fretting over these unnecessary disturbances, she was bewildered by Pen.

Pen's flying visits, treasured because of their rarity, brought news of developments in the Digby Furness situation. Digby had found a theatre of sorts in Kentish Town. He had also engaged Pen for a guaranteed four weeks to play the part of Irina, in Chekhov's *The Three Sisters*; and Constance, with deepening depression, had been glancing through the typescript while they talked in the drawing-room. Pen, meanwhile, having unaccountably produced from her handbag some cards, played a game of patience on a small table.

'But what's it all about?' grumbled Constance, who wanted Pen's undivided attention.

'This patience? I'm practising. Irina has to set out the cards; and I want to do it properly.'

'No; I mean the play. Apparently everybody's miserable, and you're going away to teach and you plan to work and work and work. But life's a great mystery to you. You seem to dress in white, although it's going to snow. People called Masha and Olga and I don't know what. One of them says "We've got to live", as if living was all wretchedness. Well, that's not true, you know. Where's the drama?'

Pen was smiling at this lament.

'Not at all like *Triple Harness*, is it?' she asked, mischievously.

'There is a mean,' objected Constance. 'Of course, a single part, without the context, is bound to read stupidly; but this hopelessness gives me the pip. Oh, Pen, I'm in a dismal enough state, as it is. I'm not going away, presumably into limbo, like Irina; but at this moment I find life very trying, and her part'— She tapped the typescript—'doesn't make it any more intelligible.'

'I don't expect you'd make much of the whole play,' observed Pen, laying one card on another.

'Don't condescend! It's growing on you. Anybody would think I was a cretin. Well, I feel a bit of a cretin. I've had fools to tackle, and I've been reading a lot of plays—all crude or pretentious, quite impossible. So my spirits are down.'

'Poor Connie! This means *Triple Harness* is on its last legs, I suppose?'

'They're talking about it this afternoon—Soames, Marrington, and Sealby; with some wretched accountant who's been brought in. They're trying to make out that Soames is a bad manager. Cuts. Cuts. Cuts. All of the meanest kind. Meanwhile Marrington's bought himself a new yacht. By the way, have you seen Tom lately?'

She had not meant to spring the question; but it sounded like one of those shot by barristers in cross-examination.

'He's in Cornwall,' was the composed reply. Pen was never taken by surprise.

'What doing? Do you know?'

'Amusing himself, I should think.'

This was infuriating.

'He ought to be like this miserable Irina; work, work, work. Do you make anything of the part?'

'Yes; it's rather colourless at first, but I've been carried away by it. You find more and more at every rehearsal. Quite marvellous. The most sharply-drawn character is Irina's sister-in-law, who's a devil. Digby's given it to a girl called Fanny Robins.'

'Oh, I've seen her. Blonde, isn't she? Putting on weight?'

'I get an impression. It's not a sympathetic part.'

'Are any of them?'

'There are some wonderful men, mostly eccentric. They gamble, get drunk, philosophise, and shoot each other.'

'Huh! What a play!'

'Tom's mad about it. He says Chekhov is so good that he feels it's useless to go on writing.'

Constance was horrified.

'Oh, we can't have that! It's just an excuse for laziness. I do wish I could get hold of him. Did he tell you about my brilliant idea?'

'Not a word.' Pen, who had continued with her game of patience, made two or three deliberate moves, and swept the pack together. 'I shall never play patience for my own satisfaction. It's a game for aged bachelors, with endless time on their hands.'

'Tom will play it when he's eighty. If he's not in an Institution by them.'

Pen smiled quietly.

'Yes, I expect he will. I'll warn him about the Institution.'

'Don't say anything that will put him against me. I want that play.'

'I hope you'll like it when you get it,' replied Pen, very ominously indeed.

'Why, do you think I shan't?'

'I haven't the faintest idea.' It was quite good-natured; but Constance, already full of trouble, suffered deeply from what she interpreted as cruel indifference. She would not protest.

'Do you play this game of patience on the stage? Does it lead to anything?'

'Completely pointless, darling. Except for its compassionate irony. I put out the cards. It's just something to do. The author's stage direction. One of the men has to be always pulling a newspaper out of his pocket.'

'Extraordinary! That's what men do in Jane Austen. Darcy, for instance, before proposing to Elizabeth. Very ill-bred, I think.'

'Yes. Carl always read a book.'

Constance refused to answer what she took to be a jibe. She said:

'What does Tom do? I mean, when he's not talking?'

Pen smiled her unreadable smile.

'He's never self-conscious. He just sits grinning.'

'Does he talk much to you?'

'Chiefly to Digby or another man, Sydney Potter. Sydney's the one with the newspaper. I like him. Digby's a curious character; one of those men who prepare impromptus overnight. He chews his words.'

'I know. He's conceited. What sort of producer is he?'

'Strict. Everything precise. His fault's a lack of spontaneity. But the result's good. Rather like a game of chess.'

'Soames is able to act what he wants one to do. It's a help; and he's always very patient. Does Tom like Digby?'

'I couldn't say. He's secretive. When he writes, he puts his hand over the paper, so that nobody, even himself, shall see what he's written.'

'A miser! That's not a good trait, is it? I wish to goodness he'd write that play. Do you think he will?'

Pen offered no reassurance.

'He's more complex than he appears. Like the other half of Carl. But it's a considerably larger half.'

She put the cards together, resumed possession of her type-script, stood up, hesitated, and prepared to leave. To Constance's great surprise, she impulsively kissed in farewell; and, without looking back, departed.

That was very strange, wasn't it? It suggested that, under the calm, there might be real affection, or even storm. 'More complex than he appears': that was true of most people, including Pen, who offered an enigma for solution. Was she in love with Tom, and in doubt as to his feeling? 'Secretive.' 'Complex.' Apparently he talked, not to Pen, but to the other men. Why? With the object of keeping her guessing? . . . No, if Pen fell in love, she'd produce infatuation in any man. But she might be in doubt as to herself? That was something new, wasn't it?

'Well, well, well!' said Constance. She did not know why she said it; several emotions were moving simultaneously in her bosom, and she understood none of them. All, however, were disturbing.

## 4

She was still thoughtful when Soames returned from his meeting with the partners and their accountant. He looked tired; but when Constance asked if anything had been decided he said briefly that the four were to meet again at the weekend. He then withdrew, to rest before the evening performance of *Triple Harness*, leaving her unsatisfied.

'Nobody tells me anything,' she reflected. 'And to somebody completely open as I am, that's humiliating. Luckily, I'm exceptionally good-humoured.'

She dwelt for a time upon this aspect of her nature, drank another cup of tea, which made her grimace, and tried to read a new novel. The book had been sent, with a flattering inscription, by the author, whom she had met at a weekend party; so as a clergyman's daughter she felt bound to read it and express an opinion. Otherwise, having lately plodded through so many boring plays, she would have preferred to close her eyes.

'These things are meant for people whose lives are meaningless,' she decided, after a while. 'Well, really empty, I suppose. Unless you take them as sedatives or anodynes. Or for stimulation, as Soames takes whisky . . . Poor Soames. He's tired; probably ill. I'm worried about him. Wretched people, tiring him more and more with their perpetual talk of money. We shall have to spend less; but how's that to be done?'

With such ponderings she filled the time until Soames came to say they must leave for the theatre; and when, during their drive, he remained speechless she was further disquieted. Reserve on his part was always a bad sign. It meant that he, like a good but ridiculous man, was trying not to frighten her.

'So stoical!' she thought. 'And so frightening! The masculine complex! I must cure myself of this habit of saying "complex." It's an evasive word . . .'

She watched Soames, whenever possible, during the performance; but she was too much engaged with her part to risk loss of concentration. Therefore she was no wiser about his state than before. Fortunately the show went smoothly, the house was good, and the audience was so responsive that there was warm applause at the end. She hoped Marrington or Sealby was in front, to draw favourable conclusions. Thank God there had been no matinée!

She and Soames embraced as usual for the final *rapprochement*, and, hand-in-hand for the calls, were again in each other's arms as the footlights darkened, after which they separated amid the bustle of stage clearance, and met again, ready for home, in Constance's dressing-room. A small knot of admirers waited at the stage door, with murmurs of applause and goodwill; the wind, she afterwards remembered, was very cold; they drove past the crowds in Piccadilly Circus and by empty streets to Chelsea. No word came from Soames.

Anxiety gave rise to foreboding. She was oppressed by a sense that everything had happened before, and assailed by sudden memory of wartime darkness. This journey had been made during an air attack, in the company of some attractive man—a lover;— and calamity had attended the drive. What had happened on that former occasion? She had never seen the man since. Rory! He had been killed. A sick feeling of disappointment and loss caused her to shiver and move close to Soames, thankful to touch the roughness of his tweed overcoat. It was necessary to break the silence.

'Pen came this afternoon,' she said quickly. 'We had tea together. Some ridiculous nonsense about a game of patience. She described Digby Furness as a pedant.' Hearing no reply, she found that Soames was leaning back with his eyes closed. 'Are you all right?'

'Tired,' he drowsily answered. 'Go on talking. I like it.'

She slipped her hand within his arm.

'I find Pen stimulating. I'm always glad to see her; but I'm depressed after she's gone. Something in her temperament. I was asking about this play of Chekhov's. It ends with her lover being shot in a duel. I remember seeing a weird performance of another play of his—what was it called? *The Seagull?*—just before the War. That ended, like this one, with a young man getting shot; but I think he shot himself. Wouldn't you call that repetitive invention? There was also a curious temperamental woman, like the one in the play about an orchard. Everybody seems to be in despair; and very bored and hopeless. You get the impression that domestic life in Russia must be one long yawn.'

As if sympathetically, Soames yawned. She saw, or imagined, that in the light of a street lamp the hand raised to his mouth trembled. She must, after all, have been boring him; and his weariness always filled her with consternation. Being tired herself, she had talked at random. Her father had always been bored by her; she had seen him—not frown, but gaze at her apathetically as he might have done at a parrot. This in spite of the fact that she had held her tongue when he was present.

She now stopped talking; but continued in reverie to justify herself.

'It's funny, because I hardly ever bore myself. I suppose it's vitality. Soames is at a low ebb after the show, poor darling. I shan't say any more, unless he begs me to. Merciful of me!' She held up her free, unringed hand, which was perfectly steady and very white. 'Not like Pen's brown paw,' she thought. 'Her skin's always been dark. I don't think white will suit her.' The words 'nor black, either' were repressed. They would suggest death. 'Not a happy subject; though people do die, of course, all the time. I shan't. I shall go on living, and acting, for another half-century. Tom thinks we're antediluvian. He's mad on Chekhov,

silly boy. That won't last. I wonder what the fashion in plays
will be in nineteen-seventy?'

The car had stopped. They had reached home. She saw that
Soames leaned heavily on Sewell's arm, saw Sewell's tanned old
face under the peaked cap, noticed how, after helping her to
alight, he turned as if to offer further support to Soames. He
had jumped to some conclusion. That was bad. Soames, of
course, waved him impatiently away; but there must have been
some cause for Sewell's turn. Probably Soames was cramped
after the journey, for his steps were uncertain; a fact which
produced an exchange of glances between Sewell and herself
and, on her part, a faintly shaken head. Then, with three 'good-
nights,' they were indoors. It was just midnight.

A dimmed light, as usual, made the hall and stairs a region of
ghostly shadow, in which a tired man might stumble; so Constance's first act was to switch on additional illumination. She
heard Soames draw a quick breath, as of annoyance at officious-
ness; but when she saw the way he gripped the stair-rail she
knew she had done right. Their progress was very slow. It
ended when both reached the drawing-room and she helped to
relieve Soames of his heavy coat.

'Well!' he cried, in satisfaction at an achievement. 'Thank
you, darling.'

That was all. A fire burned in the grate; bottles and glasses
stood on a tray, together with some evening newspapers. Soames
did not go straight to the tray, as she expected; but stood dazedly
looking round the room, as if it were an unfamiliar place to
which he had inexplicably been brought. Her impulse was to
lead him to a chair. This she controlled, for fear of evoking
further impatience. Impatience itself, so rare in this most equable
of men, was proof that he was unwell and probably much
disturbed in spirit. Evidently he was reconsidering what had
been said, or hinted, that afternoon; for she heard him mutter
some unintelligible words in an angry undertone.

Slipping away, therefore, to discard her outdoor clothes, she went into the bedroom, leaving both doors open in case he called, and moving so swiftly that she could have been absent for no more than three or four minutes. Even so, she was not quick enough.

'Connie!' It was hoarse; hardly recognisable.

'Coming!' she cried, and darted to the door.

She had not reached it when the sound of a heavy fall struck her ears and filled her with panic.

'Just as I thought! Just as I thought!' she ejaculated. 'Those brutes!'

Soames was lying as if, after calling her, he had sunk to his knees and rolled over. His face was crimson; his breathing resembled a heavy snore; he was insensible. Every fear she had experienced on his account was confirmed; and although she rushed to his side and knelt there she was too confused to decide at once what should be done. It was only after a moment of anguish that she began to tear at his collar, flinging aside the tie, muttering wildly, and trying to remember what she had read about such mishaps. She was afraid that, by choking, he would suffocate himself: but by degrees she managed to turn his head to one side, wondering all the time whether she was making mistake after fatal mistake.

Her next act was to call Sybil, who never went to bed until she knew that they would need her no longer that day, and she now very sleepily appeared. At sight of the prostrate figure, Sybil screamed and turned white; but she did not lose her head nor make any loud lament. Obeying an instruction, she brought a big jug of cold water and a sponge, kneeling and watching while Constance did what she supposed to be the best thing and slapped water on the crimson face and brow.

'Do you know if there's a doctor quite near?' whispered Constance. 'You had a doctor, didn't you?'

'Yes. Dr Jones.' Sybil's tone was hushed, as if she shared an instinctive belief that Soames must not hear.

'Could you find his name in the telephone book? Ask him to come at once? Make him understand that it's urgent. And I think we have to have some hot bottles for the feet. Can you do that? Quickly? I'll lay the sponge on his forehead, and take off his shoes and socks. Come back and tell me what the doctor says. Then bring the hot bottles. Cook might be able to fill them, if you called her.'

'I don't want to go to Cook, ma'am. She's been in one of her mad fits. I'll manage it all.'

'Good heavens! Fancy a mad cook at this time! All right. Be as quick as you can!'

Sybil scrambled ungracefully to her feet, like a hoyden. Constance, first thinking with self-reproach 'I leave everything to Sybil. Not fair,' allowed the dripping sponge to continue its work, wrapped her dressing-gown hastily about Soames, and followed to the telephone, where she was able to communicate with the doctor and secure his immediate attendance. Meanwhile Sybil prepared the bottles. The two knelt again by the insensible body.

# SCENE ELEVEN

## *Defeat*

### I

THEY had the grace to come and see her; Sealby, a little thin man whose eyes raked everywhere, from the hardly visible lobes of her ears to the new silver figurine sent recently by an enthusiast. Marrington, tall, bald, plumply pink-faced, obviously Public School, Varsity, and City, with delightful manners and a surprisingly hoarse, high-pitched voice. Marrington entered first; but Sealby was so much quicker in movement that he came from behind with a rush. He was like a busy tug under the lee of a liner.

Both assumed expressions of sympathy as she rose to greet them; but she knew they had come with their hard minds resolved, not considering her as a woman desperately in need of counsel, nor in consternation at the shock of Soames's illness. She imagined the muttered words: 'What do we do now? Button our pockets. Treat her as what she is, a widow with no claims on us at all. Think of ourselves.' What they had decided was whether it was to their business advantage to run a play, or take it straight off, now that the chief male actor was as good as dead.

Constance was tempted to say outright: 'I hope you gentlemen realise that your unmerciful bargaining and avarice brought about this haemorrhage. He was worrying all the time over his responsibility to you—not to himself, not to me—but to you alone. If he dies, you'll have killed him; and I shall never forgive you.' The words remained unspoken.

'My dear Constance.' Marrington took her cold hand in both his own warm ones. As always, he was the gallant gentleman whose manners had pleased her at their first encounter.

'Terrible! Terrible!' piped Sealby. 'Just when things were looking up!' His hand, perceptibly less warm, felt like dry bones.

'We offer you our most tender sympathy,' said Marrington.

'We do indeed!' confirmed Sealby. 'Terrible!'

'Thank you. Thank you, both. Do sit down, Claude. And you, Harold. It is very kind of you to come.'

Constance had left her cheeks pale. She had not wept; and she did not now weep. After long and sometimes despairing wakefulness while the slow-speaking Scottish doctor made his examination and insisted that Soames should be taken immediately to hospital, while further examination followed, and while messages were sent to Marrington and Sealby, she had slept until re-awakened by Sybil at eleven o'clock. Now, having rested, she was less numbed but still distraught by the loss of all worldly protection.

She was more alone than she had ever been. They would know that. She must therefore deny their knowledge by a marble composure. If, looking for weakness or instability, they thought her heartless, that would be to her advantage. She must seem hard, watchful, and resolute. They would propose—having so decided beforehand—to dictate a decision—either to use Soames's illness as an excuse to shut down at once or to insist upon their own substitute. The first would be an affront to herself—'*you* can't draw the public'; the second, unless the substitute actor were of the highest standing, would justify them in saying 'We're sorry. We must close. Goodbye. Be a good girl.' Soames would be a helpless invalid; her power, her means, her prospects destroyed, she would be back where she began, waiting for employment, as Carl had waited for employment. These men would callously leave her high and dry.

She had not, as yet, told Pen, nor consulted Blackstone. Marrington and Sealby had been roused from their beds because they were Soames's 'partners' (meaning 'exploiters'). She knew that Soames's understudy, Syd Durling, had the memory and build for the part; no more. His gestures would mimic Soames's; he would feed her with Soames's lines, but he had not the talent to give Soames's native magnanimity to the final scene. That damned scene, at which Pen and Tom scoffed, would be revealed in its true banality. It would be disagreeable to her, as a woman, to accept in his arms a shame barely tolerable with Soames himself. What then?

'Well, we've been to the hospital; he's still unconscious.' This was grizzled by Sealby, who added: 'Doesn't seem very hopeful.'

'Not, certainly, of an *early* recovery,' amended Marrington, wincing at his companion's crudity. 'But we must all hope—we do all hope—that, given rest and quiet . . . He's been taking a great deal out of himself, dear man.'

'Yes, Claude and I have noticed that.' Sealby was bent on keeping to some point of his own. 'We've discussed it. Too much, you know. Too much.'

When Constance made no reply, they were, perhaps a little disconcerted. They were clear as to their own purpose, which was to subdue possible temperamentalism in an actress of talent and reputation who exaggerated both talent and reputation. She imagined Marrington saying 'I think you'd better let me handle her, Harold. I've dealt with women shareholders, who are apt, d'ye know . . .' This would be why Sealby filled the silence by repeating 'too much'. He was parsimonious even in the matter of language.

'We have every sympathy with you, Constance,' Marrington continued, smoothly. 'We came to assure you of our sincere sympathy. It was, in fact, our prime purpose in what you might consider an unseasonable call.'

'Thank you, Claude. Far from unseasonable. A comfort to me. I expect you also wanted to say something else.'

'That, naturally, is true.' He was guilty almost of a whimsicality of manner. 'You've had a great shock, as we all have. We all expected Soames to be fully active for a number of years; but for you the personal relation is of a different order. You're a woman; and his wife. Do you think you would be able, in spite of everything, to appear tonight? It would be very painful; we quite appreciate what it would mean; but we know you're a brave woman, a splendid artist . . .'

'Certainly I must appear. I hadn't thought of doing anything else,' said she.

'Bravo!' Sealby gave a little pipe of relief. 'We're thinking of the public. Only of the public.'

'Yes, of course; the public.'

Her dryness brought Sealby to a halt.

'If we can gain time . . . gain time . . .' he muttered, revealing a love of improvisation. Constance leapt upon the fumble.

'The weekend, you mean? That was to have been used for discussion, with Soames, wasn't it?'

She detected a simultaneous movement, not an exchanged glance, which said: 'She knows that. What else does she know?' Marrington then said:

'We should like to keep the news from the Press. I doubt if it will be possible, with a man of Soames's stature . . .'

'Different if it was me!' ejaculated Sealby. He was brushed aside by Marrington.

'They're in touch with all the hospitals; your own servants . . .'

'Are completely discreet.' Good God, had they not been so throughout the War? She took grim pleasure in the testimony. 'And once the news is out?'

They were still puzzled by her cool directness.

'Ha,' muttered Sealby.

Again Marrington brought his suavity to bear. With an appearance of great frankness, he said:

'This is Friday. There are two performances tomorrow; and the bookings for both are good. In fact, during the last two days —we called at the theatre this morning—they've been promising. If the news became very bad . . . If there seemed no prospect . . .'

'You mean, if Soames dies?'

She heard a gasp.

'That's just it!' cried Sealby, explosively, striking his knee with a skeleton hand. 'Of course we must hope . . .'

'I have no hope at all. None. We must assume he'll never act again.'

Sealby betrayed his mind. He bent forward conspiratorially.

'What's your view of Durling?'

This was the most significant remark he could have made. It told Constance that they secretly believed she could carry the play alone. If they could beat her down on terms, and use Durling on his present pay, they saw the salary bill halved and a period of economy ahead. Misers! She immediately stepped into Soames's place. It should be made impossible for them to dislodge her!

'Durling is capable, and cheap,' she said, coolly; 'but no draw. Had you thought of anybody else?'

'This is an unexpected emergency,' began Marrington: but Sealby, who apparently had set his heart on economy, blurted out the truth.

'We've seen Cotton this morning. He won't. Not his type, he says. Ambrose Tiley is willing; but his idea of salary is grotesque, and he wants a three months guarantee.'

'No,' said Constance. 'That's no good. Even with Ambrose, who after all is a short man' (she threw scorn into the word 'short'), 'three months is impossible. You must consider your shareholders—and directors!'

The relief was obvious. She heard their sighs. They were in awe of her. They had been afraid she would be histrionic, refuse to go on at all, demand the earth, and have to be placated by flattery. They found her practical, seemly, and considerate of those vulnerable pouches, their pockets.

'You're a very wonderful woman, Constance,' exclaimed Marrington.

'Superb!' echoed Sealby. 'A very Portia!'

'I'll play tonight, and both performances tomorrow, whatever happens. Whatever happens. Then we can decide together—on Sunday?'

'That would be admirable,' said Marrington. 'With Durling?'

'With Durling. For a week at least. He's very willing. I'll help him through. But if Soames dies we close down at once?'

'Oh, but wait a minute! Wait a minute!' Sealby was in agony. 'We particularly don't want to lose you, Constance; do we, Claude?'

Marrington was not to be rushed by his apparently more impulsive colleague.

'It's a question of public taste, Constance. If there seemed to be a prospect . . .'

Sealby again interrupted.

'The bookings for next week . . . Excellent . . . I mean, we . . .'

'The thing would be,' replied Constance, 'to put a new play into rehearsal.'

'With you in the lead?' This was Marrington.

'If you think that wise.' She assumed an air of modesty; but her heart was full of triumph.

'Of course. Of course,' cried Sealby. 'But where's the play?'

'I think I can promise the play,' replied Constance.

They were gone. She could think once more, in anguish for Soames, and hurry to the hospital to sit, if possible, beside his bed, or, if that were not allowed, to find out what the doctor thought of his condition. First, however, she must telephone to Pen, the only other person in the world who was really dear to her. She could say to Pen what it was impossible to say to anybody else, even Soames, knowing that it would be understood exactly as it was meant. That was the astonishing thing about Pen; whereas most people brought deep prejudice to every point, she had the imagination to put herself absolutely in one's place; only afterwards judging with the full perception of truth. She was the true critic.

'I'm like that, too,' thought Constance. 'I learn the words;

I meditate on them; I create the part . . . Those two men are both in love with me. If I were a bad woman, I could lead a life of untrammelled sin. Unfortunately I'm a good woman, and only sin occasionally. Also, I want Soames back beside me—for ever.'

She thought of Soames. She thought of Pen. Her heart was heavy for the one and eager for the true sympathy of the other. But her mind was all the time scheming to get the play she was sure Tom was writing for her, and picturing the admiration of audiences, and remembering the farewells exchanged with Marrington and Sealby.

'Goodbye, my dear Constance,' Marrington had said. He again took her hand in both his own larger ones, so that it was swallowed and altogether lost; and as he did this he bent down very gracefully, almost reverently, and kissed her cheek. 'You're a great woman!'

'Constance, I can't but follow Claude's example!' Little Sealby—she believed he must have risen to the tips of his toes—likewise took her hand in skeleton fingers and gave her an avid peck which was like a bite. 'God bless you!'

When the door had closed behind these two middle-aged adorers she could laugh in safety, while ruefully feeling the cheek saluted by Sealby. It was because of this episode that she had seen herself as a potential sinner; but she had no inclination to sin today, nor perhaps ever again. Her laughter past, she returned to gravity, to Soames, and, in relief, to Pen.

'But I must see Tom *at once*!' she exclaimed, suddenly.

## 2

Constance's first impression was that the so-called theatre would never be ready for the opening night of *The Three Sisters*. She stood on what had formerly been a platform, now the stage, and looked sceptically at the auditorium. A little heap of rubble was being tackled by one man whose hand grasped the handle of a spade; an old-fashioned balcony, supported by eight pillars, ran round the hall, and behind it was a tier of plain wooden seats which she assumed to be a gallery. The ceiling above plastered walls was vaulted. But there was no sign as yet of accommodation for stallites and pittites. The floor was merely an expanse.

And yet she was conscious of excitement. Standing beside Pen, and looking down upon this expanse, she was thrilled by all the old delight in theatres. From such a stage one could command an audience in a way that was impossible in any larger building. Granted attention, an actress might count upon her words reaching everybody in that gallery. She instinctively braced herself as if for a performance.

'I suppose there's an echo now,' she said, professionally, to Pen.

'A lovely one. Digby says it will go as soon as the carpet's down and the seats are fixed, but meanwhile it's terribly tempting, as you can guess.' Pen's quick movements, for which she would have little use in a fundamentally static play, showed that she felt comparable excitement. 'Don't you think the place will be ideal for Chekhov?'

'I shiver at the name. It's like a cat's sneeze.'

'It will be graven on your heart, like Bloody Mary's "Calais".'

'Oh, Pen! I don't like to hear you use that word!'

'I know worse words than that, Connie!'

'I'm sure you do. It's prudish of me to find them distasteful—coming from you. I suppose it's the Rectory—and being your elder sister.'

'Pity there are only two of us. I wonder what a third would have been like!'

'Probably barmy. It would have killed Mother. Hullo, they want me off the stage.'

The company was assembling for rehearsal, led by Digby Furness in the now-fashionable slacks and sweater, which Constance, accustomed to Soames's businesslike clothes, regarded as pretentious informality. He was a fattish, squat man, black-haired, with a cock-like strut and a dough-like face, who through illness had seen nothing of the War but was devoted to the theatre. Constance, instinctively aware that he took no amorous interest in women, wondered to see Pen so obedient to him. There was no question of gratitude for a job; her obedience showed genuine respect for his ability. Very strange indeed, thought Constance.

They had all been very kind to her, a gratifying experience. Even Digby had indicated a wish to please. He dilated upon the theatre, and of course upon Chekhov. 'Fascinating stuff to do,' he said. 'Wonderful composition. Real psychology. None of old Ibsen's obsession with bad conscience. We're in a new era.' Constance had smilingly agreed to all this, accepting his enthusiasm, and feeling sure that Soames would have understood it without being at all attracted to *The Three Sisters*. Everybody had spoken fervently of Soames, expressing horror at his seizure as well as gratitude to herself for coming to see them.

She had not come to see them. She had come because Pen said Tom was coming. But she did not tell them that. They seemed a nice crowd, all young, all laughing and enthusiastic; and, including the blonde Fanny Robins, who was to be so disagreeable in the play, expressed admiration for Pen. She's marvellous!' they said. 'Marvellous!'

'Really, I feel quite proud to be your sister,' she afterwards commented, hiding emotion behind indulgence.

Pen, if she felt emotion, hid it behind mock impatience.

'Don't keep harping on the sister business,' said she. 'It's tiresome.'

Constance was calm.

'Ah, you feel that too. You find there are too many of us!'

She skipped off the stage as the cast assembled there, taking an old kitchen chair which had been set for her. Another chair, less attractive still, stood by its side. This was meant for Tom Waring.

He arrived late, as was to be expected, and so unobtrusively

L

that those on the stage were not interrupted. Constance, in spite of her unwillingness to approve, and in spite of constant loss of attention through dreams of Soames or memory of yesterday's resumed talk with Marrington and Sealby, did not know that he was beside her. During a pause, however, Tom made her start by speaking in an undertone of the calamity which had saddened them all.

'I knew nothing of it,' he said, 'until I saw a morning paper on the train. I've come this morning from Cornwall. Dear Connie, you don't need to be told how strongly I feel.'

'Oh God! Is it in the papers?' She felt sick. 'I haven't seen one. I was at the hospital again early. Sybil said something about people ringing up. I told her to leave the receiver off.'

'Very wise,' said Tom, in the same low voice.

'We can't talk about it here. I must go back to the hospital. There was a little sign of life this morning. I thought he recognised me; but it wasn't so. That was dreadful.'

'Heartbreaking.' There was no smile; only a warmth of kindness which affected her very much. She touched his hand with her own in recognition and thanks. 'Would you like me to come with you? I can't leave immediately; Digby wants to ask me something.'

'As a dramatist?'

'Partly. The m-meaning of one of the speeches. The translation's literal, and awkward.'

'You don't read Russian, do you? I suppose Digby wants to polish. What do the papers say about Soames?'

'Only the fact. A paragraph about his career. They always assume their readers won't have heard of a man: "Winston Churchill, the well-known M.P." Most of it was a-about you; your courage in carrying on . . .'

'Oh, good heavens! It's horrible. Couldn't they have left that alone?'

'They look for the ro-romantic touch.'

'It wasn't romantic. There was no courage. Sheer contractual necessity. I've said I'll go on all this week, unless he dies. I think he's going to die. I feel sure of it.' She could say no more.

Tom pressed her hand.

'We won't talk about death,' he whispered. 'A strain for you. Try to l-look at these kids. Digby's inspired them with his own enthusiasm.'

Constance, trying to obey, half-heard Digby deliver a short harangue to Fanny Robins between his clenched teeth. Fair enough words. Fanny was 'acting'; and Digby saw she must check a tendency to suburban flounce, because the spoken word did it all. Turning again to Tom, she whispered:

'Pen says you like this play. Is that true?'

'Yes, very much. I think it epitomises life.'

'But they're all so wretched.'

'Concentrate on Chekhov's exquisite—not a good word, perhaps—tenderness.'

'Too subdued for me. I need the robust. Shakespeare. Or Tom Waring!'

'If I could wr-write like either, I should be . . .' An irresistible smile appeared in the brown face so close to her own—'almost content.'

So close to her own. Eyes so warm, so brimming with fun, tenderness, and beauty that Constance was forced to look away. She had read, she thought, into a nature far richer than her own; and the experience filled her with the longing of a child for joy. What a friend Tom would make! She had had husbands, lovers; but never a male friend of her own calibre with whom the sweetest intimacies of thought could be exchanged. Not of thought alone.

They went together to the hospital, travelling all the way on the tops of omnibuses like youngsters engaged in an adventure. The leaden heaviness which Constance had felt since that journey home from the theatre on Thursday night was insensibly lifted. All she had done, even when battling with Marrington and Sealby, had been prompted by undefined terror of loneliness. Without fierce effort she must have collapsed. Now, drawing strength from one to whom, whatever his vagaries of conduct and opinion, fear was no more than fantasy, she awoke.

'Shakespeare sang of a merry heart,' was her reflection. 'He was thinking of himself and Tom. The secret of happiness is inner peace. With Tom I could enjoy that. Not alone.'

She speculated about Tom's childhood, and wondered if he had been born without pain, indulged, taught to rejoice. But as a boy he had been abrupt: she was tempted to ask a direct question about that wounding desertion above Wilmerton. Did he remember? She avoided the temptation to charge him with unkindness then; she was too much affected by the sense of present tenderness. Instead, therefore, she put seemingly casual questions regarding his home and parents. Once she could visualise his home, she would be able to speak of her own. This was the grandest opportunity!

There was no forgetfulness of Soames. The fact that they were going towards inevitable sorrow made a background to everything else. She referred to Soames without tears and without constraint, speaking of the exhaustions from which he had suffered; but avoiding any harsh words of his partners because they had shown considerateness towards herself. Tom listened, nodded, expressed his own gratitude to Soames, and when he did so was endearingly serious. But his eye observed all the colour and movement of the streets, and his every comment soothed her excited nerves, so that she remained what she wished that he would think her until the journey's end. There were times, indeed, when she laughed aloud.

His father had been a London watchmaker, who wore a magnifying-glass in one eye; his mother a pantomime dancer whose legs had failed. He himself, at first regarded as an interference in their curious life in two rooms at the top of an old house in Wimbledon, but, after a tumble ending in the coal-cellar, a mischance which created his stammer, a prized object of wonder. Both parents survived, living in Cornwall, where he visited them. Yes, he supported them; they were amusingly odd and devoted. No, they had never seen a performance of *Clothes and the Woman*; Dad had not wanted to sacrifice the illusion that the boy was a prodigy of some sort, and Mum disliked the theatre now that she was done with it. Mum gardened; Dad read history, and was full of information about medieval characters whose names he mispronounced to everybody's delight, including his own.

'They sound wonderful,' exclaimed Constance, fascinated by the picture of two originals. 'I wish I could see them. My father could have pronounced the names. He was rather learned; but he thought I was a monster. Well, perhaps he didn't, really; but he was so much fonder of Pen. I ought to hate Pen, from jealousy; but I'm only jealous of her at times. I'm curious to see what she makes of this part. I haven't seen her act since she was a child; but I remember how she made me furious by mimicking Blanche. Do you remember Blanche?'

'Blanche?' Tom seemed to be puzzled.

'At Wilmerton.' Constance was a little breathless at this approach to a painful subject.

When he tried to remember anything he half-closed his eyes, which thereupon became hardly more than lids in two patches of shadow. Just so must he look when at work. His brow remained unwrinkled. She recalled Pen's description of his hand over what he had written; but she now scouted the charge of miserliness. Nobody with so much candour could be a miser.

Apparently the concentration produced a result; for he exclaimed:

'Oh, yes; that girl with the furbelows. She was no good.'

'So Pen saw, and made her, while I was callowly fascinated.'

'I couldn't stand her. I thought you were the same type.'

So he had recognised her, either now or formerly.

'That was rather stupid of you. I wasn't.'

'No, I behaved badly. I'm sorry. I sometimes do. As we're talking like this I must tell you that I've always wanted to apologise.'

'Well, now I forgive you. Do you know what happened to Blanche?'

'No, I don't.' Those were the first untrue words he had spoken to her that day.

They had reached the end of their journey, and Constance caught at his arm.

'Now I need all the strength you can spare.' She was choking. A sense of calamity swept through her once again.

'I know. I need it myself; you need it much more. Come along.'

They hurried, her hand within his crooked elbow; and in this way they reached and climbed the steps to the hospital's main entrance. Once they had passed the great door every step echoed in the silence. Traffic was no more to be heard; the dust of the streets yielded to disinfected hush, and a man in uniform remained entirely impersonal. It was not his business to communicate news, whether good or bad, and as he took them to a waiting-room off the main hall Constance's teeth chattered as they had always done in moments of suspense. Tom also was pale and very grave. Words had deserted him.

'Do say something to help me, Tom,' she implored, in desperation.

'I'll say that Soames is a great man, and you're a brave girl. I imagine something of what you're feeling; not more than a small part of it, but a little. And I wish I could tell you even that. I hope when you get upstairs you'll find him conscious and glad to see you.'

'I can't forget the shock of finding he didn't know me, as I thought.'

'I know that. I'm only trying to give you heart.'

'Dear Tom; don't leave me. Don't say "I must go now. Goodbye." You've done it twice already. A third time . . .'

The man in uniform re-entered the waiting-room.

'Will you come upstairs now, Madam,' he said.

It was evident that he knew her, and that he knew the identity of the patient. What was not evident, although Constance and

Tom, both hypersensitive, tried to read his manner, was his knowledge that Soames was dead.

## 3

Everything was over; obituaries, condolences, a fashionable gathering at the cremation, with Marrington in almost unbearable attendance, correct, pressing, and full of the desire to make her burden as light as possible. Sealby, as was to be expected, took charge of what he called 'the estate', which meant the few thousand pounds left by Soames at the end of a long life of success. Constance, worn out by the demands on her strength, desired and dreaded the solitude which was to follow.

Tom had been unobtrusively kind during the hours of suffering; but after the cremation he had disappeared. She knew why. It was because he had promised to go that night to the opening of *The Three Sisters*, which had been postponed because Digby's wonderful new theatre was not ready. It was impossible for Constance to go. Convention would not have allowed it; but in any case she was too depressed to care whether the play was produced or not. Marrington and Sealby were to be there; it was a grand social occasion (for Digby moved in high circles), and they could not afford to be absent.

So Constance spent the evening alone, irked by the sight of Marrington's flowers and the memory of a clerical address which set her teeth on edge. The cast of her withdrawn play was dispersed; her cook, subdued by the disaster, had gone out to visit relations; Sybil, iron-faced with a determined refusal to weep, was the only other person in the house. And everything was reminiscent of Soames, that good man to whom she owed so much, who had been heard to mutter only one word before he died, 'Agnes', the name of his first wife, long forgotten.

'That was no compliment to me, was it?' thought Constance.

'I mustn't think of it—I won't think of it. If I did I should get obsessed; and I'm sad enough as it is. I wonder how that miserable play is going? Other people's wretchedness is no good to me. What I can't see is, why a dramatist should think it necessary to write about dismal people with nothing to live for. If I had nothing to live for . . . Why *her* name; and not mine? These grand psychologists would explain it. Sealby says the will praises me, "my darling wife". That must represent his sanest view. The other's just a throwback, representing—not senility, but the loss of control that people suffer when they're dying. Perhaps it was never said. I wasn't there; it was only what they told me; and the nurses wouldn't understand. But "Connie" couldn't be mistaken for "Agnes". Poor Soames!'

Next morning, remaining in bed after Sybil had taken away the early tea tray, she glanced through half-a-dozen newspapers, looking for notices of *The Three Sisters*. Some of them referred in their gossip columns to distinguished people in the audience: that was because Digby, being rich and pretentious, could always command the élite; and he knew how to suggest that everything he did was somehow aristocratic, far above whatever pleased larger audiences.

He was a snob; and yet what he did was evidently good. Pen admired him; Tom admired him; he'd been very courteous to herself. The snobs were curious people; out of the corners of their eyes they peeped to see what others were doing, only sneering at it from a safe distance, but as secretly envious as schoolgirls. Where were the notices?

Here they were! 'FINE CHEKHOV. FURNESS TRIUMPH AT BIJOU THEATRE.' Various names . . . 'taste . . . a little slow . . . beautiful performance by Penelope Rotherham . . . more famous sister Constance . . .' That was all right. What next? 'Lovely child . . . talented actress . . . outstanding.' 'A rare treat; play full of subtle-ty; excellent cast; not least the charming Irina of Miss Penelope Rotherham.' 'In Miss Penelope Rotherham Mr Digby Furness introduces a new star to the theatrical firmament.' 'Unless we are much mistaken, Penelope Rotherham is destined to achieve great distinction as an actress.' 'Nothing so admirable has been seen in the commercial theatre for many years . . . a talented cast without a single failure . . . the modest perfection of Penelope Rotherham as Irina . . .'

Constance could not restrain a yawn. This was what some would call 'a paean' or 'chorus of praise', and Pen had enjoyed a triumph. She was bound to do so. But how they misjudged her talent! They thought she was a zealous artist, doomed to perform in dismal plays in bandboxes like the Bijou, when in reality her *forte* was the most versatile burlesque. She mustn't doom herself to little semi-private shows and short runs before select pretentious audiences. That was the sort of thing Carl had hankered after. This was the merest beginning. All the critics singled her out for mention, although her part was relatively small. Only one referred to her more famous sister. The best comment was on her 'modest perfection'. That was true and just. And yet none of those who wrote had perceived that she could play Puck, detect and mock Blanche, Carl, and (probably) her more famous sister, and very likely be superb, later on, in Congreve and Sheridan.

'Two-faced, artful, demure, and a darling!' thought Constance, proud and jealous. 'And Tom was there. She can't have Tom. I want him for myself. How scrupulous would she be? No woman is scrupulous over a man.'

Disturbed, she threw aside the papers and the bedclothes, leaping out of bed to contemplate her own beautiful face in the dressing-table mirror. White shoulders and the further beauty of her person as it was revealed by a silken nightdress were seen without intoxication but with pleasure, and the examination was prolonged. At the end of it she turned back to the room.

'In the matter of looks, I win. In charm, no; I haven't got her *espièglerie*. But I must have that play!' she exclaimed, clenching her teeth, and speaking in excellent mimicry of Digby Furness. 'That play! That play!' Elation at Pen's success, envy of a temporarily less famous sister who had enthralled the critics, and a confusion of many unfathomed wishes and fears, made her half joyful and half melancholy. Surely Tom must see it was his duty to write a masterpiece for Constance Rotherham! 'I'd forgive him anything for that!'

He and Pen were with her for lunch. She had refused to see anybody else, although Marrington had telephoned inquiries for her health in mid-morning, and several of those whom she derisively called her 'girl friends' had offered themselves as companions or consolers. 'No, I've got Pen coming,' she told them all. 'My young sister who's such a success in the Chekhov play. I wasn't able to see her last night. Yes, wonderful. We're having a quiet lunch. I snatch at any chance of seeing her, now that she's the rage. She used to be *my* sister; now I'm *hers*.'

No mention had been made of Tom, even (as a potential dramatist) to Marrington. The truth was that Marrington, who had lost his middle-aged wife during the War, seemed to be engaged in personal manœuvre, complimentary but unwelcome; and while, because of his place in the partnership, she must not risk a wound to those highly-polished feelings, she had more urgent interests to pursue. 'Another day, Claude dear. To-morrow, if you like. And, to the girls, 'One day next week. I shall be braver then. Less bruised.'

Pen came early; but Tom was hardly later. His manner was heart-stirringly kind; and Constance detected no sign of understanding with Pen. Pen could conceal anything; Tom, more open, would surely have betrayed a special interest? He might have been a brother. Naturally they spoke first of Pen's play and its reception, raising their glasses to the new star, who radiated modest pleasure and looked, in her sober green clothes, like a woodland elf.

'How about that white frock?' asked Constance. 'I wasn't sure it would suit you.'

'I was made-up pale,' explained Pen. 'All three were made-up pale. Not Fanny Robins, who was rouged, I thought, too heavily. Digby wanted her to be the one touch of colour; rosy with sin.'

'Was Pen good?' demanded Constance, turning to Tom. 'She's not used to flattery.'

'I didn't get it, from Digby.' Pen was rueful. 'He grumbled. He was in a dither.'

'She was very good indeed,' answered Tom; 'and Digby was delighted with her. He was muttering curses on Fanny, because nerves made her too flamboyant. He said "London suburban." But she'll be splendid in a week. Digby lost control of himself; biting his nails, grinding his teeth, using language he oughtn't to know. What with the theatre being unfinished, the stalls creaking, the lighting going astray, the nobs . . . '

'And the play!' Constance could not resist a dig at that.

'Oh, the play was all right. Some of the translation was awkward; but nobody except me noticed. I did, because Digby asked me to listen for faults. Pen's tone and enunciation were ideal!

'I hope she won't go on only doing things like Chekhov. She'd be labelled, and ruined. What does Digby plan, to follow?'

'Something Spanish, I think; or Austrian.'

Constance gave a little grunt, which meant that she estimated Digby as a snob-cosmopolitan. She saw Tom and Pen for the first time exchange a smile at her patriotism; and felt a qualm. Did they really think her insensitive, or old-fashioned? She wasn't, of course; the play they had found dowdy had been chosen by Soames and Sealby. What she objected to was the new fad for everything Continental, especially everything Russian. The fad wouldn't last. They'd been bamboozled by Digby Furness, who, if he hadn't been so *Quartier Latin* in rig would have been visibly a *petit maître*. Digby's notion was that only foreigners were any good.

'Oh, well,' she said, drily: 'I suppose we haven't any dramatists of our own.'

'We've got Tom,' remarked Pen, with equal dryness. 'You and I have both played in Tom, remember!'

'Yes, I'd quite forgotten Tom.' Constance looked archly at Tom. She refused to humble herself by another entreaty. He must come to heel of his own accord. 'I wonder what Digby would think of *him*.'

Tom smiled. He apparently knew Digby's opinion. Leaving this subject, therefore, they spoke of Soames. Constance found herself describing her talks with Sealby and Marrington, who were hardly known to Tom and Pen. She impersonated both, Marrington with greater mercy than Sealby, who was in a hurry. He wanted a new production at once, his haste being dictated by concern with their lease of the Royal. This theatre could be sub-let; but Sealby's longing was to see the box office open again under his own eye. He whined—she made him whine, although in fact his voice was a complaining grizzle—that every moment was precious.

'You said you could get a play, Constance. That's why we turned down *Many a Slip*. Well, I admit we were none of us keen on it; but a bird in the hand . . . Any number of writers would be honoured to write a play for you, Constance. I don't want to seem heartless, Constance; but any number of men . . .'

That was true. And what rubbish the plays were! She said so, to Sealby, and now to Tom. But she asked Tom for nothing. She would never ask Tom for anything. He must come to her of his own accord. Now and always. She was Constance Rotherham, the darling of Wartime audiences, and still in a position to dictate.

Tom listened to the mimicry of Sealby, looking down at his hands as they rested upon the table, but not seeing them as anybody's hands. This was a favourite attitude, accounting for Pen's gibe at his secretiveness when writing. She imagined a manuscript growing under those hands, scene after scene of it, decorated by his own rather whimsical thoughts. Not whimsies, in the Barrie vein; not Shaw's garrulous glories; but his own quiet imaginings, drawn from deep-seated humour. She could have struck him, not to hurt, but with her napkin, to remind him of her presence. Was he prepared to tease her—not only as to a play, but as to their possible future relationship?

'What I'm so afraid of,' she said to Pen, 'is that Sealby will try to foist some rubbish on me; and then, if I'm battered into acceptance of it, blame me for what happens. We're deluged with drivel, witticisms from the Ark, and *dénouements*; well you know all about those.'

'I suppose everybody's the same,' answered Pen. 'In Digby's case they're all about prisoners-of-war camps, with all-male casts, or adolescents falling in love with their grannies.'

'That's probably why Digby's thinking of Spanish authors.'

'He's not interested in war plays. Nor are you, are you?'

'I should like something pre-war. That's what Claude and Harold are thinking of. They're very conventional. Their notion of great drama is Henry Arthur Jones.'

'Hm,' said Tom, awakening from reverie. 'French windows; chaps in tennis flannels; dance music "off" to dope the stallites after a good dinner; a beautiful woman with a past; strong curtains. But there's no Soames to play the wise old man.'

Constance, laughing at the burlesque, was so much affected by his final words that she cried out in protest.

'Oh, dear, Tom; don't remind me of Soames. You make me hear his grand voice. Make me long for him. If he were still here, everything would be easy. He'd decide, produce, make even platitudes sound new-minted.'

Tom demurred.

'He couldn't make them sound new-minted; nobody could do that. But he'd make them acceptable, dear old fellow. I'm sorry I hurt you, Connie. The truth is, I think of him as still alive; but in the next room. Liable to come in at any minute.' There was a long pause. At last, very slowly, Tom said: 'I've got a play finished. I don't know if it's any good . . .'

'Have you, really? For me? It's sure to be good. I'm positive. And it's always been my dream, dear Tom!' Constance ignored the fact that Pen was there, quick to mark every intonation, every slip of the tongue, and read meaning into it; but perhaps mercifully, because of her elation at last night's miracle, less ruthless than usual.

Tom gave a quick nod. She felt her heart rising to ecstasy. She left everything, now, to one for whom it grew warmer from hour to hour.

4

It had arrived, in three easily-handled sections. She drew them, almost with reverence, from their big envelope. 'BIRD OF TIME, by Thomas Waring.' Wasn't that a quotation from Omar Khayyám? She pictured Sealby's little mouth, its corners pedantically turned down in what was once called a *moue* at such a title. He wouldn't appreciate it. Claude Marrington would be more receptive. She wasn't sure she liked it herself. A title needing explanation was always suspect. But the main thing was the play itself. How lovely of Tom, with all his mischief, all his hesitation—had that been genuine or affected?—to let her have her wish!

'ACT ONE. Scene, the saloon bar of a public house, brilliantly lighted, with three men, one young, the others middle-aged, all shabbily dressed, seated at a long table. As the curtain rises, two other men enter. At the bar, with her back to the audience, a barmaid is dusting and arranging bottles on a shelf, behind which the wall is covered with a mirror. As the men talk and the newcomers enter, she turns.'

'Is this me?' asked Constance, aloud, as she skimmed the page and found the barmaid's name to be Rose. 'There ought to be a longer delay.'

She was consciously critical, imagining herself in the rôle, catching the audience by surprise as she turned; being greeted with the applause of amused recognition. Applause would be followed by an attentive hush. Yes, that wouldn't be bad. It might be just as well to get the greeting over, before the play's action began; but a bar was hardly the place . . .

An hour later, the typescript was still in her hands. She had been deeply absorbed in what she had read; but during the reading her spirits had fallen steadily; and at last, throwing the play down, she rose to her feet and began to pace the room in a state of mingled disappointment, depression, and anger.

'No!' she vehemently cried. 'No!'

That clever little fool had deliberately planned an affront. He must have known all along that the play was impossible for anybody of her standing. A pub! Good God! No wonder he had derided the French windows, the young men in flannels, dance music softening the hearts of well-fed sentimentalists in the stalls! He had been defending his own beastly notion of what they ought to be made to swallow! The nature and purpose of his artful silences were exposed. He had planned this grotesque joke, knowing that everybody, instead of coming to see, would stay away from it. What conceit! What taste! Mocking her; laughing at her! Any actress who took the part of Rose, his—you couldn't call her 'heroine'—chief female character would suffer in reputation! Impossible! Impossible!

After some tempestuous minutes she grew quieter; but more melancholy than she remembered to have been, even during Soames's illness, for many a day. Expectation had been so high, emotional confidence in Tom so powerful, that her discomfiture was as great as it had been long ago, at Wilmerton, when he left her. She heard him say: 'I must go now. Goodbye.' Because her triumphs had been continuous ever since she sang his song in *Clothes and the Woman* she was unprepared for such a shock.

'Anybody would think I was an amateur!' she exclaimed. 'Some little unknown creature creeping on to the stage for the first time! Instead of what I am; somebody rich with all the prestige of success!... This is what he thinks of me. The smile becomes a sour grin. It's terribly offensive. He sneers at me as he sneered at that precious *dénouement*! Flings me cruelly among the bottles and the dram-drinkers as if I were the very dregs of womanhood! No! No!'

She began to compose a letter which should accompany the play on its journey back to Tom. Very dignified, calm, regretful; but leaving him in no doubt that she scorned his bad joke . . . But he'd simply laugh. Whatever she wrote would seem to him contemptible. Her dignity would be seen as pompous; her calm as priggishness. He could make fun of anything—anything it, seemed, except a flash barmaid who, being carried suddenly to social heights by a flash criminal, met with disillusion, and returned, crestfallen, to her natural haunt, the bar. If not an insult, the play was insincere. More, it was sentimental. More, it was repulsive, repellent, revolting.

She would not send a letter. She must see Tom, hand him back his typescript with a smile and a shaken head. No protest; no argument: neither would be necessary.

'Thank God I'm an actress!' said Constance. 'And a good actress, Master Tom! A good actress!'

She felt better; but still melancholy.

In a little while she began to read again, going back to the beginning with a knowledge of—blessed word!—the *dénouement*, and reading with a greater sense of the play's quality as a play. She was not reconciled to it; she hated it as much as ever, and resented Tom's belief that she would be willing to act the part of Rose; but she admired the way in which the wretched man had prepared each stage in Rose's disillusionment. She even detected in Rose some dowdy nobility of character.

'But *still* it's no good!' she exclaimed, throwing down the typescript a second time.

Her brain revolved around the circumstances in which the play had come into her hands. She began to allow the possibility that Tom had not meant to throw a satirical squib into her face. He could perhaps have yielded to her unspoken importunity, knowing that she would dislike what he had written, but wishing to show that he hadn't been idle. He had said 'I don't know if it's any good.' That, however, was only an author's mock-modesty. They were a conceited brigade, shamming simplicity, when all the time they thought themselves masters and damned actors and actresses as so many parrots. He might have meant 'any good to you'.

Sighing, she longed again for the ever-cautious, ever-fair Soames. Soames would have taken a whole day over the typescript, making notes considerately on a separate sheet of paper, and weighing every word. He would then have talked to Master Tom, explaining what was wrong, and convincing him—that was the wonderful thing about Soames—of genuine disinterestedness. People had latterly jeered at Soames as too systematic, and it was true that one's first awe had been modified; but his experience was worth all the improvisations of the impatient, and she had never lost respect for him. If only he were alive now, to advise her!

Advice was necessary. She must have it before she met Tom. If the play had been by anybody else she would have sought it from him; but the mental picture of that sleepy, thoughtful, terribly attractive smile was too much. She must ask Marrington. Marrington rather than Sealby, because Marrington, although conventional, although, she believed, short-sighted, was free from Sealby's meticulousness. He would confirm her own belief, and perhaps supply words that she could use as if they were her own. And she could always quote him. If she quoted Sealby to Tom, Tom would only laugh. Damn Tom! Damn the darling, darling boy!

She might have foreseen their reaction. Claude, who was not interested in low life, did not handle the typescript at all. Sealby caught at it as a cur might have done at a bone; skimmed the first act, grimaced with his little mouth, wrinkled his pointed nose (as far as its sharpness permitted a wrinkle), hastily flipped over a few more pages.

'What do you think of it yourself, Constance?' he demanded, accusingly.

'It's very ingenious,' she loyally answered. 'Very.'

'But hardly . . .'

M

'Tell us the story,' suggested Marrington, who took delight in her voice.

'It's about this girl, Rose; the barmaid. The first act shows her on the point of marrying an Irishman who has an extraordinary gift of speech. Some of his talk is quite brilliant.'

'Rhetoric,' snapped Sealby. 'They're all talkers.'

'He does more than talk. He's a patriot, rather a poet; and he has visions of a world where all men are equal and all men are directly inspired. Rose is completely carried away by this vision. She feels she's practically marrying into the priesthood.'

'Blasphemous,' commented Sealby.

'In the second act she's ten years older . . .'

'Hm. *Milestones*,' said Sealby.

'Not quite that, Harold. It's a psychological play. They have all the husband's relations staying with them. He's just as eloquent but rather battered. She's become secretary to the man who is exploiting the husband's ideas, and turning them into a sort of religious racket. The husband captivates audiences with his eloquence; and the audiences—they're called "congregations", or "souls"—part with their savings to build up this new church of the pure spirit. Things are beginning to crack. One poor old woman comes to implore Rose's help; the husband is carried to heights of prophesy; the old woman has just one moment of disbelief. She shows her disbelief; and asks for her money back. In the midst of another oration, the husband stops. He says "You're quite right, madame; you won't get a penny, and there's no heavenly reward." '

'Hm. Cynical,' protested Sealby.

'No; the man is a fraud, but he breaks down in perfect good faith. He hasn't had any of the money. Rose guesses that the exploiter has made off with every penny; and she sticks by her husband, who begins to rant in the old way—just hollow words. She knows he's lying. There's a knock at the door. It's a detective. The last act is in the saloon bar again. She's a woman of middle age, and the husband, just released from prison, is a wreck, whom she treats as a child. He's quite childish. The man who caused all the trouble is safe in South America. He's had a fit of conscience; and without giving any address has sent them a thousand pounds in foreign currency. Of course, the idiotic husband bursts into a flow of deplorable eloquence, a travesty of his old bravura. Rose pockets the money, against his will, quietens him with whisky, and orders a gin for herself. That's all.'

'Ridiculous!' cried Sealby.

'What's it supposed to mean?' asked Marrington.

'I think it's meant to be an allegory,' answered Constance.

'I suppose he means that young dramatists are exploited by wicked managers. Young men of genius by Society; the good by the corrupt. It might be amusing to put it on for half-a-dozen *matinées*—not with you, dear Constance. That we couldn't risk.'

'We should drop a lot of money, Claude,' objected Sealby.

'Oh, yes; of course I wasn't serious. This must be a great disappointment to you, Constance. I'm sorry for that. I know you'd pinned your hopes on it. Never mind; we'll do something else. I wonder if you have anything at the back of your mind?'

It was a temptation. Constance, relieved at the decision, and yet, from perversity, despising them both for not wishing at least to explore the brilliance of the husband-victim's eloquence, answered as if they had done something more than introduce a red herring:

'Well, Claude, I've wanted all my life to play Beatrice, in *Much Ado about Nothing*. I think I'm just about ready to do it.'

'Hm. Shakespeare,' grumbled Sealby.

'They tell me he's the coming man,' said Marrington, with great good humour. 'I think you may be right, Constance. I quite long to see you in the part.'

'We couldn't do it very lavishly.' Sealby was already scheming to cut costs.

'There would be no author's royalties,' Constance reminded him.

Marrington laughed suddenly.

'Very good. Very good,' he remarked. 'Very good indeed. Well, Harold, let's go into it, shall we? Personally, I think it might be a great success.'

They left her with the typescript and a dread of parting with Tom. Sealby's head was down as he conned the questions of money, an empty theatre, authors' royalties, and the possibility of what Marrington had called 'a great success'. He had no opinion of Shakespeare as a box office dramatist; but anything would be better than the certain failure of young Tom Waring's attack on theatre managers. Under his breath, he muttered:

'These boys are all the same. They want to change everything.'

Marrington, following him from the room, stopped and looked back.

'Just a minute, Harold,' he said. To Constance, in a low tone, he added: 'I didn't want you to speak of it before Harold, Constance dear. I want to get away from him for a while. An excellent fellow; but perhaps—you know?—a little uninspired. I'm planning to take a few friends on my yacht to the Mediterranean. Just a three-weeks cruise; but it ought to be delightful there just now. Along the coast, perhaps to Rhodes, Alexandria, Constantinople. I wonder if you'd care to come? It would do you good, take your mind off things. And of course you would be studying the part of Beatrice! I wish it were in my power to play the part of Benedick! Will you? I should be extraordinarily happy . . .'

Seeing her face lighten at the prospect, he took her hand, and, as he had done once before, very gallantly kissed her cheek.

'Coming, Harold; coming!' she heard him cry as he hastened away.

There remained Tom. She took the coward's way, and rang him up.

'Good morning, Connie.' He had recognised her voice. 'How are you?'

'Tom, I've read the play!' She pictured him listening with amused composure for any sign of agitation. 'It's very good indeed.'

'That's bad. It means you don't like it.'

'I didn't, at first. At a third reading I began to see the point of it.'

'Always my ambition to be obscure!'

'No, no, Tom; don't be facetious! It's defensive; when it's I who should be defensive.'

'Darling Connie! Forgive me. I can't help being facetious. It's my curse. I won't interrupt again. You shall tell me in your own words.'

'That's what they say to children. All right, I'm a child. All women are children. I've seen Claude and Harold; told them everything about it—as far as one can tell everything to any-body in half an hour.'

She heard him laugh. He said quickly:

'Especially Harold, who hears only the chink of money! Excuse me! Go on.'

'You're making it terribly easy for me; and I thought it was going to be difficult. None of us thinks it's at all suitable. For one thing, the chief character is a man. For another, Rose isn't *me.*'

'It wasn't meant to be you. It was a part for you to create.'

'A subordinate part, when we want something where I'm a heroine.'

'Rose is a heroine. She's outwitted by fate; but she's game to the last.'

'Driven to gin!'

'Well, poor soul, she's thirsty. Needs a little something to keep out the cold.'

'I wish you wouldn't be so facetious about something very serious, Tom. It's wrong; like the play. Did you really think it possible? I mean, for me?'

'Very difficult to say. A man writes what occurs to him as worth writing. He can't judge it, and he can't accept anybody else's judgment of it. He's a spoilt animal. Well, now, I believe you could have a real success. Not perhaps a box office success; but something to impress the world; something to show your genius.'

She was desolated by melancholy self-distrust.

'I haven't got any genius; and you know it, Tom. You've always known it. And we all feel I can't risk a failure at this juncture. I haven't got Soames to produce me, or encourage me, or see me through.'

'Poor girl!' It was not ironic; it was full of the kindness he had shown all along. 'I quite understand.'

'And I do think the play's awfully good. At first I was furious with it. And with you. I thought you were making fun at me.'

'Oh, good heavens! I'd never do that, Connie. I love you.'

'Do you really? I'm revived. It's better than gin. I've passed through various hells this morning; and when Harold made his little sour grimace I proclaimed you a master.'

'That passed, I expect.' He was laughing again.

'Yes, it passed,' she retorted. 'It was just pique; and I kept my mouth shut. Claude tactfully invited me to go holiday-making on his yacht, which I propose to do.'

Tom was all spirit.

'Splendid! I shall see you before you go. Don't read the play a fourth time; or you'll be back where you started. Why not come and see *The Three Sisters* with me?'

'That awful play! But I should like to see young Pen.'

'Yes, she's worth seeing,' said Tom. 'Well?'

Once she had rung off, Constance repeated the whole conversation to herself. When she came to Tom's lightly-spoken words 'I love you' she stopped, hearing his voice again. Of course he didn't mean them. Her own love surged high, tender, exquisite, as never before. She was possessed by it.

5

Three weeks of idleness in sunshine followed. Skies were generally blue, the ports dazzlingly white, the sea, unless whipped by storm, rolling and agreeable. And when the evenings were chill there was always comfort in the yacht's splendid lounge, where the chatter of smart people on holiday and in a mood to share knowledge of history, politics, and contemporary scandal was broken by some delightful music. Claude Marrington played the piano very well; and the party of twelve included a rather sullen-looking boy from Poland who fiddled brilliantly and scowled whenever the names of famous violinists were mentioned by others.

It was a new experience to Constance, for whom the boy fiddler showed charming devotion. She was very politely treated by the rest of the party, most of whom were too wealthy to feel envy and too socially experienced to be unpleasant. Claude Marrington had made a fastidious selection, and he was equally fastidious in his considerateness of each guest. At no time did he pay any marked attention to her, although if they chanced to be alone together his attraction was evident. She had plenty to read, saw many beautiful and interesting relics of Mediterranean history, and when she was in her cabin she read *Much Ado about Nothing* in a volume of the Temple Shakespeare until she knew every word of it.

She did not rehearse; she read and pondered. She pretended that the play's scene was indeed Messina, and that Messina was just such a place as one of those they visited. When she and any of her companions walked in a street, or, turning a corner, discovered some wider area surrounded by arcades or ancient houses, she immediately peopled the neighbourhood with actors in Elizabethan costume. 'Now what was Leonato's orchard like?' she asked herself. 'That's easy for a scenic artist to paint; but I want to feel it.' And again: 'Was Leonato's house like this? If I could go in, I should know. How I wish I could draw, paint, design! I've been too busy learning parts to study art. I wonder Erasmus Hurd never saw himself as Benedick. I wonder what Bill Wyse will be like in the part. He may be ghastly!'

She had no love for Benedick. Her love was for Beatrice, the most free and daring of all Shakespeare's women. As she exclaimed ' "Kill Claudio!" ' she felt all the old enthusiasm of her childish defiance of the breakers. This, this, at last, was what she had always wanted to express; the fierce passion of the heart!

After holiday, work. They were ashore again in England, upon a cold day of misty rain; and at Southampton the party broke up.

'It's been wonderful, Claude!' everybody was saying. 'The perfect host; the perfect yacht, the perfect escape from telephone, newspapers, noise, and inconvenience. Thank you so much. Thank you. And goodbye, Miss Rotherham. We're so looking forward to seeing you in your next show.'

'I hope you'll do me one more kindness,' replied Marrington. 'I hope you'll let me entertain you at Constance's first appearance in Shakespeare . . .'

'Not quite my first appearance, Claude,' interposed Constance. 'At one time I had quite a success as Jessica, in *The Merchant of Venice*. Even earlier as Oberon.'

This information pleased them all. Little Micha, the violinist, looked pathetic in his wistful brightening at the prospect of seeing her again. The others were not wistful, but exultant.

'A very beautiful Oberon, I'm sure!' cried the richest man of the group, Hereford Wise. 'And we shall all be charmed to accept Claude's invitation. I shall send you flowers.'

Amid many smiling farewells, Constance stepped into Marrington's limousine, knowing that its owner would see her safely home after a spanking drive through the New Forest and watery sunshine to London. She sank back into the cushions with something of the pleasure she had felt after the opening night of *Clothes and the Woman*, ages ago, in Soames's car, which she had thought the grandest vehicle in existence. That had been the night when Carl left her: sudden melancholy touched her mind, Carl, Soames—and Tom? How fine Tom had been; and how exquisite Pen had been in the part of Irina . . .

Claude was beside her. They drove through the streets of Southampton; and she saw that he had been gratified by the welcome given to his invitation. Browned by the sea air, he looked very distinguished; and his courtesy to her showed pride in her success with the party.

'You made a great hit with my other guests,' he said. 'They were all enchanted with you.'

'Then I suppose you were pleased with me?'

'More than pleased, dear Constance; I shared the enchantment.'

That was all. He was in no hurry. But it was clear that his regard for her was very great. With any encouragement, this regard would reach a point, not of passion, not of infatuation, because such wildnesses were outside his temperament, but of proud and indulgent possessiveness.

Sybil could never look radiant; but as far as her natural stiffness allowed she showed happiness at the return of one whom she greatly admired. Her loyalty took the form of stubborn dumbness. Her mouth hardly ever opened wide. She was never known to laugh or sing. But into her grey eyes, which normally were hard, there crept a little warmth when she looked at Constance or Pen.

She had come to Constance in the first months of success, when the cockney song was being applauded nightly and its singer could afford a maid. Still dumb, but not at all visibly censorious, she had moved to Chelsea when Soames became her mistress's admitted lover; and the understanding between them had never been broken by temper on either side. Constance knew that Sybil had her own opinions, and that if once reserve was cracked a stream of unpleasant revelations might sully her own more charitable readings of conduct. She also knew, or believed, that Sybil's silences were the more golden because they had a certain unction.

'There's been lots of telephones,' Sybil explained. 'I told them all the same thing; but not when you'd be back. And your letters are on the table by the window. I've got the papers in the kitchen, all except this week's, and today's; they're on the other table.'

'Thank you, Sybil. Oh, heavens, what a lot! I've got some things for you and Cook and Florence in my cases. We'll unpack them presently. Meanwhile, if I could have a cup of tea I should be thankful. Sir Claude and I had lunch at a place on the Hog's Back; but I'm dying for some tea.'

'Very good, Madam,' replied Sybil, exactly as she had seen parlourmaids do on the stage. Her lips were pressed together in a remarkable smile.

Constance glanced through the letters, here and there identifying a writer, but not as yet opening any envelopes. She took her place in an armchair by the fire, and idly held the one of several morning newspapers in her hand.

'We saw no papers while we were away, Sybil,' she said, when the tea was brought.

'You didn't miss much,' was Sybil's dry response.

'I don't know why they publish them,' said Constance fretfully.

'It's to prevent people minding their own business,' replied Sybil. 'Or having any peace of mind. At least, that's what I think,' she added, rather defiantly.

Constance paid no attention to this remark; for she was scanning the headlines and simultaneously tasting a first restorative sip of tea. When she looked up again Sybil was gone.

The paper was full of politics, which did not interest her. The report of a Society divorce case, another of some robbery, and a third of a big fire could well have appeared at any time during her absence from London. More interesting was criticism of a new play: apparently that had been as boring as most plays about sophisticates, and only the names of the actors and actresses gave this one any point. Apparently Marie Biggs was in a small part . . .

She next sought the advertisements of theatres, where she found that Chekhov's *The Three Sisters* was still running at the Bijou. This reminded her that she must telephone to Pen. She also began to speculate on what had happened about the casting of *Much Ado about Nothing*, which had been left in Sealby's hands. She knew that Claude would be seeing Harold this evening, and they would all meet at the Royal. It had been thought that Andrew Cotton would accept the part of Benedick; and if he did that the rest would be easy. It would have been lovely to have Pen for Hero. Hopeless, of course; somebody insipid was needed. As for Claudio, that handsome rat, Sealby had wanted a youngster—his *protégé*, named Flinder. Well, she mustn't interfere. It was Sealby's business; and beyond an expectation that she would be allowed to veto an unsavoury Benedick she wished for no further responsibility . . .

Were there any items of theatrical news? Ah! Miss Rotherham to play Beatrice, her first Shakespearean part . . . experiment awaited with much interest . . . The Benedick will be Mr. Cotton.' So that was all right; Cotton had agreed. She would enjoy referring to him as Signor Mountanto. It was a good scornful word for one who valued himself above rubies. She was about to throw the paper down when her eye caught another, longer paragraph.

'The run of *The Three Sisters*, which was to have been limited to six weeks at the Bijou Theatre, has been extended for another three weeks. Mr. Digby Furness has been much gratified by the public interest in this play, and hopes to produce another by Chekhov, probably *Uncle Vanya*, in the Spring. The next play to be seen at the Bijou will be a new tragi-comedy by Thomas Waring, in which the important leading rôles have been entrusted to Patrick O'Flaherty and Miss Penelope Rotherham, whose performance as Irina, in *The Three Sisters*, has given her a prominent position among the most promising of our younger actresses. The play . . . '

A tumult of feeling made further concern with the newspaper impossible. Constance held it; but the type had become blurred. Tom must have written the part with Pen in mind. He had only offered it to herself with the certainty that it would be refused. Damn! Damn! For her, during three weeks of holiday, time had seemed to stand still. Here in London it had taken wing into the unknown. She was full of torment.

## 6

The next month was one of the most crowded Constance had ever known. She was in anxious consultation with Marrington and Sealby; she wrangled with Roberts, the stage manager, who had never before dealt in Elizabethan drama and could make little of a confusing text and characters whom he regarded as talkative bores; she was torn between Sealby's parsimony, a personal wish for rich and richly coloured dresses, and the designer's unaccountable preference for a Beardsley-style black-and-white production. Marrington became her only resource; and Marrington, she angrily decided, was at bottom an evasive man who, while independent of theatrical profits, was at heart a money-maker.

She saw Pen from time to time; but both were caught up in the rush of their own affairs. Pen must know that she was to play a part that Constance had refused; but she gave no sign at all of knowing. No humility; no self-consciousness; certainly no triumph. Nor did she dwell on the part: all she said was: 'Patrick's as Irish as the Little People themselves; he talks and yarns till the theatre becomes full of pixies and pigs, tinkers and fiddlers. One great dominating volume of gas. But he's awfully good. He loves Tom like a brother; he'd almost forgive him for the Black and Tans; and now that Ireland's got most of what she's wanted for centuries he's thinking, he says, of emigrating to start a revolution somewhere else. The whole world, he says, is groaning.'

'And Tom?' asked Constance. 'What does he say?'

'Tom listens, and grins. That's what the Irish can't understand about the English. In the end Patrick guffaws, too, and slaps Tom on the back. Tells him he's a "quare feller", and says the play can never be done in Dublin. "They'd lynch ye!" Tom retorts that he'll boycott Ireland.'

Children again! Children again! Constance felt the oldest woman alive.

'I wish you could knock some sense into Charlie Tower,' she said. 'I simply detest my costume. Fancy dressing a star-born Beatrice as if she were a nun! It's potty. But what am I to do? When I howl to Claude he says "Very nice, my dear," "Delightful, my darling!" and I've sworn myself to ribbons.'

'Poor Con! It's the worst of being a woman!'

'Ah, but there are compensations. If I'd been a man I'd never have been allowed to play Beatrice!'

'I must bring Patrick to see you,' said Pen. 'You talk the same language.'

'I can't bear harangues. I'm one for short speeches. You should hear me say "Kill Claudio!" It curdles the blood. I'd sometimes like to kill Cotton. Not to mention Charlie Tower and Harold Sealby.'

'What's your Hero like?' asked Pen.

'Straight from school. I wish you could have played her. That would have been splendid. She's just your part.'

'And I've got my hands full.'

'Yes. Like me. I'm frightened of dropping something. Yet we're really rather lucky. The Rotherham Sisters; sounds like a music-hall turn. I hope the first nights won't clash.'

'I'll ask Digby to see your boys, shall I?'

'Hm. "My boys," ' groaned Constance. 'Harold Sealby, Claude, Jim Roberts; ripe in sin! Yes, do ask Digby, darling.'

She returned to her own trials. They had not spoken as she would have liked to do, about Tom or the play, or what Pen secretly thought of both or either. On Pen's side the abstention must have been deliberate; on her own, tactful. Some would call tact timidity. 'Which I deny,' proclaimed Constance, to the air. 'Absolutely.'

Hopes and despairs afflicted her. There were moments when she was able to imagine a rapturous welcome, and demands that she should grant everybody the privilege of seeing her as every great heroine of dramatic literature; and moments when she was tempted to embrace the quietude of a nunnery. 'Although even there,' she reflected, 'it's said that not everything's as peaceful as it looks from the outside.'

Her chief sensation was dread. At the dress rehearsal, when, she knew, Pen was already in the other theatre turning at the bar to greet her gaseous bridegroom, everything at the Royal was in such helter-skelter confusion that she was reminded of Hurd's Players and their ridiculous flutters. Those days had been crude, with Maude joking and Carl watching the rest in satirical disdain; but this was just as bad. Nothing went right; Cotton, as Benedick, forgot his best quips; Don John was as stiff as Masefield had ever been; Claudio so obviously a cad that he should have been kicked at sight; and Hero, the key to the whole imbroglio, as insipid as a fifth-form girl at Pickering's. Ghastly!

'Well, well, well,' groaned Constance, as she crept, exhausted, to bed, and wished that Soames had been there to comfort her. 'I hope Tom's rubbish has gone better. I'm glad I remembered to send them both telegrams. Did I remember? I wish I could have been there. No, I don't. I couldn't have born it. To see Pen in my part. My part! My part! It was never my part. It wouldn't have done at all. Pen's got nothing to lose. She's committed to little theatres, and dismal plays, for another five years at least. I wonder what she'll be doing in five years. If that play's a failure, as it will be, she'll be less self-complacent. Do I want that? I'm a beast and a cad; and I don't want her to suffer as I've done. Nor, of course, to be idolised as I've been. As I've deserved to be.'

She recalled triumphs as Jessica, as the various dolls she had played in London. She recalled Carl, that poor fool who hadn't been good enough to get the jobs he thought he despised. He'd have been a far better Claudio than this wretched man who cheapened the whole drama by his obviousness and his inability to speak a great language. Why were people such fools and incompetents? And lucky and unlucky?

> ' " 'Tis all a checker-board of Nights and Days,
>    Where Destiny with Men for Pieces plays;
> Hither and thither moves, and mates, and slays,
>    And one by one back in the Closet lays."

'Blast!'

Turning and tossing for another hour, she must have fallen asleep; for she opened her eyes to find Sybil bringing early tea and a pile of morning newspapers.

'What's it like, Sybil, out of doors?'

'Very grey, Madam.'

'Yes, it would be! Heavy on the spirits!'

'Yes, Madam.'

'Pah! Get you gone; you depress me!'

When Sybil had got her gone, Constance sat up, drank the tea quickly, seized the first paper she saw, and greedily turned to its report on last night's performance. Here it was; and the headline read: 'GREAT PLAY: INSPIRED ACTING.' Pah! Only Digby's wire-pulling! Digby was a supreme confidence-trickster. An aura of quality; gentility; a tremendous pretence of 'ART'. But what was he in reality?

"We do not hesitate to say that Mr. Waring has given us a most poignant . . . Patrick O'Flaherty . . . The beauty and pathos of Miss Penelope Rotherham defies description . . . She gives a very beautiful performance indeed, which all London should see . . .'

'Bravo, Pen! Damn her! Even Digby couldn't guarantee that sort of praise! I'm not at all jealous. Not at all. Yes, I am; disgustingly. I'm delighted. Delighted . . .'

What did the other papers say? All were pitched upon the same high note. One or two suggested that Tom had aimed at something beyond reach; but all extolled Patrick and Pen. 'Miss Rotherham's versatility was a revelation. She was young, middle-aged, and old without a single false note.' 'A flawless impersonation of one of the most beautiful characters in modern drama.' 'What a pleasure it is to see really modern tragedy, bold and beautiful. Miss Rotherham . . .'

'Well,' said Constance, flinging all the newspapers to a distance, 'if I get notices like this tomorrow, we shall be the most successful sisters in the business!'

Terrible doubts crept into her mind.

The Royal was a brilliant scene, inside and out, for *Much Ado about Nothing*. The *foyer* was glorious with flowers, Constance's dressing-room—she was not the first to remark—was like a florist's shop. Telegrams and flowers, not only from her fellow-passengers on Marrington's yacht, but from well-wishers from all over England, gave her new heart. She put Marrington's roses to her face and inhaled their intoxicating scent, and when; upon opening her first telegram, she read its message, she laughed aloud.

The telegram, from Maude, read: *Happy Night Hope Erasmus Turns in His Grave Loving Memories.*

'Dear old Maude,' thought Constance. 'I really must write to her. This is an augury!'

She was alert with excitement, full of the gaiety which the part of Beatrice had always induced. Her movements were already those of a disdainful young woman ready to tease without mercy the soldier to whom she was destined by the laughing mischief of naughty conspirators. Whatever went wrong behind the scenes she knew she would carry the vivacity of her favourite heroine to its merry conclusion . . . 'By this good day I yield upon great persuasion, and partly to save your life . . .' That was the way to accept a suitor whom one was already determined to marry!

All at last were banished from her dressing-room for five minutes of peace before the curtain rose. She was alone. Only Claude, departing, had cried 'Good luck, Beatrice! You'll enchant them all; as you've already done the rest of the company—including myself.'

Including himself; yes, of course, that need hardly have been said! Now! A quick journey to the wings; Roberts taking a final survey of Leonato's orchard and turning up his thumbs to show that he was satisfied; Hero, Leonato, and the messenger waiting. Somebody whispering: 'Brilliant house. All on tiptoe. Listen!' Yes, one need hardly listen, except to catch at the last notes of a drowned orchestra. Nerves, nerves; and yet stimulation, too . . . At last! Up went the curtain. There was the usual roar of greeting which delayed Leonato's opening speech. Then the story was in motion. Old Shakespeare, if it was Shakespeare and not another man using his name, knew his business!

> 'I learn in this letter that Don Pedro of
> Arragon comes this night to Messina . . .'

That was not the Earl of Oxford's voice; it was the voice of one who knew the stage by acting on it! Bang! Right into the drama! She must remember to say as much to Master Tom!

She caught sight of Tom afterwards amidst the throng of fashionables; and while those whom she described as 'dowagers' were all screaming 'You were wonderful!' and 'Such a treat to hear the King's English—is it the King's? we used to say the Queen's,' and 'What a pleasure you've given us, dear Miss Rotherham!' she beckoned him to her side. And as he came, there was a stir among the first-nighters, and one or two of them raised their voices to show that they had seen his play on the previous evening.

'Lovely,' he murmured, as she held his hand. 'Really perfect, Con.'

She was humble, imploring, very close to him, close to his eyes, close to his heart.

'You really think that? Not pretending?'

'From my heart. You were at your best; and every word as clear as a bell.'

When she had impulsively kissed him she felt better. She could speak with gaiety.

'Not too plangent, I hope?'

'Not at all. I'll report to our friend.'

'Our friend? Pen? Was last night all they say?'

Their glances met, his laughing, hers betraying.

'You're a pair of peaches,' answered Tom. 'Both of the first order.'

They had no time for more. Marrington was at hand, bringing a stranger; and the noise was horrifying. Why was it educated Englishwomen shouted so? Well, of course, it was to make themselves heard! 'Thank you! Thank you.' This funny little man must be someone important; for Claude seemed to genuflect every time he spoke. Where was Tom? Tom was going. Her heart went with him. But he'd really liked her; been at his kindest. She would sleep well tonight, thinking of him as her eyes closed. Thank God the show was over!

In the morning she awoke late, still yawning with weariness, but at the same time eager to see the Press comments. The papers had been laid on her bedside table. Had Sybil looked at any of them? It wasn't likely, as she had such contempt for newspapers and what they recorded. Now, where were we?

Her heart gave a great bound as she saw the first heading: 'COURAGEOUS FAILURE.' She read on: 'Shakespeare's . . . Everard Cotton a spirited Benedick . . . Miss Rotherham, so delightful in modern comedy, was out of her depth : . . graceful; but never for a moment Shakespeare's Beatrice. Costumes and *décor* striking . . .' Scandalous! She was choking with disappointment, with anger. What did the next say? 'Miss Rotherham delivered her lines clearly. She could do nothing without charm . . .' A third: 'Miss Rotherham had moments of delightful archness; her Beatrice was pretty and wayward . . .'

And so the story ran. At most, the commentators—she could not call them critics, since none of them had studied her performance with any attention—praised her boldness in attempting the part; only one cordially advised his readers to see the play. He was indeed 'courageous'. All spoke well of Cotton, found words even for the Hero, treated Dogberry and Verges as a pair of knockabouts from the Circus, whereas she had entreated Roberts to keep them within the picture; but concerning herself there was practically unanimous agreement in deprecation. 'Failure!' 'Courageous failure.' 'Delivered her lines clearly.' Bah!

Tears filled her eyes. She pushed the papers away, clenching her teeth and fists, and speaking, though she did not know it, as Digby spoke. Everybody would see these notices. They would be read all over England. Maude, up in the North; all the fiends who hated her and would wish to see her mortified; the public who would stay away believing that, after all, she was a third-rate mime who had been carried to popularity by association with Soames. Harold Sealby would grumble and lose faith in her; Claude would gallantly bow himself out of her presence; the dowagers would revise their judgments and join in the general depreciation—'My dear, *so* dull! I never did think her . . .'

Why? Could it be that having extolled one Rotherham, these wretches were in reaction against the other? Having made up their minds that she was one kind of actress did they resent the fact that she could be anything else? But they had praised Pen's versatility . . . Pen! Damn! It had always been the same when she and Pen were brought into comparison. Pen was admired; she by contrast was belittled. 'One man may lead a horse to the water; another mustn't look over the stable door!' She was the one forbidden the stable door! Why? Was it simply that Digby had pulled his strings adroitly, while Sealby had let them flap? Did they think she had been too successful in the past? Did they merely dislike Shakespeare? Were they angry because the audience last night had been so enthusiastic? Were they apes who gibbered in concert? Passing each other *en route* for the bar, had they cocked their heads and signalled: 'Thumbs down?' ...

While these and other rageful questions racked her the telephone by the bedside rang. Sybil must have put the caller straight through, which she would not have done if he or she had been a stranger. Therefore it must be Pen.

'Hullo, Pen.'

'Ah, Con. Are you still in bed?'

'Yes, are you?'

'No, I've been striding about Hampstead Heath.'

'Nonsense! You can't stride!'

'Filling my lungs with the morning air. Getting my feet wet. Well, when I got back I read all those disgusting notices. I thought I'd ring up and give you a piece of my mind. Have they upset you?'

'They have, rather. I'm still fuming.'

'So am I. Tom says you were superb. He's never wrong.'

'Is he always sincere?'

'No; but in this case completely so. I'm sure of it. He's so angry he's thinking of writing a general letter to the Press.'

'Oh, heavens! Don't let him do that. He'd get in wrong with the wretches. They'd hound him.'

'He doesn't care. The arrogance of genius, you know; which is less obnoxious than the arrogance of parasites. I said not to do anything silly; so he's just going to write one article, lauding you. At least, that's his latest notion.'

'I must tell him not to. Soames always said "ignore the adverse; take it as complacently as you take praise". I never knew if he was scorning my vanity. By the way, how is it you know what Tom wants to do?'

'Telephone, darling. I saw him last night after the show, and he told me how magnificent you were. Hotly enthusiastic; which he rarely is. He said it was thrilling to hear you say "Kill Claudio!" Then he rang me at breakfast time.'

Constance thought it peculiar that there should have been this close exchange night and morning.

'Why didn't he ring *me?*'

'I suppose he knew you wouldn't be up.'

'Very strange.'

Pen was obviously amused. After a pause, the words came:

'I think I must tell you I'm going to marry Tom.'

Constance died in that moment. Everything went black. Only by an extraordinary effort did she control her voice.

'Does he know?'

This time she was sure that Pen laughed; for the lovely sound came to her ears like a linnet's song.

'Oh, yes; he suggested it.'

That was almost the whole of their conversation. She had no more breath. She was choking. When Pen, seemingly unaware of anything amiss, concluded 'Well, ta-ta. I'll be round to see you this afternoon,' Constance slid down into the bed, pulling the clothes right over her, sobbing with no attempt at further stoicism. 'Tom! Oh, Tom! How could you do it? You've broken my heart!'

The dream was ended.

# Postlude

TIME heals broken hearts. Time, and, for actresses, a multi-plicity of distractions, and added fames or misfortunes.

One day in 1963, on the eve of her seventy-fifth birthday, Constance noticed with surprise that these occurrences of long ago had slipped back into her awareness, displacing many others more recent. She happened to be alone on a bright, windy Spring afternoon, looking from the first-floor window of her house in South Audley Street; and in the anticipation of a party that night she was in high spirits. She would be queen of the party. She enjoyed being queen of any party; and as this fact was known to her admiring friends they took pains to see that her enjoyment was unsullied.

While in the mood to be amused, she saw in the street below a meeting between two young women—both unknown to her, but smartly dressed and coiffured—whom she estimated as matrons in their mid-thirties. The taller, probably also the elder, was brilliantly fair; the smaller and darker, exquisitely brown from winter sun-bathing in a hot climate, had a most seductive air of mischievousness.

'Lucky woman!' thought Constance, with envy. 'She tans to perfection. Something I never did.'

She began whimsically to invent a conversation for the pair, who shared a common gaiety; and from conversation she pro-ceeded to rather fantastic guesses about their characters and life-histories. The taller must be a wife, not a mother, married to a rich stockbroker, and content, but not enraptured, with her lot. Probably her husband was a second-best, as often happened. She was exactly three inches too tall for perfection; a fact which she unconsciously emphasized by stooping slightly and wasting energy in movements imitative of her more naturally vivacious companion.

'No actress,' thought Constance, observing the restless elbows. 'If she had come to me I should have cured that.' In making this reflection she turned almost with relief to the perfectly poised smaller woman, who, although forced to tilt her chin upward, was brimming with what the watcher was gratified to describe as malicious *espiéglerie*. 'Cleverer. More artful. Petted a lot, and therefore self-confident. Married into diplomacy; husband a consul, or something, quite satisfied with him. The blonde charms; but knows she hasn't the other's quicksilver quality. They're like Pen and me! I really mean, me and Pen; but that would sound ungrammatical.'

This identification, and contrast, brought Pen sharply to her mind.

From the adoring child who pestered her elder sister for companionship, Pen had grown into an independent minx, enigma, and supplanter. She had become their Father's pet and, at last, sole comfort. She had graduated from dramatic school to Fairy Queen, critic, and actress. A very strange progress from the seaside Rectory and Pickering's! It had carried her by easy paths to tremendous theatrical *réclame*. People spoke of her with loving delight, as their grandparents had done of Ellen Terry.

'I never did that,' decided Constance, judicially. 'Of course I saw the cleverness; but then I was clever myself, as I still am. Yes, we mustn't forget that. People tend to, I find. It's tactless of them to praise her to me. After all, I came first. There must always have been something about both of us, even at Pickering's, two bright lights. We weren't like the others. And what we've done is very creditable . . .

'She and I have always got on well together. Mutual understanding, I suppose it could be called. Even when she bewitched
Tom. But for her I should have done that. What a difference it
would have made! . . . I wonder how she feels now, the little
scamp? And he? They seem devoted enough. The children,
lovely children, the two boys and that miniature gem Connie,
all very fond of their aunt, thank God, and full of character,
seem to have made no difference. Two minds with but a single
malicious giggle! . . . Oh, dear, I envy that giggle! My husbands
were serious men; no encouragement to my *espiéglerie*! There
again she's had the luck. My husbands, bless them!'

Memory became so copious that, stimulated by typical impersonation of the two chatterers in the street below, she began
to impersonate herself, recalling things that had never happened,
speeches that had never been made, witticisms which, if they
had been uttered in time, would have done credit to Oscar
Wilde. In a dream, she saw the two women below, her puppets,
separate, laughing, with a familiarity too intimate for kiss or
handshake. Obviously they said no more than 'ta-ta'. They
would soon be meeting again; probably tonight; probably in
Kensington, or Chelsea, or St. John's Wood. Were they, as
she now assumed, sisters?

The clue to what followed was the comparison with Pen and
herself. She was back in the Rectory at Wilmerton, smelling the
old timber and the curious salt mustiness of her bedroom,
touching the sides of the twisty staircase, hiding from Pen, declaiming to the breakers, defying the mistresses at Pickering's,
and re-entering the drawing-room where her pale-faced mother
welcomed her with a smile only a little impaired by dread lest
*migraine* should come once more.

Dear Mother; pathetically modest, humble, full of secret
thoughts and amusements, too timid to show the love she felt.
Father, tall as a member of Frederick the Great's bodyguard, but
fleshless to the bone, always vanishing through the doorway to
his study. She saw him staring at her in what she supposed to be

horror. His coat-tails swirled. His dressing-gown, his 'vision', his dying disillusion and message of love for herself . . . If only the words had been spoken years before!

How much that she now knew had been hidden from her in childhood! Everything then had been repressed, not from hypocrisy, but from her parents' puritanical belief in self-control as the supreme virtue, and fear lest, in herself, knowledge of evil would destroy self-confidence and make her timid. Absurd! She had always been self-confident; some said, egotistical. That wasn't true. If she had not believed in her own gift, she would have died long ago. Died, or drifted into some home for broken old women . . .

Other scenes followed. The front-door bell rang rustily; the wind blew from the sea; there was salt on her lips. These scenes gave place to others, in less definite surroundings, which were possibly stage sets. They related to Carl, Soames, and Claude. All had taught or indulged her; and all fell short of Tom, her one natural sweetheart, with whom everything could have been shared, from the most delicious love to the laughter which those others had repressed. Pen had him now. For herself remained only that wretched echo: 'I must go now. Goodbye.'

Carl was a juvenile fancy, a mystery that proved, although incomprehensible enough, hollow. Soames was the best husband of them all. Claude had been a rich man who coaxed with gifts, took her about the world, financed her theatrical successes (never mind the failures; even *Much Ado*, in spite of a malignant Press, had run for three months), made her Lady Marrington, and left her his fortune. Other men had excited her more than these three; one alone had charmed her so sweetly, even after she had lost him to Pen, that she sometimes cried a little— hardly a dozen tears—at the memory.

Dramatic critics had treated her fairly well. They had been brutes over Beatrice, and had pretended to think Desdemona and Lady Macbeth beyond her range. The liars! No part had ever been beyond her range. All depreciation of her acting had been crass. Especially that trick of implying that she falsified parts by playing them idiosyncratically. The suggestion had been that in middle life she mangled an author's conception by imposing her own personality upon it. She often, they hinted, converted a possible success into failure.

'Not true,' she ejaculated, recalling the so-called failure. 'Bad plays; therefore disgruntled dramatists. I know who they were. The truth is, I breathed life into parts that hadn't been properly imagined. I created them, as I re-created Beatrice. If the other fools fell short of me, or the creations were outside what the pedants expected, was I to blame?'

Pen, of course, being more artful, had never shown the contempt she felt. She had gone on exploiting her charm and producing infatuation. Weary men were revived by her *gaminerie*. Walkley, silly old fellow, had called her 'roguey-poguey'. Others, hunting through their meagre vocabularies for words of marvel, wrote 'fey', 'elfin', and 'exquisite'. Ridiculous! As elfin as leather! Quick, light on her feet (that was due to Beryl Gosling, at Pickering's), charming; but as superficial as a quick-change artist. Always on the point of burlesque, because burlesque, the catching of traits, was her true *métier*. No seriousness: a ribald; and—it went almost without saying—a pet. Yes, damn it, always an irresistible pet . . .

Well, there it was. If one were to say these things, in the utmost candour, and in all love, one would be adjudged peevishly jealous. And there was nobody, absolutely nobody, capable of appreciating the truth. There never had been; there never would be. That was why the defeated turned to religion.

The Spring afternoon darkened. Street lamps leapt into radiance. The whirr of passing vehicles grew less busy; and there were short intervals of complete silence. Lovely intervals! It was almost impossible to believe that, further east, the theatres were beginning to sparkle with fascinating bright lights. The lights would again lure actors and actresses, and ordinary men and women, into a realm of make-believe. Wonderful realm, where hearts were stirred and imaginations quickened to the enrichment of life and character!

Sybil, haggard with age, and impenitently ugly, with hollow cheeks and repulsive baldness, brought the tea and made up the glowing fire.

'Shall I draw the curtains, Madam?' she asked, in her stiff voice, which concealed hell-begotten knowledge of a thousand Constantian privacies.

'Leave them, Sybil. They shut out the world; and I need the world. It's my unconsumed oyster.'

'Very good, Madam.'

The response was so unsmiling that Constance, ever sensitive, was unpleasantly impressed. She looked up quickly, seeing no more than Sybil's back as she squeezed out of the room. Why squeeze? Was it just a miserly trait? Was somebody hidden on the landing? This place was full of shadows, some of them of physical origin, a century old, others the vagaries of one's mind. Sybil was as much a skeleton as Father had been. A bag of old-maidish bones. What was her real age? Sixty-seven? Seventy? She walked stiffly; her joints ached. Well, from time to time everybody's joints ached. No good giving in to that. Death followed. Sybil was giving in.

'God send she lasts my time!'

It was to be hoped that Sybil was not thinking of going to grass. She'd had no expenses for half a century. No family to support. Her savings were probably large enough to pay for a world cruise, an annuity, or perhaps yearly accommodation in an hotel at Bournemouth or Torquay. Incredibly boring!

'And not a word!' ejaculated Constance. 'Not a word to show she loves me or would miss me! Perhaps she's not a human being at all; but a spirit sent by the Devil to spy on me and keep a tally of my misdeeds? At the last minute she may say "Catch her" as I'm whirled away, like Faust, to infernal fires. I must never be unkind to her—in case. Of course, I shouldn't dream of being unkind. I'm a kind person.'

She took a small mirror from her purse.

'Hm. Not bad.' The face she saw in the mirror was not visibly wrinkled. The eyelids were heavier than of old; the cheeks a little full, and the lips turned up at the corners in tolerant derision of mankind's incurable folly. She was not displeased. 'A bare fifty', she muttered. 'But Pen, at seventy, might be seventeen. She says I look like a satisfied cat. It's no lie. But it's not a compliment, either.'

The fading daylight was behind her. She poured tea, sipped it, and in watching the flames was amused to see how they flared and died, giving place to other flames which also, after flaring, died. They were like love. They epitomised her own history.

' "The real way seemed made up of all the ways," ' she murmured. 'That's *Sordello*. Well, my way has been pretty good so far. A queer jumble; and what point there is in all the wars and bigotries that shake the earth I haven't the least idea. But I've made a lot of people happy; and on the whole I've been happy myself. On the whole. I shall go on being happy until . . . Until what?'

The light from the window was almost gone; the admired flames wearied her eyes, which she closed. Her head drooped. Her visions became dream. She slept.